SKULL SESSION

Daniel Hecht

SKULL SESSION

Viking

VIKING
Published by the Penguin Group
Penguin Putnam Inc., 375 Hudson Street,
New York, New York 10014, U.S.A.
Penguin Books Ltd, 27 Wrights Lane,
London W8 5TZ, England
Penguin Books Australia Ltd, Ringwood,
Victoria, Australia
Penguin Books Canada Ltd, 10 Alcorn Avenue,
Toronto, Ontario, Canada M4V 3B2
Penguin Books (N.Z.) Ltd, 182–190 Wairau Road,
Auckland 10, New Zealand

Penguin Books Ltd, Registered Offices:
Harmondsworth, Middlesex, England

First published in 1998 by Viking Penguin,
a member of Penguin Putnam Inc.

Grateful acknowledgment is made for permission to reprint the diagnostic criteria for intermittent explosive disorder from the *Diagnostic and Statistical Manual of Mental Disorders*,
Third Edition, revised. Copyright © 1980, the American Psychiatric Association.

PUBLISHER'S NOTE
This is a work of fiction. Names, characters, places, and incidents either are the product of
the author's imagination or are used fictitiously, and any resemblance to actual persons, living or dead, events, or locales is entirely coincidental.

Printed in the United States of America

Designed by Pei Koay

Acknowledgments

This book would not exist without the assistance of many people who helped me formulate and clarify its basic premises and technical details. Any inaccuracies in the text are due to my own stupidity or reckless license, and not to lack of effort or expertise on the part of these individuals.

For information on Tourette's syndrome, I am grateful to the Tourette Syndrome Association, which has done a remarkable job of making the public aware of this difficult and fascinating condition. Profuse thanks are in order to Sue Levi-Pearl, director of medical and scientific programs at the TSA, and Dr. Ruth Bruun of the TSA's medical advisory board, for reviewing the manuscript and offering both accurate medical information and valuable insights on the inner experience of Touretters. Thanks are also due to Dr. Oliver Sacks for his wonderful articles on Tourette's.

For information about forensic investigation and police procedure, I am deeply indebted to the New York State Police: to Dr. Michael Baden, the renowned forensic pathologist, and especially to Major Tim McAuliffe, who over a period of two years gave generously of his time and the knowledge gained from his long experience in criminal investigation and police administration. The people of New York State are fortunate to be served by such individuals, and by an organization of such effectiveness, integrity, and devotion to duty.

Thanks also to Tom Buckles, forensic criminologist, investigator, legal educator, and friend, for his review of legal and forensic considerations, and to Dr. John Matthew for his suggestions on specific concerns of anatomy and biochemistry.

Finally, thanks are in order for Nicole Aragi, my most ferocious and lovely agent, for her unwavering belief in this book, and Courtney Hodell, my editor, whose patience and tact I have put to every test and found exceptional.

I

The sinister is always the unintelligible, the impressive, the numinous. Wherever something divine appears, we begin to experience fear.

. . . Everything that has to do with salvation possesses, among other things, a sinister, unfamiliar character; it always includes the superhuman.

It is a specifically human trait to find joy in destruction.

—ADOLF GUGGENBUHL-CRAIG

Prologue

Steve swung a cast-iron skillet through the door of a cupboard, spraying the kitchen with broken glass and china, and Dub ducked back through the doorway. In the dining room he stood picking splinters of glass off his shirt, trying to sort out the clash of feelings in his chest.

When they'd come up the hill and Dub had first glimpsed the house, he'd been startled by the sight, momentarily transfixed: the slanting light of late afternoon, the grand forlorn tall chimneys and weathered shingle walls, the September woods all around shot with streaks of bright color. Scary, but beautiful, he thought, puzzled at the paradox of conflicting impressions.

Steve had just come in and started wrenching doors off the kitchen cabinets and throwing them through windows. Earlier he had been talking about how all the shit in your life built up inside, and how trashing the abandoned house would be a perfect way to let it out. Watching him now, Dub could easily believe it: Steve's mouth kinked in a weird smile that seemed to have as much pain as happiness in it, and the way his eyes bulged from exertion, he did look like he had some kind of pressure in him.

A pot bounced off the doorframe and almost hit Dub, so he left the dining room and headed into the huge room at the center of the house. Why the fuck had he even come up here? Partly it had to do with Steve, who talked too much and moved his hands and feet too much and came from a crappy family and bitched about being poor, and inspired in Dub a mix of admiration and pity that added up to a desire not to let him down when he proposed the idea. Partly it had been curiosity, he decided: It might be nice to try throwing things around, let out all the anger and frustration or whatever. Or at least let him know if he had all that stuff inside or not.

And yet now he couldn't bring himself to smash anything. He was too nervous, too appalled at the damage, almost paralyzed. When they'd first come in he thought he'd heard a noise somewhere inside, and he couldn't get rid of the feeling that somebody was in here with them—watching, listening. Plus the house was wrecked so badly, to the point where he didn't think it could be just high school kids like him and Steve, he could almost believe the talk about weird rituals up here, or maybe poltergeists. Now every muscle in his body was drawn too tight, his senses on guard, everything made him jump.

Horrified and fascinated, he wandered aimlessly in the main room, just looking. The room was as long as a tennis court and two stories tall, and like the rest of the house was several feet deep with a mash of clothes and appliances and broken furniture and smashed paintings and books and stuffed animal heads. The walls had been broken open in places, too, leaving chunks of plaster and broken boards on the floor.

Dub prodded a stuffed wolf head with his toe, and then jumped as it rolled toward him and seemed to cock its glistening eye at him. He moved away.

The wolf's frozen snarl brought back a disturbing memory: the time when he was eight and he had climbed a tree out in the woods and after a while a bunch of dogs had come by, a German shepherd and Sue Boardman's collie and a little yellow mutt and Jamie Klein's black Lab. They weren't at all the same friendly pets he'd wrestled with and thrown sticks for—somehow, roaming wild, out of view of their owners, they had changed back into pack hunters. Every movement taut and purposeful, they combed through the woods looking for things to kill, ears upright, faces different from their usual sappy expressions. More like that wolf head. As he watched, they flushed and caught a rabbit, tossing it up in the air and then pulling it to pieces. What would have happened if he'd been on the ground and they'd seen him?

Now, as he listened to Steve in the other room, the thought occurred to him. Maybe people could change the same way those dogs did. How else could they wreck a house in this totally fucked-up way? And what else could they do when they got that different, that dangerous?

Dub shivered at the thought. That's where he disagreed with Steve, he decided: If there was stuff like that down inside you, maybe it wasn't such a good idea to let it out.

But despite the tension, despite the twisted, broken mess around him, there was still that other thing he'd felt from the moment he'd first seen the place—a good feeling, he decided, having to do with how beautiful things were, how mysterious. Now the sun had gone down, and through the tall windows he could see the sky, striped purple and peach. And below it the woods had darkened so that it felt like he and Steve were on the edge of another world. They were only a mile or two from home and yet they might as well be on a desert island: The heavy forest in the waning light had an ancient, timeless look to it, like the jungle in Jurassic Park, eerily beautiful. And the house was beautiful, too, despite being so fucked up—the fading red light gave the big room a somber, stately quality, like the inside of a church. With the same sad feeling churches had, too, always a poor dead Jesus pinned to the wall somewhere.

Dub picked up a heavy crystal vase and looked through its fluted glass at the fractured remains of sunset, puzzled by his own internal state as much as

*by the effects of light. Like his vision, his thoughts seemed especially lucid, un-
familiar and exciting. As if your mind changed when you were away from
other people, or did something new and forbidden, or maybe when the light
changed as night began to fall—*

*He jumped involuntarily as out of the corner of his eye he saw something
big fly through the dining room door, hit the near wall, and drop to the floor.
It was getting too dark to see well, but he figured Steve must have thrown the
broken-off back of the antique settee he'd noticed in there—the upholstered,
wood-trimmed back would have made that kind of knock-thump noise when
it hit. Although it would have been hard to throw that far.*

*Now Steve was really going wild—it almost sounded like two or three guys,
or someone much bigger and stronger than Steve. Something in the dining
room or kitchen crashed so loud Dub's whole body jerked in response, and
then there was a rending noise, like nailed-together boards being pried apart,
the floor shivered with it. Dub set the vase down carefully, realizing he'd really
rather go home now.*

*"Jesus, Steve, take it easy," he called. He tried to put a laugh in his voice so
Steve wouldn't get pissy about it. Steve didn't answer, but suddenly the noises
stopped, everything but a strange, rhythmic sound, like someone sawing.*

*"Steve?" Dub squinted across the big room, not able to see clearly into the
doorway thirty feet away, realizing that it got dark quickly here when the sun
dipped below the trees. A wave of anxiety sent ice into his veins, and he started
to walk back toward the door, suddenly shaky. "Hey, man, maybe we ought to
get going," he said.*

*Halfway to the door he came close to the thing that had been thrown and
now lay tumbled and shapeless against the wall, and he saw what it was. It
was Steve.*

*He turned to the dining room doorway and saw the vehement movement
inside, and instantly became empty of thought. Worst of all, the lens of strange
beauty was gone from his eyes, and all that remained was the ugly, animal
light of fear.*

1

"**The** thing about danger," Lia shouted, "is that it *simplifies* you. It strips away everything but the *essentials*. Whatever's left, that's got to be *really* who you are, right?" She was standing at the open hatch of the Piper Seneca, a wall of chaotic wind at her face, a 15,000-foot drop just below the toes of her boots. Framed against the blue square of sky, even in the baggy khaki jumpsuit, crisscrossed with harness straps and burdened by parachutes, her silhouette got to Paul. An undeniably female shape.

"Yeah," Paul shouted back. "Absolutely." Aside, he said, "Yeah! Humpty Dumpty!" A rhythmically symmetrical phrase, he thought, but definitely inappropriate right now. Luckily, he was sure she hadn't heard him inside her crash helmet, with the wind noise and the penetrating drone of the engines. Anyway, she was focused inward now, facing her jump, savoring the struggling forces of fear and will inside as she watched the forested hills sliding below. Paul knew this was the part she liked best: just *before*, when the normal, cautious, day-to-day psyche had to be torn to shreds, broken wide open, so the raw impulse or desire could assert itself and take command. Lia had a hungry soul. Danger fed it.

Paul couldn't repress a gesture, repeatedly raising one arm and snapping his fingers, like an impatient customer summoning a waiter. Lia wasn't a highly experienced sky diver. She'd readily admitted that she had insufficient qualifications for this jump. Plus it was too cold, and the thirteenth of November, an inauspicious date. The plane jittered in the wind, which was broken into erratic puffs and eddies by the Green Mountains. If it weren't for Linc they'd never have gotten a plane, and no one else would have let her jump. There didn't seem to be enough control on this particular risk.

Through the window, Paul could see the gray and dark green November woods below give way to the smooth brown of open land, then the airfield—from three miles up no bigger than a postage stamp. The jump site.

Up front, Linc slapped a thick hand twice on the cabin ceiling. "Any time," he shouted back. He dropped the Piper's airspeed. At the hatch, Lia gripped the walls of the fuselage on each side, her mouth all teeth, a grin or grimace, her eyes hidden beneath shaded goggles. She turned her face briefly toward Paul, and he felt the hot beam of her attention on him despite the goggles. Then the square of the hatch was empty.

Paul rammed the hatch shut, secured it, scrambled forward. He fell into the seat next to Linc just as the plane tilted and began to spiral sharply downward. It took him a moment to find her, a tiny form falling, a single windblown leaf lost in the big landscape of mountains and sky.

"Akathisia," Paul said. He said it again, singing it, drawing out the separate syllables: "A-ka-*theee*-zha!"

"What's that mean?" Linc said. He was steering the plane in a wide circle with Lia's free-falling body at its center.

"Shouldn't she be opening her chute by now?" Paul asked. "Christ!"

"Pretty soon."

" 'Akathisia' means an internal sensation of acute restlessness."

Linc grunted. "Like when you take too many diet pills. I know that one." He wore small sunglasses and a radio headset that covered just his left ear. He had a wide mouth with slack, sensuous lips, and round cheeks covered by stubbly gray-black beard. Despite the cold, his leather jacket was open over his bulging chest and stomach, just a T-shirt underneath. At his feet a collection of beer and pop cans rolled and clattered.

"So is this really a good idea? Lia jumping today?" Paul was just keeping his mouth moving. His eyes were locked on Lia's rigid form—face down, arms out, legs spread and bent sharply at the knee. He touched his nose, first with his left forefinger, then his right.

Linc shrugged.

Paul wondered again whether Linc himself wasn't part of Lia's experiment, one of the elements of risk in this scenario. How competent was he to judge a jumper's skills, the weather, the condition of equipment? He didn't exactly inspire confidence. If Lia hadn't befriended the pilot last year, if Linc wasn't a slob and a rebel and a loner with the perpetual hots for her, they'd never have gotten aloft today. Linc was doing this for love. They certainly couldn't afford to pay anyone for a flight.

Paul lost sight of her against some deep brown woods, then spotted her again as she came out against the lighter yellow-brown of the fields. Maybe she was too cold. Maybe something was the matter with the chute. "Fuck!" he barked. He raised his arm and snapped his fingers again. "Fuck! Fuck!" he said under his breath.

Linc glanced at Paul's flicking hand. "What's that called again? That thing you've got? Lia was telling me."

Suddenly there was something in the air above her, a lengthening strand of silver. A long, thin inverted teardrop appeared and opened abruptly into a bright blue-and-white umbrella that seemed to catch on some hook in the air, hovering almost motionless as Lia swung beneath it.

Paul took a deep breath, only now feeling how tight the muscles of his chest and shoulders had gotten, the ache in his jaw. "Tourette's," he told Linc. "Tourette's syndrome."

Linc lazily shoved the half-wheel and the plane dropped further. He nodded. "Where you have to talk dirty? Somebody said maybe Nixon had that—all those expletive deleteds in his tapes."

"Yeah, coprolalia can be part of it," Paul told him. "But I don't know about Nixon."

"It gets worse when you're tense or scared?" Linc said, not really interested.

"Seems to." Understatement.

Neither of them said anything for a while as Linc brought the plane down. Then Linc yawned. "I guess everybody's got some cross to bear, some fatal flaw, huh? An Achilles' heel. Can't say you haven't gotten lucky in other respects, though." He jutted his double chin toward the approaching field, where Lia was just touching down. She somersaulted, the chute wilted. Then she was up and gathering line quickly as the nylon blossomed again in a random wind.

Linc found a slot between the bucking mountain breezes and brought the plane in for what turned out to be a perfectly smooth landing. As the tension slid away, Paul thought of the look Lia had shot him just before going out the hatch, her mouth straight and serious, no kidding around. She'd been pausing at the edge of the impending jump, inspecting what was left in her when fear stripped away everything superfluous. He smiled. They'd been living together for two years, but it was nice to have these things confirmed: If he read her right, that look said that she'd found some feelings for him among the essentials that remained.

2

Lia left for Dartmouth early on Monday, and Paul spent the entire morning trying to crank out two job applications. A depressing task. How do you account for a checkered employment history, the years you spent being a carpenter and small-time building contractor, a career shift late in life? How do you gussie up your resume so it looks like your life has any internal logic or continuity? How do you write a cover letter that doesn't sound like an apology? *Listen, I know this sounds strange, but I can explain everything, really.*

And how do you realistically toot your own horn without sounding like a narcissistic asshole? *I'm thirty-eight, I've got Tourette's, I've never held a job as a teacher, but I've done a lot of research on the brain, I've gained a lot of special-ed experience by working with my own son's behavioral problems, I've got an IQ of 153 and a master's degree, I'm really good, believe me.* He'd already sent resumes to every high school within sixty miles and hadn't even drawn an interview.

Giving your past such close scrutiny was not a healthy exercise. When you were broke, though, you performed these little rituals.

His desk was in one of the upstairs bedrooms of the old farmhouse he and Lia rented, with westward views over a few Vermont hills and the distant White Mountains of New Hampshire. Among the clutter of books and papers next to the computer monitor stood his full-size model of the human head, the outer features molded in clear plastic so that the diverse parts of the brain showed through in various shades of pink and red, green and purple. Now the transparent face wore a pair of wraparound sunglasses, a convenient place to keep them. He'd bought the model two years before from a medical supply company as a tool to help Mark visualize the brain and all its queer little structures. The skull opened up, and you could lift away the cerebellum, the cortex, the hypothalamus, all the other parts, piece by piece. "It's like a puzzle!" Mark had said the first time Paul showed it to him. Paul had to agree: the absolute, ultimate puzzle.

By one o'clock he got tired of the head's silent, alien gaze and went out to the barn to work on the MG. He stood in the cold for a few minutes, appraising the car with mixed emotions, then lay down on the rough planks of the barn floor and crammed himself underneath.

He'd always had a weakness for British vehicles—the toggle switches, the panels of walnut burl on the dashboard, the jaunty, tall-wheeled stance. When he'd bought the 1958 Twin Cam MG junker six years ago, back when he still had enough money to restore it, it had seemed like the perfect symbol of his desire for change and fulfillment. But while the Brits had class, they couldn't figure out how to make nuts stay on bolts, how to seat screws so they wouldn't work loose. The MG's charm had lasted for about two months, until the first big mechanical problems arose. Now it had been up on blocks for three weeks, as he located and installed a complete new wiring harness. The car's recurrent electrical problems did not exactly inspire affection.

When the phone over the workbench rang, Paul was so intent that he jumped involuntarily and hit his forehead on the MG's undercarriage. It took him another three rings to caterpillar out from under and pick up the receiver.

"Yeah," he said.

"Hi, Paulie." It was his sister Kay, calling from Philadelphia. "How's tics?"

"*Screw you, bitch!*" he joked. "Actually, not bad at all right now. How are you?"

"We're doing fine—the kids are having a better year at school, Ted's business is going great, I've lost three pounds. How about you? Found work yet?"

"Not yet."

"Well, that's why I called. I just had an interesting conversation, something that might involve you. When was the last time you heard from Aunt Vivien?"

"Vivien? Hoffmann? I've talked to her on the phone maybe twice in twenty years."

"I haven't heard from her much either. I still send her Christmas cards, she calls out of the blue every now and again. Before she called this morning, I don't think I'd talked to her in three years. It turns out she's been living in San Francisco for the last six months or so. After all those years at Highwood! Apparently the lodge has been empty, and she heard from the Lewisboro police that there's been some vandalism. I guess she left a lot of her belongings there, and she's concerned things are being taken. So she wants to hire somebody to check out the house, maybe fix things up, close it off so her stuff can't be taken. She says she wants someone she can trust, preferably a family member. Which is where you come in."

"Me? She probably doesn't remember I exist."

"On the contrary. She specifically asked if you'd be interested—she remembered you'd done carpentry and cabinetry. And I suggested that the work wouldn't be, um, *unwelcome* for you right now. This could turn into a job for you. Just call her, see what she wants. You might call Mother first and see what she thinks."

Paul digested this for a moment. "Why doesn't she have Royce see to it? Why did she move to San Francisco in the first place?"

"She didn't mention Royce. He's not exactly an attentive son. Last time I asked, she said she hadn't heard from him in fifteen years or so. As for moving to San Francisco—Christ, Paulie, she's been living in that house all alone for almost forty years. It's a wonder she didn't leave years earlier."

They were interrupted by an explosion of children's voices at Kay's end. "Oop. Well," she said, "I've got to go get dinner ready for the hordes. Listen, Paulie—can I give you some advice?"

"Do I have a choice?"

"If you do this, you charge Vivien enough so that it's worth your while. I mean it. She's our aunt, but this is strictly business. Vivien can afford whatever you charge her."

By the time Paul got off the phone, it was late afternoon and the light was beginning to fade. He'd gotten chilled, standing motionless in the unheated barn. But the prospect of having a job, even a one-time infusion of cash, had improved his outlook immeasurably. What was it Mark Twain said? "Nothing improves the scenery as much as a good breakfast." A dose of material sufficiency wouldn't hurt.

3

He swung the barn doors shut and walked to the house. The weather was muted gray, raw, typical of mid-November in Vermont. Still, he and Lia had a nice setup. The farmhouse was completely isolated, private, yet was only twelve minutes from Hanover and Dartmouth College, and only twenty from Hartland, which made it easy to have Mark stay over every other week. The house and barn topped a little hill, offering views of overgrown fields surrounded by a wall of trees, now without leaves, still and dour.

After being cramped under the car, he found the open landscape very alluring. He had some things to think about anyway: time for a one-man skull session, a solo get-acquainted brainstorming interlude. He got his saxophone from the house and went out into the field, wading through brittle grass and scrub to take a seat on a granite boulder that caught the last pale sunshine. Despite cold fingers, he managed to play a version of "In the Still of the Night" by the Five Satins, and then for some reason segued into Patsy Cline's "Crazy." The pads plopped noisily over the holes.

"Crazy" was the cue. Sometimes you used a saxophone to help figure things out—a brass-voiced oracle. He needed to give some thought to Lia's jump yesterday.

They had driven back to the farm in Lia's Subaru with the heater blowing full-blast. Lia was tired and cold, still on edge from the jump. "This was a good one," she'd said. "Paul, you've got to try it! You've got to at least start the training."

"I'm doing fine just observing now. It wasn't easy seeing you dive out the hatch."

Lia smiled, shut her eyes, shuddered slightly. "I was scared out of my wits."

A high measure of praise. She could defend her controlled-risk agenda if he put her to it: Confronting your fear was essential to cognitive development, provided the rites of initiation necessary for constructive personal growth, et cetera. But on a deeper level, it wasn't rational at all. She had a longing for the ecstatic clarity, the emptiness that came with facing danger. She liked rubbing up against the darker parts of her own nature. And that was the problem for Paul: those scarier reasons or pressures that Lia didn't consciously know about or didn't want to reveal to him. Sometimes her compulsion seemed almost sexual, as if Eros and Thanatos, the life urge and death wish, both drove her. And sometimes when she talked about the epiphanies of taking risks, Paul wondered if the high hadn't become an addiction for her—a heightened craving for the neuropeptide rush, an increasing temptation to raise the stakes each time, to linger a bit longer on the brink.

"You waited to pull the chute. A little extra time?" He was just guessing: She had explained that she'd wait ninety seconds before pulling the cord, but he'd lost any real sense of time after she'd jumped. It had seemed intolerably long.

"Not that much," she'd said. She'd laid her hand over his on the stick shift, a little apology.

Paul put down the sax for a moment and rolled a kink out of his shoulders. The sun was almost gone behind the hill. He'd drifted into a cold-fingered, clunky version of "Take Good Care of My Baby." Bobby Vee, 1961. Definitely apropos. *Everybody's got some cross to bear,* Linc had said, *a fatal flaw.*

The odd thing about his resistance to her agenda was that he'd begun a similar project, struggling free of his own constraints, several years before meeting her. But they had different criteria for what constituted real risk. At one point when she'd made it clear she thought he was being more of a stick in the mud than necessary, Paul couldn't help asking her, "Aren't I taking enough risks already? I just went through a divorce—that felt pretty fucking risky. I've got an eight-year-old son who has neurological problems, and I'm risking nonconventional therapy on him. I took a chance on going back to school at the age of thirty-four, and now I've switched careers, which means I'm gambling on finding a job in a field where there are eight times as many applicants as there are jobs. I've got Tourette's syndrome and I'm cutting back on my medication. I'm unemployed and uninsured and dead broke. All of this isn't risky enough?"

Lia mimed playing a violin.

"I'm serious!"

"Those aren't risks, those are just headaches. Problems," she said, deadpan. "There's a difference." When it came to the aesthetics of danger, she had exacting standards.

"I'm living with you," he'd said. "Does that count?"

If only he could get it across to her: *Lia, it's different for me, I've got good reasons to be wary. I've got a son to think about, I intend to stay alive to be a father to Mark. I've also been burned before, I've got to take it slow.*

It was 1985, he'd been married to Janet for two years, and they'd just learned that she was pregnant. Both were very happy about it, but for Paul the impending birth brought on some soul-searching. The whole episode started with his asking a comparatively harmless question: What kind of father did he want to be? Which led to asking: What assumptions about being a father had he gotten from his own father, Ben? Eventually he was up against some large and difficult existential questions: Who was he? And that, he decided after arduous self-inspection, he couldn't begin to answer until he found out who he was without the daily consumption of a power-ful drug that controlled the chemistry of his brain.

Haloperidol was great at suppressing the tics and impulsive behavior. Between the drug and his father's training, he'd stayed stable, fairly pre-dictable. Motor tics manageable, coprolalia very rare, verbal outbursts mostly limited to snatches of song or movie lines, and usually more irritat-ing than offensive to others. Yes: stable, predictable, even-tempered, level-headed, methodical, restrained, repressed, dull, boring, bored, practically comatose. Or so it seemed at times. When he was five, he'd been considered gifted. At six he was an avid amateur scientist, working through all the ex-periments suggested by the chemistry set Ben bought him, and he could hum any tune after hearing it once—he was still playing them on the sax by memory.

But something happened to the whiz kid. He got buried under an avalanche of neurological problems, held down by decades of haloperidol drowsiness and self-restraint and the methodical habits instilled by Ben. By 1985 Paul had realized that if he wanted more out of life, he'd have to have access to all his own potentials. Was the whiz kid dead or just locked in an attic room, wearing a haloperidol straitjacket?

So a month after Janet announced that she was pregnant, he decided to go off the drug and find out who was in there, in the attic between his ears. A friend offered his remote vacation cabin, and Paul packed up enough food for several days, kissed Janet good-bye, and drove up to the Northeast Kingdom—leaving the haloperidol bottle in the medicine cabinet. He told Janet he needed to get away to think about things, but didn't tell her about the experiment; she'd no doubt worry unnecessarily. Plus, she'd probably disapprove. Janet was a big believer in playing by the rules, and her rules didn't include unsupervised medical experiments.

Mid-August: The leaves of the trees were the deep, lacquered green of late summer. The cabin stood in a little clearing at the end of a long gravel driveway, six miles of dirt road from the nearest town. No one would bother him here.

Inside, the cabin was funky and comfortable, one big room with a wood stove, a sink with ice-cold running water brought down from a spring uphill, no electricity or phone. Pleasant smell of woodsmoke, mouse piss, and insect repellent—a summer-camp smell. Paul unpacked and set out to reconnoiter, and found it to be a pretty piece of land, covered with a heavy forest of maple and birch. A stream played over clean-scrubbed rocks not far from the cabin, and a knoll just up the slope gave him views of miles of rolling hills.

Walking around, he felt a rising excitement, but aside from a somewhat manic sense of expectation he didn't notice anything different about himself that first day or the next. On the third day, though, he sensed that the haloperidol had fallen below therapeutic levels in his bloodstream. At first it wasn't much. He had gone out to cut some firewood with Bill's chainsaw, and at some point he realized that his jaw ached. In fact his whole *head* hurt. The reason was that for over an hour he'd been unconsciously playing *shave-and-a-haircut, two-bits!* on his teeth, clicking them together by shifting his jaw rapidly side to side.

Okay, that was interesting. Not exactly an act of genius, but it was the first little compulsive gesture. He had started the wild mystery rollercoaster ride. This was going to be great.

The day went fine. He worked hard, getting up a good supply of wood which he split and stacked under the long eave of the cabin. It wasn't until late evening that the first disquieting flights of morbid ideation came to him. Whole scenarios would play out in the blink of an eye. It started out with a normal, passing concern for Janet: *I hope the nausea isn't bad. I hope she's okay at home alone.* But then, compressed into a second or less, a whole scene played out in living color: Janet sitting at home, an intruder at the window, breaking in, pursuing her, hurting her. Her desperate attempts to reach the telephone, the blow to her stomach that would cause her to miscarry, they're struggling at the kitchen counter, the cutlery rack nearby—

He shook his head to clear the awful image. Just a flight of morbid fantasy, not unusual for some Touretters, he told himself. *On the other hand,* he thought, pacing around the cabin.

"No," he argued out loud, "it's just Tourette's, old Mr. T, it just seems very real because you're not familiar with the way your head works when you're off haloperidol." Then in a high, quick voice, mimicking neurotic concern, he answered himself: "But you never know, better safe than

sorry!" It wasn't a verbal tic so much as a compulsion, the pressure building inside until he had to externalize his thoughts. He shook his finger in
the air like a chiding, busybody old aunt. *"Better safe than sorry!"* It was a
funny voice, self-satirizing, but finally this was the side that won out. He
went to the car in the dark, drove six miles on dirt roads to call Janet from
the pay phone in Craftsbury.

She answered groggily after ten rings.

"Oh, hi, honey. It's me," he said. "I'm just calling to check in, see how
you're doing."

"Christ, Paul, it's eleven-thirty! Couldn't you have 'checked in' a couple
of hours ago?"

"I'm sorry. Lost track of the time. Everything okay?"

"Everything's fine," she said grumpily.

"Good, good," he said. "Hee hee." The bogus laugh escaped before he
could stop it, the two syllables necessary to "balance" the *good good,* almost
like an echo.

"Are you drunk? I thought you were going out there for some soul-
searching, not for boozing it up."

"No. God, no. Just checking in to make sure you're all right. You sure
you don't want me to come home?"

"It sounds like *you're* the one who wants to come home."

Actually, she was right: After the anxiety attack, he was nervous about
returning to the cabin, to the whole experiment. Embarrassed, he reassured
her and got off the line.

The next morning he cooked a delicious breakfast of eggs, bacon, and
coffee on the Coleman stove, occasionally making a snatching movement
in front of his face, first with one hand and then the other, like the proverbial martial-arts master grabbing flies out of midair. It felt good, pleasing, a
multisensory "tune" played on the instrument of his whole mind and
body—a kinetic melody that was very satisfying. The origin of the movement was the idea that kept coming to him at the back of his mind: *seize
the opportunity.* That's what he wanted to do with this time at the cabin,
with *life,* by God: *carpe diem.* He felt aggressively optimistic. *Snatch!* Your
thoughts and urges were always running in polyphony, like a piece of music by Bach, themes and subthemes and sub-subthemes. The normal person was seldom even aware of the subthemes, the subthoughts, but the
Touretter let them come immediately to the foreground, to be expressed in
word or gesture. *Snatch!* Consciously or unconsciously, a Touretter seized
the offbeat thought, indulged the latent impulse. Sometimes what came
out was socially inappropriate, but so what? Social convention could use a
little slap in the face. It was playful. It felt great. You had to be willing to
take risks if you were going to get ahead in life.

The parade of classic Tourettic symptoms went on, with Paul sometimes conscious of the urges and sometimes startled by them. Looking out the window at the glorious morning, he made grabbing gestures at the pretty view of trees and sky, the fresh sunlight on the leaves, and brought his fist back to his open mouth as if *eating* the beauty of it. He found his fingers tapping quickly the red-hot burner of the Coleman stove, the baited mousetraps, the edges of the kitchen knives—satisfying some hidden curiosity about little dangers, committing little violations of safety-related taboos.

The phenomenon was fascinating, but it raised some troubling questions. Where, ultimately, were the boundaries of behavior? Should there be boundaries? Themes and subthemes, conscious and subconscious—where did this stuff come from? Thinking along these lines, he improvised a comic dialogue between his conscious and his subconscious as he washed the dishes in the numbingly cold water from the sink's single faucet.

"Straighten up and fly right," the conscious mind said. "Touching knives and stove burners—settle down, guy." The voice he used was gruff and martial, the voice of a disgusted drill sergeant. Sergeant Haloperidol.

Subconscious mind's voice was self-parodying too, a limp-wristed voice, sensitive but taunting, manipulative: "Are we feeling threatened or what? Has it ever occurred to you that you'd be better off if you didn't go into a defensive *crouch* every time your *control* slips?"

"What would *you* know about control? You've never had any. You're a goddamned jellyfish. No wonder you're not in charge."

"Uh-oh: 'Who's in charge here?' " Subconscious did a great job of imitating conscious mind's voice, a parody within a parody within a parody. "Of course, Mr. Hierarchy has the answer—me, me, me!"

At one point as he mugged and postured, acting each character, he caught sight of himself in the mirror and had to laugh as he recognized something familiar in his own image. Without realizing it he had been engaging in another Tourettic oddity: mimesis. He was unconsciously imitating Robin Williams—the same elastic face, the simian gestures, even the rubbery, bouncy body. *Oh my God, Robin Williams,* he knew suddenly, *of course, he's got Tourette's, he's plugged into his Tourette's, that's where he gets his juice, his improvisatory genius!*

This was fabulous. *Robin Williams, look out.* He'd quit carpentry and get a job as a stand-up comic, an actor, he'd move to Hollywood, get into movies and TV. The whole scenario flashed through his head: big-money deals in glitzy producers' offices, movie sets, celebrity galas. Tourette's was a gift. The whiz kid was waking up, breaking free.

But by late afternoon he was beginning to fray. The humor slipped, the intermittent argument in his brain turned scary: "I want to kill you," subconscious said unexpectedly. That stopped him in his tracks. Where the fuck had *that* come from? Still chilled about the implications of it, he had another lightning-fast morbid fantasy that brought out a sweat on his neck and back: Janet driving, an accident, the baby being hurt. He argued with himself about driving into town and calling her, and only then did he realize that he had some doubt about his ability to handle the car. He was constantly snatching the air and pointing his finger, and now he'd started impulsively clapping his hands, his arms straight out in front of him like the flippers of a trained seal—what if he couldn't control the tics when he was driving?

Plus he'd begun having some compulsions. Harmless at first, they began to wear on him after a few hours. He had put on a Red Sox cap to keep the sun out of his eyes while he worked with the chainsaw. But the cap "needed" to be adjusted, had to be just so: After each cut, he'd tug the visor down, crimp it to get the right arch, push the back of the hat down further on his neck, pat the dome to make sure it had just so much loft and no more. After he'd repeated the gesture a hundred times, it had begun to exhaust him. The desire to adjust the cap was as powerful and automatic as the need to scratch a mosquito bite, the satisfaction just as short-lived.

It was coming back to him now, the work he had put in with his father, trying to overcome the various tics and compulsions of Tourette's when he was a child. For years he'd resented Ben for getting him on haloperidol so young, but now he could see why a concerned father might do so.

In fact, looking back, he had to concede that Ben had done a remarkable job in more ways than one. Back in 1963, when Paul was seven and had first started to show Tourette's symptoms, almost nobody knew about the condition. Georges Gilles de la Tourette had described the phenomenon in 1885, but mainstream medicine had virtually forgotten about it since the turn of the century. But Ben had read widely and managed to accurately identify Paul's symptoms, first inventing a practical therapy for his son and by 1965 finding out about the emerging treatment using haloperidol, which reduced the level of the neurotransmitter dopamine in the Tourettic brain.

Ben's "exercises": Philosophically, Ben was a proud son of the Age of Reason, convinced that the power of logic and thought and conscious will knew no limits. When Paul first began to tic and perform odd ritualistic movements, Ben worked with him to monitor himself, to become consciously aware of the urges that prompted his actions. It was Ben who had explained the idea that thought was always occurring on several levels at once, and that Touretters often acted upon the subthemes. And, he explained, Tourettic impulses were often *contrary*, the opposite of what was socially acceptable—or safe. So he trained Paul to "listen" to his own thoughts, to identify and restrain inappropriate impulses. And it helped. But not without a cost.

Problem: Self-restraint was a double-edged sword. Kids were *supposed* to do wacky stuff. Hell, *adults* should do more wacky stuff. You had to *play.* A lot of Tourette's behavior was playful, mischievous, based on the sheer satisfaction of movements or sounds. Snatching the air *felt good,* a catchy kinetic tune. Ben may have had good intentions, but Paul saw it as a short step from self-restraint to self-repression. And it was sometimes hard to see where Ben's resistance to Tourette's ended and where his resistance to Paul's identity began.

So then Ben found haloperidol, Paul took to the drug fairly well, and the Tourette's subsided to a manageable level. And between the drug and the habits of self-discipline Ben had imposed, Paul had from the age of eight laid the foundations of his personality. In 1985, twenty years later, it seemed that all that was left was reliable Paul, good work-ethic Paul, predictable Paul. A person Paul no longer much liked. Hence this trip to the woods.

But Tourette's was the pits too, Paul thought, adjusting the baseball cap again. In a very different way, it was just as much of a straitjacket. *Point. Clap. Snatch.* Adjust hat. Boiling random energies and urges.

"*Hi, honey!*" he said loudly. The verbal tic of the hour—a high, nasal voice like that of a stereotypical TV housewife. Where did *that* come from? Abruptly he decided to drive back home, take some medication, try to think it through from the other side.

He was relieved to find that the tics stopped as soon as he was engaged in driving, as if the sensations of steering and feeling the car's smooth flow satisfied the Tourettic itch for playful movement. He briefly felt a return of the optimism he'd felt earlier. But coming down a hill that turned abruptly left at the bottom, he saw the back end of a pickup truck, jutting up sharply, down off the steep shoulder. Driving closer, he saw that the hood of the truck was crumpled against a tree. Somebody had lost control and driven off the road.

He pulled over, leapt out of the car, adjusted his cap, ran down the embankment. The rusty blue Chevy had been heavily loaded with firewood, which had now spilled forward so that cut sections of log lay on the truck's roof and hood and on the ground on all sides. Judging from the jagged rim of broken glass around the truck's empty rear window, some of it had shot forward into the cab.

He reached the passenger side of the truck and saw a smear of blood on the shattered windshield. An elderly man lay slumped forward, face shoved between dashboard and vent window, plump body pressed against the steering wheel, logs piled against his back. Paul could imagine the savage double impact, the head striking the windshield, the logs shooting forward and battering him from behind.

Clap, adjust cap, shoot a forefinger at the sky. "Are you all right?" Paul yelled. The old man didn't move.

"*Hi, honey!*" Paul said. It was a difficult situation. He could hardly stand on the steep slope, the truck was at an acute angle, the logs still heaped on the back looked as if they could fall if disturbed. The nearest phone was ten minutes away; rescue services out here would take at least a half hour, probably more. Depending on how badly the old man was bleeding, there might not be time to go for help. Paul fought down the rising panic.

The door resisted his first pull, and on his second try he yanked the handle so hard it pulled out of the door. When he used a chunk of wood to smash the window, the logs in the bed shifted and one spun off the roof and struck his face. For an instant he almost blacked out with the pain of it. Then he reached inside and lifted the inner handle, wrenched at the door with his whole body. The truck rocked on its suspension. The door grated and swung open, then broke off the rusted hinges. Logs fell and bounded down the slope.

He climbed into the steeply canted cab, tossed away some logs, and grabbed the woodcutter's arm. His breath screaming in his throat, he pulled the old man sideways, off the steering wheel and out of the cab. The old guy, wearing a checked hunter's shirt and khaki pants held up by suspenders, was as limp as a washcloth. Paul's hands and arms became slimed with blood as he dragged him away from the truck and up the slope.

He must have weighed two hundred pounds, but Paul managed to get him up the embankment by a series of all-out heaves. His lungs were burning by the time he reached the road, laid the old man out, and inspected him. Forehead like hamburger with chunks of glass embedded in it, a flap of scalp hanging down near the base of his skull, heavy bleeding, legs making feeble movements. Not good. He'd have to get to a hospital, fast.

The old man stirred and his eyes came open. Paul's hands fluttered around his own head, making the movements of adjusting his hat, which had come off somewhere down the embankment. He clapped his hands in front of him, at arm's length. "*Hi, honey! Are you all right?*"

The woodcutter grunted, put an arm across his face, flailed it away. "Oh, God," he moaned. He lay, watching Paul with blood-rimmed, frightened eyes.

"We've got to get you into my car," Paul told him. "Okay?" His hands flew around his head, adjusting the nonexistent cap. *Clap!* "*Hi, honey!*" Paul bent toward the old man to help him to the car, only twenty feet away. He wished the tic voice wasn't so screechingly high.

The man fought off his hands, terrified.

Shock, Paul thought. What were you supposed to do? Subdue him somehow, but how? Paul's hands went to his head, made all the quick motions as if they were creatures with wills of their own. *"Hi, honey!"* he said, trying to think.

Still on his back, the old man started dragging himself away from Paul, pushing with his heels and elbows. Paul clapped and went after him. They pawed at each other for a moment until one of the woodcutter's flailing hands caught Paul on the bridge of his nose. The pain blinded him and made him sit down hard. Something the matter with his nose. Part of the nose hanging down, onto his upper lip. Even the light touch of his exploring fingers was too much too take. The log from the truck must have cut him. A lot of the blood on his hands and shirt must be his own.

That's what the situation was when the second pickup truck came around the downhill curve. It was a new red Dodge Ram, and it looked beautiful to Paul, the perfect embodiment of civilization, of order itself. Still sitting, Paul waved at the driver, feeling a flood of relief. They'd be able to get the old man to the hospital.

The woodcutter saw the truck and began scrambling toward it on his hands and knees. When it stopped and the driver leaned over to open the passenger-side door, the old man knelt, clutching the door, looking back fearfully at Paul. "Help me!" the old man said to the driver. "Please, help me!"

The driver looked wide-eyed at Paul. Then he leaned and hauled the woodcutter into the cab. Door flapping, the truck roared backward, made a three-point turn, took off in the direction of town.

Suddenly exhausted, Paul sat down with his back against his car, feet in the road, and pitched pebbles into the dust.

Then after a while the sirens, the explanations. Reflected in the State Police cruiser's window, he caught sight of the bloodied, twitching thing that he was, and he couldn't blame the old woodcutter. He labored hard to contain the verbal tics around the cops, but the pressure built inside him and he was too tired to fight it. Not knowing what else to do with him, they nailed him for drunk and disorderly. When he'd finally talked himself out of the lockup in Hardwick and had gotten his nose worked on at the hospital, he went home to Janet and more explanations that dragged on until morning.

So much for finding the whiz kid within. He went back to haloperidol.

Paul pulled back from the memory. The saxophone was a golden icicle, the sun was gone and the blue hour was upon the sky. He had never been able to convey to Lia how that episode had stayed with him. Ten years later, the story seemed a hell of a lot funnier than it had been at the time. He got stiffly off the boulder and started toward the house, fingers working the sax keys. "Who Do You Think You Are?" he decided, 1974, Bo Donaldson and the Heywoods.

Who indeed? In the short term, the experiment had sent him scurrying back to the security and predictability of Haloperidol Paul. He'd learned a basic truth: *It was dangerous to let go too much.* The memory of those two days stayed with him like a vivid nightmare. He wished he could really convey to Lia that, unlike her, he was already perpetually at risk—from within.

But the *joy* of letting go had stayed with him too, just as convincing and absolute as the risk of it. Along with the exhausting tics and compulsions had come a creativity, a spontaneity, a quickness that he liked. So after a few years he had begun to trim back the haloperidol dosage, give himself more slack, more room to be Tourette's Paul, or Playful Paul, whichever. Ultimately, this was one of the big factors in his separation from Janet: Her rules didn't include the asocial and unpredictable behavior that came with the condition.

He'd also learned that his symptoms were suspended whenever he did something that satisfied his body's—his mind's?—craving for an interesting kinetic melody. One result was that he bought himself an alto saxophone, which had been a great source of pleasure and respite in the years since.

Another positive end result was the permanent scar on his nose—a white seam that ran above his left nostril—which he found to be an improvement, lending a little dash to a face that he otherwise found too sincere and wholesome. Lia claimed it was one of the things that made him irresistibly attractive to her. Definitely worth it.

Paul cleared his mind with one last echoing blast on the sax. The depressed mood of earlier had passed. Who was it who said, "Never make a major decision indoors"? Not that he'd made a conscious decision of any kind. But he felt better. The air was fresh, the evening sky beautiful. This was the good life. *You can't say you haven't been lucky in other respects,* Linc had said.

Plus there was the phone call from Kay. With any luck, he'd be making money soon. Highwood—maybe the proposition was the beginning of the turnaround. Maybe he'd paid enough dues and it was time to collect.

4

The car door chunked and a moment later Lia burst into the kitchen, carrying an armload of books and a bag of groceries, which Paul took from her. "Wow," she said. "What a day. Ugh. I am *very* glad to be home." She kissed Paul fiercely.

"A hard day?"

"No more than usual—typical departmental squabbles, scheduling conflicts, conferences. I'm beat. I'm very, very glad to see you." She threw her books on the kitchen table and embraced him fully, her head fitting under his chin, the outdoors smell in her hair. Paul rubbed her back and felt the compressed strength of her.

"I've got pasta water on. And I got an interesting call today."

Lia turned away. "Well, you'll have to tell me over dinner. I'm going to take a nap," she said decisively. "Half an hour."

"Fine." Paul smiled, went back to working on the garlic.

"You were running in the fields," she said from the doorway, startling him. "And you didn't wear orange. Paul, it's hunting season!"

"Yeah. It was great. How did you know?"

"Burrs in my skirt." She lifted the fabric to show him a cluster of small triangular tags. "*I* wasn't out in the autumn fields wearing this skirt—they must have stuck to me when I hugged you just now. And the orange windbreaker is still hanging by the collar loop, the way I hang it. You'd have hung it by the hood." She pointed to the row of hooks near the door.

"How would anyone guess you're a police detective's daughter?"

"I wish you wouldn't do it."

"Hey, I thought you were the big apostle of controlled risk."

This didn't strike her as amusing. "That's not risky, it's just stupid."

He laughed. "I brought my saxophone. Nobody was going to shoot me, unless they thought I was a moose."

That mollified her. "If that's what moose sound like." Lia put her hand to his cheek. "You are hopeless, you know that?" She looked up at him, a heart-shaped face framed in tangled red-blond hair, cheeks banded with fatigue. Paul saw suddenly that she loved and in some way trusted the quirky, sentimentalizing muddle he lived in as much as he loved and trusted her clarity, focus, decisiveness.

Then she was heading toward the stairs again, picking at the burrs, her skirt lifted to reveal her strong calves, smooth in white tights. *I am absolutely a goner,* Paul told himself joyfully. *I am gonzo about this woman.*

Over dinner, Paul told her about the call from Kay, filling in some background. "Highwood is the house of my aunt Vivien, down in Westchester County, fifty or sixty miles from Manhattan. When I was a kid we used to spend a lot of time up there. On top of a hill, wild old woods all around—a beautiful spot. Back then, Vivien lived there with her ancient mother, Freda, and her son, Royce, who's a few years older than me."

"I don't think you've ever mentioned Vivien." Lia wrapped her spaghetti expertly on her fork and when it slipped sucked her noodles anyway. "Your mother's sister?"

"Half-sister. They weren't really in touch with each other until later in their lives. My mother's what, seventy, so Vivien would be in her early sixties. Their father divorced my mother's mother soon after her birth, and married Vivien's mother, so they grew up in separate households. More than separate—estranged. When my grandmother remarried, she didn't want to have anything to do with her ex's new family."

"Understandable."

"But then Vivien and her husband, Erik, moved to the Lewisboro area when my parents were there, bought Highwood, and they all got pretty close." He explained: Highwood had been built as a hunting lodge by some wealthy nineteenth-century industrialist, and stood alone on the top of a ridge in heavy forest. Inside, much of the decor was left over from the original owners—boar, bear, and elk heads on the walls, a stuffed bobcat, antique guns and decorative swords, Hudson River School paintings that portrayed mist-obscured, dense woods like those around Highwood. Vivien's own tastes were no less exotic. She had traveled all over the world with her husband, bringing back chairs made of antelope horns, antique inlaid chests from Milan, paint-daubed shields and spears from some African tribe. Some of her things had come from no farther away than Fifth Avenue, but those were fascinating too: Everything was surrounded with that rare—in Paul's experience—aura of *money.* The uninhabited house would be a gold mine to anyone missing a few scruples.

"I take it they were well off?"

"Loaded. Erik Hoffmann's father had made a pile in the Philippines, around the turn of the century." Paul paused, the recollection coming back to him. The hidden repositories of memory: He'd forgotten he knew any of this. "And Erik inherited it all. Major bucks."

Paul served himself some salad, ground a bit of pepper over it. "We'd all go up there, my parents and Vivien and Freda would talk, cook, drink, and we kids would run around the house and the woods. A fabulous place. It wasn't really designed to be a residence—mainly it was intended to host large hunting parties and wild-game banquets. The main room is the size of this whole house, with a balcony around three sides of it, a fireplace I could park the MG in."

"So, what—your aunt wants you to fix up the place now? What's the matter with it?"

"Last spring she moved to San Francisco. Since she's been gone, the house has apparently been vandalized, and she needs someone to spruce it back up."

"Paul, this sounds great! You're perfect for the job!" She ripped a piece from the loaf of French bread and swabbed her plate with it. "It sure wouldn't hurt to have some money coming in, would it?"

"No, it would not exactly hurt," Paul said.

It was odd, but for all the enthusiasm he felt for the memories of Highwood, there was something unpleasant in the recollections. Out of Lia's sight, under the table, one hand or the other had been ticcing constantly, the uneasiness telegraphing itself to his muscles without conscious intent.

Paul punched his mother's number and visualized the old black dial phone ringing amid the curios on the desk in her apartment. He couldn't hope that she hadn't been drinking, only that she hadn't been drinking heavily. She had taken Ben's death hard, entering a protracted mourning accompanied by fairly serious and tenacious alcoholism. Twenty-nine years later, neither the drinking nor the mourning had ended.

Now she was seventy, a plump woman of medium height, her hair mostly gray, lines of bitterness and disappointment in her face. Only rarely, in the right light, could you catch a glimpse of the insouciant, funny, gregarious journalist and young mother that the old photos showed.

"Paulie," she said. "Well. To what do I owe the honor?" A stock reproach, used even when he'd spoken to her not too long before. The exaggerated precision of her speech suggested this was one of her heavier nights.

"Profuse apologies and a spirit of repentance, okay, Ma? How're things in Philly?"

"Things in Philly have a distinctly autumnal cast. It's November. What month is it there?"

"We've finally got the cold weather. It was global warming until Friday."

"I take it you're calling about Vivien—Kay told me she'd called. What did you two cook up?"

"I haven't talked to Vivien yet. Kay said maybe I should talk to you first—I mean, I hardly know Vivien, and now I'm supposed to call her up. Kay said she's squirrely. I can't remember."

Aster laughed. "Vivien? 'Squirrely'? Vivien's not squirrely, she's nuts. Cracked. Always has been. Runs in the family."

"How so?"

"A woman would have to be cracked to live alone in that house all those years." She sounded irritated at his obtuseness. "Living up on that hill. Every time there was a storm, some tree branch would fall and bring down the power lines. Then in winter—plowing three quarters of a mile uphill. Ask Dempsey how many times he went up there to fix pipes that had frozen because the lines went down and the furnaces quit."

"We used to have a great time up there," Paul reminded her.

"Sure we did. It's a nice spot. It's a gorgeous house." She seemed about to qualify her comments but appeared to run out of criticisms. She paused, and through the receiver Paul heard the clink of ice in a glass.

"So Ma—how much are you drinking nowadays?"

"As much as I like."

"I thought you said you were going to cut back. I thought the doctor advised you."

"I have cut back. But I make an exception in November."

"I just want you to take care of yourself," he told her.

"This is how I take care of myself."

They were both quiet for a moment. "Anyway," Paul began again, "Kay is worried Vivien will be difficult to work with."

"Oh, she'll be difficult. I wouldn't do it, Paulie. Wouldn't give her the satisfaction of having a Skoglund working for her. But I know you won't listen to me. So I guess whether it's more of a headache than it's worth depends on what the job is and what you get out of it."

"Right now a regular paycheck would be worth quite a bit to me."

"Just make sure you charge her an arm and both legs—she can afford it," Aster growled. "Vivien. We used to ask her: Why live alone up there? She never set foot in the woods. But she'd rather be miserable up there for decades than ever give up the place. Oh, hell," she said dejectedly. There was something in her tone, something in her relationship with her half-sister that Paul couldn't place. Some unfathomable family thing.

"We don't have to talk about it now—"

"Just keep it businesslike, Paulie. Keep your medical history and Mark's and your divorce to yourself. And for Christ's sake, don't go talking about *me*. She'll give you the interested gaze, the insightful questions, a little flattery—but all the time she's *collecting.* Keeping files on you. She'd put old J. Edgar to shame."

"What I don't understand is what happened between you two. When I was a kid, you were pretty close. What changed?"

She exhaled slowly. "That's family for you. Skeletons in the closet—you might as well get used to it, let 'em lie. You may find yourself with your own skeletons one day, and then you'll understand."

Paul found Lia upstairs, reading in bed, Kellerman's *Radical Pedagogy* propped open on a pillow across her legs. She glanced up and made room for him next to her. "Not a good call, I take it," she said.

"How can you tell?"

"You come through the door with your chin first when she's made it difficult for you. You stump as you walk—like a chastened but defiant kid."

"It's just when she's been drinking. She lets herself go in November because that's the month my father died. She's not . . . *graceful* when she's drunk."

Lia pulled him and he toppled backward, feet still on the floor, head on her pillowed stomach. She stroked his head, waiting for him to spill.

"It's the classic psychology of the suicide survivor," Paul went on. " 'It's my fault. I failed him.' We all feel it a little: 'How did I let Ben down?' But Aster really seems to blame herself."

"Have you ever asked her about it? Why Ben did it?"

"Sure—she looks stricken for a moment, then changes the subject. Or tells me something like, 'I wish I knew, Paulie. Then maybe I could live with myself.' "

"But it's no one's *fault* but Ben's. Ultimately, we're all responsible for ourselves."

"Of course." Paul allowed himself a little tic, snapping himself in the temple with one finger. "I don't really have a problem with it. I just sometimes worry about my mother. You know."

"And Aster is Aster's responsibility."

"Yeah."

"What did she say about the project?"

"Wildly enthusiastic and supportive. No—basically she said that Vivien will be a pain in the ass and I shouldn't do it. Also that she's got lots of bucks and that I could make out pretty well."

She yanked his head around so she could bore her gaze, that diamond drill of hers, into his eyes. "Paul, your luck is changing. Count on it! Don't you get it? Things are going to go well for you. For us." She bent to kiss him. "Let's go down there and look it over. You could use a job for a while. Get the bill collectors off your back." She kissed him again. "Go call your aunt."

"Right. Okay." He heaved himself off the bed and slumped out of the room.

"Hello, Paulie!" Vivien said. "Well. Your sister said I might expect your call." Her voice was clear, each word spoken with clipped precision. "I've hardly spoken to you since you were a little boy."

"No—it's probably been thirty years since we've seen each other, Vivien."

"Tell me, Paulie Skoglund, how are you? *Who* are you? Catch me up. Of course, I've heard bits and pieces from Kay."

He hesitated, remembering Aster's warning. "Well, there isn't that much to tell. I was a self-employed carpenter and furniture maker for twelve years. Three years ago I went back to school for a master's in education. Married, divorced. Now I'm with a woman I met at Dartmouth."

"Education! Well—a noble calling. And your health is good? You're happy?"

"Yes, I'm very happy."

"I take it you've recovered from those neurological problems you had when you were a boy?"

"The early stuff went away. The Tourette's is still with me. But I've learned to live with it. Not a major problem."

"That's good. I remember how hard Ben used to work with you. He was such a devoted father. And now you're a father yourself. I understand you have a son—is he a good boy? Healthy? None of those troubles you had?"

He couldn't think how to stem the stream of questions. He hedged: "There is a genetic factor, an inherited predisposition, but Mark hasn't shown any symptoms." Not of Tourette's anyway. Mark's condition wasn't anybody's business or responsibility but his parents'—he'd be damned if he was going to elaborate for the sake of Vivien's morbid curiosity.

"Well, I'm sure the family is very glad." Vivien's voice had a smile in it, as if his hesitation had revealed something to her.

"What about you? I'm amazed to hear you're in San Francisco."

"No more than myself, I assure you. Every day I am astonished to find myself here. I'm living in a hotel now, a lovely suite. Everything is so convenient, after Highwood. It's quite delightful, Paulie. Or perhaps you'd like me to call you Paul, now that you're grown up?"

"Either one. Family calls me Paulie, everyone else Paul."

"Which leaves me to decide just how 'family' you and I are. You're very clever. Tell me—do you take after your mother or your father? Did you get the Skoglund nose?"

"After my mother, I guess." She'd turned the questions around again, revealing nothing of herself. He felt the familiar pressure building, the itch. He camouflaged a bark by turning it into a cough.

"Well, you're lucky. Your mother's a very handsome woman. How I envied her figure—those nice delicate bones. And me built like a Morgan horse."

It was true. Vivien was one of those disconcertingly large women, nearly six feet tall, like the women you sometimes saw in photos of the more obscure branches of the British royal family—the large-boned, patrician, fox-hunting type, that tribe of lady big-game hunters, aviatrixes, Channel swimmers. Even as a child, he'd noticed how dissimilar the half-sisters were, in size as well as temperament. He hadn't been surprised when his mother explained that they had had different mothers.

"Anyway—" he said.

"Time for business? Very well. I take it Kay has explained my predicament."

"She said the house had been broken into and that there was some vandalism, yes."

"The Lewisboro police called me. I understand there are windows broken, and perhaps some things taken," Vivien said. For the first time, her voice showed signs of sincere concern. "And I left everything I own at the house. You see, my California adventure was just going to be a vacation. Then I fell in love with it here, and I simply haven't had the time or energy it takes to go pack the place up."

"So why not have Dempsey do it?"

"Among other reasons, dear Dempsey is too old. Also, I'd feel better if a family member helped me with this." She paused and then continued as if choosing her words carefully, her voice lowered: "You see, Paulie, I did leave *everything* there. An old woman acquires a lot of this and that over the years. My family photos, papers, financial records. Private things. And valuable things, as you may recall. Obviously, I need someone I can . . . *trust* to help me. People one can trust seem to be in increasingly scarce supply."

Paul went back upstairs. On the surface, the conversation with Vivien had gone well. She'd been more than receptive to his working on the place and hadn't blinked at his fee. He'd agreed to go down on Wednesday, when Lia had the day off, so the whole deal could commence almost immediately.

He'd get eighteen an hour plus travel expenses just to look the place over, and for any repairs she agreed to based on his estimates. The idea of pulling in eighteen bucks an hour for a while was very agreeable.

And yet Vivien gave him the creeps: the intrusive questions, the amused, ironic tone, as if she already knew the answers to every question. Bringing up his childhood neurological problems, fishing for something on Mark.

Or maybe he was just tired, a little down after talking to Aster, being unnecessarily negative. Bad habit, time to change it.

The lights were off upstairs. Turning into the dark bedroom, he could just make out Lia, the white bedspread vaguely outlining the rise of her hips. It smelled good where Lia was: the scent of fresh laundry, sweet sweat, a faint pastiche of perfumes and smells from the mysterious alchemical pharmacy of cosmetics on her bureau.

He took off his clothes and slipped into bed beside her, avoiding touching her with his chilled skin. But she put one hand out behind her and pulled him up tightly against her, the top of his feet against her soles, his knees in the crook of hers, chest to back, every possible inch of skin contact attained. Her heat seemed to scald him.

His dark mood evaporated. Lia's presence was sweet, silky, luminous. Balm that soothed the jagged, ticcish energy the day had stirred up. He smiled into her hair. *Life hath its rewards, and none greater than this.* Sleep came over him almost instantly, as if he'd caught it from her unconscious body.

5

Their first stop in Westchester was Dempsey's. Paul had forgotten exactly where Highwood was, and the old man had agreed to come along to show them, look over the lodge, offer his professional perspective on any repairs it might need.

Turning into the familiar driveway, Paul found he couldn't enumerate all things Dempsey Corrigan was to him. More than father figure, more than friend. A source of inspiration, certainly: At seventy-two, Dempsey was living proof that you could make your own way in life, making no concessions to conventions or passing trends. He'd fought in World War II and afterward spent several years as a professional boxer. In 1949 he'd settled in Lewisboro, where he'd supported himself doing odd jobs, carpentering, museum-quality furniture restoration, all the while relentlessly pursuing his real love—painting brilliant abstract canvases—and caring nothing for his lack of commercial success. An animated and tireless raconteur, a vehement gesturer. A gruff, gentle, iconoclastic, skeptical, funny, curious, joyful man. It was no wonder he'd been Ben's closest friend.

He was also proof that living true to yourself helped you stay young. Though his bald head was marked by age spots, and the stubble that grizzled his cheeks and chin was white, he lived an active life and had kept the wiry, sturdy build of the young middleweight fighter, tiger-eyed, sleek and corded, that Paul saw in the little gallery of posters and fight bills Dempsey kept.

Dempsey's kingdom, his house and grounds, reflected his personality completely. From the driveway, the house looked like a medieval structure, with eaves close to the earth, vine-covered rock walls, small windows, a mossy shingle roof sweeping up steeply. Dempsey had built it himself with rock he'd dug out of his twelve acres, and he'd built it to last. Inside, the ceiling rose with the roofline to a high raftered peak, and the downhill side of the house was all glass, revealing a view of the Corrigans' land. Sculpted by the paths and terraced gardens they'd built over the years, the hill sloped down to a wandering stream at the bottom, a tangle of woods. It still looked like the old Westchester County, rugged and viney, which Paul greatly preferred to the succession of other images that had overlaid it—highways, shopping centers, boutiques and antique shops in the old buildings, mushrooming developments. Now just the smell of the house—rock, concrete, woodsmoke, turpentine, garlic—gave Paul a comforting sense of continuity with his own past. Dempsey was a point of reference, enduring. Somebody you could count on. Being somebody you could count on, Paul decided, was a good person to be.

Paul pulled the parking brake, Lia stretched mightily. They had barely gotten out of the car when the old man emerged from his front door.

"Welcome!" Dempsey cried, saluting them hugely with both arms—he'd never been able to resist adding a touch of ceremony to arrivals and departures. Now he wore a blue-and-white Mexican poncho, thick as a rug, and carried a gnarled, club-headed walking stick. With his big head and wise-chimpanzee face, he looked like Pablo Picasso in his later years. He hugged Lia and shook Paul's hand with the rough, strong grip of the fellow carpenter. "You want coffee, something to eat before we go up?"

Paul checked his watch. "Nah, not for me, thanks. It's two o'clock—I think we should get up the hill while there's still light. I wouldn't mind saying hello to Elaine, though."

"Not here. She's off volunteering." Elaine did almost everything: She was a superb gardener, an excellent cook, a sculptor, a substitute grade-school teacher, a fighter for various causes. Dempsey pretended to take a dim view of his wife's activism, of which he was actually quite proud. "She'll be back around five, and we're planning on you two for dinner."

Paul pointed to Dempsey's heavy stick. "Expecting trouble?"

"I was talking to one of the Lewisboro cops. Said the place was so banged up it wasn't likely local kids. Maybe gangs from the city." Dempsey smiled reassuringly at Lia. "Not that I think we'll encounter anyone up there. My own guess is, kids were goofing around there all summer—it'd be a great party spot. No one's going to bother now that it's cold out. I'm bringing my shillelagh because it's a long driveway and we can't drive up. At my age, I need a third leg."

They drove for a few minutes, catching up on things. At two o'clock on Wednesday afternoon, there was little traffic: The trains had not yet returned the commuters to the legions of parked cars that surrounded every town in Westchester County.

"Right on 22," Dempsey told Paul, gesturing. "So, Highwood! I haven't been there in years. I'll be curious to see the old place."

"Were you and Elaine close to Vivien?" Lia asked.

"Not like the Skoglunds. Mainly I went up there to fix things. At some point I got sick of trying to be both friend and hireling, and referred her to another contractor. Veer left here, then right at the dam." Dempsey pointed the way. "Can't say I missed going up there, either, except maybe the occasional hand of cards with Freda. Do you remember Freda?"

"Sure," Paul said.

"Vivien's old mother," Dempsey explained to Lia. He shook his head. "Terrible story."

"We must be getting close," Paul said. "This seems familiar." They had come to the rocky edge of the Lewisboro Reservoir. The road followed the irregular shore, overhung by large oaks which still held their leaves, now a dark ocher after the first frosts. Uphill, a tumbled stone wall paralleled the road. To his surprise, his right hand reached out and drummed quickly on the dash. A little rising anxiety.

"Just stay on the shore road. Yes, poor old Freda. You know what happened to her, don't you, Paul?"

"I can't really remember."

"Got hit by the train, just outside the village. Vivien came home, couldn't find Freda anywhere, looked all through the house, went outside and called—no Freda. Then she went into town to ask the police if anyone had seen her. They had seen her, all right—spread out over sixty feet of track. She'd gone all to pieces, you might say." He turned to Lia. "I'm sorry. Not funny."

"I'd never heard the details," Paul said. "I was only around six. I do remember something weird or scary about it—the kind of thing when you're a kid you're told not to talk about."

Dempsey nodded. "Closed-casket funeral, believe me. Nobody was clear how she'd gotten down there. But Freda was getting pretty senile by then. And deaf. Apparently she'd wandered down the hill and onto the tracks, three miles from the house. Vivien was deeply upset. Inconsolable."

They drove in silence for another half mile. "It's along here somewhere," Paul said. "Here." He swung the car onto the shoulder. He remembered it so distinctly: the gravel drive coming down steeply through the trees, the moss-stained rock pillars on either side. Between the pillars sat a battered brown Pontiac without wheels, closing off the driveway to cars.

"Typical of Vivien," Dempsey grumbled. "Blocks the driveway cheaply and effectively, but also announces to all and sundry that the place is empty. Might as well put up a goddamned sign."

They got out, and Paul belted on the waist pack he'd loaded earlier with the camera and a few tools.

"It's very beautiful here," Lia said. She looked around, inhaling deeply. "We never see big old oaks like this in Vermont."

"That's the way these old parcels are," Dempsey told her. "This land has been in a single estate for a long time. The Morgans didn't take any timber down, and neither did Vivien. Oho! Take a look at this." He had stopped at the glassless driver's side window of the Pontiac. When Paul and Lia looked inside, they saw a human head grinning up at them from the seat.

Paul jerked back involuntarily. Dempsey chuckled, set aside his cane, and reached inside to pick up the chipped marble head. "Too bad," he said. "I always found Vivien's garden statuary rather charming." He held up the head—a smiling Greek youth, his nose broken off, ears and curls chipped. "These screwball kids. Well. On that note—" Dempsey faced the hill.

Lia was already crunching up the drive.

The afternoon sun rode above the line of hills, slender cirrus clouds trailed at the zenith of a clear sky. A thin dusting of snow made the woods seem bright and open.

"No, Vivien and I didn't always get along," Dempsey went on, puffing, "and I always considered her a bit 'tetched.' But she was a smart woman, complicated, tough. You had to admire her. The one I really didn't care for was Royce—Vivien's son."

"Why not?" Lia asked.

"He liked to play mind games, even as a little kid. Once I was up there with my tool kit, planing down the bottom of a door while Royce watched. I set the plane down to do something else, and when I reached for it, it was gone. 'What did you do with my plane?' I ask him. He says, 'What plane?' 'You know what I'm talking about,' I tell him, 'give it here, I've got work to do.' He just smiled his little smile, enjoying watching the hired-handyman-cum-family-friend cope with the ambiguities of his role. And this was when he was about six years old.

"On the bright side," Dempsey continued, "he hasn't been around here for twenty, thirty years. Never kept in touch with Vivien after he went off to school. I think it broke her heart, but I say good riddance."

The driveway turned again, lined by snow-dusted, lichen-covered boulders. The land sloping away on either side was rugged, corrugated by ravines. Explosions of white birch trees, growing in clusters, alternated with the darker trunks of old oaks and maples. Through the bare branches they could see a vista of hills and the far end of the reservoir, an uneven line where the land met the plane of water.

They rounded a last, steep turn and suddenly the lodge was there, incongruous in the heavy forest, like an ocean liner beached on the hill. Most windows were broken, but a few remained, the diamond-shaped mullioned panes Paul remembered. The gaping windows gave the house a forlorn look, and yet it still struck Paul as a well-proportioned structure, set nicely in its fold of land near the crest of the hill, big trees grown close on two sides. Out of the massive stone foundation rose three chimneys, one at each gable end and a huge main hearth in the center of the long wall. Just uphill, a terraced garden with marble statuary lay beneath a patch of bright sky.

"Has it changed much since you were a kid?" Lia asked Paul.

"Well, it didn't have its windows broken out. As I recall, the statues used to have heads." Set at bends in the garden path were statues of Greek youths and maids, some fallen, all headless.

Looking at the scene, Paul felt a wave of revulsion overtake him. Oddly, it was only partly the yawning windows, the headless statuary, the sense of abandonment. There was something else too, something left over from before, as if the emptiness had always been there, not far beneath the surface of the dinners and gatherings they'd had. His hands checked the zipper of his jacket, then came to his face, tugged his nose, touched each eyebrow.

The driveway curled into a circle at the end, between the lodge and a small carriage house, also brown-shingled. Paul led them up the short, broad steps to the flagstone terrace that ran the length of the lodge. The main entrance was at the center of the terrace, a tall oak door with an iron-barred window, but when Paul tried the handle it wouldn't budge.

"Locked. Well, we never came in this way anyway—Vivien always had us come in the kitchen door. This way." He headed to the left, down the terrace.

"You too?" Dempsey snorted. "I thought she reserved the rear-entrance crap for us tradesmen."

They walked the length of the terrace, crunching on broken glass from the windows above. The terrace wrapped around the far end of the house and ended at another short flight of steps leading to the kitchen entrance. The door there hung open, off the top hinge and canted back into the room.

"Make a note to Vivien," Dempsey joked grimly. "Next time you leave, shut the damn door." He paused and hammered the slanted door with his stick, as if even with the house abandoned it deserved some ceremony of admittance. They listened to the echoes die away inside and to total silence afterward. "Better we don't surprise anybody in here," Dempsey said.

6

The kitchen was a large room divided into two aisles by a row of three sturdy iron gas stoves. Along the right wall, beneath the windows, were two double aluminum sinks and the deep, angled soapstone sink, the size of a small bathtub, that Paul had marveled at as a boy.

Now, all the surfaces of the room were covered with splinters of broken china, curved shards littering the floor like seashells on a beach. Dented pots lay scattered, and one of Vivien's copper baking pans, big enough to roast a boar, had been flung at one of the north windows, where it hung half inside and half out, caught in the mullions.

"A-ka-*theee*-zha!" Paul said involuntarily, feeling it rising in him.

They picked their way down the aisle, stepping over domed copper lids and a tangle of drawers that had been yanked from cabinets, then through a wide door into a dining room. The table there had been broken into two halves, making a V where an old Electrolux vacuum cleaner lay tangled in its own hose. Beyond, the main room opened, full of light from windows on both sides.

Lia walked out into the big room with her hands held out from her sides, turning left and right as if savoring the light and spaciousness. The room was as impressive as Paul remembered: nearly fifty feet square, three stories high at the peak of the raftered ceiling. Around three walls ran a second-floor balcony, oak-railed, with doors to the upstairs rooms.

Paul's first impression was of disorder on the scale of an airplane crash, like the television news clips of scattered chunks of twisted metal, seats, clothing, unrecognizable tangles, humped bodies. Furniture was over-turned, flung, dismembered. Antlers of deer and elk stuck up from a tangle of clothes mixed with broken furniture, papers, books, tools, appliances. A jumble of whitened, dried vegetation and shattered pots. A cheetah's head, leaking sawdust from an empty eye socket, raged from the innards of a dis-emboweled, upended couch. An old-fashioned bathroom sink, enamel over cast iron, was embedded at head height in the wall opposite the kitchen door.

A breeze blowing in through the blasted windows lifted the pages of countless magazines and eddied among drifts of canceled checks, letters, receipts. Far above, three circular iron chandeliers hung from dust-frosted chains, but now the back of an overstuffed chair was tangled in the spokes of one, dangling shreds of stuffing and cloth. Paul spotted several conical straw hats in the rubble, which he remembered Vivien had brought from the Philippines, and a nose flute, the very concept of which had once amazed him. A refrigerator door was shoved through the railing of the wide oak staircase that rose to the balcony. In places the debris had drifted, mounded, several feet deep.

The three of them stood silently, momentarily paralyzed. Then Lia bent to pick up an inverted umbrella that seemed to proffer its handle. "On the bright side, you're going to make a lot of money putting this back together."

"Weeks of work," Dempsey said. "Just to close the place off and pick things up. Months and months if you repair anything." He bent and pulled a heavy, carved table leg from the rubble and disengaged a woman's slip from the splintered fretwork at the end. "Look at this. George III period— intact it'd be worth maybe twenty Gs. Very much worth restoring."

"Lots of goodies, actually." Lia had found a broad-brimmed maroon silk hat, dusted it off, and settled it on her head. "Where's a mirror?"

"Look, this isn't a rummage sale," Paul reminded her. "This is Vivien's stuff." *This had been here too,* he thought, *the violence and disorder. Somehow always just beneath the surface.*

The smoking room, surprisingly, was comparatively intact, although they found another of the garden statues' heads, which had apparently been used to shatter the large mirror above the fireplace mantel. Royce's old room was guarded at the door by a dead raccoon, its head mashed to a pulp. A glance inside was enough: more heaped debris, knee deep, covered with a drifting layer of goosedown.

The library was as bad or worse. "Vivien didn't want us in here," Paul said. "Once we pulled about half the books out of the shelves and built walls and steps out of them. 'Forts.' Vivien hit the roof." It had always been a warm, bright room, especially in the late morning when its tall windows caught the eastern sun. Vivien had been an avid reader, and the brown backs of leather volumes and the bright spines of paperbacks had filled two walls, floor to ceiling.

Now it was a shambles. No book remained in the shelves. The floor was covered with them, splayed open, spines broken, pages torn. A long-handled garden shovel had been pushed through the screen and out the back of a big Motorola television. Vivien's desk and big wing-back chairs were smashed and gutted. There were a number of tall file cabinets too, drawers gone and contents heaped and scattered among the drifts of books.

Lia stooped to pick up a photograph from the litter on the floor. "Who is this?" she asked.

The photo showed a young, dark-haired woman, stylishly dressed in the fashion of the early fifties. She was standing with a baby in one arm, and holding the hand of another boy of two or three who stood beside her. Behind them were the landing gear and riveted undercarriage of an airplane. The woman was making a forced-looking smile, while the little boy, wearing shorts and dressed in a suit jacket and tie, stared vacantly off to the left with wide-set eyes.

"It's Vivien," Dempsey told her. He turned the photo over, where a date was written. "Nineteen fifty-one. They must have been off on one of their jaunts. The baby would be Royce."

"Who's the little boy?" Lia asked.

Dempsey shrugged and handed the photo back to her, prodding the pile of litter with his cane. Paul could see other photos in the rubble—Vivien, an older Royce, Erik Hoffmann, groups of people he didn't recognize, parties, babies, weddings. There were letters on translucent airmail paper, envelopes with exotic stamps and postmarks, yellowed newspaper clippings, receipts for trivial purchases. Poor Vivien: sixty-two years old, her past in tatters and exposed to the world.

Dempsey voiced it for him. "This is what gets me the most. This stuff— the family papers. Photographs, letters, bills. Recipes. I don't know. It's so . . . intrusive. That someone would throw this stuff around. It's Vivien's whole goddamned life."

Lia had picked up another piece of paper and was looking it over closely. "Look at this," she said. Dempsey and Paul went to her side to read over her shoulder. The letter was undated, typewritten.

Dear Vivien,

 Aster and I would like to thank you for the lovely evening on Tuesday. It was such a pleasure to have an adult dinner without the children running amok; we'll have to do it again soon.

 I confess that until Mr. Vincentero brought it up I had no idea Erik's father was acquainted with such luminaries of Philippine history as Aguinaldo and Bonifacio. I'd enjoy hearing more from you about Hoffmann Senior's connection with them.

 Yes, I disagreed with Mr. Vincentero about the Huks and other collectivist movements. Sorry, but I thoroughly enjoyed offending your guests with my vociferousness; I hope what I said sticks in their craws and chokes them. I hope, however, that my contentiousness didn't spoil your

enjoyment of the evening. You were oddly silent on the issue; is it far-
fetched to assume you didn't entirely agree with Mr. Vincentero's ver-
sion of "let them eat cake"? I would be curious to know your opinion.

Ben

"From your father, right?"

"That's Ben," Dempsey said. "You can just see him ambushing some stuffy upper-class type at what was supposed to be a formal dinner." He grinned bitterly and passed the letter to Paul. "He was always a big letter writer."

Paul looked it over again, folded it, and put it in his pocket. A memento of the past. He was entitled.

Finding Ben's letter seemed to darken Dempsey's mood still further. His face glowered with disapproval as they toured the rest of the house.

Paul was surprised at how well he remembered the lodge. Main room at the center, a single open space rising to the full height of the roof and running the full width of the building from east to west, smaller rooms arranged on the north and south walls of both floors. Downstairs, the north rooms were the kitchen, dining room, and library; on the south were the smoking room and a pair of bedrooms. Upstairs, accessed by doors leading from the balcony, were two bedroom suites on the north end, where he and his family stayed when they spent the night, and Vivien's bedroom on the south.

They went up the broad oak steps at the northwest corner of the balcony. On the second floor, the story was the same—drawers pulled from bureaus, papers and toiletries strewn, furniture dismembered, mirrors shattered, sections of the interior wall broken open, moldings smashed away from door frames.

Dempsey began to trail behind Lia and Paul as they moved from room to room. By the time they reached the door to Vivien's bedroom, he'd apparently had enough. "This stirs up a bunch of stuff for me," he said. "The photos, Ben's letter—all the things a person accumulates. When you get old, your junk takes on significance. A way to remember who you were. You try to honor your own life for what it is. Seeing it all spread out, ripped up—it trivializes everything. Makes it all seem arbitrary. Inconsequential." He shook his head, then seemed to make an effort to rally. "Let me check my pulse. No, not dead yet. Okay, that's my morose quota for the day." He didn't quite manage a smile, and Lia moved to his side and took his arm.

"Anyway," Dempsey went on, "I think I'm going to go outside, sit on a rock, and ponder fate." He turned toward the door and then paused. "Paulie—don't forget to take snapshots of this. You'll have a hard time getting Vivien to believe it. You're going to need weeks here, and substantial cash up front for expenses. Take the photos. And don't forget to check the pipes." He stepped over a fallen coat tree and left, walking the length of the balcony erect and dignified, as if consciously holding himself aloof from the surroundings.

"How about you? How're you doing?" Lia asked. With her eyes she followed his hand as it checked the zipper of his jacket, top to bottom. The hand had been up and down a hundred times, like a spider, since they'd entered the house.

"I've got some of the same feelings Dempsey has. Finding the letter from Ben really brought it home to me. There's other stuff here too. It's complicated." He turned and started through the door, then paused to lean against the door frame and take a deep breath. He was glad to feel Lia's hand on his back. "Anyway," he said, "this is Vivien's bedroom. She didn't like us to play in here, either. I seem to remember her keeping it locked."

"After what you told me about the library, I don't blame her."

Paul's first response upon stepping into the room was surprise: Vivien's bedroom was no bigger than those on the north end. He'd assumed it would be larger because there was no other door on the balcony's south wall.

The room was flooded with light from the lowering sun, streaming in through the empty windows on the west wall. Here the destruction was thorough—it reminded Paul of television news scenes of shops devastated by terrorist bombings in Ireland. Mattress ripped and gutted, cotton batting tossed in heaps like entrails. Clothes, books, jewelry, curios, cosmetics, lamps, broken legs and boards of furniture covering the entire floor. Interior wall punched open in places, broken lath showing in the gaps like ribs. A red high-heeled shoe, pitched or hammered against the wall so that the spike heel had penetrated the plaster, leaving it pinned alone on the white stucco.

"Good God," Lia said softly.

All the little items of a life were there, jumbled and broken: prescription pill bottles, a pair of glasses, a clock radio, a hot water bottle, small photographs in frames, a felt slipper, a scattering of pens, pantyhose, a woman's watch. Splayed paperback novels, copies of *TV Guide* and *National Geographic*, an electric space heater. And papers everywhere. A large armoire had been smashed into splinters by a thick slab of marble—the pried-loose mantel of the fireplace on the south wall. Through the gaping south window, Paul could see a bureau that had been flung outside and had exploded against a boulder downslope.

From the bedroom they went into a large windowless room, without as much debris as the other rooms. In the dim light, they could see metal shelves along two of the walls, bent and twisted, emptied cardboard boxes, and piles of clothes on the floor. Paul snapped a photo, and they went back into the bedroom.

Lia lifted a fox stole from the rubble, her cheeks red, eyes flashing. Catching fire.

Of course, Paul thought. The cop's daughter, who liked a mystery so much that she had for a time considered a career in criminology. Plus she had to feel the buzz of danger here—for Lia, irresistible. "You're getting that forensic look," he told her.

"This is interesting. It's like a riddle, a crossword puzzle."

"What's there to figure out? A bunch of teenagers have been having a good time up here for the last six months."

Lia scanned the room thoughtfully. "You're not noticing the same things I am. Look—a jewelry box, right? It's been thrown around and broken open, but what's the matter with this picture?"

Paul took the box from her. It was made of ebony, inlaid with ivory and chased with silver, the lid cracked and dangling by one hinge. In its one remaining drawer lay an assortment of jewelry—a pearl necklace, several rings, an opal brooch.

"You mean that it's still got jewelry in it. Prompting the question, Who's going to come up here, trash the place, but not make off with valuable, portable loot?" Looking around, Paul could see other things in the same light: another necklace hanging from the splintered window sill, a tangle of silver earrings and bracelets, the fox stole. "So what's your explanation?"

"I can think of several, but there's another thing I noticed that makes me think of one in particular. In the kitchen—did you notice the stoves?"

"Not really. Lia, I need to get going on my damage assessment. Also, I don't like being in here. I want to get the fuck out of here. Tell me as we work our way back to the kitchen." He took a couple of photos of the bedroom, then went out to the balcony and snapped several overhead shots of the big room.

Lia put her arm around his waist as they walked back around to the head of the stairs. "Here's what I was thinking. You probably did some vandalism when you were a teenager, right?" she began.

"Sure. When I was around twelve, thirteen. Loved it. There was an abandoned factory where we'd go have a free-for-all once in a while. One time we stole a shopping cart from the Grand Union and rolled it down a hill lined with parked cars."

"I did too, a little—with my brothers. Why did you do it?"

Paul thought as they descended the stairs. From the windows above the driveway he could see Dempsey, sitting on the terrace steps, poking at the gravel with his cane. The sun was still above the tree line, but the light outside had started to pale as a high haze formed. It seemed to be getting cooler. "Same as any kid. Maximum effect for minimum effort. Throw a rock, get the reward of a loud smash, a hole in the window. And there was the thrill of danger—'What if we get caught?' "

Lia steered him into the kitchen. "Exactly," she told him. "Instant gratification. Maximum effect, minimum effort. Loud noises, something in pieces, run away convinced you're another Al Capone. That's why this doesn't fit." She brought him to the stoves. On all three, the knobs had been systematically broken off, the steel shafts bent flat against the iron facing.

Paul tried to straighten one of the finger-thick shafts, found it immovable. "Right. This was a lot of work."

"Work? After the first few, this must have been downright *tedious*. There must be two dozen shafts here. How about the couches in the big room? They were slashed dozens of times. It's too systematic. Lacks the spontaneous touch of the vandal. And there's nobody around to hear any of it. What's the thrill?"

"Point being?"

"The motivation wasn't casual vandalism."

"What then?"

"Revenge, maybe? Someone who had a grudge against Vivien, wanting to make sure this place is really in ruins."

"So why not just burn it down? Maximum effect, minimum effort, right?"

Lia frowned. "I don't know. Maybe there's an aesthetic to revenge—something to draw out and savor, especially if you've waited a long time."

While he thought about it, Paul took a few photos of the kitchen from the doorway. "I've got to take a look at the basement rooms," he said finally, "and see about the pipes and whatnot. But I'm a little worried about Dempsey. You don't want to go out and cheer him up, do you?"

"Sure. But first—" Lia turned to him, took the camera out of his hands and set it on one of the dented stoves, unzipped her jacket and his, then placed his arms around her. She pulled their bellies together hard and leaned back to survey him. "Paul, this is fascinating. In a way what we'll be doing is *archeology*. Digging down through the layers."

"What do you mean *we*? You're still in school. You've got a job."

"All I'm really doing at school is my thesis and little end-of-semester errands, and my hours at work are flexible. Are you kidding? I wouldn't miss this for the world!"

"If Vivien agrees to hire me," he said, trying to sound discouraging. "If she gets me money up front."

"She will."

Lia burrowed against him and he grudgingly succumbed to the warmth and softness of her. After a few moments she let go of him, waved, and stepped outside, over the canted door. Paul pulled his waist pack around to the front and got out the flashlight, a little Maglite with an adjustable beam.

He sighed, checked his zipper, touched his nose, eyebrows, zipper again.

When they were kids, they'd gone in and out of the basement through a flight of steps near the outside kitchen door, but there was also an inner stairway that ran down from the pantry between kitchen and library. Now the door was open, black as a pit.

As Paul remembered it, the basement was divided by a corridor that ran the length of the building and opened into a half dozen rooms, including a pitch-black coal room directly under the kitchen, the furnace room, and a workshop. He checked the furthest north of the rooms, which had been set up as a game-hanging closet with hooks in the ceiling beams. Vivien had kept her gardening equipment in there, and now it was a tangle of tools, broken shelving, exploded bags of potting soil, peat moss, and manure, kinked garden hoses snaking in and out of the mess.

The pipes had obviously not been drained before Vivien left, judging by the icicles that hung from the joints of many. Ruptured pipes—another thing to take care of before he could turn on the heat. He snapped a photo of a cluster of icicles, and after the flash was dogged by purple splotches in his vision. The flashlight seemed dim and yellow.

He navigated the debris-choked hallway to the furnace room, where two huge oil furnaces gripped the ceiling with their ducts, spread like the arms of a galvanized-steel octopus. Paul played the flashlight beam over the scene, wishing he'd thought to bring a bigger and brighter light, or at least checked the batteries in this one.

The furnaces hadn't been spared. The oil pumps had been ripped out of the floor, the sheet metal housing around the fireboxes badly dented and torn. Many of the galvanized steel ducts were slashed, wide jagged rents two or three feet long, and he found one of the iron firebox doors broken off and stuffed through one of the rips.

Lia was right. It wouldn't be any fun to vandalize a furnace. It'd be work.

He located the fuse boxes and inspected them carefully: Getting power back would be an important first step. There were five boxes of differ-ent sizes and vintages, now buckled, doors gone or hanging awry, fuses smashed in their sockets, breaker switches pulverized and dangling on their wires. On the floor beneath them he found one of the oil pump mo-tors, still on its mount, which had apparently been torn from the concrete and used to smash the fuse boxes. On impulse, he put the Maglite in his mouth and bent to lift the pump. A hundred pounds, he decided, maybe more.

The light dimmed and brightened again, the batteries truly failing now. Not much of the basement remained: the corridor, a couple of miscellaneous rooms. And the workshop, where the slope left the foundation above ground and permitted an outside door and two windows—at least there'd be some light there.

Paul followed the dark passage to the south end of the house, his lips moving soundlessly, *fuckfuck!*, a little song of anxiety, the rhythm of his heartbeat. Associative gibberish ran through his head: *Who's afraid of the big bad wolf?* He was relieved to emerge into the comparative brightness of the workshop, a large room lit by windows and a door that faced the sloping woods to the east. Along two walls stood workbenches, much as he remembered, but now sections of the four-inch-slab benches were cracked, splintered. Tools had been tossed around, and a Sears Shop-Vac had been flung through one of the windows, its gray hose trailing back through the opening like some groping plastic annelid.

He'd always liked this room. Sometimes Dempsey had been here, fixing a broken window or lamp, planing some board. Paul had loved seeing the curl of raw wood coming up in the plane, spiraling in on itself until at last it dislodged and fell to the floor, arch, stiff, thin as paper.

And that's how your life works, Paul thought. You observe something, it makes an impression on you, and unbeknownst to you it shapes your life forever. Little Paulie had admired the curls in the plane and Dempsey's command and pleasure in his work, and years later had become a woodworker himself.

Something fell and clanged in the corridor. A cold sound. His heart was suddenly racing, the muscles of his abdomen clenched. "Lia?" he called. No answer. He shined the flashlight down the hall, its feeble light revealing nothing.

No one had brought it up, but there'd been a hidden tension this whole time: *What if they found someone here?* "Dempsey?" he called. *But there would have been footprints in the snow. Unless they came up through the woods. Or unless they'd been here all along.* A grisly thought. How easily nostalgia turns to nightmare.

But there was no more noise. His heart stopped punching his chest. Just something falling over, something he himself had disturbed in passing. He took a photo of the workshop, then unlocked the outside door and stepped with relief into the open. The woods were still, reassuringly normal. He crunched his way around the outside of the house to the terrace, where Dempsey and Lia stood, swinging their arms, puffing steam, talking.

He used the last of the film to snap the two of them, both red-cheeked and cheerful now. Dempsey appeared to have recovered. Another of Lia's many talents.

On their way out, they stopped at the carriage house that faced the lodge across the circular drive. Paul quickly checked both floors and was pleased to find the building largely undamaged. The upstairs rooms were empty, and Paul made a mental note that they would make a good temporary staging area for the work, at least until the main house got straightened up a bit.

The sun disappeared behind the hill as they went down the driveway, leaving the woods glowing a watery blue. Lia and Dempsey continued their conversation, but Paul couldn't get involved. Seeing the house had stirred up an odd mix of feelings, an upwelling of the past. Mainly family stuff—the brighter early years of living here in Westchester, then Ben's death and the dark years of grieving and poverty, moving away, Aster's withdrawal from the world. Lia could manage her ebullient mood because for her this had nothing to do with past, parents, death in the family. It had only to do with the future, a puzzle, a little morsel of danger to be savored. Paul doubted that he could find her point of view. "Fuck it," he said out loud.

Dempsey turned to him. "Coprolalia, or just plain old regular profanity?"

"Maybe a little of both," Paul told him.

7

Paul drove on the four-hour trip back to Vermont, Lia next to him in the dark car. They'd eaten an early dinner at the Corrigans' and promised to stay over when they came down again, which would be soon if Paul could come to an agreement with Vivien. Now Lia leaned against the seat back, talking about Dempsey and Elaine.

Paul grunted replies.

At last Lia took his hand off the gearshift knob and held it loosely on her thigh. "So," she said. "What's going on?"

"I'm not sure." Paul tried to put his thoughts in any order that would make sense. The evening with the Corrigans had been mostly very pleasant—a fire in the Franklin woodstove casting a warm light on the room, Elaine's terrific scallops, a lot of laughs. But none of it had succeeded in dispelling the sense of unease that the visit to Highwood had brought on. "Maybe I shouldn't do this job," he said.

"Why not?"

"I don't know. It brings up a bunch of stuff for me."

"Like?"

"The old days. There was a sort of golden age—then my father died and it all got complicated." He drove without turning his face toward her. "Fuck. It sounds like I'm feeling sorry for myself. I guess going up there put me in one of those 'look at your past and wonder what you've done with your life' moods."

Lia waited for him to continue. After a moment she carefully placed his hand palm-down on her thigh and traced his jaw with one finger. "You have a beautiful chin," she told him. "Look at this beautiful line. Brave. Like the bow of a fine ship." *The sweet non sequitur that only the woman you love can pull off.* He was grateful for her touch, circumventing words and logic to remind him of all that was good in his life. Lia waited expectantly, as if she knew there was something else.

"And," he went on reluctantly, "it disturbs me to think of someone smashing the place up that way. Your revenge theory—what if the people who did it come back?"

"While we're up there? With plumbers and furnace repairmen and electricians and Dempsey and you and me there? Not the perp's pattern, as my father would say. Let me ask you something—did you see the mouse turds in the mess? The mildew that was all over anything made of cloth?"

"Yeah, I did. Another reason why Vivien had better hurry up and do something about it, if she wants to salvage anything."

Lia nodded. "True. But you're missing the implication. If there's that much mouse and mildew damage, it means that stuff has been lying like that for some time. It's been too cold for mildew for at least a month. Whoever did it hasn't been back."

"Maybe not. And maybe they'll get a hankering for that particular kinky thrill again. I can't believe you aren't more concerned."

Lia was quiet for a moment, as if considering how to reply. "Once when I was eight," she said at last, "my father and I went to a shopping center to get me some shoes. It was summer, and when we drove home at around seven-thirty it was still light. My father was off duty, but while we were driving home he got a call on the radio that he was needed at a crime scene. When he parked the car, he told me absolutely not to get out. I sat there for a little while, watching the lights of five or six police cars and ambulances, and then got curious and wandered down there. It was a beat-up neighborhood. Everyone was clustered around a little white clapboard house with peeling paint. Someone had stabbed to death a woman and her two kids. The mother was still on the porch stairs when I got there. Head down, tangled in her own arms and legs. Every drop of her blood had drained out onto the stairs and sidewalk. The way she was lying—it was like she'd . . . she'd been wrestling with herself."

"Christ, Lia."

She took a moment to pull back from the memory. "My point is, after that I'm not going to be upset by some broken furniture."

Paul imagined the little girl, trying to integrate the horrible scene into her world view. Somehow she'd miraculously emerged as the Lia he knew. In the long run, maybe it was something that strengthened her. Or maybe those images were part of what drove her, rode her. Because something *was* riding her, a desperation she revealed only very rarely.

He'd seen it the first time they'd really spoken to each other, a little over two years ago. For two months he'd been auditing a night class in Adolescent Psychology at Dartmouth, and covertly admiring her from across the room. She was in her first term as a special student pursuing an independent project for her master's in social work.

That Wednesday night, after class, he wasn't ready to return to his apartment, and had stopped for a beer at Murphy's Pub. He was surprised to see Lia at a table alone: It had never occurred to him that a woman that pretty would ever be unaccompanied. Seeing her there was a revelation, like a window to some long and gorgeous vista opening in his mind. He got a beer from the bar, walked to her table, and asked if he could join her.

Lia took his intrusion gracefully, made him feel welcome. They talked. She told him she was working twenty hours a week at a family advocacy organization where she investigated claims of spouse and child abuse, plus doing full-time graduate school work. Despite her vitality, her clarity, he could see the fatigue in her.

She'd been telling him amusing anecdotes about being a police detective's daughter. But at some point the tone of her stories and the timbre of her voice had changed. "There were a lot of nights," she said, "when I'd be at home with my mother. My father would be at work. I knew he was a police detective, but I didn't know exactly what he did. My mother would clean the kitchen, and my brothers and I would stay up doing homework at the kitchen table. She kept a police scanner on the counter. I hated it—the sharp-voiced messages, all the static, once in a while my father's voice, sounding like a stranger. I see now she couldn't help herself, she needed to know where my father was, what he was doing. Some nights I'd say something to her and she wouldn't answer. One night I figured out why. On the scanner, there was some dangerous thing going on, a holdup, a gunfight, calls for assistance, officers down at the scene. My mother had her back to me, not moving. I finally went up to her. When I saw her face, her eyes were glittery like a rabbit's, and it finally dawned on me: *She's afraid my father might not come home.*"

Lia stopped in her narrative to blow out a breath of air. "Until then it had never occurred to me that anything could happen to him. I didn't know that *people could die.* I didn't know that my mother couldn't control everything. After that, I hated those nights. I'd be really cheerful and I'd be good, helping her in the kitchen, cleaning my room, being extra nice to my brothers. As if that could help my mother feel better."

She shook her head, adjusted the man's dress tie that held her lopsided fountain of hair, smiled a ragged and apologetic smile. "Wow. I must be tireder than I thought. I'm really sorry. I'm really not like this."

Then she surprised him again, switching gears completely. "What's it like to have Tourette's syndrome?" she asked.

Paul was taken aback. It was his first real glimpse of her observational powers. "And here I thought I was doing a pretty good job of keeping it under control," he said, laughing uneasily. This wasn't particularly good first-date material.

"You are. But I've been watching you in class for a while," she said.

She grabbed her nose, stroked her upper lip and her eyebrows, one quick, practiced motion, a perfect imitation of Paul's most unconscious and persistent tic.

Paul was a bit drunk by then, enough to plunge past the momentary discomfort her mimicry brought on. "I've been observing you too," he told her. "But probably for different reasons." Why not? He had nothing to lose.

"Oh, I don't know about that." She looked away, gorgeous in her embarrassment. It was a beautiful moment, the best, teetering on the brink of falling in love, letting it start to happen, letting the wild hopes run crazy in his heart. Suddenly he wanted her, more than he'd ever wanted anything.

Later he often wondered about the side of her he'd glimpsed that night. She let it surface so seldom, yet he knew it was always there: those innumerable nights of feeling fear stalk the house, knowing that no one was safe from it, no one was any protection from it. How had that affected her? And how did it tie in with her hunger for danger? He couldn't say. Maybe it had to do with *people die*: Lia jumped out of airplanes because she wanted to get all she could out of life. Or having hidden from fear then, she was driven now to face into it, master it, stare it down. Or maybe it was just Thanatos, the death wish.

Paul shook his head. Freudian explanations made him vaguely ill. They were so Viennese, turn of the century, self-indulgent. Reality was always both more straightforward and more mysterious, more elegant, more pathetic. He might never know what made Lia drive herself as she did. But clearly, until he understood, until he could experience the revelatory edge of it himself, he couldn't know her. Thus his willingness to share her self-imposed dangers, come with her on her strange missions. Along with this line of thought came a troubling corollary: Until he knew what danger did for her—and until he embodied some measure of this thing that meant so much to her—he'd never believe he'd won her love at all.

Lia's voice brought him back to the present: "I need to drowse out," she said. The mumble of sleepy lips. "You going to be okay? Need me to help keep you awake?"

"I'm fine," he said.

Actually, it wasn't a bad time to be left alone with his thoughts. The motions of driving satisfied his need for a kinetic tune, the controls under his hands as gratifying as the saxophone keys. The dark highway was a strange landscape of white and yellow dots against the black background of the night—the dividing lines, reflectors, approaching headlights swinging toward him in a relentless, smooth, hypnotic arc.

At dinner with Dempsey and Elaine, they'd chatted and joked about Highwood and about their respective family histories. Elaine was nine years younger than Dempsey, a plump woman in an enormous blue sweater and clogs, her dark hair cut short to reveal turquoise-and-silver earrings. They sat on tall stools at the kitchen counter, sipping wine as Elaine deftly sliced vegetables.

It was nice to be in a well-lived-in house. The Corrigans liked bold, warm prints, unstained wood, smooth white walls counterpointed with sections of bare rock, an eclectic mix of furniture that Dempsey had built or that they'd bought during trips to Mexico. Dempsey's paintings on the walls, Elaine's plants in pots she'd turned and fired herself. Order, pretty things, a comfortable space beneath the high, raftered ceiling.

Dempsey proposed toasts to health and happiness, and they had a fine dinner, the pleasant room lit only by candles and the gently flickering light of the fire. Paul had begun to feel his dark mood slip away: The past wasn't all grief and knots. After the meal, while Lia and Elaine were deeply involved in a discussion about education, Dempsey asked Paul if he'd like to see some of the projects he was working on in his shop. Paul agreed immediately.

Dempsey's woodshop was attached to the house on the far side of the garage, a large room with a good collection of milling and woodworking equipment. As always, the shop was filled with wonders: strange shapes of wood that had been by-products of other projects, weird jigs and templates, the unusual furniture restoration commissions Dempsey took in. Paul admired Dempsey's impeccable work on a pair of rare Linnell chairs he was restoring for a museum in Philadelphia. When he glanced up he found the old man looking at him appraisingly.

"Paul—you think you'll do the job at Highwood? You seem to have your reservations."

"Can you blame me?"

"No."

"But on the other hand," Paul went on, glad to have Dempsey to bounce this off of, "I've got a lot of reasons to do it too—not the least of which is I'm dead broke. I've been sponging off of Lia for the last few months."

"Never a good idea. To tell you the truth, I'm in the same boat myself."

"You? What do you mean?"

Dempsey took down a brush and dustpan and began sweeping one of the workbenches. "I'm getting *old,* can you believe it? Treason. Betrayal from within. It's getting harder to do the fix-it stuff I used to do. That's been petering out for a couple of years."

"So how do you folks get by?"

"It's a close shave. Elaine substitute teaches, cleans houses two days a week. I still do fine restoration—when I can find it." He gestured at the chairs, a gilded bench, an elaborately inlaid marquetry box. "So. I'm not encouraging you to take the job at Highwood, but if you do, it'd help us if you wanted to sub out some of the furniture work. If you brought it here."

"Are you kidding? Who could do it better than you? I don't know enough about it. And I'm sure Vivien would be happy to have you doing the restoration."

Dempsey tossed the dustpan down. "God, there are times when I wish I still smoked." He shot a glance at Paul from under lowered eyebrows. "No—I'd as soon you didn't tell Vivien I was doing the work. At least not right away."

"Why not? You two have a falling out?"

"It's nothing important. It's just another of the stupid things between people that by the time you're my age you've got plenty of. It's a long time ago, it's trivial. Simply put, I'd just as soon not resume the hired-man role with Vivien. Maybe it doesn't matter anymore, but nobody needs old headaches. And right now I could use the work. I'm not up for lifting sheets of plywood all day, I don't trust myself on roofs or ladders. But I can sure as hell restore fine furniture in my own shop. So if you take the job, toss me the furniture work. If you want to."

"Of course." It had been painful to see Dempsey so ill at ease. He had felt oddly distant from the old man, an unusual and unpleasant feeling.

Paul slowed for the turn onto 91 north, the lights of Hartford slanting through the windows and casting trapezoids which slid over Lia's motionless form. Her head was turned toward him, and she breathed slowly, releasing air through her lips in gentle explosions.

His thoughts spun in big slow circles, spiraling in on the letter from Ben, still folded in his shirt pocket. The voice in the letter was absolutely Ben, yet so different from the man he usually recalled. The Ben in the letter seemed almost mischievous, *playful,* but the man he remembered was so often urging restraint, self-control. It would be nice to know which was the real one. For that matter, it would also be nice to know why the real one chose to jump off the cliff at Break Neck, had chosen to break apart not only his own body but his family as well, on the rocks below. Aster gave up on her career as a journalist, drank, became embittered and isolated. Kay sought refuge in a sort of deliberate amnesia, the calculated and shallow normalcy of middle-class life. And Paul himself, with his various sad and secret wounds. What malaise of the spirit caused Ben to bequeath such a legacy? In Paul's darker moments, he wondered whether he might have inherited the same worm in his soul.

After Springfield the traffic died down and there was just the dark highway, the speeding white and yellow dots swarming toward him, mesmerizing, like tracers fired from a machine gun in the darkness ahead.

He had all the reasons to do the job, yet he still felt a reservation. What was the problem? It was a nice place. He could remember it vividly.

Looking back at the great long high bulk of the house, deep in the shadows of big trees. Dark shingle walls, stained slate roof, white-trimmed windows, lightning rods. In the garden, the marble cupids' disingenuous gazes.

Running in the cool high woods. Vivien's big white sheepdog runs alongside. Sun through the treetops, straight beams in slightly misted air. Upthrust granite shelves covered with intricate embroidery of moss and lichen in greens and grays. The dog ranges, snuffles, glances back with his friendly toothy smile. Brambles and ravines. Birds swoop in the lattice of branches. Past the spooky dark under a massive overgrown rock shelf, a little scared, then into the sun again. Sitting resting on a boulder, feeling the dutiful deep heartbeat slowing, calming. The big dog scratches his ears with a hind leg, then licks his pink incongruous penis.

Moving on, deeper, moist mossy ground squelches in the low places, gnarled birch roots grip elephant-skinned boulders. Stands of white birch in bright contrast to the background forest gloom. Dog sees something ahead, whines uneasily, ears perked. Chill tingle of fear, feeling suddenly alone and too far from the house—

Paul was startled alert when Lia spoke, the thick voice of someone just awakened. He had been so deep in memory he was almost asleep.

"Something that occurred to me," Lia said. "It seems strange that Vivien just left everything as it was. You'd think she'd have taken more of her personal things with her, or put them in storage or something. Ask the neighbors to look after the place—" Lia yawned hugely. "You'd think she'd take better care of her property." She burrowed down into the swell of her jacket.

Paul waited for her to say more, but she had drowsed off again. She was right. Vivien's seemingly abrupt departure was strange—yet another anomaly about Highwood. Yes, one of several strangenesses. He thought back on the times he'd installed furnaces, and how hard it could be to cut that old heavy-gauge galvanized steel, even with the right tools, and of the weight of the furnace oil pump he'd hoisted in the basement at Highwood. There was the heavy marble mantelpiece in Vivien's room too, ripped out of the fireplace masonry. The bureau thrown out the window. The smashed piano he'd spotted in Royce's old room—even the cast iron, trussed string harp had been broken.

Something tugged at his memory, something not from the distant past but from recent times. Maybe about Mark? Too tired. The thread of thought evaded him. It was connected to another realization that had been growing on him, something Lia hadn't mentioned: *Whoever did it was one strong son of a bitch.*

8

Morgan Ford parked his car, shut off the ignition, and paused to massage his eyes and forehead. It was 8:05 A.M. Starting a day's work always brought on a moment of extreme fatigue that he had to overcome before he could open the car door, grab his overstuffed leather briefcase, and head into the one-story, pseudo-colonial brick building that housed the New York State Police barracks at Lewisboro.

It was Thursday and felt like it. The fatigue was his body's rebellion against facing another day of his job as investigator for the Bureau of Criminal Investigation. This stemmed in part from working in an environment where he was the new boy on the block, low man on the totem pole, preceded by the fucked-up reputation he'd gained at White Plains. But mostly the exhaustion originated internally. He wasn't certain that this job was doable, that he really had the stuff for it, or that this was what he ought to be doing with his life. Every day at this hour he thought the same thought: Maybe he should talk to his doctor, ask about chronic fatigue syndrome or something. He was thirty-five years old, a regular exerciser, nonsmoker, moderate drinker. He shouldn't feel this bad every day.

He went down the hallway to his so-called office and spotted what appeared to be a conference in the BCI senior investigator's office at the end of the hall—Barrett, Tommy Mack, Joe Matarini, Sue Trenton. He was glad to get his door open and slip inside without anyone noticing him. All he wanted was to get started on his day's work without encountering, too early, any of the other BCI staff, especially not his supervisor, Frank Barrett. Barrett was in his mid-fifties, with heavy jowls and a thick middle, a face as drooping and lugubrious as a basset hound's. Mo didn't need to look at those pouched eyes this early in the day.

His office was commensurate with his status: not good. He'd come on the job a month earlier, replacing detective William Avery, who had reached sixty and retired without burning out, getting shot, or drinking himself to death, although he'd apparently given that a good try. The barracks nickname Wild Bill was intended ironically. He had a bland face, thinning reddish hair, big clumsy limbs, a drinker's veined nose. He'd avoided getting killed on the job by not pushing anything too hard. Especially in the last few months before his retirement, he'd nursed his cases along at a leisurely tempo, basically killing time until the buzzer went off, he took his ceremonial retirement badge from the Police Benevolent Association, and went home.

They'd worked together for two weeks in the transition, Avery explaining the cases Mo would inherit, walking him through his files. Maybe Avery's golden-years-on-the-force aura had protected Mo during the transition period, and the staff had seemed friendly enough at first. But once he was gone, things changed. Mo got Wild Bill's files but not his desk in the main office, which faced windows overlooking a nice view of fields, woods, the hills across the valley. The day after Avery's farewell dinner, they'd begun installation of some new heating and plumbing in the ceiling over that half of the main room, and Mo's desk had been "temporarily" relocated into a tiny utility room with one narrow window opening onto a view of whatever vehicle had parked in front of it. Being isolated from the others right away suited Mo's disposition but was probably bad managerial planning by Barrett. His banishment coincided uncomfortably with the changing tone of his exchanges with his fellows in the two weeks since Avery left, the snatches of overheard conversations alluding to his problems at White Plains. Now people seemed to approach him with either a chill or, worse, a smug sort of sympathy.

Mo listened to his voice mail, opened his calendar for the day. He was supposed to meet with Barrett at eleven and had several interviews scheduled for the afternoon, dealing with the missing kid thing, one of the cases Wild Bill had been coasting on for the last six months. This promised to be at least marginally interesting, unlike most of the cases he'd been given, which concerned crap like burglary, a small-time car theft ring, a hit-and-run vehicular homicide with absolutely no leads, and so on. He spent an hour reviewing case files, jotting some notes, and by the time he was done felt up to encountering his colleagues.

The conference in Barrett's office had ended. Mo could see Barrett at his desk with his half-lens glasses on, reading from a thick sheaf of papers. He passed by the doorway without being noticed and turned into the main office, where the other BCI staff maintained desks in half-wall cubicles and where two civilian secretaries worked at their computer terminals. Mo got himself a cup of coffee, then paused at his mailbox. He separated the junk mail into the recycling bins and tossed the window envelopes into the trash.

Louise, one of the secretaries, returned to her desk and sat down. "How are you today, Mo?" she asked.

"I'm as good as can be expected under the circumstances, which could be better and could be worse," he said. "How about yourself?"

"Same." She stood up partway and raised the lever on her hydraulic chair so that the seat came up under her, then pulled her skirt under her thighs and sat back down. "I think the shock absorber on this thing leaks," she complained.

Mo opened a piece of mail and pretended to read it, watching Louise settle herself. When he'd first come into the office, he'd done the single man's offhand inventory of the female staff. With the exception of Louise, the women were ten or fifteen years older than he was, a rather colorless bunch. Grasping at straws, he'd entertained speculation about Louise for a few days because she was about his age and had a graceful if extremely slender figure. At first, the very plainness of the clothes she wore—slim-fitting, gray wool skirts, white long-sleeved blouses, sometimes with a pastel sweater thrown over her shoulders, low-heeled black shoes—had seemed to set off the sensual grace of her curves. She had a languid quality about her that had struck him as sexy too: the way she'd pause at her typing, tilt her chin back and roll her head to one side and the other—presumably to work out neck tension—or would push her dark hair back from her forehead not with her hand and fingers but with the back of her bent wrist.

But after a few days he'd decided that she was just a slightly anorexic woman with chronic hypoglycemia. She handled her work with only moderate competence, and during breaks had been working her way slowly through *The Bridges of Madison County* ever since he'd arrived. Though he could still appreciate the wan sweetness of the shape of her hips as she settled onto her chair, he had accepted that she was neither particularly sexy nor particularly interesting. Nor particularly interested. It was now over a year since his divorce from Dara, and he'd faced into his longing for another relationship, but after only a week at the new job he'd had to accept that if he were looking for love, he wasn't going to find it at the Lewisboro State Police barracks.

"Mo." He was startled out of his thoughts by a deep voice immediately behind him. He turned to see Barrett, glasses in hand, blue eyes staring out at him from the layered bags around them. "I've got a few minutes now," Barrett said. "You want to make our eleven o'clock a little early?"

Mo followed Barrett to his office, where the senior investigator sat on the edge of his desk and Mo took one of the plump vinyl-upholstered chairs. Barrett's office had a nice view of scrub sumac trees, a deep dried-blood purple, and above them a series of folds of pleasant brown fields interspersed with woods. The white rectangles of a new subdivision were scattered on the furthest hill, looking like spilled ice cubes.

"So," Barrett began, putting on his glasses again. "We're just basically checking in, I guess." He looked at Mo over the glasses, a surprisingly piercing glance as if Mo's response would be deeply revealing.

"Yes."

"Well, generalities first. The office working well? Copier code working?"

"Everything's fine. I'm still sorting out the"—Mo paused, about to say *shitheap,* then thinking better of it—"files that Avery left me."

"Wild Bill was tired out, wasn't he? I'll buy that he didn't keep a tidy house. How bad is it?"

Mo wasn't sure how revered Wild Bill's memory was with Barrett, but he felt compelled to be at least marginally truthful. "Pretty bad. The main problem is that he didn't do a lot of legwork for the last few months. There are a lot of leads he didn't follow up on."

This was an understatement. Wild Bill's inattention had bordered on nonfeasance. He'd done a pretty good job with everything you could do over the phone, but he hadn't gone into the field enough. In the case of the missing kids, Wild Bill had contacted missing persons agencies, juvenile detention centers, family resource agencies around the state and the country; he'd called relatives and checked with cheap hotels in the city, the FBI, other police departments, morgues and hospitals within a couple of hundred miles. But when none of these efforts had turned up any sign of them, he hadn't gone and talked to their buddies, their girlfriends, the local low-level drug dealers, the liquor store owners. Mo could see why: It would be hard to visualize old Wild Bill, with his bland, pleasant, over-the-hill face and big soft body, making much headway with suspicious, paranoid teenagers.

The pattern of his last few months' work was plain: If it could be done with the telephone propped between ear and shoulder, size twelves on the desk, he did it. If it meant driving all over Westchester County in the lousy weather they'd had this fall, he didn't get around to it. That left a lot of this sort of work for Mo. Which he didn't mind—he'd rather be out in his car or talking to the citizenry than shuffling papers in his office, getting the chill from his colleagues.

Mo told Barrett some of this, and Barrett nodded approvingly. "Bill didn't plan to be a hero," he admitted. "Not his style to die with his boots on." Both men chuckled at this image and then Barrett went on, raising his sad, penetrating eyes to Mo's: "Listen, Mo, here's the thing. You know and I know that you're coming here with some problems left over from White Plains—the thing with Wolf Dickie, your other disciplinary problems. You and I know you're hot shit but an uneven performer. And you and I also know what a mess Wild Bill left. Frankly, everyone else in the office knows it too. But Bill was well-liked—had that sort of, what do they call it, Teflon, and no one was going to complain, not with him out of here so soon. But what's going to happen now is, if I don't start giving you some new work, I've got to redistribute cases. People are going to complain about their caseloads, think you're not pulling your weight."

"You mean you don't think I've got much Teflon?" Mo said. He intended it as a joke.

Barrett continued, expressionless, the irony lost on him. "No, you don't seem to. So your best advice is to wrap these up soon and get in the line like everyone else. On some of Bill's I'd like to see results. Some of them you may just have to put to bed. Dead letter office."

No case was actively pursued forever. When no one had made headway on a case in a reasonable amount of time, the file was placed in a sort of holding pattern—available for any new information that might come in but not actively pursued on a daily basis unless something significant warranted reactivation. After a while, the investigator's reporting period for a go-nowhere case got longer and longer, and the case file was put in progressively deeper and more obscure storage repositories, along with the paper flotsam and jetsam of other state bureaucracies, until it was truly forgotten.

"Okay," Mo said. "I plan to do a lot of legwork this week and next. If nothing budges—"

Just then the phone on the desk wheedled, and Barrett leaned over to pick it up. "BCI, Barrett," he said into the mouthpiece, "hold on a minute." He punched the hold button with a thumb. "Okay," he went on to Mo, "sounds like you've got the right take on this. And listen, play by the book this time, Ford. Keep in close touch with me, am I being clear? The word is *teamwork,* right?" He hit the hold button again. "Yeah," he said.

Mo let himself out of the office, to his surprise feeling rather good. He was somewhat affirmed by Barrett's apparent faith in him, despite the Teflon comment and his closing reminder that Mo's status was tentative and he was to run his cases strictly by standard procedures, not go off on his own or indulge his instincts. He poured a cup of coffee, brought it back to his office, and sat down at his desk.

Okay. The vehicular homicide would be the first case to be put to bed. He opened the file and reviewed it as he sipped the coffee. The hit-and-run had happened about four months before, in early August. The twenty-three-year-old victim, Richard Mason, had apparently been out with friends earlier in the day. Around midnight, for some reason, he'd parked his car on Highway 138, at the top of the Lewisboro Reservoir, and gone for a walk. Someone had struck him hard enough to kill him and then had driven on, leaving the body in the eastbound lane at a sharp bend. Which was where, at around half past midnight, Betty Rosen and her husband ran over it again with their Ford Taurus stationwagon as they drove home from dinner and a play in the city. Betty was driving because Theodore's night vision was not good. They came around the bend and had no time to slow before hitting the body. After the impact, they had stopped long enough to look back at the remains, and then, in shock, they'd driven on to report the incident.

According to the accident report, it was a gory scene the Rosens had viewed in the glow from their taillights. Mo had read the report carefully but had not looked at the photos, a couple dozen eight-by-tens, which were in the file in a white envelope. The episode in White Plains had shown him that he didn't have much stomach for blood, and if at all possible he intended to work on this case without ever looking at the photos. There was no need—the crime scene team's report, the medical examiner's report, the accident reconstructionist's report were very detailed, and he trusted their expertise and judgment. Anyway, his imagination was quite good.

When the accident scene team arrived, they found the guy's body at the end of a trail of blood and body parts almost a hundred feet long. He had apparently been struck hard by the first car or truck or whatever, hard enough to kill him and sever one leg. Then the Rosens had come along and the body had been dragged beneath their car, rebounding between the pavement and the vehicle's undercarriage, probably getting "processed" by the tire, up and around a wheel well. So when poor Betty and Theodore had looked back, they saw a tangled heap of soft wet stuff, 180 pounds of chopped liver with some gristle in it. No, Mo would skip the photos.

When Betty Rosen had become coherent enough to be interviewed, she estimated that she'd seen the body in the headlights for less than two seconds before her car hit it. She further testified that some dismemberment had already occurred—she had seen "two lumps" in the road. The accident team's report verified that the Rosens had struck Mason when he was already dead, and that in fact his left leg had already been separated from his torso prior to the Taurus's impact. The ME's report also said there was some alcohol in Mason's blood, 0.06, a mild drunk, which concurred with friends' testimony that he'd downed a couple of beers earlier. The Rosens had been cleared of any wrongdoing.

The problem for Mo was that the body bore no clues about the vehicle that had done the killing—no automobile trim or rust or paint, no telltale wounds, and, most disappointing, no tire tracks other than the Rosens' in the blood fan. And none of the standard means for locating a hit-and-run had revealed anything: No car body shops had reported suspicious damage or tissue residues. No tips had come in to the anonymous hotline the county maintained. And at almost four months after the fact, they never would. The incident was a good candidate for the dead letter office.

Mo looked at the photo he had clipped to the folder, which showed the victim with his mother, father, and younger sister standing in front of a fireplace. Apparently the father was some exec at IBM, so the family did all right. The sister appeared to be much younger, around twelve, a plain girl with an awkward mouth and thick glasses. Somewhat strained smiles all around. The younger Mason had just returned from college in Syracuse and was staying with the family until he got a job or otherwise figured out his life. With his well-fleshed body, his tailored suit, his big face and thick lips, at once macho and babyish, he looked a typical young man of his generation: a bit spoiled, a bit ashamed of his inability to live up to expectations, a bit resentful of his parents' generosity and the emotional strings attached to it. The little sister had a history of psychological problems, and her brother's death had apparently really set her back. No doubt, like any family, they were all often more aware of the daily tensions and pressures, the little feuds and grudges, than the important bonds that really mattered. It's a shame, Mo thought, how often it took something like this to make people remember their priorities.

Mo closed the file, spun his chair to look at the hood of a blue pickup parked in front of his window and at the gray day outside, then spun back and opened another folder.

The missing kid thing was another situation entirely, not one to put away yet. At least four local high-school kids had disappeared from the area during the last few months. There were some signs that their disappearances were connected—they had vanished during the same period of two months, a couple of the kids had known each other slightly at school—but this was speculative. Wild Bill had run a File 6 check on NYSPIN, the New York State Police Information Network, and had met with an interagency task force, but nobody had gotten anywhere. Wild Bill's idea, which the Westchester district attorney's office apparently shared, was that the whole business was probably nothing more than an epidemic of running away from home among the well-off but rebellious upper–Westchester County teenagers. For Bill it had been a good excuse not to push the case.

Wild Bill's theory appeared to have been borne out by recent developments. Originally, they'd thought five teenagers were missing, but in a lucky coup for his first week on the job Mo had located one of the kids. By talking to friends and girlfriends, Mo had figured out enough of the family dynamic operating in this case to make a few deductions. It was typical divorce stuff, which Wild Bill should have known—the kid had turned up at a relative's house in Pennsylvania. The case was now what it should have been from the start: just another ugly custody battle, pricey gladiators battling in a walnut-paneled arena, making everybody's life hell.

But that still left four kids. All were between the ages of fifteen and eighteen, and all had disappeared within a seven-week period during August and September. It was the times of their various disappearances that interested Mo most.

For two of the kids, pinning down the exact date of disappearance had proven impossible. It had to do with family structure and the values prevalent in Westchester County, New York, U.S.A., in the late twentieth century.

One kid, Mike Walinski, came from a very well-off family in which the parents—because they didn't give a damn or through some misguided theory of child rearing—didn't keep track of their son's comings and goings. The kid had his own car, his own apartment above the garage; the parents had a busy social calendar, traveled a lot, spent nights away, left the kid on his own. In general, Mo had decided, they pursued their careers and their various indulgences with more diligence than they applied to their parenting. When Wild Bill tried to establish exactly when Mike had gone missing, the parents admitted that there were problems in the family, they hadn't seen much of Mike lately. They justified their inattention by claiming a great respect for the kid's need for independence. They had returned late at night from three days on the West Coast, hadn't seen Mike that night, although his car was in the garage. It was only after two more days that they got concerned enough to call the police. As a result, nobody could pin down exactly when Mike disappeared. At eighteen, Mike was the oldest of the missing teenagers. He was an only child, just graduated from JFK High School.

The second kid's background was very different, but the end result was oddly similar. Steve Rubio was fifteen and lived alone with his father, an alcoholic who held temporary landscaping and repair jobs and barely scraped by. Strange, Mo thought, how the family structure of both rich and poor, highly educated and uneducated, could end up being so similar. Mo wouldn't be surprised to find that these kids had run away, and he couldn't blame them either.

But the other two kids' parents had called the same days their kids had gone out and not come back, so it was easy to ascertain when they had last been seen. Essie Howrigan was sixteen, a pretty girl according to the class photo Bill had procured for her file. Her parents had last seen her on the evening of August 6, when they went out with some friends to a movie. The boy was Dub Gilmore, real name Allen Jr., who was also sixteen and had just completed his sophomore year at the high school. Lived only a mile from the Howrigans, but the two families didn't know each other. Dub had taken off around seven weeks later than Essie, in mid-September. To Mo, these two kids didn't fit the profile of probable runaways. The parents certainly didn't think so, and the local papers had made a thing of it for a while. In his file were a half dozen newspaper clippings, some about the disappearances, some about the school-sponsored community meetings at which dozens of parents had spoken about the "teen crisis," social fragmentation, erosion of the family, etc. The BCI school liaison officer came to talk about "normlessness," the current big buzzword at the Bureau. For all Mo's cynicism about the jargon, he tended to agree with what they said.

Mo checked his watch, closed his files, left the building. Outside, a breeze blew through the parking lot, carrying a chill as if it had blown off the ice-cube subdivision on the distant slope. He was glad to get into his car.

Driving to the town of Purdys, he thought about the case some more. The individual cases came together into a pattern in that the dates fit into two clusters. Mo had filled in a calendar, marking the days when Essie and Dub had disappeared, then shading in a band of days when it was probable Mike and Steve had gone. Essie's X fell on August 6, in the middle of the period when it was likely Mike had vanished; Dub's X filled in September 19, at the tail end of Steve's band. It was suggestive.

His next job was to explore the possibility of links between the kids. In his notebooks, he had started to draw a tinkertoy pattern, four circles representing each kid, with lines connecting them—knew each other, went to school together, friends in common, overlapping interests. So far, there weren't many connecting lines.

Today's interviews were the ones he'd decided were most likely to give him something useful: the families of Dub Gilmore and Essie Howrigan. These were parents who could be expected to know something about their kids' lives, who had demonstrated enough concern to call the police right away.

Mo checked the Gilmores' Briar Estates address in his notebook, found the number on a mailbox in front of a recently built two-story house, one with some architectural flourishes, stylishly faced in brown clapboards. Each tree in the yard was surrounded by a neat circle of redwood bark. When did that fashion start? More to the point, he wondered, when would it pass? An overly neat, professionally maintained yard, a Honda Accord station wagon parked in the drive: Mo decided that the Gilmores were doing all right.

Before turning into the driveway, he glanced at the dashboard clock. Ten minutes to one—he was early. It wasn't a good idea to be early for an interview like this, when families needed to brace themselves. He turned up the heater another notch and continued past the house, out the Lewisboro Reservoir Road, along the bottom of the reservoir.

It was pretty country up here. He remembered coming fishing with his parents to one or another of these reservoirs when he was a kid and loving it. In the last twenty years, the landscape had changed as the commuter population burgeoned and as old farms and woodlots were sold off as subdivisions. Yet on a day like today, when the bare trees were gaunt and dark, when the wind seemed to press the water of the reservoir into a flat slate-gray sheet, he could still feel the way it had been. There was still the feel of Washington Irving's Catskills here—hoary old woods, meandering tumble-down stone walls, dark, shingle-faced houses barely visible through the trees.

Mo checked the time again and pulled into a wide driveway to turn around. Two squat pillars of mossy stone flanked a wrecked car that had been placed to block access to the driveway, which rose steeply away from the road and disappeared into the trees. Another of the old family homes, most likely run on hard times, estate litigation, high land taxes, or generational transitions. By next year or the year after, there'd be more neat houses clustered here, marked by a stylish sign: Saxony Village or Briarwood Manor. Something cute, pretentious, and Anglo. Mo chided himself for his cynicism, then pulled a U-turn back toward the Gilmores' house.

9

Mrs. Gilmore was a short woman, around forty, with a washed-out look: wispy blond hair in a cloud of curls, a pale face, no lipstick. Her husband was already in the living room when they came in, standing and pretending to read a newspaper, clearly too nervous to sit down. Mr. Gilmore was tall and thin, slightly hunched, with dark, thinning hair and a look of both weariness and hostility. He shook hands with Mo, a hard, quick grip, his eyes never leaving Mo's face. Mo wondered how much the last two months had changed the way these people looked.

"Please sit here, Mr. Ford," Mrs. Gilmore said, gesturing at an armchair near a fireplace containing some logs that, Mo guessed, were purely ornamental. They had prepared for his visit: Two other chairs were drawn up to make a neat triangle. "Can I get you some coffee?"

Mo hesitated, then assented. If it would help put Mrs. Gilmore at ease, he'd sit there with coffee at his elbow, although he didn't really want to drink any. He wished he'd eaten some lunch.

"You have a fine house here," he said. "This is a very nice area."

"Well, we once thought so," Mr. Gilmore said.

"My family is from Scarsdale. We used to come up here to go fishing. I always liked it up here." Mo felt as if everything he said was the wrong thing, each statement wounding Mr. Gilmore. He was glad when Mrs. Gilmore reappeared with three cups of coffee on a tray, served him, and sat down.

"Mr. and Mrs. Gilmore," Mo began, "let me begin by repeating what I said on the telephone: I'm not here to tell you anything new. I'm here to find out what I can, hopefully to find something that can help us locate Dub. Detective Avery has retired, and I'm taking over this case. If I ask you things he's already asked you, I'm sorry, but please try to answer as completely as you can. Something may come to mind that didn't when Detective Avery spoke to you."

Mrs. Gilmore nodded encouragingly. In Mo's limited experience, parents of kids involved in crimes, either as victims or perpetrators, tended to have one of two attitudes toward police: either angry and accusatory, or apologetic and embarrassed. It looked as if he had one of each in the Gilmores.

"I don't know if Detective Avery made it clear the way we're viewing this situation."

"He told us some other kids from the area had disappeared," Mrs. Gilmore said. "That maybe the disappearances were connected."

"It's suppositional, but yes. So my goal is to talk to you and the other parents—"

"With all due respect to the other families," Mr. Gilmore broke in, "I want to see someone working for *our* kid. For *us*. We had one detective, one old *rummy*, frankly—"

"Dear," Mrs. Gilmore cautioned. She looked to Mo for sympathy.

Her husband was just getting going. "—one old rummy trying to find five or six kids. Now we've got you, a new guy coming in cold, doesn't know a goddamned thing about the case—"

Mrs. Gilmore raised her voice, surprising Mo. "Allen!" She turned to Mo again, almost in tears. Mr. Gilmore subsided, chastened.

Mo cleared his throat. "Let me see if I can address your concerns. First of all, yes, I'm new in the area, but I think there's a certain advantage to having a fresh pair of eyes to look at things. Second, there's an advantage to working on related cases as a group. With your son's disappearance alone, we don't have much to go on. But if you add information from the others, you might see a pattern. Third, I'm not really alone on this. We've got an interagency task force with some very sharp people on it, and I assure you, your son's disappearance is high on the agenda."

Mo paused to get his thoughts in order. What he wanted to do was get the Gilmores talking, telling him about their son, without having to interrupt or overtly steer them. Probably Wild Bill had been trained before the newer cognitive interviewing techniques had become part of basic investigative procedure—he'd sit down, ask 'em the who what when where and why, take his notes, draw his conclusions. The problem being that memory doesn't work that way. If Mo wanted to get details that Bill had failed to turn up, his best bet was to encourage in the Gilmores a deep state of recollection, stream-of-consciousness remembering.

Mrs. Gilmore seemed to need to unload, and Mo let her talk, her husband interjecting comments occasionally. From what they said, Dub was a pretty average kid: sports, girls, buddies, some mischief, medium student at school. No indications of drug use, but he'd pilfered scotch from the liquor cabinet on a couple of occasions, watering the whiskey from the tap so the bottle wouldn't look depleted. Mo smiled as they told him this: He'd done the same himself at Dub's age. He had a slightly punk haircut, Mrs. Gilmore said, but he didn't have that cynical attitude: He'd spent half the summer teaching his little brother to ride a two-wheeler. Once this spring, after Mrs. Gilmore had had a stressful day, he'd given her a neck and shoulder massage. How many kids his age would give their moms a massage, Detective Ford?

After half an hour, the Gilmores wound down, having failed to reveal anything of particular use.

Mo waited until he was sure the flow had stopped. "I'd like to ask you some questions about Dub's personal life." He read through the questions he'd prepared, about Dub's friends, about kids he may have spent time with in extracurricular activities or sports, about what kind of mood he was in before he disappeared, about what he liked to do when he did things by himself. Pen pals, friends who had moved away, people they'd met on vacations. They gave him a few new names, which Mo wrote down. Dub sounded like a pretty normal kid. His mood when he disappeared was not unusually depressed or distant.

"I know you've been asked this before, but please tell me—do any of these names mean anything to you?" He read them the names of the other missing teenagers: Mike Walinski, Essie Howrigan, Steve Rubio.

"The Howrigans we have met," Mrs. Gilmore said. "At dinner at some mutual friends'. I think Essie was in Dub's English class last year, but not this year. We already told Detective Avery."

"Do you have any reason to believe they spent time together?"

"No. None." Something in Mo's face must have caught her attention. "Mr. Ford," she said, "we were a fairly close family. There were girls Dub was sweet on. We've told you their names. As a family, we always tried to keep communication open. Dub wasn't shy about telling us who he was interested in. But he never once mentioned Essie Howrigan. I'm sorry."

Mo asked a few more perfunctory questions, but he could see that it was time to wrap up the interview. As memories of Dub awoke, so did the grief, and both parents began to look drained. He stood up, closed his notebook, thanked them, and promised he'd stay in touch.

Mr. Gilmore ignored Mo's hand when he offered it. "So," he said, "you got nothing at all from us. Not a goddamned thing, right?"

"It's too soon to tell. You've given me a lot to follow up on."

" 'Too soon to tell'? My son's been gone for two months, Mr. Ford. How long is long enough for you guys?" He went to stand at the window, his back to Mo, slapping his thigh with the folded newspaper.

Mrs. Gilmore led Mo to the door, not saying anything until they got to the entrance hall and Mo turned to shake her hand. "Mr. Ford," she said, "I'd like to apologize for my husband's tone."

"That's not necessary. Not at all."

She looked into his eyes beseechingly and continued in a hushed voice, as if desperate for his understanding. "You see, when something like this happens, it . . . it violates your trust in the whole world. That it's really not . . . a very nice place. That you can't have faith in what will happen anymore. And you stop trusting anybody. Even the police. Even"—she looked back toward the living room—"each other."

Mo went down the sidewalk to his car. So that was it, Mo decided, the look the Gilmores had in common, despite their different responses: a marrow-deep caution, a holding back. The foundation of basic trust knocked out from under them. For a moment, the morning's fatigue came rushing back upon him, and he fought it off by taking deep breaths of the cold air. He wasn't cut out to be anyone's marriage counselor.

Mo steered with one hand and wolfed down a couple of stale vending-machine packages of peanut butter–and–cracker sandwiches, which he kept in the glove compartment for blood-sugar emergencies. By the time he got to the Howrigans' neighborhood, his stomach was beginning to process the food and he could feel his energy returning.

The Howrigans lived on one of several looping streets of a subdivision that had been built in the early seventies, cheaper homes in shades of pale green and blue aluminum siding, middle class without much pretension. Marty Howrigan was a thick-set man of medium height, with a beer-drinker's hard paunch and an aggressively projecting mustache the same red as his hair. He gave Mo a firm handshake in a square, muscular hand and led him back into their living room, where his wife and daughter waited.

"Girls, this is Detective Ford. Mr. Ford, my wife, Janis, and my daughter, Brittany." Howrigan tossed himself down into a wing chair.

Mo shook hands, immediately experiencing discomfort at the proximity of Janis. She was heartbreakingly beautiful. She looked too young to have a sixteen-year-old daughter. Over her jeans she wore a man's blue work shirt, untucked but held to her slim waist with a thin red leather belt. She had rich dark hair that set off her pale skin and startlingly blue eyes. A true Black Irish beauty, Mo thought. Flawless eyebrows and cheekbones. And the thing that really nailed him: the sadness in her eyes, around her perfect mouth. The hint of uncertainty and melancholy that awoke his chivalrous feelings.

After seeing Janis, it took a conscious effort to keep his eyes where they ought to be, looking to each of the three as they spoke. Mo cursed himself for his vulnerability.

The Howrigans clearly weren't planning to let him take the lead. "We did some homework based on what you told us you wanted," Janis Howrigan said. She handed him several sheets of paper on which names were listed, each followed by a paragraph of text. "These are the names of every one of Essie's friends and acquaintances. Everyone she baby-sat for, people she worked with in our church group, kids she worked with washing cars for the school teams." Janis leaned across the coffee table to point to a paragraph, and Mo caught the sweet scent of her hair. "We all made notes about what we knew about her relationship with them, and I compiled them. I thought it would save you time."

"My wife has a computer database and this on-line network to help us find Essie," Marty Howrigan told him. "Not that we don't trust you guys to do a good job. We're just determined we'll find her. One way or the other."

Mo scanned the list, then brought out the new list he'd compiled at the Gilmores' and compared it with Janis's meticulous notes. It was disappointing.

"If you wouldn't mind, I'd like to briefly go over each of these with you. Brittany, I'd like your help on this. Often a brother or sister knows things a parent doesn't. Okay?"

Brittany nodded. She was about eleven, a tall, skinny girl with braces.

They went down the list, which Janis had alphabetized, the Howrigans filling in any missing details as Mo asked questions. Essie was an active girl, belonging to various clubs and youth groups, and the list of people she'd associated with was quite long. After several entries, Janis had noted "T.C."

"What does 'T.C.' stand for?" Mo asked Janis.

"That's 'Teen Companion.' It's a program at our church, where teens go out and spend time with the elderly or people who are sick or who have other problems that a companion can help with. Some of them are housebound and just need company."

"It looks like Essie was very active in the group."

"Yes, this last year especially."

"Ella Marbin, Dorothy McKenzie, Heather Mason, Wally Graham—do you know all these people? Are they all members of your church?"

Marty Howrigan answered: "Some are. Some are referred to the T.C. group by one agency or another—Social Rehabilitation Service, Senior Wheels, that kind of thing."

"Ella is a member of our church," Janis put in. She leaned close again and put a slim finger on the entry. "She's seventy-six and broke her hip last fall. Essie went to her house once a week to play cards and help with cleaning. Dorothy McKenzie we don't know personally but is also elderly. She has vision problems. Essie read to her."

Brittany spoke up. "Heather Mason isn't old—she's like retarded or something."

"She's not retarded, Brit," Janis said. "I understand she is a teenager with behavioral problems. Essie was spending a lot of time with her—two or three afternoons or evenings a week. We don't know the family."

"What about this last one?"

"Wally. I've met him. He's cute," Brittany said.

"Wally is a seven-year-old who has muscular dystrophy. He's in a wheel-chair. A very nice little boy who can't do much and as a result doesn't have many friends. Essie just played with him." When Janis leaned back into the couch, her eyes were brimming despite her iron resolve.

Marty Howrigan spoke again, forcefully: "Maybe you can see why we think Essie is a very special kid. We want her back."

They went on through the laborious process of discussing each friend and contact. Only when they reached the end did it dawn on Mo that something was missing from the list.

"Mrs. Howrigan, I hate to bring this up, but I have to ask. Doesn't Essie have a boyfriend? I mean, she's sixteen, she's a beautiful girl, surely—"

Janis hesitated, looked uncomfortable. "No. No boyfriend."

"Never? You've done a fine job of listing every last friend and acquain-tance, I've got ten pages of notes, but I don't even see any *old* boyfriends here. Guys she *used to* like."

The parents looked at each other, and Brittany became very interested in the ribbon at her collar. The micromomentaries—sudden activation of small muscle movements, like Marty's mustache twitching, the changeable weather of Janis's eyes and brows—told Mo he'd hit a topic of concern. Probably, therefore, of value.

"The fact is, we don't know," Marty admitted. "Essie is very reserved about that aspect of her life. We respect that. We don't pry."

Janis looked distressed. "Brittany, honey, can you do me a favor? Get me a drink of water? With ice, sweetie."

Brittany stood up, frowning, and stumped out of the room, aware that she was being gotten rid of.

"Part of it was the church group, Mr. Ford," Janis said. She glanced at her husband, eyes brimming again. "They are so thoroughly . . . clean-cut. Such good, *traditional* values. Essie took it all to heart. At first I was glad. But I think the new pastor went too far—I mean, this emphasis on chastity and virginity and all that. They never mention sex without mentioning dis-eases or—"

"Janis, Mr. Ford doesn't want to hear it."

"Essie was a good girl," Janis said, crying openly now. "She really, deeply, wanted to be good and virtuous."

"She *was* good and virtuous. She *is*," Marty Howrigan insisted.

Mo coughed. "Excuse me. This may be uncomfortable for you, but I'm afraid I have to ask: To your knowledge, was Essie sexually active?"

The Howrigans were silent for a moment, looking at each other. Some gulf had opened between them, a mistrust. The look Marty Howrigan gave his wife seemed slightly fearful, as if he saw for the first time that whole areas of his daughter's life might be secret from him—and that his wife might not, in fact, always tell him everything.

"Not to my knowledge, no," Marty Howrigan said cautiously.

Janis wiped her lovely eyes with the sleeve of her shirt. "I don't think so. I mean, I don't know either. That's my point," she said, looking at her husband. "It's not whether she had boyfriends or not that bothers me, it's that she didn't feel she could ever, *ever* talk about it to us. Ever. Don't you see, Marty?"

"This is an old discussion," Marty said. He threw himself back against the chair, started to speak again, then clapped his hands on his thighs and shut his mouth.

"Then let me ask you this," Mo put in, not willing to let the revelations stall, "what sort of mood was Essie in when she disappeared? Was she different in any way? The day she left, the weeks preceding her disappearance?"

"I don't know," Janis said dully. "Maybe."

"Maybe how?"

"She was, I'd say, preoccupied," Marty said.

Janis nodded. "Just a little off. Not always paying attention. I just thought it was, you know, a developmental stage."

Brittany returned with a glass of water for her mother and sat again on the couch. Janis Howrigan took the glass absently. She had withdrawn, not looking at anything, lost in her thoughts. That tragic inwardness—another mannerism that always got to Mo, pierced him to his heart.

Mo asked the three of them some more questions, but it was clear the interview was effectively over. When he stood to go, Janis was staring at her glass of water, which she hadn't taken a drink from. She nodded vaguely but didn't speak to him or look at him when he said good-bye.

Driving around the reservoir for the third time that day, he fumed at himself. His heart felt wrecked in his chest, simply because a beautiful woman had not shown any special interest in him when he left. What had he expected? A lingering, meaningful gaze from a woman mourning her lost daughter? He was as vulnerable as a lovesick boy.

He'd liked the Howrigans, but he should have known that there was buried stuff there. Like every family. So the two parents had very different politics, especially when it came to issues of sexuality. Unless Essie turned up, they could wrangle over it for the rest of their lives—whose fault it was, whose philosophy was right, which of them had failed her as a parent. And how would Brittany deal with it when her turn came? She'd see the fork in the road soon enough, and have to choose.

Mo raged at himself and then found himself venting his anger on the Howrigans. *Brittany:* another one of those idiotic, pretentious names that were so in fashion, along with Chelsea, Tiffany, Heather, Courtney, et cetera. Cutesy, turn-of-the-century, pseudo-Anglo, yuppie. It wasn't until he'd driven another five miles that he realized the explosion about Essie's sex life, or the lack thereof, had deflected his thoughts. Something important had slipped through. Something about the names—another fashionable name. He thought back. One of the Teen Companion people: the teenager, Heather Mason. He'd have to check the files as soon as he got back to the barracks. If he remembered right, Heather Mason was the name of Richard Mason's sister—Richard Mason, the hit-and-run victim, the young man who had ended up at the end of a ninety-foot blood fan. On Route 138, not two miles from the Howrigans'.

10

"I'm not getting it," Paul told Lia. "I don't get clear when we do this shit, the way you do. Like right now I'm *swarming*. I'm full of maggots." His abdomen seized in wrenching tics, explosions of air choked in his throat. A vaguely threatening tune was playing in his head, so loud he could hardly hear. He couldn't place the title, another growing irritation. When Lia had first planned the dive, a month before, it hadn't seemed such a bad idea, but now the danger had begun to seem all too real. Maybe it had something to do with visiting Highwood, feeling the darkness there.

"Just see to your gear, I guess," Lia said. She wasn't unsympathetic: When she had the wild light in her eyes, that was philosophy, not advice. She wore a heavily insulated, hooded wetsuit, glistening black and neon blue with purple knee pads, that made her look like a female Master of the Universe. She checked over her tanks, her regulators, her lights, the curved hip weights, the specialty tools on her belt, hands flying. Obviously keyed up.

Lia had borrowed the equipment from another friend, a fellow member of CDA, Cave Divers Anonymous. The name of the organization was indicative, Paul thought, suggesting compulsion and addiction. He wished the diving gear, with its dials and tubes, rubbery straps, molded shapes, didn't resemble medical apparatus quite so much.

It was early Friday afternoon. They had left the Subaru parked by the side of a narrow dirt road, then packed the gear through the woods two hundred yards on a small path that, presumably, only CDAs knew about. The entrance to the cave was a low triangular cleft in a tumble of granite chunks at the base of a cliff. Though Paul could hardly squeeze himself through, the passage opened inside to a room-size cave that Lia called The Foyer, where they stopped to dress and to perform the last equipment check before the dive. At the far end of The Foyer, another small hole opened, black and wet-looking.

"It's not *just* the element of risk." Lia cinched her tanks, made small adjustments. "There's curiosity too. And it's beautiful in there—it's strange and magical. You'll see."

Paul looked again at the map Lia had provided him, a Day-Glo yellow sheet of tough thin plastic with the winding labyrinth of the cave marked in black. It reminded him of something anatomical. They were about to slip inside the body of some giant creature.

"And the great thing is, it *registers*," Lia went on. "So often we're so cluttered with day-to-day concerns, preoccupations, we don't really *see* what's around us. It all gets filtered through the morass of daily crap, we miss a lot. The beauty of fear is that it cuts through, forces you to live in the moment. Watch how well you remember everything, later on."

"I'm feeling *more* cluttered. Damn it, Lia, I've got Tourette's."

"But you've said yourself when you're focused it goes away. I've noticed that after stress, you're calmer. Could it be that exposure to risk or tension desensitizes you to stressors? Who knows, Paul, maybe this is a way to reduce your symptoms."

It was possible. But Paul's resistance was also connected to Lia. Her intensity, the *hunger,* was as frightening as anything here.

When they were both suited up, three-fingered gloves on, forehead lamps in place, Lia led the way to the slot at the end, flippers slapping the rock. "I'm given to understand this is a rare structure for the East Coast, a remnant of volcanic action—chutes and tubes and pockets, often enlarged by the action of water. This one is pretty small, only a mile or so of passages."

"Meaning we might live."

She seemed unconscious of his sarcasm. "Yeah." She slid through the opening and disappeared, and Paul followed her, his tanks scraping on the granite edge. *You could get caught on something in such close quarters. Things could go wrong.*

Inside was a second chamber, smaller. Lia waited on a sloping shelf of rock, her forehead light illuminating a tapering funnel that ended abruptly in a sheet of utterly black, motionless water.

Paul stared at it, appalled. "On one condition, damn it. We—*you*—do not push the envelope. You do not extend your dive time. You do not explore anything that's not on the map. You do not play games."

She met his gaze and clearly caught the look in his eyes. "Okay," she said softly.

They waited a moment. Lia was spiraling in on her fear, finding the clarity and whatever else it was that so fascinated her, that she so needed. Paul tried to do the same, trying to become transparent to the anxiety, to let the tics and urges boil through and pass out of him.

"I think," Lia said at last, "I think it has to do with *surrender.* There's a paradox here—when you surrender to it, to the moment, to the fear, to your mortality, that's when you have the greatest power." She looked at him again, and he could see she meant it, deeply. And he could see how much it mattered to her that he see it.

This has got to be love, Paul thought. He pulled down his mask and respirator. He slid into the black water before Lia had moved, a way of saying he'd understood her. *This is love, and it will take you to the strangest places, and you'll go willingly.*

None of the limited diving he'd done before prepared him for this. Those few days had been in the sunlit, shallow waters off Key West, other divers all around, boats above. The water had been alive with fish, the play of sunlight, the metallic whine of distant propellers. This was just a yawning throat, disappearing into darkness, green-black rock walls at arm's length on all sides. The massive granite weight of the Green Mountains, the hiss of intake and the bubble of exhalation, the subliminal drum of his heartbeat. Above, Lia descended gracefully into the column of his bubbles, her light gyrating as she moved in eerie slow motion. A soft mist began to obscure the water around them, eons' worth of slowly accumulating superfine silt, swept from the walls by their movements. Cold, pressure, darkness. *Fear.*

After a vertical drop of fifty feet or so, the chute widened and canted, gradually becoming nearly horizontal. The horizontal stretch was worse: *no up or down.* The weights gave him neutral buoyancy, and without a surface above, without an external source of light, he couldn't always tell how to orient. It made his nerves shriek. *Which way was up?*

Paul rode the crest of his panic, controlled his breathing, which had gotten quick and shallow. Bubbles *rose*—that was up. His exhaled air hit the ceiling and scuttled away over the rough surface like living drops of mercury. He paused to stabilize himself and let Lia reach him, and together they clumsily unfolded the map. Lia traced a route with one finger, then led the way through one of several openings.

This tube seemed to have a somewhat different structure, rounded and molded of yellowish igneous rock that sparkled in their lights. Humps and globs and folds of rock, like hardened wax, stretched away ahead. *A bile duct. A cholesterol-clogged artery, a small intestine.*

The route Lia had traced led to a large chamber, marked on the map as an irregular oval, the biggest of the cave's spaces. As she'd explained earlier, the chamber had originally been above water and still trapped a bubble of air, which meant they could emerge there and rest for a time before heading back. The air would be breathable: Wherever there was water, there'd be oxygen.

Paul took the lead as they negotiated the final passage leading to the chamber. Obviously, this tube had once been above the water level too: Stalactites and stalagmites hung from the ceiling and sprouted from the floor, jagged teeth. Some filaments of accumulated mineral were as thin as soda straws, tapering to needle points. Paul navigated with care, occasionally gripping the rock and using it to propel himself. The irregular tunnel was a shifting shadowland in his forehead light, distances became difficult to gauge. The panic he'd controlled earlier began to rise again.

Ahead, the tunnel began to widen, the beginning of the big room. Paul felt a moment of relief until he noticed that the light around him had changed. He turned awkwardly to see Lia's forehead light panning wildly in the hanging forest of rock structures forty feet behind him. Something was wrong. Abruptly the light flashed through a swirl of bubbles, outlining a dark, struggling shape.

Paul catapulted himself off the base of a stalagmite and dove back through the maze of tapering rock, grappled and swam toward Lia. She was twisting and arching, reaching up behind her with her arms, repeating the same convulsive movement again and again. A hideous dance, a slow-motion ballet of death. Bubbles poured up from her tanks, scattering on the ceiling, a silvery tornado.

The pattern of it registered: Lia had caught some part of her apparatus on a spine of rock, her air tube had broken or dislodged, she couldn't turn to free herself. Again and again, the reflexes of her body made her try to reach and turn. An animal in trap. If she'd already inhaled water, death throes.

Hating the stubborn resistance of the water, Paul dove for the side of the tunnel, dodging Lia's flailing limbs, then came around behind her. In the flurry of bubbles it was hard to see what had caught, but he brought his shoulder against the pillar of rock and heaved. On the second try, it broke with a sharp *clack!*, and he was able to twist it free of her regulator housing and air tube. Lia came around again, felt her freedom to turn, found Paul's arms with her clutching hands.

He yanked her mouthpiece out and gave her his extra respirator, then reached up to cut off her air flow. The cacophony of hissing and bubbling air abruptly stopped. Lia calmed slightly, taking air, then got her own spare reg into operation.

After an agonizing few minutes they broke the surface in the big chamber. Paul paddled, treading water and turning to cast his beam around him. They were in a high-vaulted room, perhaps a hundred feet long. Against one wall, a massive formation resembling a cluster of organ pipes rose to the ceiling, its base melting into a shelf that extended into the water like a small beach. Paul pushed Lia ahead of him, then boosted her onto the shelf. They both collapsed, flinging off the masks, breathing the air of the cave.

No thoughts, no talk. Just air, some space overhead.

After a time Paul sat up and looked at Lia. What was she feeling? Relief, remorse, shame, gratitude? Was she at some level savoring this? She was clearly focused inward, inspecting whatever had been revealed. Or maybe just in shock. She'd pulled off her hood, and her wet hair lay tangled around her. He wished she weren't so beautiful: He wanted to stay angry with her. He'd be damned if he'd let her off easy this time.

"You know what I was thinking the whole time?" she said at last. Her voice was hoarse. "I mean, not that I was doing any actual 'thinking,' but there was one sort of idea that came to me."

"Has it ever occurred to you there might be other ways to get at these great ideas? I don't want to listen to any of the revelations this earned you. Whatever they are, they're not worth it."

She ignored him. "The thought was, *I want to have a baby with Paul. I've got to get unstuck so I can live and make a baby with Paul.* I know it's nuts. But there it is."

Paul didn't answer. Some big, nameless feeling was rushing to fill the aftermath. A good feeling, strong. He scowled at it.

She didn't push her luck, just looked around the room with him. Their lights set fire to the rocks, a rainbow of pastels, luminous. Still gently disturbed by their swimming, the water reflected and fragmented the ceiling colors, scattered the beams of their lights. An enormous, lustrous opal.

"There's a word for the way it looks," Lia said. "*Chatoyant.* It's in the dictionary. It means 'of changeable luster.' Isn't that a beautiful word?"

He didn't answer, didn't look at her. He kept seeing her struggling, caught and convulsing like a gaffed fish.

"Thank you for helping me," she said. "For saving me. I never saw anyone move so fast. I don't know how you broke that stalactite."

"How much air did you lose, Lia?"

"There's enough to make it out again."

Lia worked on her gear, small hands deft and certain. Paul looked away again. They'd lived. With any luck they'd make it out alive too. He couldn't stay mad at her forever. She was right about too many things. The Big Nameless filled him, almost euphoric. He felt completely empty of tics, centered, simplified. He almost wanted to fake a twitch or two, just to spite her. God damn her for being crazy, and for being right. Terror therapy for Tourette's—the latest cure. After his panic, his unthinking effort to save her, he felt oddly sensual, conscious of his body, aware of the blood circulating in his veins, the well-used feeling in his muscles. He could feel Lia's body heat next to him, the electrical energy of her. The hall they were in was astonishing, the throne room of some underworld king. He'd never seen anything so beautiful.

It slipped out of him before he could stop it: "So maybe fear is a barrier," he said. "Beyond which is *wonder.*"

She looked at him. "If I'd said that now, you'd get mad."

Paul lay back again, staring at the ceiling. *Surrender, just surrender.* It was hopeless. He knew from experience that after her near escape she'd be charged with sexual energy. And he felt it too. Maybe there was truth to the theory that an organism's procreative urge was strongest during mortal threat, an ancient, primal instinct to assure survival. Paul didn't go looking for it the way she did, but he wasn't immune to it either.

After a time he gave up and reached for her, slid open the long zipper of her wet suit. They stood and undressed each other. Beneath her clothes, her skin was taut, soft curves taking some of the opal light. He was achingly erect, swollen, ready to burst, needing to bury himself in her. The cave felt supremely private, intimate. He spread their suits on the rock and laid her back down on them. She guided his face to her breasts, and he took one nipple in his mouth, drawing on her. Still suckling, he slid up between her thighs and drew exquisite circles in her wet folds until she pulled against his buttocks and slid him full into her. One of her hands found its way to his balls, cupping him lightly there, and then pulling him in, always in, massaging the root of his erection, the throbbing shaft that now connected them. She was a cave, she was the mountain, the earth. She arched until he had reached the limit, socketed into her. Her body rippled, impossibly supple, as she drew upon her recent panic, her own mortal fear. And then all the pressures rose and converged and he became a volcano, bursting explosively into her as she writhed in her own orgasm, arching up to receive him. The tectonic plates shifting. Earthquake.

When he spiraled back, she was crying softly. Her eyes met his, pooling and overflowing. Some deep part of her, upwelling and becoming tears. Delayed reaction to her close call? Remorse? Some deep sorrow? Sheer wonder? Sheer surrender, maybe. How amazing that you could feel so supremely close and yet understand nothing. The limits of intimacy: You could only get so naked, so revealed. Ultimately you were alone inside your own skin, your own skull.

Maybe she'd kill herself one of these times. Maybe that's what she wanted. *Eros, Thanatos.* And yet he had no choice but to love her, go with her there too if that's where she had to go. Or maybe he'd find some key, some healing magic. He held her until she was done crying, alarmed at the mystery of her, knowing that he would remember this vividly for years, just as she'd said, and yet probably never understand.

11

"**Aunt** Vivien, I have bad news, I'm afraid," Paul said. He straightened the notes he'd prepared for this conversation. Having devoted Thursday to the dive with Lia, he had spent all day Friday developing photos, making dozens of calls to the Lewisboro area—electricians, building supply outfits, dry cleaners, tool rental houses, heating specialists—and taking exhaustive notes. Looking down at his materials now, he found himself incredulous, despite having seen it with his own eyes.

His hand flew to his nose, moustache, and eyebrows, quick smoothing motions. "I have photos and a written description, and I've prepared a preliminary estimate for you. Bottom line, your house is a wreck. I don't know how to convey what it's like there. Structurally, it's not too bad, but inside it's as if a tornado hit it. There are holes in the interior walls big enough to walk through. The floor is two or three feet deep with your belongings, your clothes are everywhere, there's rodent and water damage. There are broken pieces of furniture in the driveway and on the ground around the house. Your papers are blowing around the house."

He heard her inhale. "My personal papers?"

"If your papers were in the file cabinets in the library or bedrooms, yes. There are literally heaps and drifts of papers."

She didn't respond, and he waited, listening to the ghosts of other conversations on the satellite line.

At last he cleared his throat. "I'm sorry." He made himself go on: the furniture, the windows, the plumbing, the furnaces, the wiring, continuing the recitation of destruction until he ran out of things to say.

"Well," she said. "Well. And where does that leave us? What do you recommend?" Her voice sounded tentative, dazed.

"First, you'll need to close off the house against further intrusion and the weather."

"Yes."

"Then you'll need to get electricity and some kind of heat source—the furnaces, preferably. Whoever is going to sift through your things will need a long time, and it's cold up there. The driveway won't be passable if it snows, so we may need plowing. And before we can bring the heat up inside, you'll need to see to the plumbing. At the very least, you should drain the remaining water in the pipes."

"It will have to be you," she said quietly. "Just you."

"I'm not really a plumber, Vivien, I—"

"No. I meant going through my things. It will have to be you." Vivien's tone stiffened, a touch of the hauteur returning. "I can't have some local tradesman in there, looking over my papers, my belongings. I'm not going to hire some . . . some chatterbox *Kelly Girl*. It's completely out of the question. You can have Mr. Becker in, from the village, for the pipes. He's done our repairs before. And Mr. Cohen for the wiring."

"Okay." Paul made a quick note.

"I'll want you to stay with them, of course. These people from town—I assure you they would not think twice about putting something they took a fancy to into their little pockets."

"All right." Her mistrust and contempt for her neighbors, he decided, were not endearing traits.

Paul took several minutes to outline his strategy for repairs. "Vivien," he concluded, "before I can pin down a final estimate, I need to ask you what your long-term plans are for Highwood. If you plan to live in the house again, it'll have to be restored fully, which will take longer and cost more. If you plan to sell the house, you don't need to fix every last piece of furniture or get the kitchen operating and so on. We can just close it up, clean it out, make structural repairs."

"My long-term plans?" Her bitter laughter rang over the line. "I haven't made any. I hadn't planned on my house being torn to pieces. It will take me a little while to include this trifling fact in my plans. It won't make any difference in your work, will it? For the first two weeks or so?"

"Not immediately, no."

"Then let me wait to decide. Perhaps you can do me the favor of preparing two estimates, one long-term, the other short-term. We'll review the possibilities when I see you."

"I'm sorry?"

"We'll need to meet, of course. I haven't seen you in thirty years. I'm certainly not going to arrange anything as important as this without a face-to-face meeting. Our familial connection notwithstanding, I've learned the hard way not to trust people unless I've had the opportunity to take their measure first. And I simply don't negotiate over the telephone. I'd like you to fly out here. I'll pay for the flight, of course."

"Wouldn't it be better for you to come here? You could take a look at the house yourself. You could help sort things—"

"Good Christ, no," she said without hesitation. "I don't think I could bear it. Not with the house as you describe it." She sighed and went on in a dry, desolate voice. "I'm sixty-two, Paulie. At my age you begin to wonder about your life—whether it meant anything. Whether it was worth it. The best you hope for is a *maybe,* a delicate balance. Seeing my house, my things, every last *keepsake*—for *God's sake!*" She sobbed the last two words, as if choking on the indignity and sorrow of it.

"I understand," he said gently.

"Now, we need to determine when you can catch a flight to San Francisco. As you pointed out, the sooner the better."

"It's very short notice—"

"I'll pay for your tickets and a fee for your time."

"I'll have to look at my calendar. We've got Thanksgiving plans for next week."

"Then perhaps this week. Today is Friday. You may still be able to get tickets for this weekend."

"Maybe, if there are seats available—"

"There are always first-class seats available." A little jab, reminding him of an important difference between them: money. Paul had never flown first class in his life. "What else, Paulie? This discussion has exhausted me."

There were still plenty of questions he could ask, but probably those were best left for later. "I guess that's all," he said.

"Then you'll let me know your flight schedule." The timbre of her voice changed as she spoke, becoming harsh, strident. "And Paulie—in the future you needn't waste your breath telling me how difficult winter is at Highwood. How cold the house is, how hard it will be to get vehicles up and down the driveway. These are topics I am *very* familiar with. As I'm sure you can imagine."

She hung up before he could reply.

12

Paul tried to relax and suppress his tics as the jet tilted and slid into its final descent. Since talking to Vivien on Friday, he'd been in constant motion, arranging his schedule, making more calls to Westchester, preparing his estimates, working on the MG. He'd been skeptical of finding tickets for any flight this close to Thanksgiving, but Vivien had been right—there were first-class seats available on a flight out on Saturday and, miraculously, a return flight Sunday.

Through the window, he saw the wing flaps extend. Beyond the wing, the water of the bay glinted, the clustered hills of San Francisco took dimension. Further to the west, the sun threw a blinding slash of silver on the Pacific. Saturday afternoon, still two hours from sunset.

It was all happening very fast. One of the few advantages of being unemployed: a flexible schedule. He had no pressing reason *not* to take two days to fly to the West Coast. Mark was still at Janet's until Tuesday, the MG needed only a couple more hours of work. With the end of the semester imminent, Lia had so much work to do that she'd have no time for him over the weekend anyway. Actually, the timing couldn't be better.

Before he left, Lia had reminded him to probe Vivien: "Try to get her to tell you who would go to such lengths to wreck her house. Who might have a grudge they'd try to settle that way."

"Lia, she's not hiring me to be a detective, she's hiring me to fix up the house. Anyway, Vivien's a regular Medici, if what everybody tells me is true. She's a lot more accustomed to intrigues than I am. I'm not sure I can be that subtle."

"Why be subtle? Just ask her," Lia said. "Also ask her if I can have that maroon hat." She'd come into his arms then and kissed him sweetly. "Just be yourself with her. Don't let her push you off balance. She can't do anything to you if you relax and stay your easygoing, lovable self. Keep your sense of humor. Let *her* worry about being subtle."

Paul felt the first lurch of the jet's deceleration. He'd never subscribed to any particular religion, but on seeing the landscape tilt crazily, hearing the rising whine of air over the lowered wingflaps, his mind flinched into a sort of prayer. Within seconds, just as Lia said, the fear distilled out of him everything superfluous, leaving only the essentials: *Let me have more life to live, I will use life more wisely, let Mark and Lia be okay and know how much I love them.*

The landing was uneventful. How fast, he thought, your concern for absolutes gives way to the petty details of disembarking, claiming bags, navigating the airport. What fickle creatures we are, how short-lived our humility.

He checked the bus schedules, but then remembered that Vivien was footing the bill, and found a row of taxis. Ahead of him, a young woman in a short skirt swung into the backseat of a cab, showing briefly the best legs Paul had ever seen in his life. He took a breath of California air, eucalyptus mixed with diesel exhaust, and was glad he'd come.

The Royale was an old five-story building just off Union Square, constructed in the era of elaborate cornices and lintels, when builders were glad for any excuse to use decorative masonry. Paul stood briefly on the sidewalk, savoring the bustle of the street for just a moment before facing Vivien. It was five o'clock, the rush-hour traffic was heavy, people were hurrying past. Still lit by the sun just over the horizon, the sky was a vast dome of deepening turquoise, and the streetlights had come on. San Francisco had always been one of his favorite places—if he hadn't been scheduled to meet Vivien tonight, he'd have gone to the Savoy Tivoli for a meal and wine, visited the City Lights bookstore, then wandered for a time in Chinatown, buying trinkets for Mark and maybe catching a kung fu movie. He'd reserved a room at a cheap hotel on Columbus Avenue, and for a moment he considered going there for a shower and a change of clothes. But that was just an excuse to put off seeing Vivien. He'd agreed to meet her as soon as he got in, she'd insisted on treating him to dinner, and he'd accepted. He shrugged: This was a business trip, not a vacation.

She stood aside for him to enter. "You are right on schedule, nephew. I do appreciate your punctuality. Welcome to my western redoubt."

"Hello, Aunt Vivien," Paul said. He held her shoulders briefly and smelled the lavender scent of her.

Paul followed her into a large living room, where Vivien sat in a burgundy upholstered armchair. "My Lord, here you are. When I last saw you, you were perhaps eight and had rips at the knees of your dungarees and snot running down from both nostrils. And of course, I was not a wrinkled-up old lady."

Paul started to object, but Vivien waved him to silence. "Now, we can exchange tiresome pleasantries and covertly inspect each other for a time, or we can express our reciprocal curiosity frankly over a glass of wine, whichever you like. Personally I would prefer the latter."

"The wine sounds wonderful." Paul smiled. There was a certain charm to her imperiousness.

She turned to a small table, which held a bottle of red wine and two stemmed glasses. "I took the liberty of opening this to breathe before you arrived. Isn't this a lovely suite? Every day is a luxury for me after those many years at Highwood."

As Vivien poured the wine, Paul looked around the high-ceilinged room. Victorian-era elegance, only slightly faded: a huge oriental carpet on the floor, royal purple drapes on each side of the windows, a small fireplace framed by carved white oak and topped with a heavy black marble mantel. Crowded bookshelves rose from floor to ceiling on each side of the fireplace.

Vivien was much as he remembered her, a tall, broad-hipped woman who projected an aura of authority. With her vital manner, the fashionable cut of her brown hair, she registered as younger than her actual age. Her facial features clearly resembled Aster's, but while his mother's face had sagged into wrinkles of disappointment, resignation, and self-pity, Vivien's was the face of a woman accustomed to having her way, used to privilege, lined with pride, anger, impatience. Her eyes were a piercing blue, hungry and alert, set in nests of fine wrinkles. They were the eyes, Paul decided, of a bird of prey. No, a dragon. Vivien the Dragon Lady.

"Your wine," she said.

He took the glass and brought it to his nose, inhaling the strong tannic scent. Vivien watched him closely, eyes penetrating and darkly amused. "You have no idea how much I have looked forward to seeing you," she said. "It has been so long since I've seen a family member, someone of the same blood. It has to do with my narcissism, of course—a blood relative can provide a convenient mirror of oneself. An opportunity to find out what sort of stuff one is made of."

"I suppose," Paul said. "For better or worse."

"Absolutely! In fact, I suspect we learn most from that which is least flattering."

"Perhaps."

"Oh yes. Every time. The blood tells. Let's have a toast, shall we? To family. To the blood." She raised her glass and struck it hard against his, then sipped it thirstily. Paul lifted the rich red liquid to his lips, vaguely ill-at-ease with her toast.

"I must ask you to indulge me," Vivien said. "For years, I've gotten only bits and snatches of family news, from Kay. I am eager to hear all about you Skoglunds."

Be yourself, Lia had said. *Keep it businesslike,* Aster had warned. "Tell you what," Paul said, hedging. "I'll be happy to tell you about the Skoglunds if you tell me about the Hoffmanns. If it's reciprocal."

"You mean I'm not to get out the Klieg lights and truncheons?" Vivien said. "That seems fair enough."

Paul told her about his sister and about Aster, avoiding anything too personal or too funky. Vivien sipped her wine and watched him closely as he spoke. Outside, the muted noise of city traffic ebbed as rush hour passed.

"You've omitted one of the Skoglunds—yourself," she said.

"I've already told you the basic saga. There's not a lot else."

"You have told me only the material data and have studiously avoided anything substantive."

"Such as?"

"Such as what you believe, what you aspire to. What it is you *want.*"

"What do I want? I'd like to be a good father to my son. I want to build a good relationship with Lia. I'd like my family to be happy. I want to do work that I believe in, that I can excel in, and that makes me enough money to live on."

She looked at him incredulously. "You don't want wealth, fame, power, lots of women—?"

He smiled. "Occasionally. Not so much anymore."

"You don't want to, for example, experience bliss, know God, probe life's mysteries, give wings to your own creative genius—"

"I don't think I'd recognize any of that if it came my way. In the existential department, I'll settle for being a decent person and keeping my worst impulses in check. A good marriage, a happy family, a vacation to someplace warm once a year. I figure that if I get that far, those other things will find their way into the equation."

She looked at him as if he were some exotic animal. "Astonishing!" she said. She took another sip of wine and then sighed. "Well. It all sounds lovely. You Skoglunds are such normal and decent people. It sounds as if you have all done quite well, considering."

"Considering?"

"Tut-tut! I'm speaking with admiration. The death of a father, especially by suicide, can have such difficult and lasting repercussions. There are whole books written on the subject."

"I'm not sure we exactly escaped unscathed, Vivien," Paul said carefully.

She must have noticed his hesitation. "Perhaps Ben's death isn't a topic you're comfortable with."

"It's been thirty years—it's territory I've gone over fairly thoroughly. You might say I feel the way you do when I tell you how long the driveway at Highwood is."

Her eyes narrowed and she smiled faintly, approving. "Point taken."

They both sipped their wine, and Vivien's expression softened. "Dear Ben. You may not know it, but your father and I were quite close." She gazed for a moment into space, remembering. "There was a wonderful period when the four of us spent a great deal of time together, Ben and Aster and Erik and I. And even after Erik . . . took his leave, there were Ben and Aster and I. And of course Dempsey. We shared similar interests. We were young enough to be optimistic still. We sincerely believed our thoughts and ideas and our . . . our *style* were so splendid that everything would turn out as we planned. That our meals and conversations, our games, our walks in the woods, the books we read and discussed, somehow *mattered* to the world, were *significant*. With such *élan* we would accomplish all sorts of meaningful things. Such arrogance! But for us it was—how can I express it?—a golden era."

A golden era, yes, Paul thought. But with odd shadows on the periphery.

"Do you know, Ben and I even corresponded? Right up until the last. It seems silly, with us living so close by, but Ben was a great believer in the gentle, scholarly art of letter writing. I still have his letters. I save all my correspondence." Her face twitched suddenly, mouth pulling downward sharply, a bitter frown. "That is, if they're not destroyed. Along with everything else at Highwood."

"I have a confession to make—I stole something of yours. Borrowed, anyway, from the floor of the library. This." He unfolded Ben's letter from his jacket pocket and handed it to her.

More than anything he'd said, the letter seemed to affect her. Her hands shook slightly as she held it to the light. When she was done reading, her face looked suddenly weary, eyes opaque, distant. Without saying anything, she folded the letter and handed it back to him. *You wonder about your life, whether it meant anything,* she'd said. *You struggle to maintain a delicate balance.*

"Yes. Well. We had many fine dinners together," she said.

Paul gave her a moment. "Maybe we should talk about the house."

Vivien stirred in her chair, as if she'd just remembered he was there, then checked her watch. "I suppose I can endure it whenever you're ready. However, it's now half past six, and I made dinner reservations for seven. We can talk about it after dinner. I hope you like Chinese food—I reserved a room at the Xi'an, which I have found to be the finest in the city." She rose, crossed the room to pause in a doorway. "I will need a few minutes to get ready," she said over her shoulder. "Please have some more wine."

He poured another glassful, then stood to look out the window. Below him in the street, traffic cruised past and several cabs waited at the curb. A siren whooped close and faded, the night sky glowed with the lights of the city. The thought of Chinese food brought a flood of saliva to his mouth.

Vivien was a powerful personality and would no doubt be an unpleasant person to have as an enemy. But she was also interesting. She enjoyed being provocative, she didn't talk around a subject. If she often managed to hit a nerve, it was due to her obvious aversion to small talk, her preference for matters of substance. And however the letter had affected her, she had rallied quickly: She had come back, speaking with precision and formality, mustering the dignity, the stubborn arrogance, that sustained her. You had to admire that.

Still, he didn't trust her either, any farther than he could throw her.

Paul strolled around the room, sipping wine, and stopped in front of the bookcase to scan the titles idly. Judging by the books she'd purchased in her six months in San Francisco, Vivien had maintained her eclectic reading tastes. Agatha Christie, the Castaneda books, a row of le Carré novels. History: books about the history of San Francisco, the Crusades, the Vikings. Several histories of the Philippine Islands.

There were maybe two dozen slick contemporary paperbacks on topics such as alien abduction, angels, channeling, and life after death, and he wondered if these were interests Vivien had acquired since coming to the trendy credulity of Northern California. Further down were a dozen or so textbooks on biochemistry and anatomy. Surprised, he found a whole shelf devoted to psychology and neurology, and pulled a book at random, finding it to be a fairly detailed layman's text on the brain.

"One can learn a great deal about a person by observing his bookshelves," Vivien said, startling him. She had appeared at his side without his hearing her approach. "As one can by observing what a visitor takes from the shelf. Apparently you share my interest in neurology." She had put on a brown coat trimmed with mink and had applied lipstick to her mouth, a bright, unflattering crimson.

"It comes with the turf," he said, tapping his head. "With having Tourette's. What prompts your interest?"

"Right now I'm looking into how your brain works when you get old. Quite fascinating. Luckily, they're finding ways to keep your brain young. I've started taking 'smart pills' every day, guaranteed to improve your cognition and completely legal. Here in San Francisco, there are even smart-drug cafes where you can order a malted milk with L-pyroglutamic acid and phosphatidyl choline and 2-dimethylaminoethanol, and so on. Lovely brain-nurturing chemicals."

"If you can remember the names, they must be working pretty well."

Vivien smiled slightly. "I'm probably not the best judge. Perhaps you can tell me. Now, we had better go." Paul instinctively offered his elbow, and she gripped his arm firmly above the biceps as they left the suite. "But Paulie—you won't start shouting obscenities at the restaurant, or anything of that sort, will you?" It was a gentle teasing, a flirtation.

"I'll try to restrain myself," he said.

13

He was surprised when she suggested they walk back to the Royale from Chinatown.

"You must understand," she explained, "this is the San Francisco I love most. Mysterious, timeless. We could be in old Shanghai. I don't often have a willing companion for evening walks, and I intend to take full advantage of your presence." She gripped his arm, steered him to the right, into the labyrinthine streets on the edge of Chinatown.

A fog had rolled in, occluding the city. Vivien inhaled deeply of the moist air, and Paul did the same, savoring its strangeness. The smell of the ocean mingled with the exotic stink of restaurants and groceries: butchered meat, dried fish, strange herbs, incense. Through the windows of darkened storefronts, Paul saw plucked corpses of geese hung in rows by their long necks, doomed carp hovering in their packed aquariums, bins of contorted roots and bulbs and dried squid. A few other pedestrians, faceless in the fog, walked hurriedly past them.

They had lingered over an excellent dinner of central China's regional cuisine, drinking plum wine and conversing on a wide range of topics—everything but what had brought him to San Francisco. The walls of their small private room were decorated with panels of intricately carved wood, lacquered a deep red, depicting scenes at the court of some Chinese emperor. Sitting opposite Vivien, Paul felt that the setting perfectly framed her: There was an imperial, Oriental quality to her, with her incongruously dramatic red lips, the cynical arch of her eyebrows.

"Now, where were we?" Vivien said. She walked easily, still gripping his arm. "Oh yes. It was your turn to explain *your* interest in neurology. Per our agreement to be entirely reciprocal."

"As I said, it comes with the territory. When I was a kid, Ben taught me about the brain so I could understand my own neurological problems. Now I try to stay current on Tourette's syndrome research—there's been a lot of progress in the last twenty years. Also, I thought I should understand how the brain works, how brain functions develop during childhood, if I wanted to understand the learning process. For teaching."

"And it has nothing whatever to do with your son, Mark, and his behavioral problems."

He didn't try to hide his irritation. "I guess Kay has kept you pretty well informed."

"You are so wary of me, Paulie! Have you heard such terrible tales about me? I'd think you'd be glad to compare notes with another amateur scholar of the brain."

"Mark has been variously diagnosed as autistic, epileptic, and about half a dozen other things. Since the medical community couldn't agree on what his problem was or how to help him, I thought I'd give it a try. I've done a lot of reading, but I don't consider myself a scholar so much as, basically, a parent."

They turned again, onto a darker residential street where the streetlights cut cones of light in the fog. In a dark doorway, what he'd thought to be a shadow stirred as they passed, revealing itself as a homeless man, lying on his side, swaddled in blankets. Paul felt tension begin to twitch in the muscles of his shoulders.

"Is there any similarity between Mark's condition and what you once had? Before the Tourette's?"

At first he was hesitant to go into details with Vivien, but then decided the hell with it. It was a relief to explore this difficult area of his life, to unburden himself. Vivien nodded encouragingly as he talked.

Yes, he explained, there were a lot of similarities between Mark's symptoms and the symptoms he himself had shown as a child. Dealing with Mark's condition, Paul had learned only a little from the failed programs the child psychologists and neurologists had prescribed, and mainly by negative example. He'd gotten more from his own reading, and still more from remembering his own childhood experience. Though his first symptoms had been later eclipsed by Tourette's and had never returned, he remembered distinctly the same micropsia Mark complained about, and the strange, remote, frightened mood that seemed to accompany it.

"Remind me what micropsia is," Vivien interjected.

It almost always had come on near bedtime, when Paul would be reading or playing with toys, getting drowsy. He remembered being fascinated by the slippery play of light on the shiny paint on one of his toy soldiers. Suddenly it was as if he were looking through the wrong end of a telescope: His own feet looked tiny, tapering with the distance, the soldier nearly imperceptible in his faraway hand. A fascinating change of perspective, making him feel like a giant of geological proportions. But also frightening.

He'd shake his head violently in an effort to clear his sight, which never worked.

Thirty years later, he watched Mark suddenly start shaking his head as he played with some small toy and realized his son was experiencing the same thing. If Mark got up to walk then, he'd topple uncertainly, as if having difficulty balancing on those tiny, distant feet: a feeling Paul remembered well.

Since micropsia was one symptom of temporal lobe epilepsy, he and Janet had taken Mark for EEGs and CAT scans, but nothing definitive had ever shown up—no unusual spikes on the EEG, no sign of dark, mysterious structural abnormalities on the CAT scan. Definitely a mixed relief for parents wanting a name and a cure for whatever it was that tormented their child.

But the micropsia was only a signal, the beginning of what might be hours or days of altered behavior, when Mark would be sullen, uncooperative, unpredictable. Withdrawal, long periods of immobility with some toy forgotten in his slack hand. Reversion to infantile behaviors: nagging whines or imperious shrieks, throwing things, arching and flailing. They couldn't send him to school when he was in one of these periods, and though he was an exceptionally bright child, his academic progress suffered. As did his social development.

Some seizure activity occurs deep in the brain, the neurologists told them, and wouldn't necessarily show up on an EEG. On the assumption that Mark had some undetectable activity, they'd given him antiepileptic clonazepam, but it had little effect on the symptoms. And neither Mark nor Paul could endure the side effects of drowsiness, torpidity, disorientation. After the fifth drug had done no better, Paul had insisted that they try alternative therapies.

The key, Paul felt, would have to be conscious acts on Mark's part. He needed to sense in himself the beginning of the slide, and resist. Once in the state, he needed to let his parents or teachers know, and find ways to get out of it. Talking did nothing to help; what seemed to work best were activities that reached Mark through other senses: massage, structured play with brightly colored blocks, interactive drawing, and large-muscle kinetic activity like dancing together or walks outdoors—anything that countered the tendency to focus on little things and the affect of anxiety and isolation. Mark's taking an intentional role in governing his own mental state was not only his best hope in combating the seizures; it was essential to his sense of self, a way to assert that he could make choices, that he had some control over his life.

Vivien listened intently, nodding slightly, and in a doorway light she stopped him to look sharply into his eyes. "Do you know the most fascinating aspect of what you've told me? That your response has been so like Ben's, when he was wrestling with your various conditions. The role of conscious, intentional behaviors. Self-observation and self-discipline. That marvelous faith in *reason*. That marvelous arrogance again."

"I suppose so," Paul admitted.

"You say that rather grudgingly."

"It's just that I'm not always and exclusively *grateful* for some of the long-term effects of Ben's training. I hate the thought that I'm visiting the same sins on my own son."

Vivien's face was immobile, but her eyes glinted. A greedy light. He regretted letting her see this much of his feelings toward Ben. The knowledge was something she'd salt away, hoard. To what end? He smoothed his moustache and eyebrows with a flick of his free hand.

"Do you remember all of his treatments?" Vivien turned and began to walk again. Muffled in the fog, the sounds of the city were faint, just their footsteps and the occasional dull hoot of foghorns from ships on the bay. Behind them, another pedestrian had appeared on the otherwise empty street.

"For the Tourette's. Not for the earlier stuff."

"I ask because, your resentment notwithstanding, I seem to recall he felt he'd found some very effective ways to help you when the medical community could do nothing. He wrote to me about it in great detail. It is too long ago for me to recall the specifics, but perhaps among my letters—" She let the thought hang. Even in the darkness, he could see her lips draw down. "That is, if any of them are recoverable."

At the thought of a cure for Mark, Paul's hopes leapt. He coughed, trying to conceal the desperate interest she'd certainly perceive in his voice or his face. He'd be sorting through the letters soon enough. And, with or without her approval, be looking at them very closely.

Several blocks ahead, Paul was relieved to see a brighter cross street, mist-blurred, and the occasional passing car. He knew San Francisco fairly well, knew they were heading generally in the right direction. But in the fog, after the wine, he felt disoriented, not sure where they were. He glanced back to see the bulky shadow of the person behind them, closer now. A sudden tic caused his hand to rise and rang an invisible bell.

"You do realize," Vivien went on, "that in your prognosis for Mark you have set up a rather classical equation? The hidden, unconscious, 'animal' processes of mind on one hand, the conscious, intentional 'human' self on the other. All sorts of lovely resonances!"

"I hadn't seen it in such exalted terms," Paul said. "I'm just trying to give my son a chance for a normal life."

"In any case, I think you are wise to take the prognostications of the medical experts with a grain of salt," Vivien said. "There is a great deal we don't know about ourselves." She laughed humorlessly, a dry cackle.

They made it to the cross street, and as they turned Paul glanced down the street they'd just come from. Their fellow traveler had vanished.

Again Vivien steered him, turning toward a bench. "Do you mind if we sit, Paulie? I'm afraid I'm not used to so much exercise."

Paul guided her to the seat, then sat down himself. A few cars passed, occupants invisible. The fatigue of the long day began to catch up with him. The thought of his hotel bed began to seem very alluring.

"I understand you are no longer with Mark's mother," Vivien was saying.

"Janet and I separated three years ago and finalized our divorce two years ago. I'm living with a wonderful woman named Lia McLean."

"Mmm. My, how lightly your generation seems to take such things. Tell me: How does Mark get along with your—what is the term nowadays?— significant other?"

"There've been a few minor adjustment problems, but she and Mark generally do just fine together."

"And you feel that Lia is a better match for you than Janet?"

He paused, uncomfortable. Her voice had become brittle, full of veiled accusation—issues of marriage were obviously something to avoid with Vivien. He wondered if her own divorce had anything to do with her attitudes. And their conversation had begun to resemble an interrogation again. Still, he found himself liking her for her outspoken curiosity, which seemed to invite the same in return. "Frankly, yes," he said. "But now I think it's your turn, since we're being reciprocal. Royce—tell me about him."

"I am not in communication with him."

"Your choice or his?"

"I'm not sure it was anyone's choice. Royce found me a difficult mother, I found him a difficult son. Perhaps it is because we're similar people."

"How so?"

Vivien tilted her head and gazed at him. "Similar outlooks on life, perhaps. Or similar disappointments with ourselves—and therefore with each other."

"I'm not sure I understand."

"For many years, when Royce was a boy, I was a victim of what I call Rimbaud's disease. A term your father coined, actually. After Rimbaud, the French Symbolist poet. Are you familiar with him?"

"I've read his *Illuminations*. Frankly, I don't think I understand it that well."

"He was brilliant, a prodigy. By the time he was seventeen, he was acknowledged as a genius who had changed the world of poetry forever.

Then, when he was twenty, he gave it up. Stopped writing. Became rather a rough fellow, ended up running guns in Africa. Died at thirty-seven."

"So what's Rimbaud's disease?"

Vivien brought her voice low, as if confiding a treasured secret. "It's what killed him. Not physically—he had cancer. I mean *metaphysically.* At his deathbed, his sister called in a priest. Rimbaud was in anguish, and the priest sat by the bedside, prepared to administer extreme unction. Do you know what Rimbaud's last words were?"

"No. Sorry."

" '*Show me something.*' Do you see? *He'd exhausted the world!* It had nothing left for him. He'd given up poetry, a life of literary celebrity, and had gone on an increasingly desperate, violent quest for novelty and sensation—but could not find it anywhere. 'Show me something.' The most terrible death of all!"

For a moment Paul could see it in her face, just below the mask of pride and command: desolation, emptiness. A disappointment on the deepest level: *Life has no meaning. Nothing is real enough. There is no purpose.* He shuddered involuntarily.

"But you aren't dead," he said.

"No. I have escaped. At least so far. I have certain pleasures to sustain myself with. In any event, I'm afraid dear Royce caught some of that dread disease from me. It's no wonder that he needs to keep his distance, or that he harbors less than fond feelings for his mother."

A thought occurred to him: "Do you think it was Rimbaud's disease that killed my father?" he asked.

Vivien looked at him shrewdly. Again, she seemed to save away whatever she gleaned from his question. "I can't answer that for you. Perhaps if you encounter more of his letters as you're sorting my things, you'll find an answer for that as well. Certainly Ben loved to ponder such metaphysical questions and to write letters about them. You may be surprised to find how much you have in common with your father." She observed his reaction with a small upturn at the corners of her mouth, her eyes steady on his. "Or, if I understand your predicament correctly, you might be relieved that you have so *little* in common with him."

They had taken another turn, a short block between commercial streets, lit by angry orange vapor lights, the curb lined with trash cans and glistening plastic garbage bags. Abruptly a shape rose up in front of them and stood, blocking the sidewalk.

"What the fuck?" Paul said. Absurdly, his first feeling was embarrassment for using profanity in front of Vivien.

"Indeed," the man said. He was bearded, long-haired, big, dressed in layered rags. Paul pulled Vivien to the left, to walk around him, but the man moved to block them. Vivien recoiled, disengaging her arm and falling behind Paul. Paul was glad to have both hands free. He stood facing the man, appraising him. Tall, beard and hair matted, face dirty. Hands out and forward, ready.

"Stand and deliver," the man said. "Your purses or your lives." There was a crazed pleasure in his face. *Only in San Francisco*, Paul thought. *Years of LSD and who knows what else. A mugger who inhabits a private world, who fancies himself a highwayman of old England. A nutcase.* The thought did nothing to reassure him.

"Leave us alone," Paul told him.

Suddenly the man rushed forward, his gap-toothed mouth open in a joyful rage, and Paul had no choice but to meet his charge. The mugger's weight hit him and he fell backward, hard against a lamppost. The stinking beard was in his face, and then Paul's head rocked as a punch nearly crushed his cheek. The next punch hit him in his Adam's apple, and an explosion of pain burst in his windpipe, gagging him.

The pain seemed to wake Paul up. He broke free of the mugger's grip, ducked another punch, hit him with an uppercut, felt the shock of impact in the bones of his hand. He swung him by the rags on his shoulders, hurtling him with all his strength into an iron railing. The mugger hit hard, fell, was up immediately. The look of joy was gone, replaced by a glowering anger. A trickle of blood ran down from a cut on his cheek.

"Your mortal moment," he hissed, "is upon you." A knife appeared in his hand, long and very thin, sparking in the orange light. And then he was lunging at Paul, the knife moving almost too fast to see, up and under, going for the soft places below his rib cage. Paul dodged backward, avoided the blade, avoided a counter-slash, almost feeling the parting of his own flesh, the burning blade in his guts. His veins surged with adrenaline, a toxic mix of fear and hate and anger.

As the mugger came on again, Paul's hands found a steel trash can and swung it suddenly up at the snarling face. It was a lucky blow, hitting the arms, sending the knife spinning away into the fog. The can upended, spewed garbage.

Paul picked up another can, swung again, connected solidly, followed up, shoving it at him, knocking him down. The mugger fell onto his back, head cracking the sidewalk, and Paul was on him immediately, putting one foot on his neck as he gulped for air.

"Mother*fucker!*" Paul said, panting. "Fucking screwball nutcase!" Pain throbbed in his cheek and his outrage flared. He felt an urge to stomp the guy's throat but checked it in time. Anyway, the bearded face that stared up at him was full of fear now, as if staring through a crack in the stage set of his Robin Hood world. *The scariest sight of all,* Paul thought: *the reality we deny every day of our lives. Poor son of a bitch.*

He settled for a token kick in the ribs, just a reminder, then glanced back to Vivien, trying to catch his breath. "You all right?"

"I—I think so," she said. She stared in unabashed fascination at the mugger as he moved tentatively on the littered sidewalk. "Oughtn't we call someone, or whatever one does under such circumstances?"

Paul glanced up and down the empty street. He didn't like the idea of Vivien walking on her own to find a phone, and he couldn't leave her with this twisted fuck. "If we can find a phone."

The mugger was up and gone by the time they reached the end of the block. Knowing it was pointless, Paul called the police from a pay phone, declined to leave his name, gave them a description: big, bearded, crazy. It was dark, Officer, foggy—there wasn't much time.

He hung up and turned back to Vivien, who had waited, leaning against a wall, hugging her arms to her chest against the cold, observing him with a disconcerting intensity. His own hands were still shaking, but she seemed to have recovered completely. In fact she looked refreshed, almost pleased. Of course, he thought: The evening's excitement was a nice short-term respite from Rimbaud's disease, an unexpected but not unwelcome dose of novelty and sensation.

When they reached the brightly lit portico of the hotel, she paused, arched one ironic eyebrow at Paul. "Thank you for a most *stimulating* evening," she said. "What is the expression? 'You certainly know how to show a girl a good time.'"

14

Paul spread his notes and photos under the spotlight of Vivien's desk lamp. When she'd inspected each one closely, she clasped her hands in her lap, listening to him passively. Although she'd been confrontational all evening, the sight of the damaged house seemed to wound her. She'd poured them wine again when they sat down—maybe it was beginning to get to her.

Despite his growing fatigue and the bruises he'd gotten in the fight, he plugged ahead, outlining his plans. First, get the house closed off against the weather, then subcontract out the repair of the main systems—electricity, heat, plumbing. Install a permanent, lockable gate at the bottom of the driveway. Inside the house, her papers would be the first priority. Paul would set up a temporary heater in the smoking room, sort Vivien's papers, get them safely stored. Then begin work on the monumental task of sorting and assessing the rest of her belongings, and disposing of them or taking them for repair as needed.

Paul handed her one of the estimates he'd prepared. "This is just for the short term, basic repairs. Bear in mind, my estimates for subcontracting costs are very rough and could go a lot higher. But my own work won't exceed these numbers. So, for closing off the house and putting your belongings into basic order, I expect I'll need four weeks, about four thousand dollars. Subcontracting and materials expenses come to around ten thousand, which I'll need in hand before I begin. I also need two weeks' advance pay for me—say two thousand." He slid several sheets across to her. "This is a personal-services contract between you and me, based on the estimate. There's a copy for each of us, and I've also made a copy for your insurance company. They should also get notice soon, since they'll want to look the place over before I start."

"Insurance!" Vivien laughed darkly. "What a lovely, sensible idea! I have no insurance. I stopped paying those crooks ten years ago when they doubled my premiums for the third year in a row. No, this will be coming out of my pocket—which I hope you'll remember when you are billing me. Fourteen thousand—that's a lot of money."

"That's just for the first phase. A rough estimate for the longer term work might be $50,000 to $100,000. It'll depend on your decisions: Do you want to pay to have paintings professionally restored, or for taxidermy? How far are you willing to go to repair your furniture, clothes? And some things won't be repairable—how much will you choose to replace at value?"

She digested it all in silence for a time. "Very well. I'll expect you to keep costs down wherever possible. After the first phase, I'll look for a more accurate estimate, and we can decide at that time about the rest of it." She found a pen and signed the contracts with a jagged signature. Her movements were listless, careless. Paul wondered if it was the shock of seeing the house, or the attack, or the cumulative effect of the wine they'd drunk.

"One other expenditure you should consider," Paul said, folding his copy of the contract, "is a security system. Until you've got one installed, the house just isn't safe. In the short term, while we're doing repairs, I'll camp out in the carriage house. At least until the gate is up. I expect to be working long hours anyway—it'll save me money and commuting time."

"I'd be very grateful. But why not sleep in the house?"

"The carriage house is in much better shape. I can set right up. I won't get in my own way."

"You're not afraid of ghosts, are you?" She was rallying already, finding a way to goad him.

"The idea of ghosts hasn't figured large in my planning."

"Perhaps *presences* is a better term. Forces. But you don't believe in ghosts?"

"I'm really not sure—"

"Maybe spending time at Highwood will help you make up your mind." A cunning voice.

Paul had to smile. Suddenly the pattern of it came clear to him. "My sister warned me that you enjoy being difficult," he said. "I can see why she thought so."

"Is *that* what I enjoy."

"Maybe I should say you enjoy challenging people, provoking them. Surprising them. I think you're asking to be challenged and provoked in return. Asking to be surprised. To see something that reaches you. Maybe you're still not entirely free of Rimbaud's disease."

She looked at him, pleased. "I didn't claim I was free of it. Only that it hadn't killed me yet. But yes, you're correct. Very insightful. Your father understood that about me also."

The weary pleasure in her look told him something more: that she solicited confrontations because she wanted engagement, companionship. That was there in her face too, he realized: *loneliness. Almost forty-five years,* Kay had said, *alone on that hill.*

"What happened to Erik Hoffmann? Where is he now?" The words were out of his mouth before he could stop them.

Vivien pulled back, the pleasure gone from her face. "My husband is dead. He died in 1985."

Your ex-husband, you mean, Paul thought. "I'm sorry," he said. "I suppose a person never really stops caring, even after all those years apart." He went on, trying to change the subject, aware that he'd somehow offended her. But she interrupted him.

"Tell me, Paul, are you really such an innocent?"

"I don't think of myself as—"

"All that compassion, that virtue. Doesn't it ever bother you that no one really seems to appreciate that supposed virtue of yours?"

He was unprepared for her intensity, the change in her. He took a moment to answer, trying to decipher the reason for her sudden change of mood. "You're talking about supposed virtue. You seem to believe that the real thing doesn't exist."

"Unalloyed goodness? With no sordid underbelly of mixed motives and greed and self-interest and who knows what? Show me some." Vivien drank again and with one hand caught a drop of wine from her lower lip. "You seem to believe you can banish all your dark feelings, leaving only the good, wholesome Paulie Skoglund. But you can't really shed those feelings—all you can do is suppress them. They're still there, inside you. Can you really tell me otherwise? Anger, pain, resentment, frustration, set aside every day, never dealt with? Bottled up and stored away deep? You drop your eyes—you know I'm right. You very nearly crushed that man's windpipe, didn't you? And another question: What has this philosophy, this idealism, done for *you?* How has it empowered you? Are you using your full potential? Are you particularly happy? Fulfilled?" Vivien's voice had been rising, her eyes catching fire. "I wonder, nephew, whether your philosophy has provided you with any advantage at all. *How do you know what's inside if you suppress it all the time? How do you know what you're capable of unless you let it loose?* I suspect many of your ideals are nothing more than ways of rationalizing your paralysis, justifying your self-deceit."

He had begun to accept her sudden and extreme changes of mood, but this unexpected attack threw him off balance, left him uncertain how to respond. "You know, I came to San Francisco ready to be solicitous of my aunt's sense of propriety and her concern for her house and possessions. You've done a terrific job of putting that behind us." He swigged some wine and put his glass down harder than he'd intended. "Maybe I'm not as angry as you are."

"Perhaps not. And perhaps you've just buried it more deeply. Hidden it, along with your tics and your creativity and half your IQ, beneath a medication-induced stupor. What is it, still haloperidol? Or are you on Prozac and Prolixin?"

Paul stood up. More than anything else, he hoped he wouldn't tic or show any other sign of stress, which would no doubt gratify her enormously. "Well," he said, "time for me to go." He brushed the sleeves of his tweed jacket, straightened his collar. "Been a long day for me. It's been lovely, Vivien. We'll have to do it again in another thirty years. Good luck with your house."

He walked to the hall.

"Your control is admirable, but you're only proving my point," Vivien said.

Paul turned. "I'm impressed that you've done your homework on Tourette's. I'd respond to your goading, but it's never hard to get advice on how to live, and you're not the first to offer it to me."

"So you'd rather dodge conflict. I take it running away is something you're accustomed to doing."

"What I'm accustomed to is more courtesy. Maybe, while I'm reflecting on the value of letting go, *you* ought to consider the value of some restraint. For example, you might find that if you indulged your anger or bitterness or whatever a little less, you'd have some *friends*. Or maybe you haven't yet come to grips with why you're so alone."

He immediately regretted saying it, using her most obvious weakness against her. For an instant her eyes looked startled. Her chest started to rise and fall rapidly, as if she were starting to sob. When she took a sip of her wine, she swallowed it with a grimace that shook her cheeks, and the wine tilted crazily in her glass before she set it down.

Paul went to stand at the window, his back to Vivien, thoroughly sick of the sight of her but unwilling to leave it like this between them. He felt as he did after his occasional arguments with Aster: No matter how awful it had gotten, you waited for a while, you tried to bring it around to some kind of peace before you parted ways. Because this was your family. You swallowed your pride when it came to family. Whether he liked it or not, he couldn't deny that Vivien was, felt like, family.

Outside, traffic had died down, the city had started to go to sleep.

When he turned around, he found that Vivien had subsided again, as if their battle had exhausted her. To Paul's surprise—he'd never have believed her capable of it—tears rimmed her dragon eyes and slid down her cheeks. Sitting awkwardly in her chair, she looked suddenly pathetic, her face streaked. She rubbed one of her wrists as if it ached. Her resemblance to his mother was stronger now that her fragility had been exposed. He felt a stab of pity for her.

"What can I do for you?" he asked. "Can I get you something?"

"I'll tell you what you can do for me. You can restore my things, put my house in order. Restore my possessions to me. Give me back my life. I need my things, my papers. *I need to have something to prove I've had a life.* Can you understand that?"

"Of course. Why don't I get you some water or—"

"You can get me some Kleenex. On the table near the bookshelf."

Paul brought the box to her and waited as she mopped her eyes and blew her nose. When she was done, she looked somewhat better—forlorn, empty, but in control again.

"Have we concluded our business? I am quite exhausted," she said.

"There's just one other thing. Given the extraordinary level of damage, I wondered if you had any idea who might have done it."

She was silent for so long he wondered if she'd heard him. "Aunt Vivien?"

"Why should you care?" Her voice was flat.

"I'd feel better if we found out, if only to assure that it doesn't happen again, maybe while we're working on the house. On a practical level, if you're going to have the police in, they should come before I clean the place up. I'll be effectively disrupting a crime scene, destroying evidence."

"No. No police. Absolutely not. I'm not going to have my house invaded by yet another bunch of strangers, with prying eyes and gossiping tongues. I've had my dealings with the police over the years. I'm entitled to more discretion than they're capable of."

"I'd think you'd be eager to know who did this."

Vivien waved her hand. "Don't misunderstand me. Of course I am. But I've made up my mind, Paulie. I have been exposed and invaded enough. You're not to bring the police into my house." She locked her eyes with his, driving the point home.

Paul took a frustrated turn on the carpet. "It occurred to us that maybe it was someone who had a grudge against you. Someone who would use your absence to take some kind of revenge on you by smashing the place. Can you think of anyone?"

"I have no doubt accumulated many such grudges. Some people seem to consider me less than tactful."

"Anyone in particular?"

She stared blindly into the middle of the room for a moment, apparently searching her memory. "There was a fellow in the town. He worked as my gardener for a time, and then I had to fire him. A great big bull of a man. A terrible temper."

"Why would he—"

"He stole things from the house, so I fired him and called the police. He blamed the trouble on me. This was many years ago, but he told me he'd never forget."

"What was his name? Is he still in the area?"

"An Italian. Falcone—Salvador Falcone. Yes, I believe he's still there. Although I can't imagine why he'd suddenly fly into a frenzy at this late date." Vivien walked to the window and stood looking out, her back to him. "Now it is time for you to go. I will have my bank send you a check immediately. You will excuse me for not seeing you to the door."

She didn't lift her eyes as Paul said good night and embraced her briefly.

"Look," Paul said, "try to relax now. I'll do everything I can to make sure your things are preserved and put in order." He left her at the window, then paused in the hallway and turned to face her. "Are you sure you're okay?"

She turned her head and glared at him. "Save your pity for someone else." The hard edge had returned to her voice. "I have no use for it."

15

Rock 'n' roll, Paul thought, wading through the dry grass, *whatever happened to the roll?* Rock and *rollll*. The roll was an important part of it, a smooth and sensuous counterpoint to the sharp downbeat of *rock!* Something modern bands would do well to remember. The world was going to hell.

A light whirling snow fell from a thin overcast, but the air felt just warm enough to do some sax work outside. There'd been no time to think since his return Sunday night. He came to the boulder, sat down on cold granite, and played an ornate version of "Tossin' and Turnin'," Bobby Lewis, 1961.

Even the sax didn't offer any escape. More than she knew, Vivien had put a lance through his armor: *You've buried your tics and your creativity and half your IQ.* When he was a kid, the whiz kid, he'd been a musical prodigy, listening to records or the radio and learning all the tunes by ear, playing them on Ben's piano like a little Mozart. Then in 1965, he started on haloperidol. Which smoothed him out. And dumbed him down. He'd given up music for twenty years, feeling no urge, no particular affinity, before he started playing the saxophone. It was no accident that now he played exclusively fifties and sixties rock 'n' roll: Those were the same tunes he'd picked up from the radio back then. He could force his way through any tune, but the ones that *flew* he'd learned before he was eight years old.

He and Vivien had held to their compact to be reciprocal, all right. In the final analysis, they'd traded blow for blow pretty well. The problem was that *he'd* feel guilty about beating up on a lonely old woman. And he would stay wounded. *How do you know who you are, what's inside you, what you're capable of?* He should have told Vivien: "Hey, fuck you, when you've had Tourette's for thirty years, you get used to asking yourself what's inside. And you get used to not coming up with a simple answer." But the sudden change in her, the disproportionate heat of her, had caught him off balance. Now he was just left with more woulda-coulda-shoulda, the slow-witted person's lonely pleasure. More proof of what she'd suggested. Yes, she had hit the nerve. He was hearing the same thing, more gently expressed, from Lia. From his own inner voices as well.

Since he'd returned, he'd been festering with various tics and urges. "Submit to the dark side of The Force" was the most persistent vocal compulsion. It would play in his mind, building until he had to say it, mimicking exactly Darth Vader's deep, mask-muffled bass. If you didn't get it just right, you had to say it until it had just the right pitch, timbre, tempo, nuance. When you got it right, the itch was satisfied—for about two minutes.

Paul stirred uncomfortably on the rock, licked the sax reed. All that came out was "Get a Job." The Silhouettes, 1958. On the other hand, he thought, he'd come out ahead on the question of Rimbaud's disease. Flying back, somewhere over the bald landscape of Utah and Wyoming where such thoughts always seemed to come, he'd taken a good hard look. There were moments, of course. But in the final analysis, no, he wasn't dying of weltschmerz. He didn't envy Vivien that.

At two, Paul trotted down to the town road and opened the rusted mailbox. Among the flyers and bills was a letter with an unfamiliar New York return address, which he opened immediately. It contained a check for $12,000. For a moment he experienced a flash of relief: two thousand big ones to keep the wolf at bay. But immediately the feeling evaporated. For the first time, he realized that he had indeed committed himself to the Highwood job. He stood at the mailbox, holding the check and feeling a wave of trepidation. The very look and feel of this check seemed intended to induce a sense of seriousness, a weight of responsibility—long, narrow, printed with a somber typeface, drawn on a private bank in Manhattan. With such a check came an obligation to do things right, to not make mistakes—to *deliver*.

Plus, it just occurred to him, he'd been so caught up in getting his estimates ready and flying to the West Coast and the rest of it that he'd forgotten about the impact of the job on his arrangement with Janet and Mark. She lived in Hartland, twenty minutes away, and they shuttled Mark between them, a week at one house and a week at the other. He was lucky she hadn't made custody an issue—things could have gone much worse. But she liked to make things difficult. Now she'd take his need for scheduling flexibility as yet another indication of his unreliability, his lack of commitment to anything, his self-absorption, et cetera, et cetera.

According to Janet, his own stupidity, arrogance, innate cruelty, short attention span, selfishness were to blame for everything—for their divorce, his poverty, even Mark's behavioral problems. "These things run in families," she'd said, reminding him that whatever gene produced Mark's problem had come from his bloodline, not hers.

He returned to the house and sat on the front porch, looking through the mail, breathing deeply of the good air that came off the fields, trying to banish the buzz of anxiety that had come up. "Submit to the dahk side of The Fawce," he said.

Janet's black Saab Turbo flashed among the trees along the road, then turned and came up the driveway. When she pulled to a stop and opened her door, Paul wondered when, if ever, he'd stop being disarmed by the graceful, willow-supple shape of her, the unusual silver gray of her straight hair, the seriousness of her patrician features.

Behind her, still in the car, Mark stirred in the passenger seat, rubbing his eyes. Paul waved.

"We had a bit of a difficulty over the weekend," Janet said. She opened her purse and rummaged in it for a cigarette, leaning back against the car, beautiful and out of place against the rough uneven beard of the dry fields, the frozen ruts in the driveway.

"How bad?"

"Saturday was a write-off. I tried some of the stuff you recommended, but we didn't get anywhere."

"Just the withdrawal or—"

"No tantrums, thank God. He's fine now." She looked at him levelly, cool gray-blue eyes, the self-possessed gaze he'd once found so magnetic.

Mark joined them, and Paul bent to give him a hug. As always when he first arrived, he simply took the hug and returned none of it, as if with his mother watching he was unable to decide where his loyalties lay. Later, he'd loosen up. He was dressed in a blue down jacket, jeans, black basketball shoes. His dark brown hair was shorter than last time Paul had seen him, ten days ago, but the tail he'd been growing for the last three years—eight inches of wispy tangle—still hung down his back.

"Nice haircut," Paul told him.

"I got it Friday," Mark said. In the sunlight, the skin on his serious face seemed too pale, too delicate. In general appearance, he'd taken after Janet—the long, aristocratic nose, straight eyebrows. If Paul hadn't seen him often enough goofing around, red in the face, laughing wildly, he'd never guess that there could be another side to the reserved child he saw now. Whenever Mark returned from a week with Janet, he resembled her even more—the poise, the restraint, a hint of disdain for the routines of daily life. But after a day or two with Paul and Lia, he changed. He seemed to get younger, more outspoken, finding humor in absurd things. More than once Janet had complained about the bad habits he picked up at the farmhouse: leaving toys around, not making his bed, thinking up jokes involving farts and boogers. Paul countered by telling her he thought that's how kids Mark's age were supposed to behave, and complained that Janet was trying to make him into an adult prematurely. Mark had a lot to deal with, bouncing every week between two increasingly different parental styles.

"We're going to have a great time," Paul told him. "We'll buzz down to Philly, see Grandma and Kay and your cousins. Old-fashioned Thanksgiving. Eat ourselves sick."

"Okay." Mark looked quickly to his mother, as if to find a cue to an appropriate response. "Can I go play?" He asked Janet, not Paul.

"Yes. But first get your things from the car. And give me a kiss—I'll need to be going soon."

Paul got Mark's suitcase from the trunk and set it on the porch, while Mark gathered an armful of things from the backseat: a book bag, a small brown backpack, his school lunch box, a gaudy plastic race car. After he'd put them down on the step, the kiss he gave his mother was a genuine one. Janet stooped to receive it, one arm around her son, the other holding her cigarette away. Mark let go of her reluctantly but was off immediately, opening from a composed walk into an elbow-pumping trot.

"He certainly loves his mother," Paul said.

"Yes. Contrary to your impression of things, Mark and I are very close."

"I'm sure you are. I'm glad you are."

She looked at him skeptically. He'd learned early not to be too virtuous around her: It infuriated her, giving her no legitimate object for her anger. She did much better when he kept their relationship mildly antagonistic, which her every action solicited.

"Listen," he began, "I've got a problem that we should talk about now."

She rolled her eyes as if she'd expected it.

"I've got a job coming up that'll take me out of state—not far, just to the New York area. But it'll get in the way of our schedule with Mark."

"Terrific." She flicked her cigarette disdainfully onto the drive and gave it one quick scuff of her boot. "Just how badly in the way?"

Paul explained about the job at Highwood, stressing the value of the house and furnishings, the degree of damage, the idea of familial obligation, as if that would soften Janet's resistance.

She looked at him, deadpan. "You sure you can handle it?"

"Thanks for the vote of confidence."

"I thought you weren't going to do any more of that kind of thing. I thought that's what graduate school was supposed to accomplish—you were going to be free of the blue-collar treadmill. I seem to recall us saving every penny for several years with that end in mind."

She knew all the buttons. He locked eyes with her, barely resisting the urge to counterattack. Then he gave up and smiled. "Ah, God, you're marvelous. Touché. Let's concede I'd rather be doing something else, then let's abandon this tack for now. I'm broke, Janet. I need the money badly. I've contracted for four weeks. It might turn into something longer, an additional month or two. It's impossible to be sure at this point."

"So I'm supposed to be a single mother the whole time, no backup? And what excuse are you planning to tell Mark as to why you're never around?"

"Maybe I could come back on weekends, take Mark every Saturday and Sunday. If it lasts until school gets out for Christmas break, I'll bring him down there—he can stay with Dempsey and Elaine during the day. I don't know. I want to see him, but I need the money too. How about helping me figure this out instead of opposing me?"

They both watched Mark at the far end of the barn, using a stick to swat dried milkweed pods, filling the air with drifting puffs. Janet checked her watch. "I've got to go. When are you supposed to start?"

"As soon as possible. I should go down next week."

"Great. Terrific." She got into the car, shut the door, and rolled down the window. "Paul, don't think this can go on forever," she said.

"What do you mean by that?"

"I mean that habitual insolvency, erratic behavior, unmarried cohabitation, and the rest of it aren't exactly assets when it comes to custody proceedings." She pulled away before he could respond.

Paul stood for a while after the car disappeared. She'd never threatened him before, and he reeled with the implications. Erratic behavior because he needed to change their schedule temporarily? She had obviously been thinking about it. Just how far had her thoughts taken her?

Mark swung by and stood near him, busy trimming twigs off his stick. "So what were you guys talking about?"

"Just regular stuff," Paul lied.

"I was playing over there so you'd have a chance to talk."

"That was very considerate. But you don't have to do that."

"Not just for you guys. I don't like to listen anyway. It's like there are always problems."

Paul grabbed him and hugged him to his chest, feeling the wiry body through the plump down jacket. "You know what you're doing? You're worrying about things you don't have to. I think you should leave any worrying that needs doing to me—that's my job. Okay?"

"Okay."

"You know what else? I'm glad to see you. I missed you this week—ten days was way too long."

"Yeah."

"Let's mess around out here for a while and then go in and get some lunch and then head into town. We've got to get some errands done before we head south."

They wandered outside for a while. Paul showed him some coyote prints he'd found in the frozen soil behind the barn. Mark got the idea of taking a plaster cast of a print to take to science class, and they spent some time searching for the perfect one to use. It was remarkable, Paul thought, how having Mark to think of put his own problems in order, made his own tangle of concerns more manageable. Having a kid to consider made your priorities clear. As Mark crouched to inspect another print, Paul felt a surge of nameless emotion. Something like gratefulness. Gratitude that Mark was in the world. But then, on the heels of that feeling came anger: If Janet planned any shit about custody, she'd better be ready for war. It was a grim thought. But he meant it—fucking Armageddon. Paul had to consciously relax his hands, which had balled into fists.

16

They took the MG into Hanover, where Paul deposited the check, got some cash for the drive to Philadelphia, and paid off the most pressing bills. Mark warmed gradually and talked about school, his friends, his projects. Paul told him about getting the job at Highwood.

"I was thinking we should celebrate and get something special for dinner tonight—what do you think?"

"You always want to get shrimp," Mark said without enthusiasm.

"What, you don't like shrimp? Unheard of! When I was a kid, shrimp was the best possible food in the world. We only got it when something good had happened—my father got a raise, or my mother sold an article, something like that. Most delicious possible food, and my own son doesn't like it?"

Mark tilted his hand back and forth equivocally. "I don't *not* like it. It's okay."

"What would you like instead?"

"Dessert stuff—cake and ice cream and Jell-O for the whole dinner." He laughed at himself.

"Fat chance," Paul told him. "If we ever did, I'd make sure we had brussels sprouts and liver and boiled cabbage for dessert."

They were quiet for a moment as Paul drove. Some of their banter had seemed forced, deliberately flip and upbeat, as if Mark were covering for the feelings they both always felt when Janet and Paul traded him off. But though it had started out somewhat artificial, their chatter had established a familiar and reassuring rhythm they both knew. They sat watching the road, feeling content with each other.

"So, Ma said you had an episode on Saturday. What happened?"

Mark shifted uncomfortably. "Same stuff."

"You've got to be specific. How'd it start?"

"I was writing a story and I was thinking for a minute, so I started clicking the pen in and out. I was watching the point come out of the hole at the bottom."

There it was again: the visual focus on minute things. Also the phenomenon of rhythmic stimulus, the regular clicking of the pen.

"Did you try any of the things we've been working on?"

"I remembered to breathe for a while, but then I mostly forgot."

Paul had noticed that a diminution of respiration, to the point of apnea, often signaled the onset. They'd practiced a breathing exercise, exhaling fully from the diaphragm on the chance that a buildup of carbon dioxide in the bloodstream was the trigger, inhaling and exhaling erratically to avoid any of the repetitious rhythms that might induce or reinforce the hypnogogic state. Mark was great at it when they practiced, puffing like a martial arts fanatic, but so far had not done well in the clinch.

"So what was it like this time?"

"Same stuff," Mark said dully, as if disgusted with himself. Then he quickened slightly. "There was like a thought I wanted to think but couldn't, that I kept trying to think? Sort of like when you forget a word and it's on the tip of your tongue."

"What kind of thought?"

Mark held his hands in front of him, as if trying to grasp something invisible. "I don't know." He pedaled his hands in the air. "It was jumbling around. I couldn't stop trying to think it, but I couldn't do it either. It made me mad."

"You can't remember what the thought was?"

Mark just scowled and tumbled his hands again, as if wrapping string on a spool.

"So what did Ma do?"

"I think she tried to dance with me. She kept pulling me up and making me move around. Poor Ma, huh?"

"True, you're not exactly Fred Astaire when you're in there," Paul told him. They both laughed, relieved to get some distance on it. "Well, Ma said you didn't start throwing things, though. That's a step in the right direction, right? How'd you come out of it?"

"I just suddenly remembered that I had my homework to do. Only it was night now."

"Did you write in your journal?" The question was part of the routine debriefing they went through.

Mark looked at his feet. "I forgot."

As part of making Mark's problem consciously correctable, Paul had insisted that he keep a journal, writing down everything he could remember about each episode as soon as possible after its conclusion. Paul read the journals, looking for patterns, hoping to find the loose thread that would unravel the knot. "You have to keep the journal going until we get a handle on this. Sometimes there are clues in things you write even if you don't know why you wrote them."

"I know. My subconscious writes them."

"More or less, yeah," Paul said. Mark had picked up some of the terminology. Like any eight-year-old, he was proud of the big words.

Mark rubbed his eyes with his palms. "I don't *like* my subconscious!"

"Whoa! Don't like your subconscious! Why not?"

"It's like it's down inside me, where I can't know anything about it, and it's—it's *sneaky,* the way it has to come out when you're not paying attention, and you're never sure what it really means. It's like there's someone else living inside me."

"It's not like that at all! Your subconscious is always telling you things, it's just that your conscious isn't always listening. Sometimes your subconscious is the only part of you that's really telling you what's going on!"

He didn't sound convincing. Mark shrugged, stared out the window.

Lia was home when they got back, sitting in the kitchen sipping a glass of Poland Spring water with a pile of papers and ring binders on the table beside her. A covered pot was starting to simmer on the stove.

"Looks like you've already started dinner," Paul said.

"I'm starving. I just put on some rice to go with the shrimp."

Paul took the carton of shrimp out of the bag. "How'd you know we'd have shrimp?"

Lia laughed. "The mail—an empty envelope from a private New York bank. I figured you got the check from Vivien and that you'd want to celebrate. I'd be very surprised if you brought home anything but shrimp." She looked at Mark for confirmation, but he didn't meet her eyes.

"It's nice to know I'm so predictable," Paul grumped. He started putting the other groceries away. "So what else did I get?"

"A nice white wine to go with," Lia said dreamily.

Paul put the bottle in the refrigerator to chill.

As always, it was hard for Mark to adapt to her presence immediately. First he had to go through the ritual of re-entry they had inadvertently cooked up. Paul had learned to stay out of the transaction that had to happen between Mark and Lia. What Lia did so well, Paul realized, was to harness the momentum of Mark's feelings and gently deflect them into a positive, harmonious affect. At first she'd mirror his mood, not talking much. She washed lettuce leaves and cranked the salad spinner without looking at him, then started chopping carrots.

"So how was your week, Max?" she said in a flat voice.

"It's *Mark*," he said angrily. Act one: She'd engaged his hostility and would let him vent it on something contrived and trivial, something they could soon discard.

"That's right, that's right. *Mac*—how stupid of me."

Mark played along. "My name is *Mark* Skoglund. My week was okay."

This went on for a time, until they both laughed and Lia put down her work and gave him a hug.

"We missed you," she told him. "This old farmhouse feels awfully empty when you're not here." She went back to the counter. "What's your mom doing for Thanksgiving? Is she going to Manchester?"

Another strategically chosen topic: By expressing an interest in Janet, in a way allying herself in a friendly way with her, Lia had decreased the emotional distance Mark had to travel. He wouldn't be disloyal to his mother by accepting and befriending Lia. Mark took the bait willingly, glad to have it all aboveboard.

Later, he'd thawed completely. They played Monopoly on the living room floor, sitting cross-legged around the board, spending their pastel cash lavishly, wrangling deals.

At one point, when Paul had collected a fat rent from Lia, he stupidly expressed his satisfaction by saying "Dudical!", slipping inadvertently into eight-year-old vernacular.

Which got Mark going: "Dudical? Did you really say *dudical?*"

"Why not? I thought that's what you kids said when something was good—was, I don't know, cool, a stroke of luck."

"Oh, my God. *Dudical* went out with *tubular*. God, you might as well say *gnarly!*"

"I think he's suggesting it's an archaic expression, Paul," Lia said mildly.

"Prehistoric," Mark affirmed. "If you want to sound like an airhead surfer nowadays, you've got to say *bonus!*"

"I don't know if I'm up for *bonus*."

"I mean, what if I started saying *groovy*? 'Wow, groovy, man,'" Mark said. "Oh, my God!"

He rolled the dice and moved his top-hat piece. When he landed on one of Lia's properties, thick with hotels, he clutched his chest in a mock heart attack, threw his money into the air and pitched forward, face-first onto the board. Houses and pieces and money and Community Chest cards scattered. Paul tickled him, Mark kicking and squirming, until Lia gathered him protectively into her arms, sat him on her lap.

He went willingly. "My evil stepmother," he said. A real term of endearment.

These were the good moments, Paul decided. This was what he lived for, right here.

"You're very lucky to have such a wonderful kid," Lia said. After putting Mark to bed, they had worked downstairs until their eyes bleared, Paul making preparations for Highwood, Lia doing reading for her thesis. Now they were in the big bedroom, where a single candle threw a fluttering light on the walls.

"I know."

"I'm lucky—we're lucky," she said.

Yes, Paul thought. He paused while untying his shoes to watch Lia taking off her clothes in the chill room. In Vermont in the cold season, there were a lot of layers. When she at last loosened her brassiere and stood before him, naked, the cold pulled her skin taut over every smooth curve of her. He stood and cupped her breasts, marveling at how every volume and line and weight seemed perfectly suited to his body. Her left breast had a faint scar rising from the nipple, about two inches long, the result of a bicycle accident she'd had as a teenager. The scar tugged at her areola so that it was slightly teardrop-shaped, and stroking her lightly he realized he had a different relationship with each of her breasts—the right seeming chaste and demure, the left just a bit wanton, a little streetwise. An irresistible combination. He put his face between her breasts and kissed her sternum, feeling the turgid curves against each cheek. Then, unsure of the source of her shiver, he pulled aside the blankets and sheets, laid her down, covered her up, slid in beside her.

Their love-making grew out of the quest for warmth, seeking heat from each other's bodies with growing urgency until anything less than absolute intimacy was not enough. Lia came quickly, giving herself readily to it, smiling rapturously into the waves of sensation as he rode her, then after a few moments relentlessly drawing him into it too. When she knew he was close, she held his face between her hands and commanded his gaze with hers. "Look at me," she whispered breathlessly. "I want you to look into my eyes when you come."

Feeling her feel the moment, his soul exposed to her, he did, he held her eyes and poured himself into them.

Afterward, they lay together for a time, drifting, empty of the pressure of desire, empty of thoughts. Lia's breathing slowed into her sleep rhythm.

Paul lay with his arms behind his head. A wind had come up outside, sending little drafts through the eaves and making the candle flame bounce gently. A calm had replaced the anxiety, his tics had vanished. Lia was very wise. She knew that seeing Janet was hard on him. Whenever he seemed in

danger of being caught up in some tangle, she brought him out of it by reminding him of love and desire and the good things they had. And he always felt better with Mark safely tucked in his bed: There was a
contentment, a sense of completeness, that came of knowing the people
who mattered most were safe, all under the same roof.

He began to drift toward sleep. Mark—what would become of him?
Sometimes it seemed that they were making progress, and yet it was so
hard to really know. Their conversation in the car came back to him, and
he wondered about the tumbling thought that Mark had been "trying to
think" and what it might suggest.

Then there was Mark's comment about not liking his subconscious.
Paul knew something of what Mark had been feeling. If you lived with
Tourette's, you knew what it felt like to have an "it" that lived in your head,
sometimes completely at odds with the "I" you thought you were. And in
fact every human being had parts that operated independently and se-
cretly: anatomical and neurological and psychological systems and forces
that the conscious self knew nothing about, had no control over. Tell your
heart to stop beating, your ears to stop listening, your stomach to stop di-
gesting. Couldn't be done.

"Submit . . ." he began out loud, then choked it off, weary of the feel of it
in his mouth. It was a chilling idea: that there lurked some furtive, unpredictable, irrational presence in your brain, in your personality, waiting like
a snake or a spider in a dark place. *How do you know what's inside you?*
Vivien had asked. Was that becoming a goddamned tic too? *How do you
know what you're capable of?*

Do we really want to know? Paul wondered.

Even as he thought of explanations and arguments for Mark, he found it
hard to dispel the unsettling image he had conjured: some shadowed para-
site, living its secret life inside your head.

17

Depending on his state of mind, the first phone call of the day could take on an oracular significance for Mo. If he got through, he took it as an omen of good luck. In his experience, success ran in cycles. There were days when everything clicked: when you called and the people you wanted were there, and you made the appointments or got the assistance you needed, when the gods smiled on your efforts. And there were days when every call got a busy signal, or no answer, or a machine, or resulted in being caught on hold listening to sickening canned music, or some other dead end or ambiguous closure.

Mo got lucky when he called the Masons' number first thing on Wednesday, the day after his interview with the Howrigans and the Gilmores. A woman's voice answered after only a few rings.

"Mrs. Mason," he said, "we haven't spoken before, but I'm the new person in charge of the investigation of Richard's death. I was hoping I could speak with you and your husband and daughter sometime soon."

"We've been over this and over this. Have you found out anything new?"

"I may have. I hope so."

Her voice hardened. "That sounds awfully vague, Mr. Ford."

"Any sort of prognostication would be premature, Mrs. Mason. If you don't mind, I'd like to meet with you and your family as soon as possible. Frankly, I'm especially interested in talking to your daughter."

"I don't think that's a good idea."

"May I ask why not?"

"Heather is going through . . . a difficult phase right now. As you may know, my daughter is emotionally disturbed. She is diagnosed as schizophrenic, Mr. Ford. She has been psychologically . . . fragile . . . for a long time. And then Richard's death—" Mrs. Mason paused, as if gathering her resources. "It started a deterioration. For her sake, we've tried to avoid the subject. Unless you can assure me that this is absolutely necessary, I'm afraid I can't let you speak to her."

"Mrs. Mason," he said, trying to sound certain, "I wouldn't have called otherwise."

She reluctantly agreed, but then tried to postpone their meeting, saying her husband, Victor, was in San Jose for three days. Mo persisted, told her he'd like to meet sooner to speak to the two of them, that he'd speak to Victor later if it were necessary. She settled by arranging to meet him at eleven o'clock. At one, she said, they'd have to leave for Heather's regular therapy session in Mt. Kisco.

After he hung up the phone, Mo opened his desk drawer and took out the toothbrush and toothpaste he kept there. Most early mornings were difficult enough without the tedium of brushing his teeth, so he usually waited until he got to the office and picked up a head of steam. And this morning had started off worse than most. After leaving the Howrigans' house last night, he'd felt nothing short of despondent. Janis Howrigan had reminded him of the condition of his heart, which ached with longing like a caged bird yearning to fly. He'd lain awake for hours, trying to avoid thinking of her face, of the rise of her breasts. At the alarm he'd gotten up feeling as if he had a hangover. He'd been too demoralized to brush at home. Now he slipped the brush and the tube of Pepsodent into his jacket pocket and walked down the hall to the men's room.

When he swung open the door, he spotted Pete Rizal standing at one of the sinks, working his hair with a comb. Trooper Rizal clearly liked to look at his own face.

Rizal was one of the people at the Lewisboro barracks who had made a point of making things hard for Mo. A career policeman, he had grown up in Golden's Bridge, and Mo had decided he was one of the species of local boys who had become cops originally for the prestige it had given them in the eyes of their high school buddies. Later on, when playing cop began to mean less and less to anyone, the type tended to get mean and pushy, milking the position for whatever little powers it conferred. Mo could see it in Rizal's narrow face.

Not long after he'd started at Lewisboro, he had glimpsed Rizal at the A & P with a pretty Asian woman who he assumed was Rizal's wife, pushing the wheelchair of a teenaged boy all knotted up with muscular dystrophy or something. He'd heard some talk about the kid's problems, and the sight of the three of them gave him a quick pang of sympathy. Living with that couldn't be easy. With an offhand solicitude, Rizal had presented the boy with a box of strawberries for his inspection. Mo assumed the guy was human, although it was easy to forget.

Mo took a stand at the sink next to him and pulled the toothpaste tube from his inside jacket pocket.

"Whoa, Mr. Mo Ford," Rizal said, starting to put his hands up. "You got a fast draw. Take it easy with that thing—I'm on your side." This was a nasty little jab, in the context of the White Plains thing, but not a bad joke under the circumstances.

Mo managed a smile. "Morning, Rizal," he said.

"So how's our resident sharpshooter doin'?" Rizal kept working the dark hair back on his head, watching Mo in the mirror.

"I'm doing about average, as usual. How about yourself?" He took the top off the toothpaste tube and squeezed some onto his brush.

Rizal turned to look at him, feigning amazement. "Don't have a sink at home? Or are you just one very fastidious guy?"

"Got an interview. Standard procedure," Mo lied. "Wouldn't want to offend. You know."

"She good-looking?"

Mo grinned around his toothbrush, then made a point of being engrossed in his brushing.

Rizal slid his comb into his back pocket and leaned against the sink, arms crossed. "I've been meaning to ask you something. You know. About White Plains. I mean, we hear so many rumors."

Here it comes, Mo thought. The asshole: Leave it to Rizal to wait until a guy has his mouth full and can't tell him to fuck off.

He'd first run into Rizal at the State Police firing range, during his last firearms qualification. By that time, stories about the incident in White Plains had made the rounds of the various law enforcement agencies, and Rizal had apparently conceived some sort of competitive thing with Mo. Rizal had his own little reputation as a martial arts fanatic and an artist with a pistol, anything macho and lethal. After the qualifications, they'd stood next to each other, ostensibly just getting in some practice but in fact checking each other out. Both were using standard Glock 17s. Rizal was scary fast, *pak-pak-pak-pak-pak*, eighteen shots in a matter of seven seconds. Some of the other troopers and range personnel drifted over to watch, and Mo couldn't help but get into the competitive mood, picking up the tempo of his shots. He didn't consider himself an expert marksman so much as an instinctive shooter who often got lucky. Which wasn't bad but had its drawbacks in the long run. As he'd learned painfully at White Plains.

They both put holes in five targets, fishing them back along the overhead cables as they reloaded, the other cops calling out totals to each other and exclaiming about their clusters. Rizal was a good shot, but Mo had ended up ahead. And though he tried to act like he didn't care, Rizal had made a face like he'd sucked a lemon. He'd been pushing Mo ever since.

"What I want to know," Rizal said, leaning back with exaggerated casualness, "is why you didn't go up when you knew Dickie was in trouble. Why you couldn't be bothered to keep Dickie alive."

Mo brushed thoughtfully for a moment longer, then spat into the sink. He ran the tap and cupped a handful of water to his mouth, sluiced it through his teeth, spat again. He wiped his mouth. "I've got a question for you too, Rizal," he said. "What are you doing hanging around the men's room? I mean here at the barracks—I thought you preferred the rest stops on I-84."

"Fuck you," Rizal said.

Mo yanked a paper towel from the dispenser and turned to the door, wiping his hands. "Sure. But be gentle," he said. He balled up the towel and tossed it into the trash, then shoved open the door and went out.

Driving to the meeting at the Masons' house, Mo tried to relax his stomach, which had knotted up and was giving him heartburn. It wasn't the tension of dealing with a lightweight prick like Rizal, it was the recollection of that afternoon in White Plains.

He wondered how long it would take before he was off the hook for what happened. Officially, the matter was closed, and he'd been cleared of wrongdoing, but among the other BCI staff and troopers—and in his own conscience—it was a different story.

He'd been one of a four-man team sent to an apartment building in an older neighborhood to collect a witness, Harold Wallace, in a case against a small-time cocaine distributor. Actually, their game plan had been to corner Wallace, a balding, soft-bellied counter clerk at a discount electronics store, and persuade him to testify by threatening to pick him up on his own trivial involvement with the operation. It wasn't supposed to be a risky job that Saturday. Mo and Wolf Dickie and two agents from the DEA went over as a group because it was an interjurisdictional case, and to make sure Wallace didn't try to dodge them—he'd expressed reluctance to testify against his boss at the electronics store, the little-league coke kingpin. What they didn't know was that the enterprising boss had just finalized some ambitious partnerships with bigger-league players, that Wallace was in it deeper than they'd thought, and that he had visitors that day.

Dickie and one of the DEA guys went upstairs, while Mo and the other agent covered the front and rear entrances to the building. It was a sunny but chilly day, and Mo waited in the brick gangway near the back entrance—four stories of wooden porches and open stairs—trying to keep his hands warm.

The first thing Mo heard was the slap of one of the wooden screen doors on the third floor. After that came an odd sound, not loud, that he first took to be a pneumatic wrench from some nearby gas station. He didn't realize what it was until he heard the second short burst, louder, and got the sudden, salty whiff of cordite. He scuttled to the bottom of the stairs and would have gone up if the DEA agent who'd gone with Dickie hadn't come down in front of him and partially blocked the stairs. The guy had apparently toppled over the third floor railing after being hit with the second burst from the MAC-10. With brutal force, he hit the wooden banister not ten feet from Mo, spun and bounced. He ended up in a loose sitting position, propped absurdly on one elbow as if he'd been hanging out on the back steps and had downed a few too many beers. But the top half of his head was missing, tilted toward Mo so that he could see the interior of his brain case, empty, an oddly smooth, clean pink bowl that contrasted with the ragged edges of his skull and scalp. He'd left his brain on the second-floor landing.

There was another quick burst of fire from the third floor, but Mo didn't move or flinch. He was too stunned at the sight of the DEA man. It wasn't fear. It was just an immediate and complete paralysis. *That's what's inside our heads.* He stood for several seconds, thinking vaguely about Dickie, still upstairs. Charging up the stairs exposed to fire from above didn't seem like a good idea, so he started down the gangway to alert the man at the front. He hadn't gone halfway, maybe forty feet, when he heard footsteps and turned to see two men leaping down into the gangway behind him. One carried the MAC and the other what appeared to be an Uzi, although Mo didn't consciously notice these because his arm was already coming up and then he was putting what turned out to be an incredibly tight cluster of three holes in the first man's chest, just below his left nipple. The second man put on the brakes and was bringing up his gun when Mo did the same thing again, a little more to the center, through the sternum. *Pop-pop-pop,* all reflex.

At the inquiry conducted by Inspection, and later at the grand jury hearing, the DEA agent who'd been in front said he'd come around the corner of the building to see Mo standing in the gangway, popping the two guys a few more times. It was these extra shots, plus the tight constellations he'd gotten lucky with, that caused doubts to be raised about exactly what had happened. Why had Mo abandoned his post? Why hadn't he gone upstairs as backup to Wolf Dickie, when he could clearly surmise Dickie was in big trouble? Why, if he had such a revulsion for gore that the sight of the DEA man paralyzed him, had he repeatedly shot the gunmen when they were clearly already dead? Was it really possible that a guy could hit a moving target with three bullets spaced no more than two inches apart—not once but twice in rapid succession, under great duress?

The press had a great time with it, all kinds of scandals were suggested, even a rumor that Mo was in some way involved with the cocaine ring and was finishing off witnesses who might expose him. It wasn't long before it became public knowledge that Mo already had two reprimands in his file and was known to be a difficult guy to work with. Even his admirers admitted that he'd operated too independently on a couple of cases, was prone to running with his gut instead of slogging through conventional investigative procedures, and tended to get obsessive about his own ideas, impatient with the conferences and task force meetings that were standard.

But ultimately it was the thing with Wolf Dickie. And there his worst sin, in the eyes of his superiors, was the public scrutiny he'd called down on the department, the demand for an uncomfortable level of accountability.

Mo's detractors in White Plains had been critical of him for not supporting Dickie, who was popular and had an excellent record, or for one or another violation of procedure, or for weakness or cowardice. But counterbalancing this was a secret respect for the shooting he'd done. Paradoxically, the extra shots, which gave him trouble at the official level, earned him back some respect among the rank and file. At some primal level, his supporters wanted to believe that Mo could shoot the balls off a housefly and would pay back in spades any fuckhead who messed with a brother officer.

The problem for Mo was that he could remember it all far too well, he didn't need the odd looks at the barracks or the comments of pricks like Rizal to remind him. He didn't think of himself as particularly tough or cowardly, he hadn't felt either fear or anger. There was just the unexpected, brutal impact of the DEA man hitting the railing, the oddly fascinating and revolting hollow bowl of his brain case, the Rorschach splash of blood and fluids on the stairs. The almost-complete cessation of conscious thought. The cottony deafness that followed his own explosive shots in the narrow brick gangway.

And none of that mattered anyway. After a lot of sleepless nights spent sifting through what had happened, he'd distilled out the three things that really bothered him, the three nasty gritty facts that wouldn't go away. One was that he now knew that even though he'd gotten his feet wet before, he could react unpredictably to gore—there was a strong possibility that, faced with anything like the DEA man's empty head, he'd freeze up again.

The second was the possibility, however slim, that he might have done something for Dickie and had failed to do it. If he'd even called out. Although they hadn't been particularly close, he'd liked Dickie. He wished Jane, Wolf's wife, had said something to him at the funeral, one word of understanding, but she hadn't so much as looked at him.

But worst was the frightening secret he'd managed to preserve through all the inquiries and hearings and debriefings by lying slightly about what

he saw when the gunmen came into the gangway. The truth was that his reflexive firing, those six lucky shots, would have been directed at anyone
who had come off those steps at that moment—a kid, say, or Dickie himself. Or anybody. The big drawback of his reflexive, instinctive shooting.
Eating away at him was the sense that he could no longer trust himself. Nobody, not his partners or bystanders or victims, nobody was safe around a
guy who'd shoot like that. If he had any real integrity, he'd quit, get a job
that didn't put a weapon within his reach.

18

"**Heather** is upstairs in her room," Mrs. Mason said. "I told her you would be coming to talk to her, but I thought you and I should talk for a little while first."

"Sure." Mo put his briefcase down on a wrought-iron chair and leaned against the counter. The Masons lived in one of the exclusive subdivisions built since the IBM offices moved in, a large pseudo–Tudor style house on a road that looped through heavy older forest. Now they were standing in a solarium, filled with plants of every description, which extended the length of the house on the south side. Mrs. Mason stood at a long counter set against the sloping glass wall, working a trowel in a large terra-cotta pot. A slim woman, dressed in peach running sweats and blue denim apron. Dark hair streaked with gray, pulled back into a loose ponytail. Mid-forties, Mo guessed. He was relieved that although she was a pleasant-looking woman, she wasn't another Janis Howrigan. He would be able to concentrate on business.

The air in the solarium was agreeably warm, filled with humidity and the smell of green leaves and blossoms. He waited as Mrs. Mason went on working, not speaking, wetting the soil occasionally with a watering can.

"As I told you," she said at last, "I'm ambivalent about meeting you today. On the phone I said I was concerned for Heather, but that's only part of the truth." She looked at him intently for a moment, with deep brown eyes that carried that almost mystical light of sorrow or fear or loss he'd seen in the eyes of the other parents.

"Okay," Mo said, feeling she expected him to say something.

"The rest of the truth is that it's hard for me too, and for my husband. Of course we'd like you to find the person who ran over Richard. But it's been four months, Mr. Ford. We've spent it grieving, and coping with Heather, and wondering whether we were good enough parents. Whether it was wise to have encouraged Rickie to come back and live at home after college. Wondering what we could have done differently that would have somehow put him anywhere but where he was that night."

She placed a small tree into the pot, sorted its roots, and began spooning more soil around them. "So," she said, "after you do this for a long time, after you feel like hell every day for a long time, after your marriage almost falls apart, you have to either decide to grieve forever or try to live again. Just in the last couple of weeks, my husband and I have decided to try to do that. It's still a very fragile effort, Mr. Ford. It's all too easy to fall back into"—she made a slack, hopeless gesture with the trowel—"all that."

"I understand. I'm grateful you agreed to see me." He couldn't help liking her, the resigned, patient, determined way she spoke and moved.

Mrs. Mason removed her apron and sat at a small wrought-iron table where a silver coffee service and cups waited. She poured two cups of coffee.

"So, I'd like to know what brought you here today. Have there been . . . developments? You have some sort of lead or clue or—?"

"Not exactly. Actually, no. None of the regular investigative channels have turned up anything new. At this point, the odds are remote that they ever will."

He'd thought she might get angry, but she just took a sip of coffee. "We assumed that much. Then why are you here?"

"Two reasons. One, to meet you, see if I can pick up on something Detective Avery might have missed. Two, to see if you or Heather can provide me with any information about what may be a related case."

"All right."

"Let me start with some general questions. How would you describe Richard's mood in the period preceding his death? Happy? Unhappy?"

"He'd had a disappointing year. He didn't really want to come home. I think he wanted to find the right girl at school and find a good job. And none of it had quite happened yet. So he came home for the summer."

"Were there family tensions?"

"Of course there were. We had our problems. I wish we'd sorted them all out when Rickie was alive. But we didn't." She paused, blew her nose into a napkin. "I'm not, not, *not* going to start crying. I have done enough of it." This she said like a chant, to herself, a little mantra of self-control. It seemed to work. When she went on, her voice was level again. "But Mr. Ford, every family has its problems. If anything, Richard seemed to be in a better mood the last three or four weeks."

Mo sipped his coffee, allowing her time to regroup.

"When you talked about connections to a related case, what did you mean?" she asked finally.

"I think there may be connections between Richard and some other young people who disappeared around the time he was killed. There's a chance that what I can find out from you and Heather may help save the lives of some of the others. It's probably a long chance. But if there's any chance at all, I've got to give it a try."

"What connections do you mean?"

Mo told her the names of the missing teenagers, saving Essie Howrigan until last. Mrs. Mason shook her head no for each of the names until he mentioned Essie.

"Essie—she was the girl who came to visit Heather."

"Yes. What can you tell me about her?"

Mrs. Mason thought for a moment, and again Mo was impressed with her, the control she maintained. "Essie was part of the Teen Companion program. She visited Heather twice a week. At some point she stopped coming, and they sent over a different girl."

"Did you know the Howrigans?"

"No. Victor and I meant to introduce ourselves to her family at some point. It just . . . we never got around to it. With all that happened."

"What was your impression of Essie?"

"She was wonderful. She was extremely pretty, but she wasn't vain or spoiled as so many pretty girls are. Intelligent, very courteous without being tense or artificial. Mature for her age. Heather can be . . . difficult. Essie did a fine job of staying with her, weathering the rough spots. We're not associated with the Howrigans' church, so at first we had concerns about the Teen Companion program, whether there was some intent to proselytize. But we never saw any sign of it from Essie."

Mo took notes in his own illegible shorthand. "And what sort of relationship did she have with Heather?"

"As far as we could tell, a good one. As I said, Heather can be very hard to relate to. Essie seemed to do quite well. Of course, I wasn't always here when she came. I stayed home to be here for the first few visits, but once I got to know Essie I took the opportunity to do things out of the house. I felt secure that Heather was in good hands with Essie and the Gonzalezes, my household staff, here. In the past five years, with Heather at home a lot of the time, I have often been housebound. For purely selfish reasons, I was very grateful to have someone like Essie here. I took a weekly dance class, Mr. Ford, Victor and I could go to movies or visit friends at *their* houses. Then Rickie was killed. Right around then, they called to say Essie wouldn't be coming." She massaged her forehead, which had slowly drawn into furrows. "Oh," she said, realizing what she'd just said. "So there's one of the connections, right? Of course."

"How long had Essie been coming, at that point?"

"It's hard to remember. I'd say three months. Yes, I think she started coming in April."

Not long before Richard Mason would have come back from college,

Mo was thinking. He wouldn't ask her about that, he decided. Not yet. He poured himself another half cup of the superb coffee and swigged it, not sure whether the excitement he felt was the edge of caffeine hitting his bloodstream or something else. It just might all connect. If he remembered correctly from Wild Bill's notes, the Masons had gone out the night Richard was killed, returning at around midnight from dinner with friends.

"Mrs. Mason, before I meet Heather, I'd like you to tell me about her. I know the clinical definition of schizophrenia, but I don't know what it means in terms of Heather's behavior."

She drew a deep breath, let her shoulders slump. Clearly a big area, full of pain. "Schizophrenia is just a name. The fact is, everything has a name, but names don't necessarily mean anything. What does 'love' mean, Mr. Ford? Do you 'love' your wife? Your dog? Pizza? Do you 'love' America? How many meanings does the word have? The same is true with psychological terms. Only there you have complete disagreement to compound the issue. No one can list all the ways schizophrenia manifests in behavior." She had a lot of anger here, Mo saw. "The term ends up not meaning anything. No one knows all the types of craziness."

"You said she's bright."

"She's mathematically gifted, she reads at an adult level, mainly clinical texts about psychopathologies. Yes, she's very intelligent. Maybe that's one of her problems."

"You keep referring to the degree to which Richard's death affected Heather. Were she and Richard very close? Or do you think the particular nature of his death—"

"We told her almost nothing about the accident. No, it wasn't that. He was important to her. You have to understand that she lives in a type of isolation you and I can only vaguely imagine. When Richard came home from school, I think he filled a gap in her life. He was her own flesh and blood, someone who could understand her, at least a little. They often did things together."

"What sort of things?"

Mrs. Mason opened her hands to each side. "What young people do. They went to movies, went swimming sometimes. Shopping. Concerts at Caramoor."

"Did Essie ever accompany them?"

"Once or twice. Essie could control Heather better than Richard, if she got difficult in public."

Mo nodded, taking notes. Mrs. Mason continued, slipping inadvertently into reminiscence, and he let her go on, looking for the lines that converged. At last she shook her head, as if to clear it.

"I'm sorry," she said. "I have probably gotten off track. If you'd like, we can go up to Heather's room now. I think you'll have more luck with her if she feels like she's on her own turf, but I can't promise she'll cooperate, and I don't have any way to compel her to."

"Understood." Mo followed her through the house and up the broad staircase.

Heather's room turned out to be a small suite—one large room, a bathroom, and a bright alcove facing the backyard. It was a reassuringly normal, adolescent girl's bedroom: white carpet, white curtains trimmed with pink, stuffed animals ranged on shelves and bureaus, a boom box surrounded by piles of CDs. On the walls, among pinups of musicians, posters of Freud and Einstein. The only really jarring element Mo could see was a large, framed print of Munch's *The Scream* over the bed.

Heather was seated at a table in the alcove, bent over and writing studiously with a pen. She was wearing jeans and a gray sweatshirt. Though he couldn't see her face, Mo remembered the photo of her with her family, the straight blond hair, surprised eyes and loose, thick lips.

"Heather, this is the man I said would be coming—Mr. Ford."

Heather didn't lift her head or stop writing. "Why didn't you come up before? He's been here for an hour already. What were you doing, prepping him for me?"

"I wanted to talk to your mother about various things," Mo said.

"You can go now, Mom," Heather said, still not looking up.

Mrs. Mason glanced at Mo. *You see what I mean,* her eyes said. "I'd like you to be polite to Mr. Ford. He thinks you may be able to help him. Don't forget, we need to be ready to go by one o'clock. And I want you to eat some lunch before we go." She went to the door, where she paused as if she had more to say, then turned down the hall.

Mo stood in the bedroom, waiting for Heather to say something. Through the windows of the alcove, he could see that the sky outside had cleared and a bright sun shone down into the backyard. With the sun had come a wind, tossing the tattered oak leaves that still clung to the trees. He looked around the room for a moment, then back at Heather. She still had not lifted her head; all Mo could see was the curtain of her hair, almost touching the spiral notebook she was writing in.

"What are you writing?" he said at last.

"A story."

"Oh yeah? What's it called? What's it about?"

"I don't have a title for it yet—that's the hardest part for me. It's sort of a detective story."

"Ah. What kind of a detective story?"

Heather jotted another line. "It's about a detective who comes to talk to a schizophrenic girl."

Mo stopped, feeling out of his depth. He wasn't certain how to approach this. She was playing with him. He had been with her three minutes and had already lost control of the interview.

When he didn't answer, Heather looked up for the first time. She had pale skin, a child's face. She hardly looked fourteen, more like ten or eleven, Mo decided, with her skinny legs, narrow shoulders, undeveloped chest. The loose and unguarded look of her mouth was made more awkward by the braces on her teeth. Only her eyes looked older. "Don't you want to know what happens?"

"Okay. What happens?"

Heather smiled coquettishly at him. "I'm not going to tell you. You have to guess."

It would be useless to fence with her, Mo decided, to humor her or condescend to her. Better to challenge her, throw her off balance, take a gamble. "Fine." He cleared his throat, put his hands in his jacket pockets, and paced while he talked: "I'd guess it's about a schizophrenic girl whose older brother is in love with a girl, a girl who's a friend of the schizophrenic and is almost her age. The brother often takes his sister with him when he goes out with the other girl because neither the brother nor the other girl want anyone to know they're hanging out together. Am I warm?"

Heather's eyes had narrowed. "I don't like you," she said.

"Sometimes the three of them go out when everybody thinks the other girl is visiting the schizophrenic girl. But other times they go out when nobody knows, and they bring the schizophrenic girl along so she's not alone at the house, or in case any of the parents find out."

Heather climbed awkwardly out of her chair and went to the window seat, where she looked out at the backyard. All he could see was the curtain of hair again.

"I really don't like you," she said again. Her voice was shaky, and Mo felt at once a rush of excitement and a stab of pity. This kid was messed up. She'd been through a lot. Mo could guess only so far, and then he drew a blank. He had no idea what had happened or what Heather knew or didn't. At some point, he'd have to have her cooperation, or he'd get nothing. "Anyway," Heather continued bitterly, "she wasn't really the schizophrenic sister's friend."

"Why do you say that?"

"Because she just came because she was supposed to for her religious club. Because she just came to see Richard."

"Couldn't she do both of those and still really be a friend too? I think she could."

"And the brother just went places with the sister so he could be with the girl."

"I don't think it has to be that way either." Mo had to repress the urge to reach out and touch her, comfort her.

Heather shook her head. "You think you're very smart, but you're really stupid. If the schizophrenic girl thinks things like that, she can't be mad at them, and if she can't be mad, then she'll have to be even more sad and it will all be much worse. You get mad so when you think of it, all you can think of is how mad you are. You don't have to think of what happened."

Mo waited, hoping she'd go on, his heart thudding so hard he was sure she'd hear it. He wished he'd brought a tape recorder. This was rich stuff, ore to be mined and processed thoroughly, material to be analyzed by a forensic psychologist. She sat silently, working her hands together as if they were fighting, so much tension and force in the knotting motions that Mo had to look away. "What did happen, Heather?"

"How should I know? I was talking about a story. I haven't written it all yet." Heather turned to face him, and he was shocked to see her smiling, an incongruous, horribly artificial ear-to-ear grin.

"That's not true."

The smile went away. "Besides, there's another thing behind the mad, not just sad, that's even worse."

"What," Mo said quietly. She seemed to want to tell him, tell somebody.

"Scared. *Very* scared," she whispered with a round-eyed, childish certainty.

Mo's skin prickled. "What kind of scared?"

"Very very. But you have to guess."

Mo knelt in front of her. He had to overcome the desire to take her by the shoulders and shake it out of her. "Heather, you need to tell me. I need to hear you. But I can't do this. I'm not as smart as you are, and this isn't a game. And it isn't a story. You know it isn't."

"And the brother said never to tell. About them."

"He never thought all this would happen."

"Sometimes he'd park the car and they'd go up. I'd wait. Sometimes I'd walk partway too. You couldn't park too close because people would see the car there."

Mo waited, his eyes locked on hers, trying to keep it flowing between them by force of will. Heather seemed to draw into herself, her eyes watching some scene he couldn't imagine. She didn't continue.

Mo let several minutes pass. "And?" he prompted at last.

"What?"

"And what happened then?"

She looked across the room, her eyes suggesting resignation, as if she were disappointed with him. "See, you think it's just a detective story. I said *sort of* a detective story."

"Well, what kind of story is it then?"

"It's much, much more than that. It's very important. It's about when we think we know what's real and then find out we didn't know. How we didn't know hardly anything. How people can do things nobody ever, ever imagined they could. *Ever, ever, ever, ever, never, never, never, never, never.*"

She chanted the last words as if they were a warding ritual from which she took some desperate comfort. Mo felt lost again. Heather was drifting into abstractions that he couldn't fathom. He'd have to bring her back.

"Heather, what happened then? They parked the car and you waited, and they went up. What happened after that?"

She looked at him as if surprised. "When?"

"In the story."

"What story?" She stood up and went to the table, where she picked up the spiral notebook. "This? This isn't a story. You were right, it's not a story. See? I was fooling you." She brandished the book at him, and he could see that the lines weren't script at all, just a series of uniform squiggles neatly filling each line on the page. She tore four or five pages from the book and began ripping them neatly in half, then in half again.

"Heather, please," he said.

Heather pointed at a wall clock over her table. "It's time for me to be getting ready for my therapy session with Dr. Kurtz. I call him Dr. Klutz."

"We will have to talk again. Would that be okay?"

"Probably not. If I tell my mother or Dr. Kurtz how much I don't like you, they won't let you see me again."

Mo stood and watched her as she brushed her hair in front of the bureau mirror. He tried to think of the thing to say, the one right thing that would provoke her, crack her open again, but couldn't come up with a guess. If he ever slipped, guessed too wide of the mark, she'd know she could dodge him forever. It was safer to let it ride. For now.

"Okay," he said. "Heather, you've been very helpful. I'm going to go. I hope you'll consider talking with me again." He went toward the door of the bedroom and stood, wondering if she'd say good-bye.

To his surprise, she turned quickly. "Wait," she said. She came toward him, smiling a little smile now. "Don't look so sad. I'll tell you a clue. A secret." Standing close to him, she tilted her child's face up toward him, and he automatically bent toward her. She put her lips next to his ear, so close he could feel her breath on his cheek.

"It was Superman," she whispered, her voice lisping slightly because of the braces. The skin across Mo's back drew taut with a sudden chill. She pulled away and looked at him round-eyed, awed, shaking her head up and down with that childlike certainty. "*Superman.*"

"Great," Mo said. He had no idea what was going on at this point. He just felt a strong desire to get away from this demented, pathetic, frightened girl and try to sort out what he'd learned, if anything. He couldn't keep track of the levels of truth, deception, denial, manipulation, and whatever else she was working through. The hell with it. He wasn't cut out for this.

He turned to go down the hall but stopped when she spoke again: "Don't you want to know what happens to the detective in the story?"

"Okay. I'll bite, Heather," he said wearily. "What happens to him?"

"He gets killed," she said, still round-eyed, certain.

19

"Royce did it," Kay said immediately.

They were all at the big dining room table at Kay and Ted's house in Philadelphia, the feast spread out before them. Paul and Lia had been describing their visit to Highwood, and Paul had recounted his visit with Vivien. The whole group had relished the story—Kay and Ted, their two children Alexis and Ben, Aster, and a younger neighbor couple, Jim and Francette, with their eight-month-old baby.

At the head of the table, Ted sat next to Kay, serving the turkey he'd carved when they first sat down. He'd put on weight since Paul had seen him last, and his wide shoulders were now offset with a broadening belly. His dark, thick hair and bristly moustache were shot with gray.

Kay was plumper too, but she looked vigorous, happy, her skin pink from the heat of the kitchen. Now she worked next to Ted as the plates came around again, serving seconds of mashed potatoes and stewed onions from gigantic bowls.

Down at the far end of the table, the three children were still acting shyly toward one another. When they'd first arrived, Mark had barely been able to greet his cousins. Alexis was now twelve and had begun to get her growth; Ben was nine, stocky like his father, an extroverted, good-natured boy. Seen with his cousins, Mark seemed smaller and paler, his uncertainties obvious. Between the divorce and his neurological problems his confidence was weak, especially in this rather staid, well-off household.

Only Aster hadn't enjoyed the talk about Highwood, scowling when the others made jokes or appeared to be enjoying the narrative too much. She'd had her hair permed recently, a tight curl that made her hair stiff and too sculpted, a smooth gray sphere like a ball of steel wool. It emphasized the age lines in her face.

"Yep—Royce," Kay said again. "He's our cousin, the son of the woman who owns the house," she explained to Jim and Francette.

"Why Royce?" Lia asked.

"You'd have to know him," she said. "He was always a creep. He also hates his mother. Always has."

"You two used to be very close friends," Aster said. Then she addressed Ted and the neighbors, as if looking for support: "The two of them were inseparable from the moment we set foot on the hill to when I had to pry Kay away. You never heard so much laughing and carrying on."

"He was spoiled rotten, he was neurotic and manipulative. And he made sure we never forgot that they had money and we didn't."

"We all had a perfectly lovely time at Highwood." Aster put her fork down pointedly, as if to signal the end of the discussion.

"We ran around like loonies, it's true. It would have been hard not to have fun up there. But I pretty well had to do what Royce wanted. It wasn't always very nice. More turkey, anyone?"

Jim held out his plate, and Ted forked a piece of meat from the platter onto it.

"Ohhh, bay-buh!" Paul said. It was the tic of the day, the Big Bopper's voice. Nobody paid any attention—the family was used to it, and he'd taken a moment earlier to explain to the guests.

Ted thoughtfully rubbed the short bristles of his moustache. "Why do you say he hated his mother?"

"Because he often said so. There was always this strange antipathy. It's easy for me to believe he'd take it out on her, on the house, even all these years later."

"Chilling idea," Jim said. "An adult man harboring such a deep resentment that its expression takes such a vehement form, even after thirty years. Pathological, really." Jim was the guidance counselor at Alexis and Ben's school. At the far end of the table, the three children were eating silently, following the conversation.

"Fantasy, really," Aster said, disgusted. "Royce has been a successful and responsible businessman, with interests all over the world, for many, many years."

Ted had been stirring his food with the tip of his fork, listening thoughtfully. "There are other possibilities that fit what you've described. Think about it—someone's been slashing the ducts, poking holes in the walls, busting open bureaus, emptying out file cabinets. Sounds to me like they've been looking for something."

Lia nodded. "The thought had occurred to me. Not that there isn't a lot of other damage that doesn't fit that pattern—"

"The real question for you," Francette put in, "then becomes whether or not they plan to come back to continue looking for whatever it is. And how they'll react when they find you there, dutifully trying to put things back together."

"Have you talked to the police up there yet?" Ted asked. "Maybe this should be looked into from a crime perspective before you disturb the scene. There may be evidence in the rubble."

"She made it clear she doesn't want the police to come in," Paul told them. "She keeps stressing that it's a job for family. All her private papers and so on."

"Completely understandable," Aster said.

Ted shook his head. "I wouldn't touch it if I were you, Paul. Don't ask for trouble. Stay clear of the whole deal."

Kay laughed and slugged his arm. "Oh, Ted! It's not like that! It's a nice area, it's a lovely house. Don't scare Paul off—he needs the work."

"Ohhh, bay-*buh*!" Almost always when Kay was talking: some residual sibling thing.

No one was ready for dessert. They cleared the table and made a token stab at the mess in the kitchen, then moved into the living room. Ted stoked the fire in the fireplace, the kids began a complicated card game. The adults took chairs, sipping drinks as they talked and watched the flames.

Paul wished she wouldn't keep at it, but Kay brought up Highwood again. "Do you remember Vivien's weird gardeners?" she asked Paul.

"Aha—the weird gardeners," Jim said in a Boris Karloff voice.

"Well, she had a succession of gardeners up there," Kay explained. "There was that Italian, the great big one? He had the bushiest eyebrows I'd ever seen—they made him look mad all the time. He was so strong! Once Vivien asked him to remove a boulder from the garden, assuming he'd hire a bulldozer to come up from town. So a half hour later, she looks out the window and there's this guy, leaning into the boulder and rolling it up the hill himself, like Sisyphus. It was practically the size of a . . . a *freezer,* so help me, and he dug it up and shoved it uphill a hundred feet by himself."

"Actually, Vivien mentioned him to me," Paul told them. "Apparently he stole some things from the house. She had him arrested."

"That's not how I remember it. Or rather, there's more to it than that. He had a temper. Remember, there was that shack at the top of the garden? One little room, where they kept the tools and wheelbarrows and so on. I thought Vivien had him arrested because he went bananas and tore the place apart. This is what Royce told me, anyway. He said the gardener got mad and threw the wheelbarrow through the window of the shed."

"You just can't get good help nowadays," Jim quipped.

"Personally, I can't blame the guy," Kay told him. "If I'd had to work around Vivien and Royce all day, I'd have wanted a little cathartic self-expression too."

Everyone laughed but Aster.

"There was one more weird gardener when we still lived in the area," Kay went on. "He worked there for such a short time, I hardly remember him. A smaller man, younger. Asian—Indonesian or Vietnamese."

"Haven't we heard enough yet?" Aster complained.

"What was his claim to the weird-gardener hall of fame?" Jim asked.

"Apparently he got into the habit of coming into the house at night, shall I say, *unannounced*. Back then, Vivien's gardeners used to live upstairs in the carriage house. So it wasn't unusual for them to come into the kitchen during the day. But this guy liked to come into the rest of the house when everybody was asleep."

Kay paused, and everyone waited expectantly. "And?" Jim prompted her.

"One night Vivien saw him coming out of Royce's room. Tiptoeing in his bare feet—"

Ted cleared his throat, a deep rumble, and glanced meaningfully at the kids, who appeared to be deeply engrossed in their game. Paul knew they were listening intently.

"He was never tiptoeing out of Royce's room!" Aster said. "You've been watching too much television. He was from the Philippines, he'd been a farmer there, and he often preferred to be barefoot in the summertime. Vivien was concerned he was taking things—"

"Anyway, they got another gardener *very* quickly." Kay let them digest the scandal and then went on, clearly enjoying her rumor-mongering role. "And you know how Freda died, right? Run over by the train. The question in my mind is, did she fall or was she pushed? And where was Royce that afternoon?"

"Oh, Kay, for the love of God!" Aster said indignantly. "This has gone well beyond the bounds of good taste."

"Sounds like the kid in *The Addams Family*," Jim said.

Aster stood up. "Well. If you people can't figure out some topic for adult conversation, I'm going to retire. I really don't think I can take any more of this rubbish."

Kay put her hand on her mother's arm. "Oh, Mother. Don't get so upset. You have to admit, there are some dark things in that family's past."

Mark and Alexis looked up from their cards, unable to conceal their interest.

"Of course," Aster said. "Certainly. There are dark secrets in every family's past. But one doesn't have to parade every last one before the public's eye, does one?" She stalked out of the room.

20

Paul wandered back to the kitchen, where he picked at the ravaged turkey for a while, thinking. He was startled when Kay appeared next to him at the counter.

"The best part of Thanksgiving, isn't it—picking at the turkey." She pinched off a piece of white meat. "Why do you think it tastes better like this?"

"Because we get to use our fingers," Paul said. "Gives our monkey hands something fidgety to do."

"I think you're right." Kay peeled another strip of meat, put it primly in her mouth. "So what are your ruminations out here in the solitude of the quiet kitchen?"

"I think you should try to be more sympathetic to Mother. She has a right to preserve whatever image of her past she wants."

As he'd expected, Kay didn't back down: "I agree we have to respect her sensibilities, but I also think we have to not let her drift away from reality completely. This thing of sanitizing, idealizing the past—she's getting to the age where she needs to be called back to earth now and again or she'll get off into her own little universe."

"She comes from a generation that simply didn't discuss certain things over the dinner table, Kay. The way she sees it, a person's most intimate details are not appropriate subjects for casual conversation."

"What you're saying is that our outspoken, radical, bohemian mother has a wide Victorian streak and we should indulge her contradictions."

"She's entitled to her contradictions."

"Sure. So is everybody. But she has to stay anchored in *reality,* for Christ's sake. Otherwise she'll get isolated, and when someone her age gets isolated they go into a final tailspin."

"Ohhh, bay-*buh*!" It had always been impossible to win an argument with Kay. She had the Viking warrior-woman in her—with her eyes sparking, her hair on one shoulder in a thick gold braid, all she needed was a steel helmet with horns. "So now she's off by herself in your guest bedroom," he said, "as isolated as she can be."

"I'm not going to start censoring my conversation because my mother needs to launder her past," Kay said. But her voice had lost conviction. Aster's withdrawal had gotten to her too.

They both took another bite of turkey. "I found a note from Ben to Vivien, in the mess up there," Paul told her. "I'm kind of curious to find more letters."

"Yeah, Dad was a big letter-writer. I think he was determined to leave lots of interesting material for his future biographers."

"You don't have to be so cynical. Aren't you interested in what he had to say, in who he was?"

"Not as much as you are. My present is about all I can manage. The less of my past I have to lug around with me, the better." Kay looked quickly to the door to the dining room, then swung it shut on the gentle hubbub of voices and continued in a lower voice. "Listen. I'll tell you another reason why I don't feel I have to defend the glorious Hoffmann family, or feel inclined to let Mother smooth everything over. It wasn't always Walt Disney up there. Royce was a little rotter, and Aster never could see it. Partly because I never told her everything."

"Like what?"

"Like the fact that when I was thirteen, Royce decided he wanted to have sex with his cousin Kay. At first he just liked to grab me where he shouldn't—when we'd be wrestling or climbing or whatever. Then he started making me kiss him and let him put his hands on me."

"For Christ's sake!"

Remembering, Kay became indignant. "That sleazy little shit! When I told him cousins weren't supposed to do that sort of thing, he basically told me that was precisely what made it so much fun."

"How old was he?"

"Fourteen."

"So—"

"So I lost my virginity to Royce Hoffmann. Don't look so shocked—it wasn't rape, really. I didn't want to go along, but at the same time I didn't want Royce to think I was any less daring or knowledgeable than he pretended to be. I have to take responsibility for that. It wasn't traumatic, just sort of disgusting."

Paul waited, not knowing what to say.

"Really, I wasn't a victim. I didn't feel any different afterward except that I was nauseated by the very sight of Royce. You know what the most sickening thing was, though? That Royce threatened to tell on me if I didn't do what he wanted, or if I told anyone about the things he did. Ooph!" Kay shivered in disgust. "Little ratshit creepoid!"

"Tell on *you*. What a son of a bitch!"

Kay picked absently at the turkey again. "Anyway. You can see why I don't go along with all of Aster's stuff."

The kitchen door swung open and Ted came in backward with both hands full of empty beer and soda bottles. "Aha. Picking the carcass. I had the same idea."

"Proving that human beings aren't omnivores really, they're carrion eaters," Paul joked.

"Is everybody happy out there?" Kay asked. "Is it time for dessert?"

Aster was sitting on the neatly made bed of the guest bedroom, massaging her face. Paul hesitated in the hall, then knocked on the door frame. "There's pie and ice cream."

"Paulie," she said. "Maybe in a few minutes."

"I'm sorry the conversation upset you. I'm sure they're done with the topic now."

"Safe for me to come out?" She snorted. "I just needed a few minutes alone. I don't know why Kay has to go on like that, airing the dirty laundry. Honestly."

Paul came into the room and half-sat on the dressing table. "She just sees it differently. It's not dirty laundry, it's just amusing conversation."

"Well, she doesn't have to sensationalize things." Aster coughed, wiped her mouth with a tissue, and then stared at the wall as if looking into the distance. "On the other hand, Ted may have something there—that someone was looking for something. I think it's much more likely than Kay's utterly fantastic ideas about Royce."

"What would someone be looking for?"

"Who knows? Paulie, you should know by now that wherever large amounts of money are involved, people's behavior changes. Different rules apply, values and priorities shift. Your father used to say that large fortunes have a gravitational field, one that attracts things to it for better or for worse—usually for the worse." Aster looked very tired. "What were they looking for? Probably nothing. When I was a little girl, there was an old woman who lived by herself in a big old house at the end of our road— Mrs. Williams, or Willard, something like that. She kept to herself, never went outside, had her groceries delivered. The whole town was convinced she had a mattress full of money. Classic small-town folklore. Kids would talk about going in and stealing some of it. So when she got very old, she didn't pay her taxes, and the town finally came in and seized her house.

She'd been living in squalor. There wasn't any money. Never had been. My point is, it doesn't matter what's true, it only matters what people believe. Somebody's probably going to Highwood convinced there's something hidden that isn't there and never was."

Aster coughed harshly, her cheeks swelling. When she recovered, she went on: "And there's something else. There are a lot of things I don't like about my sister. But when you're older, a woman who lives alone, people are willing to believe anything about you. It's a treacherous aspect of human nature. Remember the witch-hunts. God only knows what people in my neighborhood say about *me*." She wiped her eyes with a tissue, then squared her shoulders. "Anyway. Vivien is too smart to keep anything hidden at Highwood. She always used some private bank in Manhattan."

"I know—they sent me a check."

"Don't you get caught in that gravitational field. Don't let it pull you or deflect you or bend you around. And don't make the mistake of thinking Vivien isn't aware of the way people around her are affected—she is, and she likes to make good use of it."

"I've noticed."

Aster's voice grew bitter. "Maneuvering people. Playing on their hopes and expectations. That's how she gets what she wants."

There it was again: Whenever she spoke about her half-sister, she seemed to oscillate between two opposite emotional poles—on one hand sympathy, loyalty, pride; on the other bitterness, envy, mistrust. He sat across from her on the bed. "Can I ask you a question?"

"Maybe."

"What happened between you two?"

She looked at him shrewdly. "You asked me that before. The answer is, nothing."

"I mean, I have to work up there, I've taken the check. I've got to deal with Vivien. If there's something I need to know, I wish you'd tell me now."

"Really, you and Kay have the most fantastic ideas." She stood up briskly and caught sight of herself in the mirror over the bureau. "God, this haircut! Am I ever going to have normal hair again? This was Kay's idea of therapy for her depressed old mother—get a perm." She tugged at the kinked mass. "Yes, I think I would like some dessert now," she said.

Paul sat on the bed next to Mark, the darkened room lit only by the light leaking around the hall door. "So. Was it a good night?"

"Pretty good." Mark's voice sounded uncertain.

"Only pretty good? Didn't you have a good time with your cousins?" He tucked the sheet under Mark's chin.

"Yeah. Alexis cheats, though."

Paul had to laugh. "I think all cousins cheat at games. It's a tradition. Anyway, I thought I saw you pull a little fast one."

"Who, me?" A little smile flickered. "You *saw* that?"

"You'll never put one past me, boy."

Mark thought about it, then got serious again. "Is it true?"

"Is what true?"

"All that stuff about Highwood—the son murdering the grandmother."

"I don't think anyone murdered the grandmother. Kay's exaggerating because it's entertaining. You know, how you sometimes like a scary story, especially when you know you're perfectly safe. The same reason people like roller-coasters."

"But you really *are* scared." Mark said it matter-of-factly.

Was he? He had some attention on the possibility of risk, certainly. He was constantly suppressing tics. He also had that odd, nagging feeling, the strange familiarity of the emptiness at Highwood. There was fear there, but something else too. Loneliness? Darkness? He couldn't think of a word for it. "What makes you say that?"

"Because you listen so closely when Kay's talking about it. Because you don't laugh when everyone else thinks it's funny."

"No, I'm not scared. If I'm quiet, it's because I'm thinking about practical things like how many yards of plastic I'll need to cover the broken windows."

Mark rolled his head away on the pillow, and for a moment Paul thought he was signaling his readiness to sleep. "I think Alexis and Ben are spoiled," he said.

"Spoiled? What do you mean?"

Mark rubbed his forearm across his eyes and left it there, concealing his face from Paul. "They're so . . . I don't know. Like they're used to everything being okay all the time. Nothing to worry about."

Paul felt a stab of anguish. Mark was saying that their mother and father were still together, and that they didn't have to worry about what was inside their heads. That they were *secure,* for God's sake, which made them relaxed and confident. He felt his throat tighten, an abyss opening before him.

"Everybody has about the same number of problems in the long run," Paul told him, not really believing it. "And everything *is* going to be okay. You've got a lot on your mind tonight. You know what I think is happening? Sometimes when you're tired, everything seems like a problem. Why don't you just be quiet for a while, I'll rub your head, and next thing you know it'll be morning." He massaged Mark's temples, tugged gently at his hair, willing him to be at peace. Before long, the boy's exhalations slowed and whistled in his throat, a gentle snore.

Friday, heading back to Vermont, Paul drove the Subaru as Lia read another volume of Piaget. Mark fell asleep in the backseat within minutes.

After glancing back to see that Mark was truly out cold, Lia put a shoe
box on the seat next to her, opened it, and took out a snub-nosed, chrome
revolver.

"What the hell is that?"

"Ted's old .38 police special. He offered to lend it to us, and I accepted.
It's a nice little gun." She deftly opened the cylinder, spun it, looked through
the barrel, snicked it shut again.

"Fucking terrific. Jesus, Lia." The sight of her savoring the heft of the
gun set off unpleasant reverberations in his nervous system.

"Seems clumsy until you fire it," she said. "Then you're glad for the
weight—absorbs some of the recoil. We got Ted worried. He was talking
about gangs from the city coming up while we're at the lodge. Says we
should make sure we've got an equalizer. He's right."

"Nobody's going to come up there."

"Fine. Then what're you so bent out of shape about?"

"Look, if it's so dangerous that we have to fucking pack a gun to work
there, I don't want the job."

"It's not like that. I agree with you, nobody's going to come up there. It's
just insurance, Paul."

"I don't know how to use one of those things."

"I do."

Of course she did. Cop's daughter. Connoisseur of risk. Paul scowled at
the road as she inspected the boxes of bullets Ted had included with the
gun, then wrapped it up again and resumed her reading.

He had looked forward to the open road, but the gun put him back into
the black mood he'd awakened in. It had been a good visit, generally, except
for the way Highwood had cast a shadow on things. Now he found he
couldn't stop thinking about something Kay had said while putting away
the dishes that morning. "I was thinking about Highwood," she'd said. "I
probably made it sound like it's some kind of haunted house, but of course
it's not—it's a charming, pleasant place. No, it's not like the house is
haunted. . . . It's more like that *family* is haunted. Do you know what I
mean?"

He'd found himself inexplicably susceptible to the idea: that scary things
could live within a clan, a bloodline, terrors that survived through genera-
tions. Kay had gone on with the dishes, blithely unaware of his discomfort.

21

Damon Karadwicz rolled his head slowly off to the right, face grotesquely contorted, and then snapped upright, his wild eyes taking a second to stabilize when he came out of the tic. "Good to see you, buddy," he told Paul. "What's the rumpus?"

Paul clapped him on the shoulder and took a seat on the stool next to him. Terry's Taproom was quiet, unusual for a Saturday night—they'd have no problem getting one of the pool tables later. A businesslike, hard-bitten woman Paul hadn't seen before tended bar, washing glasses and staring up at the television, ignoring them. The television screen showed some news program, a SWAT team or some such smashing into an urban building, armed men running and dodging with adrenaline-packed movements. Or maybe it was Chechnya.

"Terrific haircut," Paul told him. "You've traded the Rasputin look for the Nazi skinhead look. *Très chic.*"

"Fuck you too." Since they'd last gotten together, Damon's dark hair had been cut so short it was little more than stubble, the same density and length as his beard. From his collar to the top of his head he was five-o'clock shadow. "I've got seborrhea, had to treat my scalp. The hair was getting in the way." Damon repeated the neck roll, coming out of it with his face grimacing around his protruding tongue.

"Maybe a Catamount Amber," Paul told the bartender, who had come up to their end of the bar with a look of calculated disinterest on her face. She turned back to the tap.

Damon was ugly: squat, flabby and unkempt, short-necked, with a wide face dominated by a broad, flaring nose. Though he shaved, he had facial hair so heavy that from the eyelids down his skin had a bluish cast. He had the most difficult and offensive Tourette's imaginable. He was also one of the most intelligent, gentle, perceptive people Paul had ever known. They'd been friends for ten years. Since moving to Norwich, Paul had been driving up to visit Damon at least twice a month, meeting him at one blue-collar bar or another in Burlington's old North End.

"How is Rosie?" Paul asked. Rosie was Damon's daughter, a bone-skinny, precocious twelve-year-old. Maggie, Rosie's mother, had died of lymph cancer six years ago.

"*Bitch!* I am well-pleased with her. *Shitfuck!* The Rose is obsessed with Sojourner Truth this month," Damon said, wiping his lips with the back of his hand. " 'Ain't I a woman?' I'm getting a feminist, Quaker education from my daughter."

Paul got his beer, and they compared notes on the kids. Damon's explosive vocal tics were offensive not just because of the coprolalia, but because they all seemed calculated to deride, disrupt, or intimidate a conversational partner. Whenever Paul spoke, Damon's tics went wild: swearing, guttural noises in his chest and throat, abdominal contractions that produced strangling sounds, exaggerated facial distortions and hand gestures. The most disruptive was his loud, deep-voiced, *"Yeah? So?"* which he repeated almost continuously as Paul talked. The demon of Tourette's.

By the bartender's tight, disapproving face, Paul could tell that she considered Damon to be about midway between a complete asshole and an escaped maniac. Most people assumed the same.

It was a source of anguish for Damon. "No one can see *me*," he'd once moaned. "All anyone can see is *it*." This was some years after Maggie's death, when Damon was beginning to think no other woman would have the strength and stamina to look past the tics and the blue face and squat body to love him. "How could anyone? Sometimes even *I'm* not sure who's Damon and who's just fucking Igor, the hunchback in my belfry."

"Everybody's both," Paul said at the time. "It's just that *we* get reminded of the fact every day."

It was an offshoot of this issue that Paul wanted to discuss with Damon now. Last time they'd gotten together, Damon had been talking about a theory he'd developed, based on his reading in Jungian psychology. Since seeing Vivien, fragments of that conversation had been coming back to Paul.

"Damon," he said, switching topics gracelessly, "tell me where you've been going with your ideas about Jung's *shadow*."

"Aha. Existential problems looming large?"

"Maybe." Paul told him briefly about the Highwood job, his visit with Vivien, the questions she'd raised.

"Okay," Damon said. "So Jung developed a theory of personality: that we all have two sides, one being our regular self and the other being what he called the *shadow*."

"Sounds like the old radio show—'The Shadow knows,' " Paul said.

"*Shitfuck!* Actually, that's not a bad paraphrase of Jung's thinking. The shadow *does* know a lot. It's a sort of anti-self, containing all the parts of our personalities that we banish from our conscious minds. The parts we consider undesirable, unworthy, bad, antisocial."

Paul thought about it as he finished his beer and raised his glass to get the bartender's attention. Behind her on the TV screen a pretty blonde brushed her teeth with an excess of glee.

"How do these parts of you get banished?"

"A lot of ways. For example, when you were a kid, your parents told you to share. So to win their approval you acted generous, put away your selfishness and possessiveness. It was still there, but your conscious mind held it in check, hid it, denied it. Then maybe your parents said, or society said, not to hit your friends. So you had to hide away your anger. Later on, you started choosing your own stuff to hide away, things you didn't feel were worthy. Eventually, you've got a lot of feelings, all hidden away in the same box. That's Jung's shadow self. Still there, still alive, but only able to express itself when the 'good' self slips up."

"And the problem being—?"

"*Guh!* The problem being that *Fuck!,* one, a lot of *good* things get hidden away there too. If your parents said, 'Don't stare, you'll hurt that paraplegic's feelings!' you probably banished some of your natural curiosity. If you got the idea you weren't supposed to play with your wiener, even though it felt good, you hid away some of your sexuality. And so on. *Guck! Guh!*"

"So you've locked away some valuable stuff too."

"So the theory goes. Jung said that to be truly empowered, to act with all our resources, we had to be in touch with our shadows."

"You mentioned two problems. What's the second?"

"*Suck me?*" Damon came out of a ghastly tic that gripped his whole upper body, his hands mangling the air. "The second is the distortions caused by packing things away. This is where a lot of psychopathologies come from. Repress normal sexual urges, they'll show up later as sexual perversions. Or take anger—lots of little angers, bottled up, may explode as one big, violent rage. You name it, a lot of things get twisted."

"So you think Tourette's may be a way that some of the shadow expresses itself?"

"*Shit! No!* Sure. In some cases, anyway. Look at me—my tics are all contraries. Just then, because I *wanted* to say yes, Igor said no. When you talk, because I *want* to listen, because you're my valued friend and I want you to tell me your thoughts, I screw you up as much as I can. The neurochemical theory of Tourette's doesn't answer an important question: Why should the excess of dopamine in your synaptic cleft selectively produce only oppositional social behaviors? Some social behaviors are hard-wired into our brains, but we'd have a pretty sad vision of mankind if we believed that everything we are is pre-established by the biological equivalent of a soldered circuit board. There's got to be a psychological component—the personality plays some role. That's where the shadow idea makes so much sense."

Paul sipped his beer, thinking it over. In Damon's case it was believable. All his competitive urges, all his negative thoughts, all his self-aggrandizing desires had found their way to his Tourettic impulses, leaving the conscious Damon clean, a deeply sincere, compassionate, well-intentioned person.

"*Suck me?*" Damon said to the bartender. "I mean, how about another one of these?" He raised his glass. When the bartender turned away, he called after her: "It's a neurological disorder!" He turned back to Paul, shaking his head. "The perpetual plea for understanding," he said.

Another couple had taken seats a few stools down, and the bartender took their order. They averted their faces at Damon's outburst.

"So," Paul said after a time, "what about that librarian? Making any headway? The one you said looks like Jessica Lange?"

"Ahh," Damon said sadly. "I was trying to ask her out. Got too tense about it. Igor went bananas."

"Shit."

"Yeah. Heads were turning. She asked me to leave the library. Politely."

"You should have explained."

"This was *after* I had explained." Damon chugged the beer the bartender had set down. "I've got too many strikes against me, Paul. We're talking the princess and the frog here. I didn't get the good facial bones, like you." Seeing Paul's expression of commiseration, Damon rallied. "But I met this lady ski instructor. Her body's out of this world, but her face, she could be my sister. . . . Maybe I've got a chance. Seems understanding. A sense of humor, anyway."

"Tell her you're an incarnation of the archetypal mischief maker—Loki, Coyote. Or Krishna—he had a blue face too. Tell her there's a long and honorable tradition of monkey wrenchers in every culture."

"Nah. I tried that one on the librarian."

They sipped their drinks. Damon: a good friend. Like Dempsey, but in a very different way, a point of reference. In Damon, Paul could see one example of severe, uncontrolled Tourette's. Damon didn't respond well, physically or philosophically, to medications. As a result, he was an odd, often lonely person. He didn't hold jobs long, if he could get them at all. Not much luck with women. Nobody's idea of a success. An example to consider when thinking of cutting back on his medication.

Was that what he was thinking about, cutting back even further? Apparently. Vivien must have gotten to him more than he knew.

But Damon managed to love his life, to enjoy living "wild and woolly," as he described it. He played keyboard in various bands, in a brilliant, uneven, extemporaneous style for which he was highly respected by Burlington's musicians. He was an avid reader, a philosopher. He loved his daughter absolutely and was a terrific father. He was as good a friend as anyone could ask for.

"But what about me?" Paul finally said. "Given that my tics aren't so contrary. People aren't all that offended by quotes from old rock 'n' roll songs and little finger dances. What's my shadow doing? Where are all my banished feelings and behaviors going?"

Damon shrugged. "We're all different. So you're parking it someplace else. I guess I just got lucky, huh?" He lifted himself off the stool, stretched his long arms, ticced convulsively. "How about some pool? Before someone else gets the table?"

Driving home, Paul abruptly made up his mind that, yes, he'd cut back dosage. No big fanfare, just quietly taper off. Over the last few years he had cut back from eight to six milligrams daily and had been able to live with himself; maybe now he'd try a few days at four, a few more at two, then maybe skip a day now and again. See what bubbled up out of the primordial ooze. Maybe see where his shadow lived, maybe have an occasional chat with the whiz kid within. You could only ask yourself who the hell you were so many times, and then you had to have some kind of an answer.

Yes, Vivien had gotten to him—not wounding him, really, just mercilessly reminding him of the wound he carried with him always. It was time to see what he'd be like with just his unadulterated, natural brain, the juices he was born with, without a factory-produced substance dominating his neural chemistry.

That idea got him thinking about his brain, and soon he found himself suffering from a full-blown case of what he called the *brain blues*. This was a mood, or a sensation, a Tourettic *idée fixe*, when he'd become conscious of the living brain pulsing in his skull. It nauseated him.

He could see it, *feel* it in him: spinal cord thickening into the brainstem. Cerebellum, hypothalamus, pituitary gland. The arching fornices, the baked potato–shaped thalamus, the caudate and lentiform nuclei, the little egg of the amygdala. The corpus callosum, exactly like an extended tongue, covered by the proverbial gray stuff, the wrinkled cerebrum, and the cortex, only an eighth of an inch thick, intricately folded upon itself. The whole thing just the size and shape of your two hands if you put them over an apple.

And all of it made out of billions of tiny octopi, the neurons and dendrites, each with tentacles branching hundreds or thousands of times, connected to each other in an incalculable number of ways. All jittering with tiny electrical currents, squirting minute releases of chemicals that made up your thoughts, feelings, memories, reactions.

And that's your brain. That's where you live. That's *you.*

The problem was, it wasn't that simple. Or that nice. Paul's stomach churned, picturing it. He'd dissected a fresh human brain in a class at Dartmouth and could never forget the feel of it on his hands, the grayish-pink clots clinging to his scalpel and his skin. *Forget the cute analogies to potatoes, eggs, apples. Think of a raw clam: gray, wet, quivering soft stuff, hiding in its hard shell. Think of the swollen bag of muck that's the clam's belly, the queasy, stringier stuff.* That's *the brain.* That's *you.*

He sighed, wishing he'd skipped the last round he and Damon had drunk.

Then there was the philosophical concern. Maybe "self" was nothing more than that collection of twitching nerve cells, squirting and oozing glands, chemicals brewing and recombining. Even the best feelings, the most noble impulses, love, joy, reverence, awe: just more juices.

A pretty sad vision of mankind, as Damon had said. A lousy way to look at yourself. Unfortunately, Paul thought, no matter what you believed, you still had that devious clam between your ears to contend with. The question of *I* versus *it* wasn't just for Touretters.

22

With a low, blank sky over it, slate roof darkened by rain, the lodge seemed especially forlorn, brooding on its own emptiness. Paul sat in the idling car for a moment, savoring the hot air from the heater, letting the intermittent wiper clear his view. It was only one o'clock on Monday, but the day was dark as twilight. A light rain fell from the gray sky.

"A-ka-*theee*-zha," he said.

Lia was at Dartmouth, finishing up her errands before joining him. They had traded cars so Paul could use the station wagon to carry down his tools and camping equipment. Now the back of the car was jammed with his gear: two long wooden carpenter's toolboxes, power tools in their cases, levels, squares, nail belts, several metal toolboxes, extension cords, sleeping bag, tarps, Coleman white-gas stove and lantern. Lashed to the roof rack was his thirty-foot aluminum extension ladder. The car rode low on its burdened suspension.

He'd called Martin's Garage to have the battered Pontiac removed from the bottom of the driveway. Paul had watched as old Sandy Martin winched the hulk screeching up onto the tilted bed of his tow rig, and then had paid him from his subcontracting account. The old man had climbed stiffly back into his truck and then rolled down the window.

"What're you goin to do, keep kids from drivin up there now?"

"I thought I'd put up a gate. Know anyone who can install one for me fairly soon?"

"You want to put up a good gate, my boy Albert sells 'em. Best price around." Sandy handed a business card to Paul. He put his rig into gear, then paused. "See, it's different around here now. You seen the security services everybody uses? Little signs out front? There's a good reason for that." He paused again, frowning, as if he had more to say, but all he managed was, "You take care now." Then he'd eased out the clutch and pulled away.

Paul jotted a note to himself on the clipboard he kept on the seat beside him: *Call Albert Martin re: gate estimate.* Then, with resignation more than decisiveness, he shut off the car. He swung open one of the carriage house's bay doors to give the downstairs some light, and stumped up the narrow staircase. Upstairs, the building had served as living quarters for grounds-keepers or servants. The smaller back room, facing the trees uphill, was set up as a kitchen; the large front room, with windows facing the main house and down the driveway, was empty but for a fine wooden bed frame and a gas heater. Not unpleasant: a view of the distant hills out the downhill win-dow, nice yellow oak floors. If the gas heater still worked, it would be easy to keep the room comfortably warm.

Paul piled his gear in the front room, then unpacked the lantern, pumped it up, and lit it. He brought a broom from the car and thoroughly swept both rooms clear of dust, cobwebs, mouse turds. In a closet he found a mattress that had been stored in a heavy plastic bag and was free of mouse damage. He dragged it to the bed frame, and when he was done he fluffed out the down sleeping bag and laid it on the bed.

With his gear ordered he felt a little better, and carrying things up the stairs had gotten him warm again. This was just a job to be done, he told himself. If he could keep this up, if he could banish the dark and chill and disorder by little increments every day, the house would be restored.

His neck ticced irresistibly, pulling his head around.

Paul glanced at his watch. Two o'clock—about three hours until sunset. The next step was to take a tour through the house, reconnoiter the area. Mark was right: He *was* afraid, although he couldn't say just what he was afraid of. Whatever, it would be wise to confront the fear, keep it from tak-ing root.

The heatable, undamaged carriage house rooms helped. He'd planned to sleep at Highwood in part to discourage further vandalism or theft, and in part to speed things along: It would be easier to work twelve or fourteen hours a day if his headquarters were here on the hill. The long work days would be necessary if he wanted to beat out the really cold weather. But more important was his schedule with Mark—Janet's barely veiled threat had made it clear that this change in their schedule wasn't something she'd put up with for long. He couldn't let the job drag on.

Looking out the windows at the lodge suspended in the weak light and sifting rain, Paul realized he had another reason, just as important. At some level, he'd taken on this job as a personal challenge. It had to do with what Ben had said about understanding the terrain, even if it scares you. "Face into it—otherwise your own fear will put a cage around you," he'd said. "Face your own demons, and face them down." One of Ben's favorite homilies.

Ben had been an avid outdoorsman. Paul remembered particularly a summer when he was around eight—possibly Ben's last summer alive. A beautiful day in late July. Father and son had left the women at home and had driven together to Adirondack State Park, where they locked the car and hiked out. They both wore backpacks, jeans, and Vibram-soled boots, and they'd smeared themselves with insect repellent to keep off the biting black flies. Paul had started on haloperidol, which made him almost normal, if a little sluggish, with just an occasional simple motor tic.

After several hours on a marked trail, they cut off along a ridge, following a game trail. Ben had a destination in mind—an outcropping of ledge that looked over "five counties and two states." Three hours later, Paul had begun to whine and complain. He was exhausted, harried by the bugs that orbited his head relentlessly, dive-bombing his eyes. The pack straps chafed his shoulders.

They didn't reach Ben's cliff until sunset. Though Paul was too cross to admit it, Ben had chosen a beautiful spot, an unbroken sweep of forest below, falling away steeply nearby and then rising to another crest several miles east. Lake Champlain was a distant slash of light, the Green Mountains a dim band of misty green.

But Paul was cranky, footsore, tired of his father's exuberance. And a gnawing tension had begun in him: They had come many miles from help if they needed it. The woods had begun to darken. They had seen bear scat several times on the way in.

Ben set down his pack, helped Paul out of his—and then immediately suggested they go for a walk.

"I don't want to," Paul told him. He plopped down on the ground and stared at his legs stretched straight in front of him.

"Tell me why."

"Because I'm too tired. And I'm hungry and I'm sleepy."

"Are you scared?"

Paul hesitated before answering, suspecting he was being led somewhere, but not sure what his father had in mind. He looked at Ben, standing uphill, legs apart, somehow professorial even in his checked shirt and short-brimmed straw hat, even in this wild setting. Behind him, the boulder-strewn slope of woods had slid into deep shadow.

"Yes," Paul said in a small voice.

Ben crouched next to him. "You know what? I'm scared too. So rather than lie here, scared to death of bears and bogeymen all night, let's take a little tour, make sure we know the ground, no surprises for us later. Right?" He stood and hoisted Paul up with him. "Come on. Five more minutes."

They went uphill, away from the cliff, and in the near dark began a wide circle around their campsite.

"See, Paulie," Ben said, "most of the things you're afraid of are inside you. They're not real. But they'll hold you back if you don't *show* yourself they're not real. So you reconnoiter your campsite. You get your eyes used to the dark, you figure out how to ally yourself with the terrain rather than ignore it or try to hide from it. You wouldn't want to camp twenty feet away from a bear's den, would you? It's better to face the scaries than have your back to them, right?"

"Yeah," Paul grunted. He felt very sorry for himself: On top of everything else, he had to listen to one of Ben's lectures.

Ben walked quietly, almost stealthily, for a time, pointing out in a near-whisper the branching game trails, the burrows of little animals, the trunks of dead trees ripped apart by woodpeckers and bears. They explored the shadowed base of a tremendous boulder, then entered an area of pines where the branches grew close together, almost impenetrable and very dark.

"Face into it," Ben whispered.

Paul hated the brittle, clutching branches. He felt claustrophobic, blind, every nerve screaming. But when they finally broke free, he found that his eyes had adapted to the dark. He felt electrified by the mystery of night in the remote mountain woods. He could sense the animal presences, and the gently shifting trees seemed sentient, awakened by the onset of night.

"So," Ben said, "we've made a little map in our heads of the immediate vicinity. We know what kind of animals we're likely to hear later, what kind of noises they'll make when they do come around. We've made the woods accessible to *reason*."

Then Ben put his hands on Paul's shoulders, put his face close in the dim light, speaking with intensity that startled Paul. Clearly this was life-lesson time. "Paulie, the same thing applies to what's inside you. *Don't ever run from what's scary or from what you don't understand about your own mind.* Go into it, get to know it. Then you're really safe. Only then. Will you remember this?"

Ben started walking again. "If you think about it," he went on professorially, "it's the root principle of rational humanism. . . ."

Paul tuned him out, trudging behind him. But when they got back to their packs, the open cliff edge seemed abundantly light. Thanks to the mental map their walk had assembled, he could now gauge the distance of the shifting and scurrying sounds all around, the size of the creatures that made them. They had a fine dinner of dehydrated beef stroganoff and canned peaches, and slept soundly beneath the bowl of stars. Sunrise the next day was spectacular, royally extravagant, worth the hike and the momentary fears of the night before.

The lesson had stayed with him. You had to face into yourself—reconnoiter the campsite, as it were.

On the surface the philosophy was not unlike Vivien's. The difference between Vivien's view and Ben's seemed to be that Ben believed the light of reason would prevail, that the conscious mind would bring light and order to the mind's darker places, civilization enlightening the barbarians. Whereas Vivien seemed to think the barbarians would, and should, storm the walls and conquer the city. Of course, it would be a hell of a lot easier to believe Ben's view if he hadn't demonstrated the deep loss of his own faith—if he hadn't jumped off the goddamned cliff at Break Neck.

Was that part of what he was facing into here? When he'd told Lia he'd decided to sleep at Highwood, when he'd insisted on coming down on Monday rather than caravanning with her on Tuesday, she'd nodded and laughed understandingly: He'd arranged this solitary first day and night to challenge himself, face down the growing anxiety. She certainly knew that need quite well.

Paul stood up, stretched, and looked over the room. It was okay. It would do. Whatever had broken in Ben, that had been Ben's challenge. This was his own. He'd made base camp at Highwood. Now it was time to reconnoiter.

23

Outside, the air had cooled slightly, enough that the rain had started to freeze. Little pellets of ice slid down the windshield of the Subaru and hissed softly in the woods. Paul opened the tailgate and found his clipboard and the big battery-powered floodlight. No winking Maglites today.

Inside, things were just as they'd been the previous week. In the main room, he squatted to inspect closely a tangle of cloth—drapes, judging by the rings sewn along one edge. Again, Lia was right: There were mouse droppings in every fold, showing that the cloth had lain just this way for some time. Paul straightened and made a note on the pad in his clipboard: *Mousetraps? Exterminator?*

He took his time now, deliberately ignoring his body's yearning to get out of the cold, crazed interior. In the library, the sea of paper stirred in a faint breeze from the smashed windows—torn pages of books and the papers that had been spilled and flung from file-cabinet drawers. Vivien had obviously saved all her receipts and correspondence: There were half a dozen four-drawer steel cabinets here, along with several lateral files, all crushed and twisted beyond repair. He'd noticed several more among the wreckage in her bedroom. *File boxes,* he wrote.

On his way out of the library, he spotted the headline of a yellowed newspaper and stooped to pick it up. *North Salem Man Falls to Death at Break Neck.* Below the headline was a smiling picture of Ben, in his early thirties, the same photo used year after year in the faculty section of the Columbia catalog. Paul's heart seemed to stop, then to pump dully, straining, as if his blood had thickened in his veins. It was the sort of thing he'd suspected he'd find here, wanted to find—yet confronted with it at last, he could hardly bring himself to read. Years ago, helping Aster move, he'd come across a collection of Ben's obituaries, which had detailed Ben's academic accomplishments and had avoided specifics about his death. This was different: just a regular news item, reporting another morbid incident in all its grisly detail.

He carried the clipping to the smoking room, sat on the rug, and made himself read it.

Cold Spring, November 19. A prominent professor of history at Columbia University died today in a fall from the cliffs at Break Neck, north of Cold Spring. Dr. Benjamin K. Skoglund, of North Salem, fell three hundred feet from the steep rock faces above Route 9D, in an apparent suicide.

According to Putnam County coroner Harold Vanderlass, the fall was witnessed by several members of the Peekskill Outing Club who had paused at a bend in the popular hiking trail, below Skoglund.

"We saw him come out on the rocks about fifty feet almost directly above us," said Peter Melcher of Peekskill, president of the hiking club. "We had just stopped to regroup and rest when he showed up at the very edge of the cliff. Next thing you know, he backed up, out of view, like he was getting a running start, and then came charging out and off the cliff."

Melcher and other club members descended the trail, called police and helped a medical team recover Skoglund's body from the rugged terrain where he had fallen. Skoglund sustained severe head and internal injuries and was pronounced dead at the scene.

According to his wife, Skoglund was an experienced amateur rock-climber who regularly climbed at Break Neck. He had reportedly been upset and depressed by family problems in recent weeks.

Paul set the article aside, lay back on the rug, and crossed his arms behind his head, staring at the ceiling. Without feeling any particular sadness, he found tears sliding out of the corners of his eyes and pooling in his ears. An ancient, ancient pain, so familiar as to be imperceptible. An underground lake of tears.

At some point in the distant past, Aster had mentioned the people who had seen Ben jump, the Melchers. Nice people, she'd said, an older couple. They'd attended the funeral, expressed condolences. Melcher was a dentist or an orthodontist or something.

What bothered him most was the line about Ben being "upset and depressed by family problems." After all these years, he really had no idea what those family "problems" were. Aster must know—if she told the reporter there were problems, she must have had something specific in mind, not the vague generalities and evasions she'd offered whenever Paul had brought it up. Sooner or later he'd confront her about it.

Paul began to feel the fatigue of yesterday's events, the long day, the drive, the initial tension he'd felt in the house. A spacey, floating feeling descended on him, and he lay, almost drowsing, remembering: Ben, Aster, and Vivien, sitting in this room at the leather-topped table, playing cards or doing the *New York Times* crossword puzzle together. Paulie lying in a square of sun on the Persian rug, looking at magazines and half listening to their meandering conversation. Or going off on expeditions in the woods near the house—

A humid haze suspended in the woods. Father away, work to do. Vivien says it will be a warm day, but it's chilly where the mist is thick. White dog snuffles along with. Out above the garden, then over and down into the boulder-strewn woods. A folded handkerchief Mother gave, with a whole Cracker Jack box and a little sandwich made of bread and butter. It's a special sandwich because Mother cut the crusts off the bread and then cut it in half, corner to corner.

Finding a flat-topped boulder jutting over a ravine, lying stomach-down, face close to the rock. Ants trickle across the miniature landscape of mosses and lichens, carrying tiny larvae and dead insects. In books everything has a mom, but you never see bugs with their moms. Mist slowly thins, sun coming out, bright shafts, dark tree shadows. Forest like a big house, winding hallways.

Heading down into the ravine and up the other side. Socks full of tag burrs, ankles itching. A big mushroom with part of its thick red cap broken off, flesh still pale and fresh. Suddenly the dog stops, alert, ears arched, making a thin whistling, just air. Then a sound down the hill. A bad sound. Something moving. Not supposed to do that. They're not supposed to. No one is supposed to see. Turning quickly back, then tripping, getting up quickly, afraid, running, catching at the rough sides of boulders, tearing skin off hands. Crying now. Everything in the way, everything catching, feet slipping.

Then seeing the house and running down through the garden. Shins scissoring, badly scraped. On the terrace, Mother stands up quickly, face full of concern.

"Baby, what happened?" Wanting to run to her and hug her, but then stopping, holding back. "What in the world happened? Are you all right?" Knowing you're not supposed to see, not supposed to tell. Crying, letting her gather you into her arms, letting her calm you, but knowing you can't ever tell her.

Paul recoiled from the memory, shook his head to dispel the trance of recollection he'd fallen into. Deeply chilled, he stood up and swung his arms, then checked his watch. No wonder he was cold: He'd been sitting without moving for almost twenty minutes. The vague terror fluttered at the edge of memory, indistinct images already slipping away from conscious scrutiny.

He shadowboxed vigorously to get his circulation going, trying to clear his head. *Face into it,* he thought: The disordered mansion of memory was another scary terrain that would have to be braved. And, he decided, some-day put into order.

He continued touring the house, adding to the list of items he'd need to buy to start the job. *Large trash bags.* He wrote down questions he'd need to remember to ask Vivien, next time they talked: *Animal heads to taxider-mist?* Some of the repair work would be highly specialized. *Furs?* How do you restore a floor-length sable coat that mice had been nesting in for six months?

Upstairs, he looked into each of the rooms, counting broken windows. Vivien's room was the strangest of all—seeing it now, the violence of the destruction astonished him. The contents of the room were broken into small pieces and stirred together as if it had all been put in a big blender and ground up. And the windowless room next to it, although it apparently hadn't contained much, was the same. Paul switched on his big floodlight and looked around the room they'd barely been able to see before. Tangled metal shelving, twisted, knotted onto itself, took up most of the floor. Cardboard boxes of linens had exploded, and several boxes of glassware had been emptied and thrown, the pieces trampled, pulverized into a coarse sand that sparkled in the flashlight's beam and gritted beneath his feet.

It was a strange room, far too large for a closet, yet clearly not designed for living. A darkroom? But there was no sign there'd ever been any plumb-ing. And the door from Vivien's bedroom: solid oak, four inches thick, decoratively paneled on only the outside face, steel plate on the inside, a single lock at the handle. When he levered the handle, he found that it slid thumb-thick bolts at the top and bottom. The hinge was continuous, a heavy steel flange the full length of the door. The room was very nearly a vault. If that's what it was, why hadn't Vivien bothered to put her impor-tant things inside before leaving? Another question for her.

On the way down the stairs, Paul paused on the landing to look closely at the broken end of one of the thick oak newel posts, one of two dozen that supported the banister and the railing around the three sides of the balcony. They were all alike: paneled oak columns, fourteen inches square in cross-section, that rose to chest height and then tapered to a short, lathed neck, topped by a traditional pine-cone finial—a knob of oak the size of a bowling ball, elongated and pointed at the top, carved with overlapping leaves or scales. All were intact but the post at the front of the landing, which was missing its finial.

The break was odd. Though it was at least three inches thick at its nar-rowest point, as thick as a baseball bat, the neck had been wrenched apart. A jagged bristle of oak fiber stood up where the ball had been. Fascinated, Paul tried to visualize how that much force could be brought to bear. From the direction of the broken fibers he could see that the ball had been broken outward, away from the stairs, toward the other side of the room.

Lia would have a name for what he was looking for, he thought, forensic terminology like *ballistic trajectory* or some such. If the ball were broken off with a lot of force, it would travel in the direction the broken wood indicated. And, if no one had found some other use for it, like using it to smash mirrors, it might still be where it fell.

He sighted across the break and selected the most likely trajectory—straight across the big room—then picked his way across, scanning the rubble. At the opposite wall he found it, a pinecone of oak with a brighter yellow beard of torn fiber at the bottom, lying among the shards of a shattered vase. He lifted it, morbidly engrossed, his heart starting to thump. A good swing with a sledgehammer might have dislodged it, but it was inconceivable that the ball would travel fifty feet. And the hammer would have left the imprint of its head deep in the wood. Yet the carved edges were still sharp, the finish unmarred except for a smudge of white—paint or plaster. Paul scanned the wall and found the print of the ball's scalloped leaf impressed into the plaster.

He glanced back at the post. It looked as if the ball had traveled across the room and had hit the wall hard enough to dent the plaster. He couldn't imagine the level of force required to accomplish the act. *Vivien's "presences,"* he thought. *Ghosts.*

He shivered, almost seeing it: patterns hidden in the room, lines of motion, arcs and trajectories revealed in the way things were smashed, the scatter of pieces, the direction of bends and breaks. The meandering paths of tornadoes left destruction like this, leaving whorls and bends, roofs twisted, farm implements flung, trees fallen, all revealing the route and shape of the angry winds. He could almost feel a system of turbulence lingering in the air, like a retinal afterimage of a dancer's gyrations. Yes, it was as if some impossibly wild dance had happened here, mad giants spinning with dire abandon, leaving in the debris a record of their steps and leaps, the arcs of their flailing arms and legs. There was a kinetic melody here, a tune played in three-dimensional space, vastly satisfying, vehement beyond imagining.

Paul hefted the carved ball, wondering what it would feel like to open himself to that release, to feel that much energy channeled through him, a hot electric arc down every nerve.

Something tugged at his memory, something fairly recent. His reading, his research. School? No—it had to do with Mark. He paused, trying to find the thread of his thought, but it was gone. Thinking about the finial had set it off, but weighing it in his hands now he could find nothing. With all his strength, he flung the ball back toward the staircase. It was too heavy to throw overhand, and his body compensated, shoving it through the air like a shot put. It fell short of the steps by ten feet, bounced and rolled.

The noise echoed in the house like a gunshot, shocking him out of the mood he'd drifted into. The fact was that what remained was a squalid, mouse-infested mess, a pointless waste of beautiful and valuable things. An unacceptable violation of his aunt's house and her life. Which had fallen to him to remedy. He found his pen and made a note on his pad: *Total 44 windows—39 broken.*

He looked around at the room again, then jotted another note: *Look up Salvador Falcone.*

Golden's Bridge was quiet: The commuters' cars were still parked along the roads, but the bad weather had discouraged shoppers. The pavement felt greasy beneath his wheels. Paul stopped at a pay phone and managed to reach Albert Martin, who told him to come on over.

Martin's Garage in Somers had been there since time immemorial, a ramshackle cluster of clapboard buildings on the side of Route 100, with an old-fashioned portico over the pumps, a repair shop with a lift, and a separate body shop surrounded by collision-damaged cars. Sandy Martin had lived in the apartment on the second floor when Paul was a boy, but in his old age he'd moved elsewhere and turned the apartment over to his son. Paul parked alongside the garage and walked to the back of the building. Near the end of the lot, a square of wire-mesh fence surrounded a collection of fencing materials, including heavy swinging gates of the sort he envisioned for Highwood, stacked haphazardly. He scanned the lot, then knocked loudly at a wooden door in the main garage building. A muffled voice shouted for him to come in.

He went up a steep stairway into air thick with the smell of frying onions and stuffy with heat, and was greeted at the top by a short, wiry man in his mid-forties, wearing a mechanic's coverall. His forehead was beaded with sweat.

"I'm Albert. Come on in. Have a seat in the living room." In a quieter voice, he said to Paul, "Sorry about the heat—Granny gets cold if the thermostat's below eighty. Dad's mom."

He showed Paul through a narrow hallway into a living room, where Paul took a seat on a hard, red vinyl–covered couch that had probably once served in the filling station's office.

"I was just making lunch," Albert said. "Lemme grab a bite and I'll be right with you." He disappeared back down the hall, and Paul heard the clatter of dishes.

The living room contained an unusual mix of furniture and objects. On the walnut coffee table in front of the couch were stacks of papers, auto-repair invoices on clipboards, automotive magazines and catalogs, a used distributor cap, and a new oil filter, along with a delicate porcelain vase holding some dusty fabric flowers. Across the room was a large overstuffed chair, its back draped with a piece of yellowed lace. Next to the chair, a handsome antique side table held a glass of water containing a set of false teeth, shocking pink plastic gums absurdly magnified by the curve of glass.

Paul had been sitting alone for a few moments when the door behind the chair opened and a little old woman came out. She couldn't be a day under ninety, Paul decided. Her hair made a thin white halo around her head, her back was humped beneath a faded purple shawl, the skin of her face hung in loose folds. There could be no doubt whose teeth were in the glass.

She closed the door carefully behind her and then, taking many small steps, turned and sat with difficulty in the chair. When she noticed Paul, her face broke into a wide-eyed smile.

"Oh, hello," she said. She said it with such warmth that Paul thought for a moment she recognized him.

"Hello," he said. "I'm just here to talk to Albert."

"Oh," she said. She nodded approvingly. "And who are you?"

"I'm Paul Skoglund."

"Paul Skoglund, Paul Skoglund," she said, frowning, shaking her head. "No, I don't know who you are. I don't think I've seen you before."

"Well, we moved away from the area a long time ago. Maybe you knew Ben and Aster Skoglund, my parents? I'm back here to fix up the old lodge at Highwood."

She kept shaking her head. "Scofield, Scofield. No—no, I don't think so." Then her face brightened. "Here's Albert!" She spoke as if she hadn't seen him in a long time.

Albert came out of the kitchen carrying a plate of fried onions and sausages, and took a seat at the other end of the vinyl couch. Even with the smell of the onions in the air, Paul caught the chemical scent of auto body filler emanating from his clothes.

"My granny," Albert said, pointing with his chin at the old woman. He took a bite of sausage and chewed hastily. "Sorry," he said when he'd swallowed. "So you need a gate over at Highwood."

"Yes. I've got the measurements here." He handed Albert a rough sketch of the end of the drive with the stone pillars marked on it.

Albert set down his plate to look over the sketch. "I know the place. So, about sixteen feet between the old stone pillars. Probably you'd want to set the new posts just inside and behind the pillars."

"I'd like something sturdy."

"Oh, it'll be sturdy. We'll sink a stainless steel post, six by six, at each end. Set the posts in concrete footings that go down five, six feet. Your choice of about eight different styles and weights and so on. I got a catalog here—" Albert dug in the piles of papers, looking frustrated. "Sorry. Hang on a sec." He got up and disappeared through a doorway.

The ancient woman was holding the glass in one shaky hand and trying to fish her teeth out of it with two fingers of the other hand. She hooked one of the plates, fished it up and installed it in her mouth, then did the same with the second plate. She grimaced around her new teeth to seat them on her gums.

"I always felt so sorry for that woman," Granny said.

"Oh. Yes," Paul said.

"And the children. One just a baby, and the older one, he wasn't right in his head. So sorry for them all." She shook her head sadly.

Albert returned with a sheaf of papers, including a couple of glossy pamphlets that he set in front of Paul. "Got 'em. Take a look. This I can get you, cost is"—he checked his price list—"fourteen hundred. That'd look good in there."

Paul scanned the pamphlets, which showed swinging driveway gates of various sizes and designs. "What've you got that you could put up right away? As I told you, I'm in a bit of a hurry."

"No problem, no problem," Albert said. He took another ravenous bite of onions and sausage and rummaged on the table again. "Sorry. Damn! I know I've got my inventory list somewhere."

Granny coughed genteelly into a handkerchief she had pulled out of her sleeve. "They were quite wealthy. I was the nanny—only for a little while, when the new baby came. I don't know whatever became of the other one. Of course, they were traveling so much, those first few years."

"Here it is," Albert said with relief. "Okay." He pointed to one after another of the gates in the pamphlet Paul held. "Right now, we got this, double gate, fourteen foot, in stock. That's what most people around here get. A very successful product."

Paul asked the prices of several gates and settled on one that Albert had in the lot.

Albert claimed he could get the gate up this weekend. "This Saturday, mid-afternoon," he promised. "No problem. I've got a slot on my calendar, just opened up. Only take a few hours. Use it the next day, after the cement's set." He started to scan the table, apparently for the calendar, but gave it up and looked to Paul as if for sympathy.

Sweltering, Paul wrote out a check, then thanked Albert and stood to go.

"And then to have to live up there with no husband, all those years!" Granny said, scandalized. "That poor woman. That poor family."

"Okay, Gran, Mr. Skoglund has to go now," Albert said, just a trace of impatience in his voice.

"Skoglund—no, I don't think I know Skoglund," she said.

At the phone booth in Somers, Paul called to order delivery of some bottled gas for the heater in the carriage house, left a message for Stewart Cohen, the electrician Vivien had recommended, then called Becker's Plumbing and Heating, who agreed to send a man up Tuesday or Wednesday. Telephone company: get service restored at Highwood. Tool rental: kerosene heater. Dempsey's answering machine: yes, dinner on Thursday would be great.

That left one little detail. He opened the wrinkled telephone directory and paged through until he found what he was looking for: *Salvador Falcone*. He jotted down the Purdys' address and number, not yet sure what he had in mind for the infamous Mr. Falcone.

24

Paul awoke with a jerk, unsure whether he'd really heard a noise or whether it was part of the dream he'd been having. He listened intently, lying motionless in the down sleeping bag, covered with a light sweat from head to foot. The room was pitch black, the windows slightly paler rectangles of darkness.

He had the impression the noise had come from the back of the carriage house, the woods, and he realized that in scouting the area he'd thought only of the house. Now he felt acutely aware of the tangled jungle that stretched away on three sides. He had only the vaguest sense of the landscape back there, a hodgepodge of recent glimpses and ancient memories: big trees, vines, boulders, ravines, brambles.

After several tense minutes of hearing only the blood hissing in his ears, he calmed somewhat and chided himself for his paranoia. With a racket of nylon he brought both arms free of the bag, found the Maglite, and flashed it quickly on and off to see his wristwatch: 4:30.

Ben had figured in the dream, and Paul felt the familiar, ancient sorrow come over him. Being here seemed to be awakening his memories of Ben. Or maybe it was connected to cutting back on haloperidol.

In the dream, he had been climbing with Ben at Break Neck, up the steep trail they'd climbed so many times together. Paul preceded Ben up the mountain, choosing his footing carefully, aware of his father's scrutiny from behind. At intervals he'd turn to face the valley, the breathtaking abyss with the flat Hudson River at the bottom, winding out of view. Like toys, the commuter train followed the curves of the riverbank, cars wound soundlessly along Route 9D. A pair of hawks wheeled in the updrafts, high above the valley but on a level with Paul and Ben.

"Wait'll we get up there," Ben had said, meaning, *The view will be even better up top.* Or, *You're not out of breath yet, are you? At your age?* Well-meaning Ben, enthusiastic Ben, wanting his son to know all his joys and often robbing Paul of his own way of understanding. As if he didn't trust his son to appreciate natural beauty or to develop his own enthusiasms.

In the dream, Paul had continued up the trail, gripping gnarled tree roots and outcroppings to hoist himself, testing each hold before trusting it with his weight. Yes, and resenting Ben's unrelenting well-meant advice, yet at the same time taking comfort that his father was behind him, down-slope, to catch Paul if he lost his footing.

At one point Paul found himself with an impossibly steep slope to his right, a chasm so deep he couldn't stand to look over it. "The Chute," Ben said from behind. Paul had the sense of a bluish haze below him.

In his fear he placed a foot unwisely, then started to slide, catching at rocks only to have them give way. He scrabbled at the cliff face and managed to hook the edge of his boot on a nub of stone, and clung, panicking. When he twisted his head to call out to Ben, Ben wasn't there. The jumbled slope stretched away, the altitude unendurable. Yet more terrifying than the drop was Ben's absence. The sense of security he'd provided was an illusion.

Then as Paul hung in terror, Ben rose over the shoulder of rock to his right, body horizontal, arms outspread, floating with the buoyancy and precision of the hawks. Ben came over the near line of rocks like the rising moon, huge and vague, supported only by the air, still smiling and watching Paul, unbearably frightening.

And then the noise from outside had awakened Paul.

Paul roused slightly, remembering to listen again. It had been a stupid dream, a nice Freudian mishmash that combined infantile fear of falling and abandonment with classical Oedipal resentment.

He sat up to light a candle and immediately the room reversed like a photographic negative, the windows going flat black, the room springing bright in contrast. It was 5:30, not too early to get started. He lit the Coleman stove, filled the mess-kit pot with water from the canteen, and put a spoonful of instant coffee in his camping mug. While he waited for the water to boil, he selected his tools for the day's work. First job: hang the new kitchen door he'd bought. Then the windows. Once the windows were covered on the outside, he could remove the broken sashes from inside and hire out the glazing. Maybe Dempsey would be willing to do it.

By eleven o'clock he'd hung the new kitchen door and covered all ten broken windows on the eastern facade. He'd gone to the terrace to cut another piece of plastic when he heard gravel crunch and pop in the driveway and the low rumble of a car's motor. *Too early to be Lia.* Without thinking about it, he took the crowbar out of his toolbox, hooking his fingers through the curved end, his heart racing as a rush of adrenaline hit his bloodstream. *So near the surface: the fear that you don't admit is there.* His stomach muscles clenched in a powerful tic.

He was surprised to see a dark-blue-and-yellow State Police cruiser mount the rise and stop momentarily just above the circular drive. Without a sound, its blue strobe bar started flashing, then the car slid down into the drive. The door opened, and a trooper stood up out of the car, adjusting his broad-brimmed hat before stepping beyond the open door and facing Paul alertly.

"Good morning," the trooper said. He looked to be in his mid-forties. His uniform was crisp on a trim, compact frame, and he had a narrow face, partly concealed by sunglasses. He grinned humorlessly, as if sensing Paul's discomfort.

"Morning," Paul said.

"Don't like cops?"

Paul hesitated. "What?"

"I said, 'Don't like cops?'" The smile stretched. "Got plans for the crowbar?"

Paul looked down, surprised to see the tool still in his fist. He tossed it into the toolbox. "Sorry. You startled me."

The policeman took off his sunglasses and folded them carefully with one hand into his shirt pocket as he scanned the facade of the house, the other hand resting lightly on the handle of his gun. "You're supposed to say, 'I like cops okay. I just feel better when they're not around.' Chuck Bukowski. Funniest line he ever wrote. Funny thing is, I feel the same way, and I'm a cop. As you may have noticed." He stepped easily up the terrace stairs, and stood appraising Paul with piercing eyes set closely in a face that was handsome in a predatory way. "And your name is—?"

"Paul Skoglund."

"Mr. Skoglund, I'm Trooper Peter Rizal of the New York State Police. Now, I'd like you to turn around, put your hands against the wall of the house and spread your legs. Don't move unless I tell you to. You know the drill." The grin had stayed on Rizal's face.

"*Fuck!*" Paul barked. It started to come again and he tried to camouflage it: "*Look,* I'm supposed to be fixing this place up. I don't know any goddamned drill." His hands clapped in the air toward Rizal.

Rizal had his pistol out of its holster so fast Paul never saw him reach for it. The policeman stood, legs wide, gun held in two hands and pointed at Paul's chin. "Do the thing or I'll blow your fucking face through the back of your head," he said flatly.

Paul turned, unbelieving, put his hands on the shingles. "I'm fixing this place up!"

"Feet back! Farther!" Rizal barked.

Paul did as he was told, until he was leaning forward on his hands, well off balance. His lungs compulsively squeezed, but he bit off the *Fuck!* and made it come out as just a bark. He felt Rizal's hands slapping his body: chest, back, inner thighs, groin. When he was done, Rizal slid Paul's wallet out of his pocket and stood back for a moment, apparently looking over his identification.

"You can turn around now." Rizal handed back the wallet. The grin was back, flickering at the corners of his mouth. "You don't think it's a little early in the day to be indulging in your drug of choice?"

"I've got a neurological disorder." Paul's face writhed and knotted in a powerful tic. He panted from rage and frustration, as much at himself, his fate, as at the cop. The whole pile of shit was too much.

Rizal walked casually along the front of the house, looking around at the headless statues, the broken windows, the glass and odd parts of furniture that had ended up on the terrace. He'd slid his gun into its holster and now seemed utterly unconcerned about Paul.

"What do you want here, Officer?"

Rizal stopped to peer into the main room through one of the tall windows that flanked the front door. "Christ on a crutch! Place is a mess, isn't it?"

"*Look!* Yeah, it's a mess and I'm supposed to repair the house and put things in order. I'd like to get back to work."

Rizal glanced at him, crossed his eyes as if imitating what he saw, a real looney-tune, then continued inspecting the house. "So you're from Vermont. Nice up there, isn't it? I like to get up to Stowe three, four times every winter, do some skiing." He bent to pick up the carved mahogany arm of a chair, inspected it briefly, then tossed it down again. "Long way to travel to put plastic on windows. Plus, I mean, talk is some crackheads've been coming up from the city. Real crazies. Be unpleasant if they came back, no? Unless maybe they're friends of yours."

"I'd like you to leave now, unless you have some legitimate reason for being on these premises. But before you go, I want your badge number and the name of your superior officer."

Rizal chuckled and went down the stairs and back to the idling cruiser. "Trooper Peter Rizal, Lewisboro barracks. I'm sure my superior officer will welcome your point of view. Station Commander Sergeant Miller. By all means, call him, Mr. Skoglund. In the meantime, I'll do some thinking about what neurological condition you may have ingested." He took off his hat and tossed it into the car's passenger seat, then took out his sunglasses and polished them thoughtfully before slipping them on. "And you have a nice day."

Paul watched the car take the circle and then accelerate over the rise. The cruiser had idled so long it had filled the still air on the terrace with the smell of exhaust.

Paul's body still seemed to burn where the cop had slapped him during the frisk. The tics jerked out of him. He should have taken Ted's advice and stopped into the local State Police barracks to let them know he'd be working there. No one was ever ready for Tourette's. Fuck. But Rizal's sardonic way of talking, his insinuations and advice, had seemed almost deliberately calculated to antagonize Paul, humiliate him, get him worked up.

25

"I don't know that you've got a legitimate complaint," Lia said. "If you look at it from his perspective—"

"I don't like being at the business end of a gun! I don't like some bastard putting me up against the wall, jerking me around. It doesn't matter that he's a cop. Yeah, I've got Tourette's, but I've also got some goddamned rights."

He'd worked off the worst of the adrenaline rush of anger, ironed out his nervous system by force of will, and had gotten most of the windows done by the time Lia arrived. Now they were in the smoking room. Lia was assembling one of two dozen cardboard file boxes Paul had bought to sort Vivien's papers into, while Paul set up the rented kerosene heater, venting it through the fireplace flue. They'd agreed the smoking room would be the best room to serve as their "operational headquarters," as Lia called it, because it was the most intact room in the house and was small enough to heat. They'd swept up the pieces of the broken mirror before bringing in Paul's tools and the stacks of folded file boxes.

"But if it hadn't been *you*—if he'd come up and found one of the creeps who did this—wouldn't you want him to catch the guy, find out who he was? Wouldn't you expect him to protect himself?"

Paul fumbled distractedly in his toolbox. "It was his, I don't know, his *tone* that got me as much as anything else."

"I don't think you can complain about tone, Paul. It's too subjective. You called it sardonic—I doubt the word can be found in any police manuals. 'Avoid a sardonic tone when dealing with suspects or the general public.'"

It was hopeless to argue with Lia when she was in such a good mood. She had loved the carriage house rooms and was happy at having a few days' break from school, excited at the prospect of poking through the house, no doubt stimulated by the scent of danger here. She was dressed like a lumberjack in a heavy red-checked wool jacket, jeans, rubber-soled boots. The bulky jacket and boots only enhanced the trim lines of her buttocks and thighs, the suppleness of her movements. With her black wool stocking cap rolled to reveal tangled hair and two incongruous gold hoop earrings, it was all Paul could do to keep his hands off her.

"I keep feeling he knew exactly who I was. I've talked to dozens of people, buying stuff, getting people to fix this and that. The whole town knows I'm up here. Rizal must have known too."

"He may not have been privy to the same gossip as the clerk in the hardware store," Lia said. "Look. You know that time we came up with the exact percentage of assholes in the world? What'd we figure—twenty-five percent?"

"I believe the precise number was twenty-eight percent."

"Okay. So twenty-eight percent of the people you meet are going to be assholes. Cops are no different—same ratio as the general population. You ran into one today, that's all."

It was hard not to laugh. They'd cracked each other up that night, after Lia had come home bitterly angry at the stupidity and pettiness rampant in the hierarchy of the graduate division at school. Paul had soothed her by opening a bottle of wine, taking her to bed to make love, and then giving her the same argument she was giving him now.

"God, I'm glad you're here," he told her. He crossed the room and grabbed her, wrapping around her, inhaling her scent, relieved to have her safe and alive and nearby. They kissed, taking their time, before getting back to work.

"Paul, there's some interesting stuff in here. No letters from your father yet, but what do you make of this?" She handed him a pair of photographs.

It was now three o'clock, the sun still shining brightly through a thin overcast. A wan light spilled through the milky, translucent plastic over the west-facing windows. They had gone to the library and scooped papers and photos into two file boxes, and now Lia sat cross-legged on the smoking room floor, a circle of papers all around her. Paul had rooted in the rubble until he managed to find a pink wall phone, undamaged, which he plugged into the wall bracket in the kitchen. No dial tone yet. Then he filled another box of papers from the library floor and rejoined Lia.

He sat next to her and took the photographs, black-and-white eight-by-tens. The first showed an interior nearly as disordered and damaged as the house they sat in: a floor-standing vase, its top shattered, some clothes strewn on the floor, a broken and overturned table. The second showed a section of wall and the corner of a mullioned window with shattered panes, a broken wooden chair crumpled into the baseboard, several books torn and splayed on the floor. Scrawled crudely on the white wall were the letters *KKK*.

"KKK? What the hell are we looking at?" Paul turned the photos over. There was nothing written on the backs. But the black-and-white was faded, taking on a slight sepia tone, the corners were frayed—clearly they weren't recent photos. "How old do you think these are?"

"Twenty years? Maybe more? The real question is, *where* were they taken? That, I think I know."

Lia led him back to the library, where they stood and compared the photos to the east wall of the room. There could be no doubt: The baseboard molding, the window frame, the mullion pattern were the same. Only the rubble was different.

"So," Paul said. He held the photo up and squinted at it. "So, Sherlock. What have we got here?"

"Well, it's hard to escape the assumption that something like this has happened before. We don't know how long ago, but almost certainly since the Hoffmanns have been here. And 'KKK.' All kinds of lovely possibilities there."

"I don't think the Ku Klux Klan has ever been active in this area."

"But they may have visited."

"Revenge on Vivien? She's always been mildly racist herself. And neither her husband nor Royce could be considered civil rights activists. Old Hoffmann made his fortune off the backs of his little brown brothers in the Philippines, and his son and grandson seem to have followed in his exploitative footsteps. Not a family that's likely to run afoul of the Klan."

"You never know. It could also be a completely bogus piece of graffiti."

"Sure," Paul conceded, "but whichever, there's another point. Vivien took these photos, or at least she's been keeping them in her files all these years. Which means she knows there's some precedent for what happened here this summer—and she hasn't bothered to tell us." Paul scuffed his foot in the litter of papers. "Which pisses me off."

"False inferences and hasty conclusions," Lia said. She had her forensic look—face animated, eyes glowing. Mind in overdrive, analyzing, processing ideas and discarding them, constructing a logical equation. "These photos may show the entire extent of damage. We can't tell, from these alone, that there was ever the widespread vandalism we see now. As far as the graffiti goes, we haven't seen any here now, which means the style of vandalism, the MO, is different. No signature this time. Different psychology, different motives. We can't really tell whether it has any bearing on this situation at all."

"In any case," he said, "you're forgetting that we're here to fix the place, not figure out who did this." His tone wasn't what he intended. There was anger building in him—the unrelenting anxiety the house seemed to induce in him, the visit from Rizal, the sense that Vivien wasn't telling them everything. And he couldn't even see asking Vivien about it: She'd give him a lecture on respecting her privacy. Or fire him. He strode out of the library.

Lia caught up to him in the big room, grabbed his arm. "Look, Paul, I'm not the only one who's fascinated with this. You feel a sort of guilty, voyeuristic pleasure in this, just as I do. Even more, you're dying to find letters from your father, maybe sort out your own puzzles on that score. You're curious about what happened here. I wish you'd admit to the urge, not deny it." She saw the admission in his face and went on. "The nice thing about it is the answers are probably right here."

She gestured around her: a carved wooden shield tangled in some panty hose. A great hammered brass bowl, covered with flowing Arabic designs in low relief, containing an uprooted, dried houseplant and a shattered pocket calculator. Several balls of heavy burgundy yarn, one still pierced with an ivory-tipped knitting needle, trailing a wild snarl of wool that included in its tangle an office stapler, a toothbrush, a small pewter pitcher. Each object with a tale to tell. And over it all, the drifts of papers.

Lia let him absorb the scene for a moment and then went on. "I've sorted exactly one quarter of one box of papers from the library, one of maybe three dozen there. There are another six or eight boxes' worth in Vivien's room. There's all this. Who knows what else we'll discover?"

"I shudder to think."

"Oh, come on! Don't be a stick in the mud!" She looked at him closely. "What's bothering you?"

Paul looked around the room, carrying on an internal debate. Yes, he was drawn to the mystery of it. Part of it was the chance to find out more about Ben, maybe some suggestion about what had made him jump. And maybe there was a chance of finding something in his letters that would be helpful in the quest for a workable therapy for Mark. And, deeper, he was attracted to the idea of the release, the catharsis he'd glimpsed when he'd thrown the finial. A secret yearning. Maybe something like Lia's hunger for danger.

But another part of him just wanted to get into the cars and drive the hell away from the relentless apprehension, the disturbing fragments of memory. He wondered briefly if it would be wise to tell Lia everything he was feeling.

"Let me show you something," he said at last.

He led her to Royce's old room, pointed out the broken harp of the piano. "The harp is trussed steel, designed to resist many tons of tension, year in and year out. Now it's bent, broken."

She just nodded, letting him make his case.

Then he took her to the stairs, showed her the neck of the post where the finial had been broken loose, and explained his thoughts. He showed her the finial itself and the imprint of its leaf pattern on the plaster wall opposite the stairs, fifty feet away.

"Still think we should stay at it?" he said.

Lia had listened closely, eyes moving quickly as she inspected the banister post, the finial, the wall, the distances between.

"I think you're being a bit paranoid," she said gently. "At the very least, you're being a lousy detective. I agree that Babe Ruth with a sledgehammer couldn't hit that ball hard enough to break it loose and send it that far with enough force to dent the wall. But if that's the only scenario you accept, you've ruled out everything but, basically, supernatural forces."

"So what did happen? How else could it have worked?"

"Let's try a differential analysis. Number one: the piano. Paul, just a few years ago it was all the rage at colleges to see how fast a group of students could put a piano through a one-foot hole in a fence. You can look it up in the *Guinness Book of World Records*. It can't be that hard to demolish one."

"How about the finial?"

She took the finial and stepped over the rubble to the wall where Paul had found it. Suddenly she drew it back and with both hands swung it like a wrecking ball against the wall. The thump of impact made Paul jump and echoed through the house. When she brought the finial back to Paul, a new bruise of paint marked the wood next to the first. And on the wall, another print of its scales was pressed into the plaster.

"For starters, I wouldn't assume that the act of breaking the ball loose over there and its leaving a mark here were causally related," she said. "I've just demonstrated that you can make the imprint pretty easily."

"Okay. Point taken. But how would you knock it off the post without leaving a dent in the wood?"

Lia thought for a moment, straight-faced, and then the corners of her mouth drew up. "Hit it with a couch," she said. She laughed and he had to laugh with her. She took his belt in her hands and tugged him forward and back. "I'm glad I can always make you laugh."

Paul checked his watch. "Three-thirty. We've got about another hour before sundown. Let's get some more work done while the light holds." He'd gotten a whiff of the thought that had eluded him the day before, but then Lia had distracted him. Something to do with one of the books he'd read when trying to figure out Mark. That and the idea of swinging a couch like a baseball bat. He shook his head as if to jar the thought loose again, but it wouldn't come.

26

Outside the carriage house, the night woods were silent. Inside, the only sound was Lia's gentle snore and the scutter of mice in the ceiling and walls. Paul lay listening for a time, trying and failing to quell the tension in his body. He wished his ears would stop straining against the silence.

It had been a productive if disturbing day. They'd worked until ten by the glaring light of the kerosene lantern, sorting papers. Most were trivial: receipts for plumbing work, car repairs, a toaster, heating oil, dating back many years. An owner's manual for a Sears lawnmower, a faded pamphlet entitled "Caring for Your Goldfish," a warranty for a Philco television. It was hard to believe Vivien wanted to save these things, but without explicit instructions to the contrary they decided it best to sort them into general categories, let her decide later what to keep. Paul found some doctors' bills from the fifties and wondered briefly at a blank psychological inventory test, the Reiss Screen for Maladaptive Behavior, then started a new box, which he labeled "Medical."

"There are veins of material," Lia had said at one point. "Like seams of ore in a mine. I've been hitting a lot of stuff related to the Philippines. Account statements. Bills of lading, shipping manifests. Port of Manila. Old, though—look at the dates."

Paul leaned to look over the sheaf of papers she held in her lap, pulling aside a curl of red-blond hair. The papers were old, the ink and stamps and signatures faded, but they could still read the dates: several from 1902 and one from 1903. The bills were specific to weight but didn't mention contents.

Paul turned several pages. "It makes sense—old Hoffmann Senior made his bucks in the Philippines. He lived there on and off for most of his life."

"I wonder why Vivien has these? That's a long time ago. And you'd think if there was anything important about these papers they'd have stayed with Hoffmann after their divorce."

"My mother told me Vivien kept files. I thought she was speaking figuratively."

Paul found a few more photos, some showing Filipino men in suits, standing and posing unsmiling for the camera; one was of a two-tone, two-door sedan in front of a low-roofed house and bamboo stockade hedge.

"These are more recent," Paul said. "I seem to recall that Hoffmann Junior and Vivien lived there for a while too, when they were first married."

Lia handed him another photo. "Here's the little boy again—the one we saw in the photo of Vivien beneath the airplane. I wonder who he is?"

The photo showed a boy of three or four, with pale skin and almost white hair, sitting with legs splayed. At the angle the camera had caught him, the boy's forehead seemed too large, almost deformed, his eyes too wide apart. "Maybe some relative on the Hoffmann side? Seems like there's some resemblance."

She showed him another photo, of a young woman in a loose cotton dress, smiling and holding a broad-brimmed, conical reed hat onto her head. "And this is Vivien, right?"

"Yeah."

"She's pretty!" Lia exclaimed.

"What did you think? Have I made her out to be such a monster? I think she married Hoffmann when she was only eighteen—she was probably in her early twenties when that was taken. Everybody's young once."

"I know. I guess this just . . . it reminds me of photos of my own parents. When they were first married. They always seemed so happy, so exuberant. When I was a kid, they seemed like pictures of ancient history. This is the same sort of photo, isn't it? A happy young woman. Something she looks at sometimes, thinking, 'I looked like that once.' "

That was just after sunset, when Lia had clearly begun to flag. A smudge of blue had appeared under each eye, and she looked suddenly fragile. Light from the bloody western sky came through the plastic-covered windows, casting blurred shadows from the trees that rocked in a slight breeze, eerily alive.

"You just tired, or is it something else?" Paul asked.

"Both. You know what I'm feeling? I miss my mother." Lia gave a weary, wry laugh. She'd always been more her father's child, maintaining an uneven and difficult relationship with her mother.

"The photo?"

"Yeah. I guess. Also winter coming on. I guess I've got a severe case of existential angst. End of a long day. Low blood sugar. Time on the wing. Ask not for whom the bell tolls. Et cetera."

"You too? I've been wondering if it's something you catch from being at Highwood."

They drove into Brewster for a late dinner of burgers and fries. It was almost eleven o'clock by the time they came into the driveway and saw the dark house again. In the glare of the headlights, the blank, slick sheets of plastic covering its windows looked like cataract-covered eyes. The few garden statues still upright seemed to move as the lights swung—decapitated disco dancers. When Paul cut the lights, the sudden darkness was absolute.

"Home sweet home," he said lamely. His lungs convulsed with a tic and he caught the air in his throat.

Lia's voice came out of the darkness: "Do we really have to stay here?"

"Only until I get a gate up—a few more days. I hope. What, this isn't your idea of a good time? A stylish sort of risk?"

She didn't rise to it. "You know, I didn't bring Ted's .38 with me this time. But right now I almost wish I had."

"I know what you mean," Paul said. In Philadelphia the idea of keeping a gun with them had seemed crazy. Now it seemed more than reasonable.

They'd gone upstairs and slipped into their down bags, each thinking private thoughts and not saying much, as if they feared to disturb the silence around them.

Paul was startled out of his near-sleep by an unexpected sound, faint, shrill, stopping and starting again in measured intervals. He opened his eyes, not believing he'd heard it, but then it came again, faint but insistent, demanding. The phone was ringing in the big house.

Instinctively, he began to get out of bed, hurry to answer it, but then thought of the time it would take to pull on clothes and shoes, find his way downstairs, across the drive, down the terrace, into the kitchen. No one would ring that long. And the idea of entering the huge dark house seemed suddenly terrifying.

He lay, counting the rings, wondering who could be calling, his heart pounding. After thirty-five rings it stopped, leaving the silent aftermath oddly chilled.

27

Richard *slowed his limping run to a trot, unable to take enough air into his burning lungs. The trees above him were dark with the dense foliage of August, but ahead he could see a faint brightness where a break in the canopy opened to the night sky. Almost to the highway,* he told himself, *maybe there'd be cars, he could tell someone, they could save him, they could get the police. Somebody had to know. Somebody had to do something.*

The old road ended, and he turned left onto the paved highway and began to run flat out again despite the pain. The only sound was his feet slapping the asphalt and the little keening he made when he breathed, the high, thin noise beyond crying that came from his throat. Shattered images of the nightmare on the hill replayed in his mind: the person or thing that came out of the darkness and tossed him aside like a dirty sock and did something terrible to Essie, something indescribable. In the dark he'd heard it more than seen it, the noises her body made and the pain sounds she uttered involuntarily and the things she said. Essie! *Yes, and the noise it had made, the scraping or sawing sound that had been their first clue that everything had gone wrong.*

They'd made love just like the times before, beautiful Essie in the bed that was like it had been left just for them, the fine bed upstairs in the big abandoned house, beautiful Essie giving him everything he'd ever wanted, her love welling up from inside her. And then when they were just starting down, the sound had startled them. His first thought had been that Heather had followed them and was making the weird noise as some strange joke. But when they turned, suddenly the darkness congealed into a shape right there and Essie was ten feet away, tumbling on the ground.

Overhead the trees closed in again, and he ran into the blackness. The images refreshed the panic that sparked in every cell, the blind urge to run, no thoughts but one: Got to get to the car. Somebody had to know.

It had wanted to kill Essie. And Essie, after it had hurt her for the third time, so terribly, after he'd been flung hard against a tree and fell down and was trying to get up, Essie had said something. "Why are you doing this to me?" *she'd asked.* "I am a human being!" *Trying to reach out, to connect, to be* seen as who she was, to explain what in her goodness she'd always taken to be an irreducible and inviolable kinship. It was as close as she'd come to pleading.

Richard tried to block out the thought that came next and couldn't—the last thing Essie had said, when she must have known her body was broken beyond repair, that she would be dead soon, some kind of insight born of her own surrender: "Why are you so sad?" With the memory he began screaming, mourning her, Essie who was the one fine thing, the one truly good person he'd ever met.

Through the trees to the left he saw the flat blank gray of the reservoir, and across the water a faint rim of light that must be the roof of the car, one more bend and he'd be there, and with the relief came hatred for himself, for the little worm of gladness that he was going to live, that whoever it was had gone after Essie and not him and that's what had allowed him to get away.

And just then he heard the sound start behind him, the rhythmic sawing like some dry insect in a hidden place, but far too fast. The sound crescendoed rapidly, as fast as a car approaching, and then he knew he would die and he was almost glad. But he made one last attempt to run, thinking, Somebody has to know.

28

MO'S depressed mood began after his talk with Heather Mason and persisted through Thanksgiving Day and the weekend. After meeting with Heather, he went back to the office and tried to sort out what he'd learned, disturbed by the shifting faces of the schizophrenic girl. He had little doubt that she knew something about the death of her brother and maybe about the disappearance of Essie Howrigan. The difficulty lay in deciding what was truth and what was delusion, or fantasy, or manipulation.

It was pretty clear that Richard Mason and Essie Howrigan had fallen in love during her visits to the Masons' house. No doubt Essie and Richard were screwing, making love, when they slipped off and left Heather in the car. For Essie it was an act so taboo that she couldn't risk letting her parents know anything at all about her connection to Richard. The excuse that she was going to spend time with Heather, a mission of charity, was the perfect cover. Thus having Heather's continuing cooperation became the key to the success of their lovers' conspiracy.

Whatever, he was sure Heather had been telling the truth at least some of the time. He could readily believe that Richard and Essie had parked the car, walked to their trysting place, leaving Heather to wait as usual—the price she had to pay for their attentions to her. Later, when Heather had gotten tired of waiting and left the car, she'd seen something, maybe the accident, if it was an accident, and had fled home on foot.

The question then was: What had Heather seen?

On Wednesday night, after talking to Heather, Mo headed back to his apartment in Mt. Kisco, stopping on the way at the A & P, where he had to brave the crowds of people who were buying last-minute supplies for their Thanksgiving feasts. The only definitive plan Mo had made for the holiday was to decline a couple of invitations for dinner.

At the A & P, he picked up some ready-made spaghetti sauce, some frozen chicken, a few cans of this and that. A Spartan diet, which he consumed without much interest in his Spartan apartment. In Mo's experience, people in his condition—emotional refugees from the divorce wars—did one of two things. About half made a big ritual of starting over, setting up house on their own, surrounding themselves with the trappings of stability by decorating their apartments, framing photos from their childhoods, learning to cook fancy cuisine. These were the ones who joined art classes, exercise clubs, hiking groups. Who made new friends to replace the old ones who inevitably got lost during the divorce. Mo envied them, their resilience and optimism.

The other half did as Mo did: living expediently, not paying any attention to their domestic lives, entering a waiting mode, taking a penitential pleasure in sparse apartments and weekends spent mostly alone, the cleansing simplicity of single life. Anyway, even though the divorce from Dara had been a mutual decision, some period of mourning seemed in order. Maybe you had to be Jewish or Catholic to feel this way. Mo had both bases covered.

His apartment consisted of three rooms on the second floor of an older brick building that had been renovated a few years before. White walls, ceilings a bit too low, almost no furniture: a couch but no coffee table, his computer and printer on a stand, a few hard chairs, a folding table in the kitchen. In the bathroom, a cake hanging inside the toilet tank made the water run neon blue, like a motel toilet. Though he'd vowed every morning he was going to take the blue cake out of there, he never got around to it. Like the minimally furnished rooms, it had become another paradoxical affirmation: *This is only temporary.* The implication being that better things were in store.

He ate a lousy dinner Wednesday night, thinking about Heather and getting nowhere, and then went to bed with his thoughts drifting back to the beautiful Janis Howrigan. Then for the rest of the night he kept up an internal discussion of love and marriage, which naturally brought him back to Dara and the divorce. Mrs. Mason's comment about love came back to him. *What does "love" mean?* She was right: Love is just another term, another abstraction. Another chimera.

At its best, Mo decided, love was something mysterious, something you couldn't name, something that worked best when you left it alone, trusted it. It lived in the air between two people, and it had a life of its own.

He'd spent three years with Dara. They'd both joked about the three-year cycle of their relationships, but in the end it had proven all they were good for. She was twenty-six when they'd met, four years younger than Mo, a serious dancer with an incredible grace of movement derived from hours at the bar and mirror. They'd met at a party of some mutual friends, where from across the room he'd been caught by the ripple of energy, the bow wave she seemed to generate around her. Then he'd attended some performances her company put on in the city, and seeing her perfect legs and

hips and flat stomach and firm, small breasts he'd begun to desire her almost unbearably. When they began to see more of each other, he'd learned
that she had a complete intolerance of bullshit, not unlike his own. They'd
laughed about that a lot.

They'd both overcome a certain skepticism about marriage to actually
tie the knot. Dara's reasoning was simple: "I'll try anything once," she'd
said. For his part, Mo had joked for years that marriage was the best way to
ruin a good relationship. But he was willing to see what happened. Like the
rest of love, it was the mystery of marriage that attracted him.

As it turned out, the first year and a half was quite wonderful. Dara had
proven surprisingly adaptable, genuinely seeming to like his friends, so different from her own, showing an interest in his work despite the sometimes gruesome stories he'd bring home, putting up with the odd hours he
often had to keep. It was the memories from this period that came back to
him now to give him grief.

Once he'd come home at around one A.M. from a tense, fruitless stakeout to find her just out of the shower, wearing her yellow terry-cloth robe
and combing the knots out of her red hair.

"I'm glad you're back," she told him.

"Why's that?" he asked, feeling funky and looking for some flattery. He
couldn't help but smile at the cascade of wet, coiling hair that hid her face.
He popped a beer and slumped in a chair across the table from her.

She didn't answer him directly. "I like being married," she said softly.

"Why?"

"Oh, I don't know. It brings out a different side of me. I feel safe, and
when I feel safe I can be . . . softer. It's very sweet."

The way she said it touched him, and he went to stand near her. "Let me
see your face," he said, wanting to kiss her. He started to pull her hair aside,
but she caught his hands and wouldn't let him. He could just see her
mouth, smiling. "Why not?" he asked.

"Because I'm shy," she said. "I'm not used to telling anyone stuff like
this." He'd never thought of her as anything like shy.

That was the kind of memory that gave him pain, so he usually tried instead to remember only the last year or so, the bickering and the infidelities
and the many little ultimatums that closed off communication. At some
point he'd realized that rather than seeing more and more of that side of
her, he was seeing less and less.

Though they had started out with similar views on marriage, they ended
up with very different perspectives. Dara felt her original view had been
vindicated: Marriage wasn't for her. To his surprise, Mo found himself believing in marriage for the first time in his life—and doubting he'd ever
find the thing he now knew he wanted.

There was an endless supply of memories, good or bad, each causing one or another form of grief. Selecting the uglier memories was a way of protecting himself, he realized. Not unlike Heather Mason, holding on to mad to stay away from sad.

The thought yanked him back to the present and the problems Heather posed. All his thinking was contingent on believing one very disturbed girl's fragmented, half-taunting narrative. Yet Mo's instinct told him some, at least, was true. Intuition, instinct, reflex—he had learned the hard way to distrust these parts of himself. Yet his hunches were persuasive. He carried on an internal argument until it exhausted him and he slept.

On Thanksgiving Day, his cynicism about holidays wavered long enough to permit him to call his parents in their retirement community in Kissimmee, Florida. His father's angina had been acting up, but the new medication was helping. His mother had taken up tai chi classes with a bunch of other elderly Jewish ladies and was enjoying it enormously; her digestion had been better ever since she started. And so on. Mo promised he'd come visit them on his next vacation, in January, and got off, wishing he hadn't called.

On Monday he returned to the office to find an unusual letter in the mail. The monogrammed, lavender-tinted, excessively feminine stationery confused him until he opened the envelope and saw Heather Mason's name across the bottom. Written in ball-point pen, the letter was short:

Dear Detective Ford,

Because I am only fourteen and schizophrenic, people don't ever believe what I say. They "interpret" what I say, they analyze it. They sort of humor me but their eyes say, "This is her craziness talking." Dr. Kurtz makes a note on his pad about my paranoia, or my blunted affect, or the configuration of my delusional matrix, or my Risperdal dosage. A lot of the time even I don't know what to call the things I think, the things I remember, the things I write in my story.

But you, I think you almost believe me. So I have another clue for you: It's going to happen again soon. Probably before Christmas. But maybe you figured that out already.

P.S. I'm not sure if you believe me, but the other thing I wanted to tell you is that I said it was Superman, but that's not completely right because Superman does good things and saves people, and this one does just the opposite. But probably you know all this. If you don't, you will soon.

Terrific. What did the girl know? Had she overheard Mo's conversation with her mother? *Going to happen again soon.* Had she figured out something that related to clusters in the timing of the disappearances? *Mathematically gifted,* her mother had said. *Reads constantly about psychopathologies.*

Mo called Mrs. Mason again to ask if he could schedule another visit with Heather.

"I'm afraid not," she told him. "Heather was very upset after your last talk with her."

"Mrs. Mason, your daughter just sent me a letter that suggests she knows something. I'm more convinced than ever that she can help us locate Essie Howrigan."

"Heather can be very manipulative. It is an established part of her psychological profile, and I wouldn't advise taking what she says at face value. No, Mr. Ford. My husband and I spoke with Dr. Kurtz about this. He's adamant that you're to have no more contact with my daughter."

"Even if she can help me find out who killed Richard?"

He heard her puff air out, struggling to keep control. "I told you how we feel about that. At this point, Mr. Ford, we have only one child left. And that one child is teetering on the edge. We're absolutely determined to protect her. Absolutely."

Later on Monday he went to see Barrett to explore ways he might encourage or force them to let him talk to Heather. He assembled his notes from the interview, wrote down as much as he could of their conversation, verbatim, so that Barrett would understand the odd credibility of this otherwise unreliable witness.

"So?" Barrett said. Barrett looked harried, his desk a litter of papers, his tie loosened and sleeves rolled up as if he were about to begin some heavy manual task. He chewed on a saliva-stained cigar which he was forbidden to light in his office because of the new smoking regulations.

Mo told him his theory about Essie Howrigan and Richard Mason.

"You got all that out of an interview with a fourteen-year-old schizophrenic?" Barrett looked incredulous.

"If you'd heard her talk, you'd believe it too."

"What I just heard, what you read from your notes, sounds like gibberish."

"It's disorganized, I know." He felt the relief of a near miss, glad he hadn't mentioned Heather's Superman comments. "But it's very suggestive and it ties in with other things we know—the date the Howrigan girl disappeared. All I want is another chance to talk to her. The parents are reluctant to let me see her again. I was thinking of, you know, what other recourse we might have—"

"What, get a court order to produce her as a witness? Threaten an obstruction charge? You know, Mo—" Barrett started to get florid, then caught himself, reining in his anger. "Look. One: There's no way this office is going to sanction any of that shit on the basis of what you've told me. No way. Understand? Not a chance." Barrett began counting off his points on his thick fingers. "Two: There's no way a judge is going to hand you an order, for the same reasons. Three: If you did try to compel her to talk to you against her own and her parents' wishes, these people have big bucks and prominent friends, and they'd have a lawsuit on us so fast it'd—" Barrett had gotten wound up again and almost choked on the idea, then brought himself back down and paused to glare at Mo intently for a second. *Which wouldn't exactly increase your popularity around here,* the glare seemed to say. He put the cigar on his desk with a look of distaste. "Look," he said again. "Roll with the punches, look for something else to back up her story. Maybe you can meet first with just the parents, sweet-talk them into another interview. Okay? Now, anything else this morning? I've got a shitload here. I'm going to need a fucking forklift." He gestured at his desk.

Then on Tuesday morning the car theft investigation came to a dead end as a guy Mo was scheduled to talk to, the one guy who knew anything, died during emergency heart surgery. It was an inauspicious start for the day.

Late Tuesday afternoon, he got some news that ordinarily would have made him feel great: One of the missing kids, Mike Walinski, surfaced again, alive and well. Mo took a call from Mike's mother, who told him Mike had called. Turned out he'd run off with a friend he'd met at summer camp the year before. The two boys had hitchhiked to San Francisco together. Mo gathered that one reason Mike had been so hard to find was that he'd discovered his true sexual orientation and was afraid to try to explain it to his parents.

Mo was glad the kid wasn't dead or maimed or whatever. And Mike's reappearance would just about nail the coffin lid on the go-nowhere multi-agency task force whose meetings Mo hated to attend—more support for Wild Bill's opinion that the whole missing-kid thing was just a mild wave of adolescent rebellion in Westchester County. But in his current mood, he couldn't help feel the downside of Mike's reappearance: another chunk falling away from his tinkertoy construction. No doubt Essie Howrigan would show up at some point too, with some reasonable explanation for her absence, and make Mo's theories look like the crap they were. He'd been taken in by the wide, earnest eyes of Heather Mason, the eerie, oracular certainty of her pronouncements. The hell with it. He'd be better off selling insurance or something.

. . .

But Wednesday was different, the luck started to turn. Mo came in, went over his notes for the interview he'd scheduled, listing the questions he needed to ask and thinking about what approach he'd use. This was an interview Wild Bill should have done but didn't, a sixteen-year-old kid who had been a good buddy of Steve Rubio.

By ten-thirty he felt the need of some coffee, and took the opportunity to do a little background check on the kid he was about to interview. Code 913 hard-copy case files were kept in the main uniform office and held materials on recent juvenile run-ins with the police, including warnings and domestic troubles, and correspondence with the school liaison officer at Troop K headquarters in Poughkeepsie. He was elbow deep in a file drawer, just around the corner from the door to the uniform commander's office, when he heard Rizal's voice.

"It's like I told you," Rizal was saying. "I see the junker's been moved from the bottom of the driveway, so I drive up to see if everything's okay. I'm out there alone in the woods, the house is a wreck, the guy's yelling obscenities at me, he comes toward me with a crowbar in his hand—"

"Says he's Mrs. Hoffmann's nephew," Station Commander Miller's voice cut in. "That you had no reason to assume wrongdoing, that you were unnecessarily rough." Miller was thin, graying, a gentle man who probably should have been an Army chaplain, some man of the cloth. "He claims he's got a medical problem, Tourette's syndrome, that makes him say things. I looked it up."

"I was *rough*? He said that? I requested he face the wall, I verified he was who he said he was. He could have been more cooperative. He seemed nervous, like he was expecting trouble from me. I never heard of a medical problem that makes you tell a cop to fuck off. You believe that?"

"Was it really necessary to draw your gun?"

"When he didn't comply with my request, in this officer's opinion, definitely yes. The Rodney King scenario this was not, Chief. I said 'please' and 'thank you.' I identified myself as a law officer, I looked over his ID and returned it. That's it."

Still searching the file cabinet, Mo heard Miller sigh. "Write up what you just told me, will you, Pete? Just so we've done the formalities. I think he just wanted to blow off steam, and I don't think it's going to turn into anything. But I'd like to have the paper so we're in the clear."

"You got it," Rizal said.

"So Highwood was in pretty bad shape?"

Rizal gave a whistle. "Are you kidding? Every window is broken. From what I could see of the inside, it looks like a bomb went off."

"Fire? Or—"

"Not that I saw. Vandalism. I'd say kids have been going up there and throwing things around, in a major way, for a long time. This guy's got his work cut out for him."

"Well. It's a good thing Mrs. Hoffmann's getting the place fixed up. Sounds like a safety hazard." Miller paused, and when he spoke again his voice had turned hard: "Okay, so listen, Pete. Once in a while, keep in mind we've got our own PR to think of. We want the kiddies to like the nice policemen. You understand? I don't want to hear of another complaint about you anytime soon. And I don't want to hear that your gun's been out unless you had good reason to think someone's life depended on it."

"Gotcha," Rizal said airily. "Sir." Mo heard his heels click down the hall.

Mo did find a slim file on the boy, Terry Bannerman, which he took back to his office. But he had a hard time concentrating on it. The discussion between Miller and Rizal had gotten him wired up. A vacant house, up a hill in the woods, kids coming to vandalize it. It fit the picture perfectly.

Mo checked his watch and found that he had another hour before the interview. Just enough time. He went up front to the dispatcher's desk and knocked to get her attention.

"Carmen," he said. "You must know this area pretty good, right?"

"In my job, I sure hope so." Carmen looked at Mo disapprovingly.

"You ever hear of a place called Highwood? Supposed to be an old mansion."

"Highwood Lodge. Over near the old Reservoir Road."

"Can you show me where it is?" Mo gestured to the area maps that dominated the wall of the dispatcher's cubicle.

Carmen scanned the maps and pointed to one. In the center of the page was the Lewisboro Reservoir, an irregular kidney-shaped lake about two miles long, starting just east of Golden's Bridge. To the north of the reservoir, sometimes paralleling the irregular shoreline and sometimes veering as much as a quarter mile away from it, ran Highway 138. To the south, zigging and zagging as it hugged the shore, ran the Lewisboro Reservoir Road.

She put her red-nailed forefinger on the map. "Right about here. Just east of that new Briar Estates development."

She returned to her seat while Mo looked closely at the map. The spot she'd pointed out was just below the eastern third of the reservoir, maybe a half mile from where the old road rejoined Highway 138. He'd been on that very road only a few days before, killing time before his appointment with the parents of Dub Gilmore.

Mo's excitement sent a tingle of adrenaline to his fingertips as he traced the meandering shoreline road. Rizal had said something about a junked car that had been blocking the bottom of the driveway. He'd turned around in that same driveway, the one with the old stone pillars. He brought his finger up the line of the shore road to its intersection with 138, then moved it west until it came to the sharp bend where Richard Mason had been killed. There was not much more than a mile between the fatal bend in 138 and the driveway to Highwood.

Mo thanked Carmen, getting a distrustful raised eyebrow from her as he grinned wildly. *Screw Carmen's attitude,* he thought. Clearly, his luck was changing again.

29

Mo looked at the kid seated across from him and felt a twinge of sympathy. Sixteen was a lousy age—not yet allowed to be an adult, no longer permitted to be a child. Terry Bannerman was a tall boy, too skinny, who sat jiggling one leg and trying to look aloof and disdainful. He appeared to take great interest in the school parking lot, visible through the windows of the guidance office at John Jay High School, where a scattering of brown leaves blew between the ranked cars.

Mo had decided on the show-them-you're-one-of-them approach, rather than the impress-them-with-your-authority routine, but so far it hadn't worked. Terry answered in monosyllables. He was wearing an aviator's leather jacket that must have cost a couple of bills, khaki fatigue pants, and big Doc Martens, the boot of preference among the punk and skinhead crowd, but his slender frame and the rash of acne on both cheeks deflated his tough-guy pretensions. So far he hadn't once met Mo's eyes.

In the outer office, a secretary clattered the keyboard of her computer, and a noisy printer spit out a steady stream of paper that draped down the front of the desk and refolded itself on the floor. When the secretary got up to tend to the printer, Mo saw she was wearing a tweed skirt that came to mid-calf and drew smooth over the sweet curve of her thighs. She saw him looking her way and smiled pleasantly, and Mo felt a pang of longing.

He sighed and plugged doggedly ahead with his interview: "So you and Steve were pretty good buddies."

"Yeah."

"So what did you do? When you hung out together?"

"Nothin'."

"Like what, 'nothing'?"

"Same old stuff."

"That's not a lot of help. Look, Terry, I'm not after your ass or Steve's. I'm just here to try to find Steve, make sure he's all right. I need to know where you guys went, what you did, who you saw, who maybe Steve knew."

Terry's gaze wandered past Mo to the outer office door. "Sometimes we went to the Electric Grotto in Danbury."

"What's that?"

"Video games."

"Great. What else?"

Terry picked at his cheek and flashed an irritated glance just past Mo's left ear. "I don't know, okay? Same stuff. You go to parties, you go to games at school. Stuff like that."

They'd already been over this. Partly the kid was dodging him, but mainly he just lacked the imagination to figure out answers that might be useful. Terry Bannerman, Mo decided, wasn't Rhodes material.

Mo slogged on for another ten minutes, getting a couple of names of other friends, possible enemies, but basically getting nowhere. At last he flipped his notebook shut. "Okay, I guess that's it, Terry." He put his pen into his inner jacket pocket, letting Terry catch a glimpse of his Glock in its shoulder holster, then went on conversationally, almost as if talking to himself. "Funny, isn't it? You look around this area, everything seems like it's on the up-and-up, but there's some damn funny stuff going on behind the scenes. Like this thing with Highwood Lodge, for example, right?"

That caught the boy off guard. "You know about that?"

"Sure," Mo bluffed. "I mean, I know what I've heard. I haven't been up there yet myself. What was it like when you went up?"

Terry started to answer, then caught himself. He looked at the door as if he were considering bolting. When Mo swung it shut, he looked almost panicked.

"Look, Terry," Mo said. "You know what? I'm sick of dicking around with you. You're going to answer my questions right now. You're going to stop playing dumb. It's not cutting it with me." He went to stand over the boy. Terry leaned away from him. "What did you do when you went up to Highwood?"

"I didn't go," the boy said resentfully.

"But you know people who did. Steve did."

"Yeah."

"But he wanted you to go, right? And what did he say about it?"

"That you could just go in and take whatever you wanted. Or fuck around, smash things. The doors weren't locked."

"What else?"

"He went up there once with some other guys. He wanted me to go with him, but I chickened out."

"Why'd you chicken out?"

"I didn't want to get caught. The driveway was blocked, you'd have to walk all the way up and back. Somebody'd see you."

"Keep going," Mo said.

Terry licked his lips, started to pick at his face and then remembered not to. "He said it was all fucked up in there. Somebody'd been trashing the place. After a while he stopped going up. He chickened out too."

"Because he was afraid he'd get caught?"

"No. He said there was something screwy about it up there. Everybody knew about it. There was some kind of satanic rituals up there."

"What kind of rituals?"

"I don't know. Everybody said something different. Maybe like calling demons. They said like a human couldn't do some of the stuff that was done up there—the way the place was trashed."

"Who else do you know who actually went up there? Who's 'everybody'?"

"I don't know."

"You're going to tell me, Terry."

"I don't fucking *know*," Terry said. He seemed close to tears. "A lot of guys would say they knew something, but it's all bullshit, they were making things up so they could sound cool. It was just something you talked about. Like half-joking. You could make up whatever you wanted. After a while people stopped talking about it."

Mo went back to his chair and stood behind it, thinking, drumming his fingers on the wooden chair back.

"Okay. That's all for today." Mo took out his wallet and handed Terry one of his cards. "This has my number on it. If you think of anything else, you call me up right away."

Terry took the card and looked at it with curiosity, then stood up, putting his hands into his jacket pockets, waiting to be dismissed.

Mo clapped him on the shoulder. "Hey, Terry, you've been a lot of help. Do me a favor, will you? Don't mention to your friends that I asked you about Highwood. Okay? Let's try to keep the rumors down about this."

"Yeah," Terry said noncommittally.

Driving back to the office, Mo felt a little guilty about being so rough on the kid. Maybe there'd been another way to get him to open up, but Mo had gotten frustrated with his sullen, guarded face and posture of resentment. As he was leaving the school, he'd been relieved to see Terry talking animatedly with a very pretty girl, showing her what Mo guessed was the card he'd given him. Why are girls that age so lovely, Mo wondered, when the boys are such geeks? How do the girls manage to fall for the graceless, pretentious, self-conscious little pricks? A miracle of nature.

Hunger was beginning to gnaw at his stomach, but he felt good. Here was another possible link to Highwood, another line converging on the southeast end of the Lewisboro Reservoir. Mo could intuitively tell it was a live lead. Should he talk this over with Barrett? No. It would be better not to push his luck with him until he had something more substantial.

One thing was clear, though—it was time to pay a social call to Highwood. An off-the-record visit. Miller had said somebody was fixing the place up—the owner's nephew. Maybe he'd be willing to talk to Mo for a few minutes, let him look around the place. It was worth a try.

30

"**Paul**, I've got some goodies here! Want to see?" Lia stood at the big table in the smoking room with various papers spread out before her as Paul refilled and started the heater. The late-night call had set into motion all kinds of dire imaginings, which Paul could visualize with perfect clarity. The worst was an emergency with Mark. His hands responded to his growing anxiety all by themselves, ringing the bell, grabbing things out of the air. He'd have to call Janet as soon as the heater was up and running.

"Oh, this is juicy! Your cousin Royce was quite a young man. Look at this: juvenile court papers, complaint forms, some kind of suit settlement terms. All from the mid-sixties. Here's a letter stating reasons for his expulsion from Phillips Exeter Academy."

"I guess that's why Vivien needed someone in the family to do this— keep the dirty laundry out of public view."

"Can't blame her!"

The papers Paul picked up turned out to be complaint forms from 1965, signed by Raymond and Lois Clausen, with a nearby Lewisboro address. They claimed that they'd caught Royce Hoffmann in the act of breaking windows at their house. The Clausens stated that Royce was doing it because they'd caught him several times before, looking into their windows late at night; they had told him not to come back or they'd call the police, and he'd resented their threats.

"A difficult kid," Paul said. "Royce would have been around fourteen then. What'd he get expelled from Phillips Exeter for?"

Lia handed him another sheaf of papers, a series of letters between the dean and Vivien, along with a formal expulsion notice. "You told me Royce liked guns, right? Apparently he threatened his roommate with a loaded World War II Luger. They also thought having live hand grenades in the dorms was a bit much."

"He was just ahead of his time. No kid would go to school with less, nowadays."

Lia laughed. "What I love is that Vivien wrote all these stirring letters in his defense—that he was just sorting things out his own way, he'd never hurt anyone really." She snorted. "That he was just a very bright boy who was having a difficult time expressing himself."

Paul looked over the other papers. In 1967 Royce and some friends, not identified, had stolen a car and rolled it into the reservoir. The family of a local girl had taken out a restraining order on him to prevent him from following and harassing their daughter, for whom he had apparently conceived an infatuation. The ugliest details were mentioned in the terms of a settlement of a suit, brought by a family who claimed that Royce and a friend had killed their two show-quality Saint Bernards by feeding them lumps of hamburger filled with razor-blade chips.

"The question I have," Lia said, "is did he grow out of it, or is he still searching for new and interesting modes of self-expression?"

Paul was just heading out to the kitchen to call Janet when a white van rolled into the driveway, and he went outside to greet the electrician. Stewart Cohen turned out to be a short, compact, middle-aged man, with dark, wiry hair and intelligent, nervous eyes. He wore new blue jeans and a baby-blue down jacket, and carried a slim steel box that served as both clipboard and briefcase. His helper, in his late teens, was tall and thin, wearing a hooded New York Knicks sweatshirt and garish, high-tech basketball shoes.

"I'm glad you could make it here on such short notice," Paul said.

"Hey, send me a check and I'll follow you anywhere." Cohen gestured at the headless statues in the garden. "Looks like the French Revolution all over again. Whole place looks like hell—what happened?"

"I keep waiting for someone to tell *me*. It's a lot worse inside."

Cohen turned away and rolled open the van's sliding door, speaking over his shoulder as he sorted among the tools crammed inside. "The strong silent type here is Kenny Wechsler, my assistant. Also my sister's son and coincidentally my nephew."

"I heard it was some kind of cult came up here," Kenny said, "like one of those satanic cults. Used the place for rituals."

"Where'd you hear that?" Paul asked.

Kenny turned away and took a pair of battery-operated double spotlights from his uncle. "Friends, I guess," he said.

Paul led them inside through the kitchen door and into the main room, where he paused to let them absorb the scene. Kenny stood and gawked openly, his weak mouth open, while Cohen drummed his fingers on his metal case.

"Holy shit," Cohen said at last.

Down in the furnace room, Cohen set up the spots and gave the circuit breakers and wiring tree a quick once-over. In the bright white glare of the lights, with the distorted shadows of the three men moving over the dirty walls and broken machinery, the furnace room seemed hellish, Paul thought. All that was needed to complete the picture would be a fiery figure with horns and cloven hooves. He shook his head to clear the image, which he blamed on Kenny's remark.

"This is going to be a delightful job, I can see that," Cohen said, kicking at the rubble. "Three days at least, probably four or five."

Paul went back upstairs, intending to make the call to Janet, only to find Dempsey's old Buick station wagon, long as a hearse, pulling up at the terrace stairs. He talked with the old man briefly and gave him the floor plan he'd drawn, showing the locations of the broken windows. "A lot of them will probably need to be completely rebuilt and reglazed. Some will only need a few panes, and we can reuse the old mullion leading. I was thinking we'd clear an area of the floor in here and you could set up shop, take out the windows one at a time." Looking at Dempsey, the gray stubbled cheeks, yellowed eyes deep in whorls of wrinkles, Paul suddenly felt unsure how much he could ask of the old man. "If carrying them down's a problem," he finished, feeling suddenly awkward, "I'd be glad to—"

Dempsey's eyes caught his. "I think I can manage these, Paulie. Thanks." There was only a little reproach in his tone.

There was something uncomfortable between them, a guardedness, an artificiality. Not anything he wanted with Dempsey Corrigan. "How are you?" he asked. "Things okay?"

Dempsey clapped him on the shoulder, squeezed his muscle there with surprising strength. "Things are as okay as they can be for an old fart who's trying hard to outrun his regrets and not always succeeding. Sometimes they threaten to catch up with me."

"You've never struck me as a person with a lot of regrets."

"Yeah, well. I don't have many, but those I've got are extraordinarily fleet of foot." Dempsey grunted humorlessly. "Lemme get to work now. Best way to come out of it. Where's a goddamned broom? I've got to clear some floor space. Can't be walking on this crap every step I take."

It was definitely not the time to hit Dempsey with the questions he'd been wanting to ask: whether he knew anything about Falcone, the Herculean gardener, or about the odd vault of a room off Vivien's bedroom, or about the KKK photos and the possibility of an earlier episode of vandalism. Let alone the trickier questions: What was it between Vivien and Aster? What was it between Vivien and Dempsey? What drove Ben over the edge?

Dempsey's dark mood added another question. Something was definitely amiss with the old man—what? Paul's abdomen convulsed and he gagged violently as the tic closed his throat.

31

With everybody finally at work, Paul went to the kitchen. He had just reached for the phone when it shrilled at him. Adrenaline shot into his fingertips. *Don't let it be bad news about Mark,* he prayed. *Let it be Vivien, or Becker's Heating. Or anything routine and normal.* He snatched the receiver, cutting off another ring.

"Hello?" He could hear his own pulse in his ears.

"Hello," a man's voice said, "I am trying to reach Paul Skoglund." There was a touch of an English accent, vaguely familiar.

"This is Paul. Who's this?"

"Well! Paulie!" the voice laughed. "This is your cousin Royce!"

Paul was so startled he couldn't speak for a moment. "We—we were just talking about you," he said at last.

"Speak of the devil, eh?" Royce said. "It's been a long time, hasn't it? Do you have a minute, Paulie?"

"Sure, I've got a minute," Paul said cautiously. Hearing suspicion in his own voice, he continued: "I'm sorry, Royce. I'm—I just barely put the phone back on the wall. Frankly, I wasn't expecting anyone to call."

"And I'll bet you weren't expecting it to be *me,* were you? I assure you, it's a surprise for me to encounter you at Highwood."

"How did you know I'd be here? I take it you talked to Vivien."

Royce chuckled. "No, actually—I had a most delightful conversation with *your* mother. Who gave me the unexpected news that you were in the neighborhood, so to speak."

"Where are you?"

"I am calling from Manhattan. I own an apartment here, although in the last few years I seem to spend most of my time in Amsterdam and Hong Kong. Your mother tells me you've been living in Vermont?"

"Yes." A tic built and he barely turned it into a cough.

"And now you've come to the rescue, I understand. The old place is pretty bunged up, Aster says. How bad is it?"

"It's a disaster. Like somebody picked the building up and shook it like a cocktail shaker. It's going to take a lot of work to put it back together."

Royce murmured encouragingly. "And I'm sure you're doing a terrific job. Actually, Paulie, it's rather fortuitous that you're only an hour away. Your mother was so extravagant in her praise of your skills that I thought I'd call. To see if you'd like to do some work for me as well."

"What kind of work?"

"In my apartment here. I'd like the woodwork restored, refinished, the walls painted. Rather mundane compared to the baronial scale of Highwood, I suppose, but I need someone who can do top-quality work. I plan to be returning to the U.S. to live and I'd like to have the place in good shape."

"I've been kind of moving away from the contracting end of things—"

"Yes, so Aster told me. You're an educator now. But an unemployed educator, apparently. I would of course pay top dollar. And this is a lovely old building, Park at Eighty-sixth. I'm certain you could easily generate more work in the area. With a good reference from me, of course."

It was the kind of opportunity that five years ago Paul would have jumped at—breaking into the lucrative New York market for fine renovation, maintaining a steady group of wealthy clients. But things were different now. If he ever really wanted a career as a teacher, he'd have to commit himself to it, not be deflected by every other possibility that came his way. On the other hand, it couldn't hurt to have a source of income while he looked for the right job. The scenario Royce suggested could be ideal.

"I was hoping you and I could get together," Royce went on. "Meet for lunch here in the city, chew the proverbial fat about old times, then head over to the apartment." He cleared his throat. "One little problem though. We'd have to have our rendezvous rather soon."

"How soon? I'm in the middle of a big job here."

"I have to be heading out of the country in a few days. I was hoping to have completed arrangements for the work before I left. Can you meet me today? It's ten now—what about lunch? My treat. Short notice, I admit."

"I can't. I've got a lot to do before the weather closes in. I've got subcontractors—"

"But old Dempsey's up there with you, right?"

Paul's hand flew to his jacket zipper. "Yes."

"Well, no one knows the old place better than Dempsey. Have him steer your people for a few hours. It's only an hour to the city, cousin. It'd be worth your while."

.   .   .

The drive down was okay, the MG's handling enjoyable, and he felt more or less up to meeting Royce. But once he parked and found himself without the prop of a red, vintage British car, he felt out of place in upper midtown Manhattan. Chic storefronts, sleek limousines, resplendent hotel facades and elaborately uniformed doormen, long-legged women draped in furs, men checking wristwatches that cost more than Paul made in a year: He'd made choices in his life, and none of them had led him to pursue the bright promises here, the money, the battle for status.

Then in the mirrored pillars of Le Cirque, he caught sight of his own reflection—a rangy, moderately handsome fellow, with a too-open face, unruly brown hair that needed cutting, an old tweed jacket that didn't fit right, a stride that was at once too loose and too anxious, one hand playing crazily at his jacket buttons. As far as the people in the world of Manhattan were concerned, he might as well be wearing manure-caked boots, denim coveralls, and a straw hat. Hell, he wasn't going to fool anybody. It would be better not to try.

The maître d' led him to a table against the back wall, beneath a trompe l'oeil mural depicting a Louis XV parlor, absurdly occupied by monkeys in period dress, floured wigs, and all.

Royce stood to shake his hand. "Cousin! I'll be damned. Paulie Skoglund."

"Hello, Royce."

They looked each other over briefly. Royce was several inches taller than Paul and broad across the shoulders of his European-cut jacket. With his dark hair impeccably cut and swept back, his deep tan, his tailored clothes, the smoothness of his movements, he registered initially as a handsome man. But his face failed him. He had kept the outstanding features of his childhood, the too-broad forehead and wide-set eyes, which made his nose seem too narrow and his chin too delicate. Royce's forehead was now horizontally seamed with a single, deep crease, as if he suffered not from the many smaller worries that etched most men's faces but just one, consuming obsession. The skin above his left eye was bunched, a faint swelling of scar pushing down the eyebrow at the corner.

"You're staring at my scar. Considered rude in some circles, but acceptable among family and forgivable considering I didn't own it last time you saw me."

"Sorry—it just seems that people and places from my past have been cropping up a lot lately."

Royce took his seat again, gesturing for Paul to do the same. "I'll spare you the embarrassment of asking. A car accident. I removed the windshield of my car by throwing myself through it, neatly taking the trim or molding or whatever you call it out with my forehead. Cut some facial nerves, leaving me with limited control of the left side of my face. Thus my charming, lopsided grin."

Royce probed Paul with his blue eyes, a subtle smile coming up his right cheek, anything but charming. He selected a roll from a linen-covered basket on the table, ripped it in half, buttered it. "Splendid way to begin a conversation. How about yourself? Any true gore stories before we eat?"

"Not yet," Paul said. "I find myself more or less intact."

"So far anyway, eh?" Royce laughed. This joke seemed to amuse him enormously, and he smiled as he tore into the roll with his teeth. With his butter knife, he gestured at the bread basket for Paul to join him, and Paul took a roll.

The pressure had been building since he'd set foot in the restaurant, and Paul felt it would be better to let the cat out of the bag: "Listen, Royce, I've got a neurological problem. Sometimes I do odd things. I thought you should be forewarned."

"That's right—I vaguely remember." Royce looked at him, a new interest in his eyes. "Does this . . . condition . . . have a name?"

"Tourette's syndrome."

"Right. Oh, my. Well. Congrats—that's getting downright fashionable nowadays. Feel free to go blooie, if you must. I love a spectacle." He took another bite of his roll. "Funny thing, I just read in the in-flight magazine coming over that they think Mozart had Tourette's. You're in good company, anyway."

Paul buttered his roll, tasted it, found it excellent. Of course, Mozart. Would Mozart have composed if they'd had haloperidol back then? He allowed a tic to squeak out, a quick succession of jerks with his hand, ringing the bell.

"Fascinating," Royce said. "Well. Now that we've exchanged medical intimacies, I am absolutely dying to hear what it's like at Highwood. I haven't clapped eyes on the place for twenty years, but I have very fond memories."

Paul gave him a summary, omitting the anomalies of the damage and any of the speculations he and Lia had come up with. As he spoke, he watched Royce's face. How much of his behavior was an act? At his most genuine, most truthful, Royce had always seemed to be hiding something, savoring some secret knowledge, preserving a disconcerting ambiguity.

"My, my," Royce said when Paul finished. "Well, hats off to the culprit, for thoroughness at least. But you say the place is structurally intact? Walls still up, roof still on top, floor underneath?"

"Some of the interior walls have been broken open, but yes, it's structurally fine."

Royce's face was unreadable. "And how exactly did *you* become involved? My dear mother simply called for a white knight, did she? Out of the blue?"

Paul reached for his glass. "More or less."

"And you simply dropped everything to come piece old Highwood together?"

"As I told you, I'm out of work. It was good timing for me." Before Royce could resume grilling him, Paul continued: "Speaking of Vivien calling, what prompted you to call Aster—out of the blue? None of us have heard from you in quite a while."

Royce's eyes moved away to scan the restaurant. He raised his chin and one finger, calling the waiter. "We should order. At this time of day, it might take a little while, and I wouldn't want to keep you from your work." He paused and took a sip of water. "Why did I call Aster? Frankly, this is my first extended stay in New York for several years. By this I mean that I'm here for a week, the first time it's been more than twenty-four hours for I don't know how long. I'm planning to move back. It's all made me feel nostalgic. Of course I thought of the Skoglunds and I found I had Aster's number. We had an awfully nice chat. Odd, isn't it? How one's past can suddenly exert such persuasive power over one's emotions. As you so eloquently pointed out to me."

"I had no idea we were such a sentimental family," Paul said. "There seems to be an epidemic of it among us just now, doesn't there?" There was a way to deal with these Hoffmanns, he decided. Keep them a touch off balance themselves. Dodge and counter punch. Play a bit of their own game, the feints and bluffs and little provocations, all with a veneer of decorum.

Royce raised his water glass and smiled. With his toast, he seemed to acknowledge Paul as an equal. Or at least a respectable opponent.

Paul ordered a grilled swordfish fillet, Royce an oyster plate. The fingers of Paul's left hand explored the underside of the table, ritualistically touching the supports, finding each screw, counting, making rhythms and drawing geometric constellations.

They talked some more about Highwood. At one point, recalling his weapon collection, Royce had to laugh. "I was a wretchedly morbid little bastard, wasn't I?"

"You mean you aren't anymore?"

"Oh yes, more so. It's just that I have more mature ways to express it now that I'm of age."

"Such as?"

"In a word, business. I can get a very satisfying sadistic thrill by sitting at tables with other like-minded individuals—major shareholders and

CEOs—calculating ways to divest the unsuspecting masses, preferably in some other country, of their money or goods. There's enough intrigue and betrayal to make Machiavelli blush, because we all take great pleasure in being each other's allies one day and cutting each other's throats the next. And I can indulge my masochistic longings by joining some new committee or board and savoring the endless petty details, the tireless wrangling and infighting."

"Sounds terrific. What kind of businesses?" Royce was apparently narcissistic enough to enjoy talking about himself with little prompting.

"Oh, I own some percentage of various companies. Some I inherited, some I earned by my own perfidiousness. I employ myself at several and run errands on their behalf. The bulk of it is exporting American and European consumer goods to Indonesia, Malaysia, the Philippines. Some high-tech. Also importing raw materials from those places. I speculate. It's all quite humdrum. I hope I'm not a disappointment to you—in the face of the rather exotic possibilities that the situation at Highwood suggests."

"Speaking of which," Paul said, trying to keep Royce talking, "do you have any idea who might have vandalized the place?"

"Haven't the slightest."

"What did you mean by 'exotic possibilities,' then?"

Again Royce seemed pleased by Paul's assertiveness. "Why should you particularly care who did it?"

"I'm curious. And I'm nervous about being there if whoever did it comes back. I'd also like to do what I can to make sure it doesn't happen again the minute I finish." Paul kept the question alive with his eyes.

Royce sighed, the patient sigh of a martyred man. "My mother isn't known as an easy person to associate with. I imagine she has managed to make any number of enemies."

"Anyone specific come to mind?"

"Frankly, Paul, I'm the wrong person to ask. I haven't spoken to the old bitch in I don't know how many years. I've no idea whom she has antagonized in that time. Sorry."

Their food arrived, beautifully displayed on plates that continued the monkey motif. A warm cloud of scent rose from the swordfish and made Paul's mouth water. Royce probed his oysters with a tiny silver fork.

"Why do you hate her?"

Royce looked up at the chandeliered ceiling, as if the answer were up there, or were so vast it required a moment for him to capture the appropriate language. At last he brought his eyes down, squeezed lemon onto an oyster, brought the shell to his mouth, and sucked the puckered gray flesh into his mouth. He chewed rapturously for a moment, then swallowed.

"These are splendid—you ought to try one. Vivien? I've always hated her. Why don't you just assume it's simply a habit, a tradition, perhaps, that we both have grown accustomed to."

"You strike me as very similar people in a lot of ways."

Royce jabbed the air with his oyster fork as if catching the idea on its tines. "Yes, I'm sure that's it," he said, mimicking revelation.

"I just saw her, you know," Paul said. "In San Francisco. She said she'd had a sort of terminal weltschmertz, what she called Rimbaud's disease, when you were a boy. She said maybe you'd caught it from her. Doesn't blame you for keeping a distance."

"Sounds like her. So, how is the old black widow?"

"I found her to be an . . . amazing woman. Very observant and intelligent. She is also a very lonely person."

"I take it I'm supposed to take pity, feel contrite, and go patch things up with her?" Royce smiled sourly at Paul, then chose another oyster. "Enough about me," he said with heavy irony. "Now let's talk about you. At least give us an outrageous tic or two. I've been waiting with bated breath. Can't you give the maître d' the finger or some such?"

Paul smiled. He volunteered ordinary information about his life and about Mark and Aster and Kay.

"Lovely. And your sister—is she pretty? A man slayer?"

"Kay is pleasant and plump and looks every bit the suburban mother."

Royce got, or pretended to get, a wistful look in his eyes. "I always thought she would be a beauty. Had juvenile fantasies about her."

"So I gather."

Royce looked at him, amused, and then patted his lips with his napkin. "Oh, so we've been talking about cousin Royce? I'm flattered. What else did we say?"

"What do you think? She's my sister."

"Oh, Paul! Are you going to defend your sister's honor? Aren't you a little late? I don't know what she told you, but let me give you *my* perspective. Frankly, your sister was a little hussy. She tripped me and hit the ground before I did."

When Paul started to object, Royce reached across the table and pinned his wrist with one large hand, gripping it with surprising strength. His eyes burned into Paul's, deadly serious. "The thing is, Paul, the real thing is this: *Truth is subjective.* It's what I say it is for me. For your sister, it's what she says it is. I'll make it whatever suits me, for whatever convoluted reasons, whether I know it or admit it or not. So will Kay. *And all you'll be doing, when you decide which of us you believe, is more of the same.*" Royce let go of Paul's wrist, and the sudden flush on his face began to recede. "Something to keep in mind when the past comes back to visit us with its little moods and its little revelations." He tugged the cuffs of his shirt, glanced sharply at Paul, and went back to his oysters.

Paul said nothing for a moment. Apart from his investment in Kay's truthfulness, he had to agree with Royce. It was one of the big ones, the big ugly scaries that you had to face sooner or later: The world is a dreamscape, where things change shape, where everything is subject to interpretation and no interpretation lasts. He'd have resented Royce's outburst if he didn't feel, for the first time, that Royce was revealing something he truly cared about, something he'd had to struggle with.

"I'll take it into consideration," Paul said. His wrist tingled unpleasantly from the strange soft-hard grip of Royce's hand. Willing his pulse to slow, he turned his attention back to his meal. The swordfish was excellent, with a delicate, peppery crust and white flesh that melted like butter in his mouth. He ate the last of it slowly, determined to savor his lunch despite the company.

32

The elevator door opened directly into Royce's foyer and they stepped out.

"So this is my New York sanctum," Royce said. He took off his overcoat and hung it in a closet, then led Paul down a hallway with a high ceiling, agreeably lit by skylights. "Bought it, oh, ten years ago, only stay here when I'm in town. Only seven rooms, but I find it rather pleasant for a small place."

The hall gave way by arched doorways to other rooms: a large L-shaped living room, a formal dining room, a kitchen.

"I'm going to visit the W.C. Feel free to wander around." Royce disappeared down the short hallway, and Paul went into the living room.

It was a huge room, sparsely but impeccably decorated: white walls, floors a fine parquet of aged white oak covered with superb Navajo rugs. Sleek hardwood furniture stood in several clusters, brightly colored abstract canvases hung on the walls. Asian and African masks and weapons hung here and there, crisply isolated against the spacious walls. On two sides of the room, a row of windows and a pair of French doors opened onto a terrace that ran around the top of the building. Outside were potted trees and shrubs, white wrought-iron furniture and arbor, a patinaed brass railing, and a fine view of Central Park.

Paul inspected several rooms and after a few minutes returned to the living room, where he paused in front of a crossed pair of short swords with notched blades, thinking over what he'd seen. Wainscoting, walls, paneled ceilings: The place was in pristine shape. It didn't need any work.

Royce appeared at his side from the hallway. "Philippine headhunters' knives," he said with satisfaction. "That half-moon notch is just about the diameter of an average neck and very sharp. I got them from my father, who got them from their makers. Who knows how many necks these have severed?" He ran his thumb along one edge. "Funny—now *headhunting* is a term we use for hiring away another company's executives. Done a bit of it myself."

Royce took him on a short tour of the apartment, then led him to the kitchen, where he started water in a teapot on a stove situated in a central island. The spacious counters were white marble, scattered with kitchen gadgets in white plastic and chrome. Royce took a chair at a small table near the windows and began spooning ground coffee from a foil pouch into a French plunger coffeemaker.

"Here's the thing, cousin. I'd like you to do the work. I need to be away, and you'd be welcome to stay here while you worked on it. Good area, close to the museums and whatnot. I'd imagine it might be a relief from the long Vermont winter."

"I'm sure it would be," Paul said. "But I'm not sure how long Highwood will take. Depending on Vivien's plans, the restoration up there may take the rest of the winter." This seemed to capture Royce's interest, and Paul immediately regretted saying anything about Vivien's intentions. His fingers began moving, playing tunes on the underside of the table.

"Oh? What exactly did she say about her plans?" Royce asked, preoccupied with the coffee.

"Just that. We'll get the place into safe shape, then give her an estimate for different levels of restoration, let her decide then what she wants to do."

Royce stroked his chin, appeared to consider this for a moment. "Because I'd really need you to start work here right away. I'm leaving in a few days, as I told you, and when I return in several weeks I'd like to have the job done. I plan to hold one of those significant social events to announce my return to the old Big Apple, and I'd like the place to be perfect."

"It's already perfect," Paul said.

"The point being that whoever takes the job must be prepared to start work immediately." The water in the teapot increased its rumble and the steam began to whistle feebly in intermittent pulses. Royce stood up and waited at the stove.

"Then that leaves me out. I've already got a commitment for this time period."

Royce's eyes flashed at him, irritated. "What are you making working for my mother? Fifteen dollars an hour? Twenty? I said I'd pay top dollar. In New York City, that means two or three times what she's paying you." The water came to a full boil, blowing a cone of steam and a steady shriek from the spout. Royce ignored it. "I'd like you to do the work, Paul."

"I said I can't."

"You drive a hard bargain, don't you?" Royce forced a smile. "I hadn't figured you for the type. Okay, eighty dollars an hour. But only if you start work immediately."

It was a staggering sum, as much as most teachers in Vermont made in a day. Paul shook his head, the whistle shrilling in his eardrums. "I can't. I've made another agreement. Would you mind taking the teapot off? It's giving me a headache."

Royce didn't move. "You're more than willing to ingratiate yourself with my mother—why not with me, at four times the pay? Don't give me this crap about the professional ethics of the handyman."

Paul stood up, slapped at the stove knob. The whistle subsided. He wanted to leave the apartment, get away from Royce. There was something twisted in Royce, something awful just below the civilized surface. Suddenly being near him had become unbearably oppressive.

"*Fuck!* One," Paul said, "I'm not ingratiating myself with anyone. I'm helping out my aunt, and I'm getting paid for my professional services. Two: This place doesn't need anything. It's fine. What's your angle?"

"I'm so glad I get to witness a few of the famous obscenities. Sit down, Paulie. Why are we arguing?" Royce had regained control over himself. His voice was smooth again, suddenly conciliatory, although his hands shook as he poured the water into the coffeemaker and inserted the plunger. "Look. I agree, the place isn't in bad shape. But—and don't take this the wrong way—here in Manhattan, when your work requires you make an impression, standards are high. 'Not bad' isn't good enough. See, the whole system works on *faith*, Paulie. Faith in a company, faith in a product, faith in the value of a currency. The stock market stays up because the gamblers have enough faith to buy in, not sell out. Right? Money is no different from any other religion, it works on reverence, awe, and blind goddamned faith. Now, I regularly move money around, big sums of it, more than my own liquidity at any given point. That means I use other people's money, and that means I need them to have *faith*. Say I'm having people over, courting an investment of millions of dollars—I have to look sound. *Absolutely* sound."

Royce slowly depressed the plunger. "I need top-quality work and I want someone I can trust in here when I'm away. Who better than you? Surely you can understand that."

Paul felt himself wavering. Royce was pointing out, not without tact, that there were cultural differences between them. Maybe the standards of Royce's class and income bracket weren't something he really understood.

Paul walked out of the room. Whatever else, he needed to get away from Royce. "I'll think about it, okay, Royce? Best I can do. If you need a decision right away, there are hundreds of contractors in New York. If you want somebody you can trust, look for one that's licensed and insured. You've got a Yellow Pages."

"I can see I've underestimated you, cousin. Fine, give it a day or so. Let's make it a hundred dollars an hour, first month paid in advance," Royce called after him. "Say fifteen thousand advance. Provided you start within the next few days."

"Thanks for lunch," Paul growled over his shoulder. "You're a big spender. I'm impressed no end." The anger seemed to well up out of nowhere, and his abdomen ticced in spasms. He found his scarf and gloves in the foyer closet and punched the elevator call button.

Royce followed him into the hall. "You think I'm fucked up?" he said, speaking softly now. "Then go ahead, work for Vivien. You don't know what fucked up means. Fair warning, cousin."

The elevator door opened, and Paul stepped inside. As the doors drew closed, Royce stood broad-shouldered and agitated at the end of the hall, looking after him and still fumbling with the coffee plunger, which seemed to have lodged, the shaft bent, halfway down the cylinder. Paul's revulsion gave way to embarrassment, the sense that he'd overreacted, and a feeling for Royce less like anger than, unexpectedly, pity.

Driving back along the crowded Saw Mill River Parkway, Paul tried to smooth out his emotions. After seeing Royce, he'd driven down to Chinatown, where he bought gifts for Janet and Mark. Fighting the heavy city traffic had exhausted him. And now the MG's motor was stuttering occasionally, reawakening his perennial concern about its reliability. His stomach felt sour, as if he'd eaten something rancid, although the food had been first-rate.

His thoughts drifted back to the preceding days, and abruptly he caught the thought that had teased him that first day as he hefted the broken finial at the lodge. He sat up out of the slump he'd fallen into behind the wheel.

It had to do with some reading he'd done while tracking down an idea about Mark. Specifically, it was a reference in a book he'd read called *The Violent Personality*, by a Dr. Emmett Childers. Mark was not habitually violent; on the contrary, he was fairly mild and prematurely adult in many ways. But his seizures, if that's what they were, often ended in fits of violence, and Paul had begun looking for known neurological origins for violent behavior. He'd found a few ideas that might bear upon Mark's condition—and had also stumbled upon a footnote in Dr. Childers' book that could conceivably explain the damage at Highwood.

He couldn't remember the exact words, but the note dealt briefly with reports of hyperkinesia and hyperdynamism. The medical term *hyperkinesia* was commonly used in connection with various psychopathologies from bipolar disorders to schizophrenia to drug responses and was often associated with hyperactivity in children. Hyperkinesic individuals moved their bodies and limbs excessively, at high speed, often inappropriately and with minimal control.

Rarer was a related condition, *hyperdynamism*—spontaneous displays of unusual or "superhuman" strength. Childers claimed that although hyperdynamism was not unknown in medical literature, it was very rare, and most reports were no doubt greatly exaggerated. The footnote had concluded with the mild suggestion that the phenomenon warranted further research.

Paul had barely glanced at the footnote at the time, reading fast and screening for information relevant to Mark, and had forgotten it immediately. But now it came back to him. He'd have to find the reference again. It was a terrifying thought, but hyperdynamism was one explanation for the finial that had been forcibly broken off while remaining unmarked by any impact. "Hit it with a couch," Lia had joked. *Or, if you're strong enough,* Paul thought, *with the palm of your hand.*

33

Paul took one of the green wing-back chairs and sipped cognac from a bottle of Remy-Martin that Lia had found, miraculously intact and unopened, in the cupboard. Lia sat across from him. The lantern hissed fiercely on the table, throwing a harsh white light that cut sharp shadows in the room. Frowning, he told Lia about Royce's interest in the state of Highwood and his urgent desire to hire Paul to do something that didn't need doing for ridiculously high pay.

"A bribe—I love it. Did you confront him on it?" Lia took the bottle from him, swigged, returned it.

"Yeah. He gave me a concise overview of our cultural differences. When I said the walls were fine, he told me that different standards pertain among the very wealthy."

"Well, it's not totally implausible, is it?"

Paul sighed wearily, rolling the liquid in the bottle. "No," he admitted.

"Did you ask him if he was our midnight caller?"

"As a matter of fact, I did. 'Why, no, cousin. Didn't speak to your mother until just this morning. Didn't know you would be there.' "

"Because Janet called, and it wasn't her—I asked. She'd gotten your message from this morning."

"Is Mark okay?"

"She didn't mention anything, so I assume there wasn't any emergency. Just her usual chilly self. She said you could try her again tonight." Lia reached for the cognac again. "And then Vivien called. 'Is this Lia?' she asked. 'I wondered if Paulie would rope you into helping him.' I gave her a quick rundown on our progress. We only talked for a minute."

"Well, I suppose that's a relief."

"Yes. But before you let your shoulders down entirely, I should tell you that a funny thing happened with Dempsey." Lia scowled. "I was in and out of the library, sorting a box, back and forth, right? So one time I poke my head in, and there's Dempsey scrabbling through the papers, picking up a page, reading it quickly, tossing it down, picking up another. As if he were looking for something specific. He didn't see me."

"Oh, Christ," Paul said.

"Maybe he's worried Vivien has something unpleasant on him, along with the rest of the dirt in her files."

"I don't believe there's any scandal in Dempsey's past. He's not that kind of person. He's always been very aboveboard about his beliefs and actions."

"What, then?"

Paul's neck torqued uncontrollably, whipping his head around. "I have no idea. I'll just have to ask him about it tonight."

Responding to his agitation, Lia went to stand behind him and began massaging his neck. Her strong fingers probed the muscles there, intuitively finding the knots of tension at the base of his skull, loosening them. Paul shut his eyes and gave himself to the sensation of her hands on him.

In the silence he became aware of the big empty disordered darkness of the main hall, pressing against the closed door of the smoking room. He debated telling her about what he was feeling. But what could he say? *Strange resonances in his memory. A big, dark, webbed, shadowed thing—*

"Can I ask you something?" he said at last. "Now that you've spent a day here, don't you ever get a . . . weird feeling about it? Like something's wrong here—something very fucked up?"

"Of course. I think the people who did this have very screwed-up priorities. But that goes without saying. I take it you mean something else."

Paul leaned into her fingers. "I have these memories—being up here, going into the woods, then something else. Something that frightened me."

"Like what?"

How could he describe it? Lia was skeptical of the idea of memory repression, the recovered-memory fad that had resulted in so many recollections of satanic ritual abuse. The allegations of bloodletting rituals, cannibalism, incest, forced abortion, and murder were simply too fantastic to believe.

He gestured with his hands, trying to describe the sense of it. "It's as if I remember the feeling, or the *texture* of it, but past a certain point no visual images come to mind. Just this disturbing, unsettling, scary . . . *turbulence,* this feeling like . . ." He gestured again and then stopped, startled. He was making a tumbling motion with his two hands, the exact movement Mark had made when trying to describe the sensation of his seizures.

"Wow," he said.

"What now?"

Paul took her hands and held them, leaning his head back against her breasts. "Nothing," he said. "I've just got a lot to think about."

Again, it was a relief to sit in the warmth and order of the Corrigans' beautiful house after the chaos at Highwood. They had eaten another of Elaine's incredible dishes, a mouthwatering kielbasa stew served to the strains of Debussy string quartets on the stereo. After drinking half a bottle of rich Barolo, Dempsey seemed to have recovered from his earlier depressed mood, and he launched into a narrative about one of the odd characters who used to live in the region.

"He lived in the woods," Dempsey said. "They called him the Leather Man because he wore a suit he'd made out of scraps he'd salvaged—a crazy quilt of different colors and thicknesses of leather, roughly sewn together. He had a range about the size of a puma's, all over northern Westchester and southern Putnam Counties. You'd see him walking, sometimes along the road, sometimes crossing it as he headed overland." He gestured with a hunk of bread.

Elaine laughed. "Dempsey talks as if he'd seen him. The Leather Man died twenty or thirty years before you were born, dear."

"What did he do?" Lia asked. "How did he survive?"

"Aha." Dempsey continued. "He scavenged food some, or lived off the land like a bear. He was big as a bear too—with a heavy, evil-looking face. Parents would tell children the Leather Man would get them if they didn't behave. Paradoxically, he was considered slightly magical, strange enough that to get a visit from him was considered a good omen. There's a universal human trait for you: We revere the strange."

The old man went on, elaborating. Ordinarily Paul would have been fascinated, but the day's events, and the prospect of asking Dempsey what he was looking for in the library, made it hard for him to concentrate.

Paul waited until Lia and Elaine took off on a conversational tangent, then turned to Dempsey. "How're those Linnell chairs of yours doing?"

Dempsey's eyes caught his briefly. "Well, they're coming. Haven't had as much time, with the Highwood windows, but I've got all the new parts in place. Want to see 'em?"

In the workshop Dempsey hit the light switch, and the overhead fluorescents blinked and came on. "Okay," Dempsey said. "This isn't a casual visit to the shop. What's up?"

"I want to know what's going on at Highwood."

Dempsey's eyes wandered from Paul's face. "How would I know? Kids, crackheads, somebody mad at Vivien—?"

"I mean, what's going on for *you* there?" Paul's heart was hammering, his body was seething with tics. "You've been trying to find something in Vivien's papers. I want to know if it's anything I should know about."

Dempsey turned away, walked half the length of the workshop, then turned back. "It's nothing that bears on you or the damage to the house or your job there."

"I also hate the thought that Dempsey Corrigan is keeping anything from me."

"Look, Paulie." Dempsey threw his hands wide, a gesture of exasperation. "I'm a little drunk right now. It feels good, but it doesn't help me think straight at this moment. Part of me says, 'Hey, Paulie, it's my business, leave it be, let an old guy have his private life.' "

"So what's the other part say?"

"Aah," Dempsey growled in self-disgust. "It reminds me that your father was my best friend, and that I've always cared about your family. And yeah, I never had kids, there's a father-and-son thing between you and me, and I don't want anything to come in the way of it. Not even my old regrets, though I'm goddamned well fully entitled to them."

Paul flicked his mustache with both hands as the two men listened to the buzz of the lights for a moment. "Do me a favor, Dempsey. Let me know what's going on. I've got my own stuff to unravel. Maybe what you tell me will help."

Dempsey rubbed the white stubble on his chin, then appeared to make a decision. "Okay, fine. Fine. It's not flattering to me, but what the hell. I'd always suspected Vivien kept everything, and seeing that heap of papers proved it. I was looking for some correspondence." He coughed, cleared his throat. "Letters from me to Vivien."

"Why not just ask Lia and me to keep an eye peeled for them? We'll turn them up eventually."

"That's exactly why I wanted to find them. So that you wouldn't."

It was Paul's turn to walk away, swinging his arms, trying to dispel some of the tension. "Jesus. You and Vivien?"

"Yeah. Like I said—a long time ago."

"So what's the big deal? As you've always said, people do that kind of thing. I mean, she was divorced, you—"

"I was married to Elaine at the time. And I'd as soon my dear wife didn't find out at this late date. I lost my head, I wrote stupid letters, I'd prefer you and Lia didn't read them. Vivien was a good-looking woman, I was full of juice. Remember, this was after she'd spent ten miserable years waiting for Hoffmann to come back to her. Not to make me sound chivalrous, but after Hoffmann, that woman was really hurting." He waited expectantly, but Paul had nothing to say. "Now you know. So let's go open another bottle of wine and forget it."

"Jesus," Paul said. "You've been worrying about that? I don't care. People of my generation aren't so easily scandalized by extramarital affairs,

Dempsey. Christ, we all grew up watching it on the tube, reading about the illicit affairs of prominent people—"

"You might surprise yourself someday," Dempsey said gruffly.

Paul followed him to the workshop door. "But what do you want me to do? Lia and I have to get the papers cleaned up. Lia's looking over every piece—she's playing detective. Also, Vivien says there are more letters from Ben up there. I'm really wanting to read them."

"Of course." Dempsey stopped with his hand on the doorknob. "I just think you're going to have to figure out how to show some regard for Vivien's privacy, and mine. If it looks like a personal letter, don't read it. Lia will respect that, won't she?"

"There're a lot of letters. Were yours handwritten? Typed?"

Dempsey thought for a moment. "I don't remember. Thirty-five god-damned years ago." He opened the door and they stepped outside into the chill night air. The light over the workshop door cut a circle of brightness around them as Dempsey replaced the padlock on its hasp. "So it's a deal then, Paulie? You'll relay my request to Lia?"

"Of course," Paul said. "Look, I'm glad you told me about this. You've seemed awfully tense up there. I hope you can relax about it now."

"Sure." Dempsey flipped the light switch and the late autumn darkness came around them, but not before Paul caught a glimpse of the old man's face, his lips a tight straight line, brows lowered, eyes distant. Anything but relaxed.

34

They came over the crest and again the headlights panned the demolished garden and the dark lodge, its wet-looking, glistening window plastic bulging and going slack again in a slight breeze, as if the house were breathing. When Paul cut the lights, the blinding darkness seemed to suck into the cab. They both sat in the dark, unwilling to leave the warmth of the car.

"What happened when you guys went out to the shop?" Lia asked. "Did you talk to Dempsey about—?"

"Yeah. He says there are some letters he wrote to Vivien that he'd like to find."

Lia made a little noise in her throat. "Letters of a compromising sort, I take it. So Dempsey and Vivien had an affair."

Paul just looked at her, barely able to make out her silhouette in the blackness.

"I suspected as much, from the way he's been acting about this," she explained. "All that melancholy, anxiety, his falling out with Vivien—"

"Well, that all blew right past *me*. Anyway, he requested that we avoid reading the letters if and when we come across them. He said he thought we should respect Vivien's privacy more too, not read any letters."

"Well, I'm not *reading* anything much, really. I certainly scan each page to see what it is, where it should be filed. It's a very fine line. Anyway, how'll we ever figure anything out? Besides, now the cat's out of the bag, right?"

Paul went to the dark kitchen to call Vivien, leaving Lia in the warmth of the smoking room, sorting papers. He shoved aside some rubble and sat on the counter, blowing steam into air as still and cold as a meat locker. Leaning forward from his seat, he could see the rectangle of bright light around the smoking room door, suspended in the cavernous darkness of the big room. A series of irresistible tics pulled the right side of his face into a snarl, and he waited for them to subside before shining the flashlight on the phone and dialing Vivien's number.

"Oh, Paulie," Vivien said. "Are you calling from Highwood?"

"As a matter of fact, I am. We just got back from dinner, and I thought I should check in." He brought her up on their activities to date.

"I'm glad you have matters so well in hand," she said when he finished. "I have been worried about the old house. About . . . everything." There was a reedy, tired sound in her voice, almost a wistful quality. "Recently, I find myself feeling quite ambivalent, Paulie. There's a part of me that misses the place, that looks back fondly and wants to protect all the things I left behind. As I told you, they're the only proof I have that I've ever been young, or married, or a mother. Some tangible connection to my younger self." She sighed, then went on. "The other half of me, frankly, is relieved to be out of the lonely castle on the hill, and only too eager to shed the accumulated detritus, the confining shell of my old life."

"Yes, I sense that ambivalence," Paul said carefully.

"And what about your own existential quest? No sign of Rimbaud's disease, I hope? I've wondered if it's contagious."

"No," he said. "No Rimbaud's disease."

"What about the ghosts? I'm curious as to how being at Highwood has affected you."

"I haven't encountered any ghosts, but, frankly, it's not always a lot of fun here. Working here seems to dredge up more of the past than I'm sure I want to deal with all at once."

"Now you know, to some small degree, how I would feel were I to return. Have you found any more of your father's letters?"

"No. Just a newspaper article about his death. It mentioned that he was upset over family problems. I wondered what those might have been." Despite his resistance to her probing, it was a relief to ask her.

"You will have to ask Aster, won't you. Of course, I can understand that you might have some reticence to do so."

"Then why'd he do it? Why'd he jump? Why did he leave his family?"

She seemed to consider how to answer him. "Your father was a complex man," she said cryptically. Then her arc of emotion abruptly changed, and her voice became acid again. "Why indeed do men do such things? Ben 'went.' Just as my husband 'went'—in a different way, but just as decisively. In fact, this is something I spoke about with your lovely-sounding wife earlier today."

"About what?"

"About the difficulties a woman encounters when her husband has chosen to 'go.' "

What she was saying didn't make sense. "Wait—you talked to Lia about this?"

"Lia? Oh, heavens, no! *Janet.* I had a lovely talk with her today. I'm sorry—I should have said your *ex-wife*, shouldn't I? But being an *ex* is a concept I just can't quite grasp. Once you've had a child with someone, how could you ever really be *ex* anything? Of course, that may be a sentiment your generation is incapable of feeling."

Paul felt tumbled off balance. Calling Janet—during their ten years of marriage, he wasn't sure he'd ever so much as mentioned Vivien to her.

"Why did you want to talk to Janet?" he said at last.

"Why indeed would I do that? I didn't. She called me." Vivien's voice hardened further. "It seems she wanted to know some details about your employment at Highwood. Such as how long you were likely to remain employed and how much you were getting paid. It sounded as though you two were not, how shall I put it, on the best of terms at the moment. If I were you, Paulie, I would consider looking into legal advice. You know what I'm talking about."

Paul felt his breath go out of him. *Child custody.* Janet's making calls could only mean she was planning something ugly.

He realized he hadn't said anything for some time when Vivien spoke again. "Are you there, Paulie?"

"I'm here."

"Oh, good. One never knows, at Highwood—so often the lines go down."

Paul slid off the counter and began to pace at the end of the telephone cord, his boots crunching on the broken china littering the floor. He remembered what he'd learned about dealing with Vivien and Royce: fight back. Slip the punch, counter hard. "Vivien, I'd like to keep Mark, and my marriage situation, and any existential problems I have, or you think I have, out of our discussions. I'm here to do a job. That's all."

"Calm down," Vivien said, a note of command in her voice. "Do you feel I'm being intrusive? How do you think I feel—my whole life spread out for you and your little girlfriend and who knows how many others to paw through? You have no doubt seen many things I would just as soon keep private. I rather enjoy the idea that we're a little more even now. I never solicited any contact with your wife—your *ex*—and frankly, I'd just as soon not be drawn into your tawdry affairs. You can spare me your righteous indignation."

He wondered briefly how she would react if he told her he'd seen Royce, if he told her what Royce had said about her, but he restrained himself. It was one thing learning to spar with these Hoffmanns; it was another thing entirely to become one of them.

Suddenly the light changed in the kitchen, and Paul turned to see Lia at the open smoking room door, light spilling from behind her and silhouetting the sweet woman-shape of her body. She made jabbering motions with her hands, then stepped back inside.

"Vivien, I'd like to get going now. It's after midnight here."

"I'd much prefer we didn't end this conversation on such a sour note, nephew."

"Wouldn't that be nice."

"I had so hoped we could chat about something more pleasant. Our neurological hobby, for example. I've decided I have a problem with my glucocortinoids. They're the chemicals you manufacture to cope with stress or crisis. But too much in your bloodstream can be bad for you—high blood pressure and so on."

"Vivien, I'd love to talk with you about this, but it'll have to be some other time. I've got to go now."

"You should look into glucocortinoids, Paulie. They're very interesting."

"I'll do that." The heat of Paul's anger had given way to a chill, and he wanted only to get off the phone and into the warm room with Lia.

"Yes, do. Sometimes these things run in families." Suddenly she burst into full-throated laughter, startling him. She gained control over herself with difficulty. "Good night, nephew," she said, and hung up.

It was five after midnight, too late to call Janet. No sense in making her angrier than she already apparently was. It would have to wait until morning. He took a few deep breaths to calm himself, then crossed the main hall to the smoking room. Lia sat in one of the wing chairs, eyes shut, hands crossed in her lap.

"I thought you'd never finish," she said, not opening her eyes.

"Yeah. Well. She seemed to want to yak at me. I'm sorry. Find anything interesting in here?" Paul's voice sounded hoarse to him. They unconsciously tended to speak in low voices in here, he realized, as if not wanting to attract attention to their presence in the empty house.

"I didn't do much sorting. Got too tired." Lia yawned. "Same stuff I've been looking at all day—old bills, miscellaneous newspaper clippings, how-to pamphlets on raising bonsai. Oh, and medical papers. Apparently Vivien liked to correspond with doctors."

"Tell me about it," Paul said dryly.

They brought the lantern with them through the wrecked house, Paul uncomfortably aware of how its hiss deafened him. The harsh white light threw monstrous shadows on the walls as they crossed the main room. It was a relief to get into the simplicity of the carriage house, to dowse the noisy lantern and light a candle.

They undressed and got into the sleeping bags. Paul had just snuffed the candle when the telephone in the lodge began ringing. He groaned, Lia got up on one elbow. They listened to the ringing, on and on, in the darkness. It rang forty-three times.

Suddenly amid the sadness, spiritual darkness, and depression, his brain seemed to catch fire . . . and with an extraordinary momentum his vital forces were strained to the utmost all at once. His sensation of being alive and his awareness increased tenfold at those moments which flashed by like lightning.

Reflecting about that moment afterwards . . . he arrived at last at the paradoxical conclusion: "What if it is a disease? . . . What does it matter that it is an abnormal tension, if the result . . . gives a feeling, undivined and undreamt of till then, of completeness, proportion, reconciliation, and an ecstatic and prayerful fusion in the highest synthesis of life?"

—FYODOR DOSTOYEVSKY

35

Priscilla stood in the dark driveway, looking up nervously at the lodge's empty windows, thinking: How'd I get into this? *This was nuts, it was the second of November and too cold to be going anywhere on a fucking motorcycle. The whole idea was insane, even with Eddy's planning: how they'd make the first trip on his motorcycle, which could get around the junked car at the bottom of the driveway, and which they could park out of sight in the woods when they went inside to scope out the lodge. They'd go through the place and select the stuff they were going to take and pile it in the woods down near the road, under a tarp. It would take them several trips, carrying stuff down the driveway in the dark, but it would be worth it because the next day they'd need only a minute to stop Eddy's station wagon, throw the stuff in, drive away. Nobody would see them or get the license number. Eddy in his Mr. Slick mode had explained to her how foolproof his scheme was, how easy, how safe. He'd heard about the abandoned house from his kid brother, who had a friend in high school over here. Some rich person had just gone away and left everything inside, and the place was wide open for anyone with the brains to see what an opportunity it was. Eddy prided himself on being a guy who recognized opportunity when it knocked.*

Priscilla felt her arms getting tired, and she put down the laundry bag full of valuable things they'd culled from the wreckage inside. There hadn't been that much after all, because the place was so badly vandalized, worse than anyone could have imagined, and few things were left unbroken. The damage level was sicko, even Eddy had been taken aback when they'd first gone inside, scared but trying to hide it.

What was Eddy doing? "One last thing I wanna get," *he'd said, and then disappeared back into the house. Now he was taking his time, and she could hear the bumps and thumps of him tossing things around inside. What was he looking for? It was getting colder out here, the motorcycle ride back to Waterbury would be killer. Plus the looming darkness of the big house, so crazy wrecked-up inside, had begun to scare her. This was the last time she'd do any-*

thing even remotely crooked with Eddy. In fact, face it, it was time to ask herself whether Eddy was really a good emotional investment. His Mr. Slick facade had long since worn thin, and the real poverty of what was beneath had begun to show through: a guy whose ambition had already topped out at being a convenience-store clerk and part-time, small-time hood running little scams like this. This was nuts. The whole relationship was nuts.

A little wind had come up, stirring the trees and bushes, spooking her. "Eddy, goddamn it, come on!" she called quietly.

It was strange to realize so suddenly that she was done with Eddy, with anyone like Eddy. It was so unexpected, yet the realization had been there for months. You could live on two levels at once, knowing something but not knowing it, living one reality outside you and another in your mind and heart, and not even noticing there was a discrepancy between them until something happened to wake you up—some event that scared you or challenged you enough. On one level she made love with Eddy, told herself they were okay together, went along with his personas of Mr. Slick and Little Boy Vulnerable. But inside, she yearned to be with a man who loved her, who she could really love, she had even played a movie in her head of going to her mother with someone and saying, "Mom, this is the man I love," and being proud of him as she said it.

The problem was she'd always forget that movie as daily life made its demands and offered its little problems and pleasures. Fervently, she vowed that when they got back from this stupid trip she'd do two things: One, she'd start the complicated process of figuring out how to disengage from Eddy, trying not to hurt him but not being deflected either. And two, most important, she would never again forget that movie or any of the other important things inside her, she would notice and honor them and be one person and not two or three who hardly even knew each other.

A shape moved in the doorway as a piece of darkness detached itself from the black rectangle and took human form on the terrace. At first she felt relief: Now they could start down and get the hell out of here. Then she realized it wasn't Eddy.

For a moment the shape stood in one place, just outside the door. But it wasn't motionless, she realized. In the poor light she couldn't see well, but the person seemed to be vibrating or rippling, every part moving, dancing in place, pulsating, palpitating. It was the most horrible thing she had ever seen. With a jerk the oval shape of the person's face turned toward her and saw her and she knew where she'd seen that kind of movement before: her cat, hunting in the backyard, tracking a bird's movement instantly with that almost mechanical twitch of its head.

Then the person twitched again, moving in a blink and stopping between her and the driveway down. A strange rhythmic noise came from the indis-

tinct shape, and it seemed to exude a current of warm air, thick with a sharp, plastic smell. For a second Priscilla stood paralyzed by fascination and terror. Then it darted straight at her, and she turned without thinking and began to run the only way open to her, back into the deep black woods behind the house.

36

"**Mr.** Skoglund? I'm Morgan Ford. I'm an investigator with the Bureau of Criminal Investigation of the New York State Police. I'd like to talk with you for a few minutes, if you don't mind." Mo held out his badge.

The driveway had proven to be much steeper and longer than Mo had expected. As he followed its curves up, he realized that it would be hard to find a more likely spot for teenagers looking for a love nest or a place to cut loose in any number of ways.

At the door, a gangly kid wearing enormous basketball shoes had led him inside through a crazed junk heap that had once been a kitchen, and on into a room the size of a movie theater, where Mo stopped, stunned. It was, as Rizal had said, as if a bomb had gone off. Yet in some ways it was more appalling. A bomb was indiscriminate, creating a simple circular pattern of destruction with its locus at the point of detonation and progressively less damage farther away from the center. This was different. This damage was everywhere, and clearly it had all been done by deliberate acts—twisting, rending, smashing, ripping, throwing.

"You guys are something," Skoglund said. He was about Mo's age, dressed in jeans, work boots, and a lumberjack shirt. He raised both his hands and seemed to slap himself in the face, keeping a baleful gaze on Mo. "You going to play Rizal's game? Let me see a search warrant, Detective. I've cut you guys all the slack you get. Show me the warrant or get off the premises."

Mo was unprepared for the man's hostility. "I don't have a warrant. I'm just here to ask—"

"Then get out. Now," Skoglund said. *"Fark!"* He choked back a cough and slapped his face again, moustache then eyebrows, two quick pats with each hand.

Out of the corner of his eye, Mo saw an old man coming toward him from the center of the big room. He took a step backward and turned fractionally so he could keep an eye on both men. "There's a misunderstanding, Mr. Skoglund. I'm here because I hoped you might be able to help me locate some missing teenagers. I think some of them may have come up here, and we might find some indication of it in the house. Although, with the place like this, I can see it's going to be harder than I thought."

A woman with red-blond hair appeared in the doorway next to Skoglund, putting her hand on his arm. "At least let him tell us what he wants, Paul. Why don't you come in, Detective—the cold's getting in with the door open. It's okay, Dempsey." Behind Mo, the old man stopped and waited.

Skoglund stepped back grudgingly, and Mo went through the door. Except for the presence of a kerosene heater and a row of file boxes, and the shattered mirror over the fireplace, the room was more or less normal.

"Thanks," Mo said. "Look, I hate to bother you—I'm sure you've got plenty to keep you busy." When they continued to look at him expressionlessly, he smiled awkwardly. "Sorry, supposed to be a joke. In any case, there seems to be some confusion here. It sounds like Trooper Rizal has been by?"

"Rizal was up here hassling me a few days ago. I called in to complain about his first visit. I haven't decided what I'm going to do about today's crap. If I were really under suspicion, he wouldn't have come up here to warn me. Which says to me he's just harassing us. The only question I have is *why*."

"Slow down, please. Suspicion for—?"

"Today he was back, telling me I'm a prime suspect in some drug selling. He implied he'd trump up drug-dealing charges on me if he felt like it."

Uniform troopers did sometimes run legwork for BCI Narco investigations. Conceivably Rizal was assisting some investigation connected with Highwood. It should be easy enough to check.

"I don't know anything about it," Mo said. "As I said, I'm looking into something else. I'm not accusing you of anything, I'm asking for your assistance. In fact, I'm—" He hesitated, then plugged ahead: "This is a pretty unofficial visit. That's because this is what my supervisor considers a longshot lead. We disagree on that." Immediately he chided himself for revealing so much.

"Why don't you sit down," the woman said. "We were about to take a coffee break anyway. There's no electricity yet, but we've got a big Thermos."

Mo took a seat and accepted the Styrofoam cup she handed him. Paul Skoglund pulled a chair around and poured himself a cup of coffee, and the three of them sat facing each other. Mo introduced himself in more detail, then gave them a general overview of his investigation, avoiding details—just enough information to persuade them to give a consent search.

Skoglund and the woman, Lia McLean, explained how they came to be involved at the house. As they talked, Mo appraised them. Paul Skoglund was tall, fit, with light brown hair, and, now that his anger and mistrust had dissipated, an open, friendly face. He seemed to have a lot of nervous gestures and occasionally repeated the barklike cough. Two thin vertical lines rose between his brows, the traces of worry that Mo associated with people of conscience.

But the woman. Lia. *Oh God,* Mo thought, *not this.* He tried to avoid looking at her except to meet her eyes occasionally, as he did Paul's, consciously distributing his gaze so as not to look like the heart-on-his-sleeve asshole he was. She was wearing jeans and a thick sweater and absurd embroidered purple socks above white running shoes. A band of late-afternoon sunshine fell across her as she sat, setting her thick hair on fire. Perfect legs, exactly the kind of strength in her thighs he most admired. A heart-shaped face, youthful but for a faint band of purple below each eye which gave her otherwise confident appearance a touch of vulnerability that Mo found himself hopelessly susceptible to. And that *alertness* about her: incredibly clear eyes with a disconcertingly acute focus. There was no wedding ring on her finger, but from the way she looked at Skoglund, the way they touched each other, it was clear they were either married or at the very least shacking up. Mo felt the familiar misery of his longing come over him, and cursed himself.

"So there are several vectors that seem to intersect here," Lia said. "You're hearing indications from several sources that at least two teenagers were here shortly before their disappearances. And there's a possible connection to another case, which I'm presuming you don't wish to tell us too much about for confidentiality reasons."

"Exactly."

"There are a couple of things I'd like clarified," she said. "You have to understand, I grew up in a police family—my father's an investigator in Providence, I've taken some forensics courses, I work part-time as an investigator for a child- and spouse-abuse advocacy group. What I don't get is why you're only now looking into this. When the kids disappeared, what, three or four months ago?"

Mo cleared his throat. "Good question. My predecessor on the case retired, so there was a, ah, delay in things. I'm new up here. I was posted with a different BCI office before. It took me a few weeks to get oriented."

"You mentioned that your senior officer didn't really think there was much to go on here."

"I intend to change his mind."

Lia laughed softly. "My father used to get into trouble for playing the Lone Ranger too often. Do you often do things this way?"

"This is the first time that comes to mind," Mo lied.

Lia got serious. "When he did it, it was usually because either he didn't have a lot of faith in his superiors' judgment, or they didn't have a lot of faith in his."

It was clear he'd have to stay on the level with her: She'd catch him in any omissions or inconsistencies. At the same time, he wasn't about to tell her the whole saga of his checkered past.

"Let's just say this is a combination of both," Mo said uncomfortably.

"We're curious about what happened here too, as you can imagine," Lia said. "As you saw, there's a strange quality to the vandalism." She looked at Paul. "Detective Ford's being here might be a real stroke of luck, Paul! It would be great to have a trained forensic investigator here—he'll no doubt see a lot of things we'd miss."

The worry lines between Paul's brow deepened. "No doubt. But it's not our house. We'd have to ask Vivien." He bit back a cough, puffed his cheeks and forcefully blew out a column of air, then turned to Mo. "My aunt has made it clear she doesn't want the police looking into this, Mr. Ford."

"Just 'Mo' is fine."

"She distrusts everyone, including the police, and she values her privacy. I doubt she'll let the police in here on the basis of what you've told us."

"I'd hoped she'd voluntarily let me in. A consent search."

"Very unlikely," Lia said. "See, Mo, there's a lot we don't understand, beyond the unusual nature of the damage. Paul's aunt has done some strange things." She went on to explain that Vivien had left abruptly, without making any provisions at all to secure the house or protect her valuables. "It's almost as if she saw this coming. Knew she had to get out quick."

"Could be." Mo rubbed his chin, thinking it over. "Tell you what. Give me your aunt's telephone number, I'll call her, try to get her consent to look through here. If she says yes, I'll conduct some routine forensics. In the meantime, I'd like to ask a small favor. Bend the rules a bit—walk me through the house today. Just so I have a general idea what I'm dealing with here."

"Sure," Paul said. "If we're going to do it, we should go right away. Once the sun gets below the ridge, it gets dark in here. You won't be able to get as good a sense of it by flashlight."

Lia tied on a pair of boots, and then Mo walked behind her out into the big room, followed by Paul. Unobserved for a moment, Mo allowed himself to look her up and down: the cascade of hair down her back, the fine square shoulders, the supple stride. He looked away, thinking, *Oh God, not this.*

In the main room, a lowering sun threw tree shadows onto the milky plastic over the tall west-facing windows. A man came through the door

Mo had entered by, set down his toolbox, and rubbed his hands, blowing on them. Mo assumed he was the electrician whose van was parked out front. From outside came the roll and chunk of a sliding van door.

"We're out of here for the day," the electrician said. "Enough's enough already. Maybe you should have a refrigeration specialist come in, they're used to working in absolute zero. Myself, I'm losing the feeling in my fingers."

"How'd it go today?" Paul asked.

"Slow. It's dark and cold down there. Plus, in these old places, they ran the wiring down a central tree from the attic. Some of this conduit has been yanked so hard it's been pulled loose up there. The whole central wiring tree's screwed. I'll have to get up into the attic tomorrow. It means replacing more than I thought, more time in the up-and-down." The electrician rubbed his thumb and fingers together, the universal sign for money.

Lia and Paul introduced Mo to the old man, Dempsey Corrigan, who was just finishing packing his tools for the night.

"I take it this is an okay cop," the old guy said.

"I try," Mo told him.

"No one can do better than that," Dempsey told him. "Well, good. And good night, kids. I'll be back in the morning." He swung his toolbox up and headed for the kitchen door.

Lia led them into the library, then into the downstairs bedrooms. Mo couldn't restrain repeated whistles of astonishment. There were drifts of rubble two and three feet deep in places—torn clothes and broken furniture, wrecked appliances and crumpled papers, dead houseplants, chunks of plaster from the walls.

"Holy shit," Mo said. "Excuse my French. Have you dug through any of these piles?"

"No. My priorities have been to close the place off against the weather, get the services back on line, set up for the long haul. My aunt wanted us to start with her papers."

"I mean," Mo went on, still struck by the thought, "you could easily have a corpse or two under all that. It's colder than a morgue drawer in here, so you wouldn't necessarily—" He stopped. He'd obviously upset his hosts with the idea.

Lia prodded him: "Wouldn't necessarily what?"

"Well, I was going to say that with the cold, no decomposition, your, uh, nose wouldn't necessarily clue you. Only way would be to conduct a manual search. Or bring dogs in."

"Terrific," Paul said. "Fucking terrific."

They started up the stairs in silence, the gruesome idea still with them.

On the balcony, they stopped as Mo leaned against the railing and surveyed the room. It was an incredible scene, a picture of the aftermath of a demented frenzy. On the way up the stairs, he'd had to step around a refrigerator door that had been ripped off its hinges and thrust through the banister railing. Downstairs, he'd noticed a sink that had been shoved or thrown hard enough that it had lodged, head-high, in the lath-and-plaster wall.

"Have you ever seen anything like this before?" Lia asked.

"Nothing even close."

"What comes to mind when you look at it?"

"Psychopathology. Maybe combined with other motives—intimidation, revenge."

"We had surmised the same," Paul told him. "There's one other element that's suggested by the holes in the walls, the ripped-up heating ducts. We figured maybe somebody was searching for something."

Mo shook his head. "No. Or rather, not just that. Whatever other conscious motives, you've got to have some psychopathology here. Somebody with a lot of anger and hate, a lot of pressure inside."

By the time they descended the stairs, only a thin band of light lingered at the top of the tall windows, and the big room was starting to darken.

"You're welcome to come into the smoking room and warm up," Lia said. "Our little oasis of comfort."

"I'd like that." Mo rubbed his hands together.

"Yeah," Paul said darkly. "I know: colder than a morgue drawer."

Mo chuckled. "Sorry. I could learn to keep my mouth shut once in a while."

"No!" Lia said emphatically. "Absolutely not. Your take on this is just what we need."

They went into the warmth. Lia's compliment, if that's what it was, made Mo feel good. The three of them held their hands in the hot air rising from the heater, not speaking, until Paul turned and began pumping up a Coleman lantern. When he had lit it and set it on the mantelpiece, he looked out the darkening windows briefly, and then turned back to Mo and Lia. "Well, I'd say the sun is verifiably over the yard arm," he said decisively. "And I am going to have some cognac. I don't usually drink this early, but it's been a rotten day and I feel entitled to some self-indulgence. Who's joining me?"

"I'd love some," Lia said. "You, Mo?"

Mo stalled, not sure. "What the hell is a 'yard arm' anyway?"

Lia laughed. "No one knows. In Providence, it's called a *yahd ahm*." She mimicked the New England accent perfectly.

Paul poured amber liquor into three Styrofoam cups and handed Mo one. Mo inhaled the fumes, feeling better than he had in a long time. He liked these two. His divorce had worked an attrition on his circle of friends, the people he'd known when he was half of a couple, all of whom ultimately took one side or the other. He'd found it difficult to stand the company even of those who'd stayed with him, uncomfortable with the mix of sympathy and suspicion that seemed to follow divorce. Everybody's relationships seemed fragile enough that all of a sudden Mo became a subtle threat, living proof that a marriage could come unglued. But this was nice. Maybe there was hope for him after all.

"I've got a question for you, Mo," Lia said. She turned her eyes on him with a trust and confidence that warmed him. For an instant, he wondered if he might be letting his attraction to her bias his judgment about getting involved up here, telling them too much, bending too many rules.

"What's that?"

"What kind of investigator are you? I mean what kind of process you use—do you think of yourself as Apollonian or Dionysian? Rational and logical, or intuitive and instinctive?"

Mo laughed uneasily. He was flattered by her attention, but she had unknowingly touched upon a sore spot. "Good question," he said. He repressed a desire to tell them about White Plains and the whole chain of ramifications. "You learn one in forensic training, but you're born with the other. I guess I use both, you've got to. But probably I go to extremes. I'd do better if my Apollo and my Dionysus could work together as a team. Kind of meet in the middle."

Lia smiled. "I think we all feel the same way." She reached over and touched her cup to his. "To meeting in the middle," she said, and swigged off her cognac. Mo automatically did the same.

Paul poured another jot into all three cups. The windows were now black rectangles, and Mo became conscious of their isolation up on the hilltop, the acres of dark forest that surrounded them.

"Well, we'll need both halves of our brains to figure this mess out," Paul said. "We've run into some very interesting things among my aunt's papers. Some of them may be linked to the vandalism here."

"The problem is," Lia said, "we don't have access to other sources of information. We have an odd photo that suggests something like this happened before, but we can't be sure. We've found—" She glanced at Paul and hesitated. "Well, other interesting things." She continued looking at Paul, as if asking a question.

"I have to honor my aunt's desire for privacy," Paul said. "It's problematical."

Mo stood up. "Listen. I want to make a pitch to you. I hear your concerns, and I respect them. I also respect your aunt's desire, her right, for privacy. Okay. I can't just make your aunt open this place up for an investigation, but at the same time I wouldn't be here if I didn't feel strongly that there was something here I need to find." He found himself getting genuinely worked up about it, gesturing, pacing feverishly. "I've got some kids, some good kids, missing. Their parents and brothers and sisters are walking wounded, there's a hole in their lives. I've got another young man who was killed dead. I can't figure out who or how or why, but I've got good indications he's tied in too. So what am I supposed to do—not follow the leads that brought me here?"

He stopped pacing, turned to face them, glad to see they were listening and responsive. "And one other concern you ought to think about. The element of danger to you. This place scares the shit out of me—excuse my French. The sooner we get to the bottom of what happened, the sooner we can neutralize any danger to you while you're up here. And whether she likes it or not, to your aunt when she returns."

He paused to let that sink in. "So here's my proposition. I call your aunt, try to get permission for a consent search. If she doesn't consent, fine, then I don't come into the house. But maybe a little compromise will be in everybody's best interests, and this part's up to you. You tell me what you find, what you discover as you go along. I run the outside work."

Lia and Paul looked at each other. "It'd be just what we need, Paul!" Lia said.

Paul needed another minute to think about it. "Okay," he said finally. "But on one condition. I'd like to get this thing with Rizal cleared up. I don't want to be pushed around by him again. If you look into why he's hassling us, I'll agree to your proposal."

"That's tricky. I can't tell you about an ongoing investigation. You've got to understand, I'm not willing to cast any aspersions on—"

"I know, loyalty to the cop corps, the brotherhood in blue. But you can tell me if there is really any drug investigation or if there's some other bug up this guy's butt." A hint of the anger Mo had seen earlier crossed Paul's face. "Just as you're sure this house is connected to your case, I'm sure he's got some hidden motives in this. I'd like to know what."

Mo considered it. Rizal was a shit, Mo wouldn't put anything past him. His instinct told him these were good people. He smiled. "Okay. It's a deal." He took his notebook out of his jacket pocket, flipped it open, settled into his chair. "Okay. So tell me what you've got."

37

The candle flames thrummed in unison, dancing to some invisible draft. Paul lay, thinking, staring at the ceiling. First thing in the morning, he planned to dig into the biggest drifts, just to set their minds at ease. It would be impossible to work wondering if the next time they moved something they'd uncover a goddamned corpse.

Rolled in her sleeping bag, Lia read one of her textbooks, leaving him to his thoughts, and Paul was glad—there were things he couldn't talk about with her just yet.

Morgan Ford, for example. At every turn, the detective had confounded Paul's preconceptions of what a cop was like. He had a humility, a self-effacing quality, that made him accessible, rather charming. Never pushy, no authority games. Yet at the same time Mo had a tough side, a persistent, assertive, competent side. Clearly a person who had taken a realistic look at his own strengths and shortcomings and come to terms with both.

When the detective interviewed them about what they'd found at the house, what they knew and surmised about Highwood, about Vivien and Royce, he'd guided the discussion skillfully, listening attentively, taking detailed notes. They'd been left with no doubts as to his professional skills.

But there were aspects of Mo that Paul didn't want to mention to Lia right away. Paul had immediately sensed Mo's attraction to Lia, the way his body had reacted, unconsciously, whenever she inadvertently bumped shoulders with the detective during their tour of the house. Even his obvious interviewing talents hadn't concealed the slight modulation of his voice whenever he addressed her. Paul was willing to bet that Mo had been divorced within the last year. He recognized the symptoms: the sweet-sad yearning of the single man. Looking at Lia leaned against the end of the bed now, her T-shirt taut against the round full curve of her breasts, he didn't blame Mo in the slightest.

Had Lia noticed? In every other way she was very observant, but her single blind spot was that unlike most beautiful women she was completely unaware of the effect she had on men. After two years with her, he'd come to know that her friendliness toward men was nothing more than a tomboy camaraderie, the natural ease of a woman who had grown up with three brothers, a cop father, a bunch of uncles. He'd always cherished her lack of self-consciousness and pretension. But a man meeting her for the first time could easily misunderstand her simple gregariousness as flirtation.

Whether she'd noticed Mo's attraction or not, Paul could understand why she might respond to Mo. The cop had a good build that his trim charcoal suit flattered, thick dark hair short on the sides but a little too long in front, giving his looks a hint of the fifties rockabilly pop star. He had a generous, slightly asymmetrical nose and unwavering dark eyes with surprisingly long lashes.

In a lot of ways, Paul suspected, Lia and Mo were more alike than Paul and Lia were: Both had quick, curious minds and a direct, pragmatic approach that Paul envied. Both had the bloodhound's instinct for the trail, both spoke the language of forensics, of deduction, of police procedure. When the three of them were talking, Lia and Mo had sometimes left him behind as they skipped ahead an inference or two, leaving Paul to wonder what he'd missed.

Plus—and this he hated to admit to himself—there had been something reassuring about having Mo in the house. As Mo came down the stairs, Paul had caught a glimpse of the gun he carried in a snug shoulder holster, and he had no doubt the detective knew how to use it. Certainly Paul wasn't a source of reassurance to anybody, with his fucking tics and jitters and family skeletons.

Despite the buzz of concern, having the detective at the house had been the best part of an otherwise miserable day. It had started with his call to Janet. After a nearly sleepless night worrying, he'd tried Janet's number first thing Thursday morning, standing in the ruined kitchen, seething with tics brought on by the anticipation of talking to her.

"Janet? Paul. I'm glad I finally managed to get through. How are you? How's Mark?"

"I'm fine. Mark is mostly fine too, although he had another bad day on Tuesday. I had to keep him home from school." Her voice was flat, revealing nothing.

"How bad?"

"Micropsia, withdrawal. The problem is, this is the second time in ten days. The one before that was about the same."

"Which means that the interval is shortening up again. Christ!" Paul said, a wave of concern coming over him. "I wish I were up there to work with him. I miss him."

That managed to put a chill in her voice. "I'm sure," she said.

Paul rang the invisible bell several times. "Well, it's going well down here. I think we're on schedule for—"

"Paul, I've been talking to an attorney."

He stopped, shifted gears. "So I gather. And to my aunt. Care to tell me why?" He resisted slipping a jab in with his question. She'd only escalate it, and right now he needed her to stay reasonable. If it came to a struggle over Mark, Janet had him at a disadvantage in every way. He was cohabiting with another woman, living outside Mark's school district, unemployed. He didn't have her family money or connections to draw upon—in his current state, he couldn't begin to match her ability to stick out a legal battle. Unspoken, whenever she listed his failings, was his Tourette's. She'd use it if she could. Could a court find him unsuitable because he had a neurological disorder? How well could he control his tics and coprolalia at a custody hearing?

"I'm just exploring the issue at this point," she said.

"What issue is that, precisely?"

"Don't play the naif, Paul, please. Really, it's your most irritating habit. The issue of the rights and obligations we each assume with regard to Mark."

"Meaning custody."

"I haven't made up my mind. I'm just doing the research I should have done years ago."

"So why'd you call my aunt?"

"I didn't call your aunt. I called your current employer—on the advice of my attorney. Your long-term financial viability, what you make and what you can pay, it all factors in. I wanted to hear it from the horse's mouth."

Paul wanted to fling the phone away from him, smash Janet's chilly voice, her condescension and her arrogance, against the wall. "Why do you want to do this? You know that I love my son, that he loves me and needs me. You know I've been working very hard to figure out what's the matter with him, and we've goddamned well been making progress. You know I'm doing everything I can to make money."

"No doubt. But you don't seem to manage to make money and live nearby at the same time, do you? Any 'progress' you might've been making seems to be slipping away, doesn't it?"

"I'll come up next week."

"I've got to get going now," she said.

"I'll come up Monday. I'm hoping I can get a gate up by then, I'll have subcontractors in the house all day—I'll be able to get away. You and I can talk. I'll have Mark out at the farm for a couple of days." Paul's knuckles ached from gripping the receiver.

"Maybe. We'll see."

"Janet, why do you want to do this?" He spoke in a gentle voice, sincerely trying to reach her. "Please, reconsider whether your anger is doing anyone any good. Please don't use Mark as a weapon to hurt me."

"Don't flatter yourself," she hissed.

Paul wrestled with the conflicting impulses in him, and at last the dammed-up anger washed over him. "Janet. You listen to me: Don't try to come between me and my son. Don't even consider it. You think you have all the cards in your pocket? The legal shit doesn't mean squat to me. I'll do whatever I have to."

"Let me see—is that a threat? Oddly enough, my attorney mentioned just such a possibility. He said I should make a note of any violent or threatening behavior on your part." Her self-control was astonishing.

"You heard me. I'll be up Sunday. Have Mark ready to come home with me Monday after school." He would have gone on, but Janet had cut the connection.

Paul stirred in the sleeping bag, squirming with tension. His arms and legs moved independently, little tics in every muscle group. Next to him, Lia turned a page, absently stroking his chest with one hand.

Then, after the call to Janet, the thing with Rizal. Paul had been drinking coffee on the terrace, pacing up and down in the crisp air, working out the kinks he'd acquired from stooping over Vivien's papers, when the State Police cruiser came over the crest of the drive. Rizal swaggered out of the car, chewing a toothpick.

"I've already registered a complaint about your last visit," Paul warned him.

"Yeah, Miller said you called. He said, 'Take a good close look at this guy Skoglund.' So I thought I'd drop by again. Actually, I'm here to do you a favor."

"What's that?"

"You're from Vermont, right? Still hippy heaven up there? Food coops and farm communes? Grow your own, do you? Green Mountain Green—I hear it's very nice."

Rizal's odd turns were hard to follow. "I'm not understanding you. What's the favor you're here to do?"

Rizal came to the bottom of the stairs and spoke to him conspiratorially. "There's been a lot of speculation about drugs happening up here for some months now. Recent talk at zone headquarters is that you're bringing down some Vermont homegrown for sale to our Westchester County kids. So the favor is this: I'm giving you a little advance warning. Giving you a chance to clear out."

"I've got to get back to work, Rizal. Come on up and search the place.

Search my car. You won't find anything. But you make sure you have a warrant, because if I see you up here without due authority again, on any pretext whatsoever, I'll bring you to court."

Rizal didn't budge. "Funny—you can *always* manage to find something if you're really looking for it."

"You mean if you want to nail somebody, you bring it with you."

Rizal just looked at him, eyes flat.

Paul had turned and started walking away, back toward the kitchen door. He'd suppressed any vocal tics, but his abdomen was clenching spasmodically. If the cop wasn't off the property by the time he got to the kitchen phone, he was calling the State Police headquarters in Albany. And then a lawyer.

"But here's another thing to consider, Mr. Skoglund," Rizal called after him. "It won't make things easier for you if there's an investigation, will it? I mean, how do you think your aunt will like it if you're even accused? If we have to go through her little castle with a fine-tooth comb? And how fast do you think your work will go if you're tangled up in something like that? Interrogations, making bail, lawyers, hearings, court dates—my guess is it will not go well. My guess is you can't afford a headache like that. So I'm giving you the chance to get lost. Go home. Tuck fanny and scoot."

Paul didn't pause or turn around. He didn't want Rizal to see that he'd finally touched a nerve. Not so much that there'd be problems with Vivien, or the job. Highwood and everything connected with it could go to hell. But a drug charge now, no matter how bogus—Janet would love it. She'd eat him alive in any legal battle. Good-bye to Mark.

"Paul! Paul!" Lia was shaking him, scattering kisses on his face. "Are you all right? You were moaning and twitching as if you were having a bad dream!"

"Yeah, a nightmare—I was thinking back on the day."

"You were grinding your teeth! You've never done that before."

"What's that *splat-splat* noise? The sound of shit hitting the fan?" Paul moaned and put his head between his hands. "Oh, baby, what's going on? Why is all this happening? What am I supposed to do?"

Lia wrapped her arms around him and rocked him gently. "It's going to be all right. I promise." She kissed him beneath his ear. "It's going to come out fine."

"How? What am I supposed to do? It seems like everyone around me is nuts."

"Me too?"

"No. Not you." He put his forehead against her. "But recently, so help me, I've been thinking *I'm* going crazy."

"You're the sanest person I know! You've got to be nuts to think you're crazy."

"Explain to me how sane I am—I seem to have forgotten."

He expected more humor, but she took him seriously: "I'll tell you exactly. You remain honest when everyone else is being deceitful. You are compassionate in a time when selfishness is everywhere. You've got the best brain of anyone I know, yet you still steer by your heart. You keep a sense of humor, even if things are difficult."

It was good to hear her flatter him. "Yeah, well, neither my heart nor my humor has been helping me recently. How're they supposed to help me with this Rizal character? Fuck it—I need a forked stick and a canvas bag for that son of a bitch."

Lia laughed, still wrapped around him.

"And I didn't even tell you about Dempsey," he went on.

"I thought you'd cleared that up."

"Ah, fuck—I think there's still something going on with him." He told her what he hadn't had time to earlier: That afternoon, Paul had found Dempsey upstairs in Vivien's bedroom, furtively rooting through the papers just as Lia had described earlier. Paul had slipped past the doorway without Dempsey's seeing him, but the implication was clear—the old man was still looking for something.

Lia looked lost in thought for a moment, then stretched like a cat and yawned hugely. "I think you're getting worried about things that probably aren't very important. So Dempsey has something else he'd like to keep private—so what? Really, who cares besides Dempsey? How does that affect Paul Skoglund? Anyway, problems are just opportunities to grow, learn more about ourselves."

"Recently I've had about all the personal growth I can stand," Paul grumbled.

Lia slept. Paul lay, arms behind his head, straining to listen to the night through the sound of her gentle snores. Night wrapped the carriage house, the rugged woods seemed to breathe too. The yellow candlelight set into sharp focus tiny irregularities in the paint on the ceiling, like the pocks and craters of the moon.

A humid, hickory smell in the air. Out in the woods with the big dog. Mother packed a snack, a sandwich and a whole Cracker Jack box, all wrapped in the special blue handkerchief. The woods strange with the bright uneven light, the mist. Vivien gone to town in her Land Rover car that smells like leather inside. The house feels empty without Father, who had work to do, and without Freda who is gone away forever but you're not supposed to talk about it because it makes Vivien too sad.

Resting on the bare granite boulder, watching ants, then staring upward. The rough rock gives off heat like some big friendly living thing. The deep sky is hung with little puffs of clouds like Indian smoke signals, their meaning mysterious.

Moving farther on. A flock of startled crows rises and spirals in the air like ashes from a fire, then blows away into the valley. Then the dog stops to perk his ears, uncertain. A chugging noise, down below in the thick tangle of vines and brambles. Scared now but going closer, hearing the thrash of dried leaves, crackle of twigs. Something's moving behind a ledge of rock, then out again, in and out, back and forth, a white-pink shape, two pink shapes, wrong against the woods colors. A sapling-top jerks suddenly, then stops, then thrashes again, shaking loose a scatter of leaves. Backing away, afraid to run, starting to turn. Tripping over something, dropping the bag with the snack in it, wanting to go back for the handkerchief but too afraid. Can't look. The horrible convulsive back and forth, the hissing-chugging, the pink and red and black. The awful blind energy of it, like animals fighting. Running away now but still hearing it, the fast rhythmic noise like a knife being sharpened. A bad secret thing that you don't talk about. Running, scrabbling away. Looking back in terror, seeing the top of the sapling heave and thrash and shiver loose its leaves.

38

MO sat down at his desk, his office dark but for the little desk lamp and the glow of his computer screen. Coming in after normal office hours, he had spotted Tommy Mack in the main office, talking on the phone and intently chewing his nails, but otherwise the BCI side of the barracks was empty. He had come away from his meeting with Lia and Paul so full of jangled ju-ju energy he could hardly contain himself. Partly it was the possibilities that emerged from what they'd told him. Partly it was Lia. Trying to name the feeling, he discarded *excited* in favor of *inspired*. He felt like an idiot, a kid. He wanted to show off for her, bring her presents—which meant, in this case, to develop the leads they'd offered him.

But first one little errand. Apollonian or Dionysian? she'd asked. The answer was both complex and simple: a cop, Lia, suspicious by nature, paranoid through experience. Sorry, folks, just a precaution. At his computer, he called up NYSPIN and punched in the names Paul Skoglund and Lia McLean. No arrest records or warrants, not even a moving violation between them. Okay. Next he typed in a vehicle registration request, using the car license numbers he'd made a point of noting before leaving the driveway at Highwood. The old MG was indeed registered to a Paul Skoglund, of Norwich, Vermont, the Subaru wagon to one Lia McLean, same address. Finally, he called the Providence police and was able to confirm that Ed McLean was an investigator in the department—a lieutenant, in fact. So they were what they appeared to be, pure as the proverbial driven snow.

Next he called the number Paul had given him for his aunt in San Francisco. As he'd promised, he didn't mention that he'd been to the lodge or had met Paul, only that he was working on a case involving missing teenagers and the lodge seemed to figure in.

"I understand that the premises have been badly vandalized. What I'd like, ma'am, is your permission to conduct a thorough forensic investigation of the house to see if the teenagers in question had been up there at any time."

The woman's voice was brittle, icy. "I presume that your request for a consent search means that you are unable to convince a judge that your suspicions merit issuing a search warrant. Am I correct?"

She didn't leave much wiggle room. "That's essentially true, Mrs. Hoffmann, but only because I'm in the preliminary stages of this investigation. Your cooperation would—"

"Mr. Ford. Please don't waste your breath. You have offered me no persuasive reason to permit my house to be invaded, during my absence, and my things tossed about yet again. I'm afraid I have standards of privacy at least as high as the local courts. If and when you are able to obtain a search warrant, I will of course be happy to comply. Until then, I am sorry. You may not enter my property without legal authorization."

Mo felt like telling her that if he got a warrant he'd search the house whether she was happy to comply or not. But this was the kind of tough old rich buzzard who knew how to make major trouble for you. He'd avoid confrontation with her for now. He thanked her for talking with him and said good-bye. A first-class bitch. Cross that possibility off the list.

The next phase of this night's work was more complex. A wild thought had occurred to him, prompted by the sight of that sink lodged in the wall, the refrigerator door driven through the stair railing. He hadn't been willing to mention the thought to Lia and Paul, not without a hell of a lot more to back it up.

Mo opened his file on the hit-and-run death of Richard Mason. For the first time, he opened the white envelope and spilled the glossy photos out on his desk. He took a deep breath, then pulled over the swing-arm desk lamp so the photos were spotlighted in a bright circle against his blotter.

Ten black-and-whites, a dozen color shots, all eight-by-tens. The body of Richard Mason was caught in its final pose on the asphalt of Highway 138, brightly lit by arc lamps set up by the photographers at the scene. In one mid-range shot, his blood-slimed face—or rather the remains of it, since part of the skull was missing—was against the road surface, almost upside down on an unnaturally limp, elongated neck. He'd ended up wearing his abdominal organs like a ghastly cape over his shoulders. Another shot showed the corpse from behind, with the bloodied shirt stretched empty on the pavement, still partly tucked into the waistband and belt, the only intact parts of the blue jeans he'd been wearing.

Mo felt woozy and looked away, covering the photos with a blank legal pad as if to protect himself from their noxious emanations. He wasn't an expert at forensic pathology or anatomy, so he didn't expect to pick up anything but a general sense of the accident from the photos. An *intuitive* sense. Once he'd gotten his breath again, he looked at a few more photos. There was one of the initial impact site, where Richard's right lower leg lay in a broad smear of dried blood. Another shot gave a good view of the ninety-foot trail between the initial impact site and the body, a tangled calligraphy of blood, pieces of cloth, and unnameable lumps.

In just the few minutes he'd been looking at the photos, he'd gotten a throbbing headache, and the light felt like a dagger driven into his eyes. Mo put the photos away and oriented the light away from him. He lifted out the accident scene report, read the reconstructionist's report carefully.

Bernie Denning, the accident reconstructionist, had been brought in from Troop K headquarters. Denning had received specialized training to be able to look closely at a vehicular incident, especially a vehicle-pedestrian collision, and reconstruct the sequence of events. Using his own observations at the scene, the M.E.'s medical report, photos, charts, computer analysis, and Betty Rosen's testimony, Denning had put together a picture of what had happened. Victim hit by at least two vehicles. Second vehicle known to be a Ford Taurus station wagon, which had rolled Richard's body beneath its undercarriage, causing innumerable fractures of bones and detaching various body parts. Embedded in the corpse were small chips of rust, some mud and oil residue, all found to have belonged to the Taurus. Patterns of hair and tissue residue on the Taurus's oil pan, springs, floorboards, and both left wheel wells told the story of the body's passage beneath it, consistent with the driver's account. Comparative absence of blood at the second scene resulted from the fact that the corpse had drained at the first impact site, where it had lain for less than half an hour.

Accurate reconstruction extremely difficult, conclusions somewhat speculative, due to double impact and extremity of injuries.

Denning had found the absence of indications about the nature of the first vehicle to be unusual, although not without precedent. In his view, the lack of mud, rust, or oil suggested that the vehicle in question had been new. Given the absence of paint, plastic, or glass in the corpse or at the scene, the victim had probably not been struck by a grill, hood, or fender; it was possible that he'd been horizontal when first hit, or had thrown himself under the vehicle. Denning felt that the only vehicle that could have accomplished such extreme damage was a truck with tandem axles and double wheels or, possibly, a piece of road construction equipment.

Denning's conclusion, a best guess, was that Richard had been knocked down by a tall, wide tire and was then "processed" by multiple wheels which churned him up and under in an exceptionally clean wheel well, either brand-new or recently washed. The most problematic aspect of the whole thing had been the absence of tire tracks from the first vehicle. In his summary, however, Denning cited a similar case near Buffalo, in which the badly damaged corpse of a woman had puzzled investigators for weeks, until a guilt-ridden local grading contractor had come forward with his brand-new front-loader.

What if, Mo thought, *what if.* What if there's a connection between the anomalous damage at Highwood and an equally anomalous vehicular homicide only a mile or so away? The extreme violence both required, the extreme force.

Okay, what if? Maybe there was a way to explore the idea further, see what other violent, criminal anomalies the human zoo had produced recently. Every violent crime in the country was recorded in the FBI's Violent Criminal Apprehension Program computer database and analysis program, which he could access as a State Police investigator. VICAP described each crime by 189 separate lines of information, each line of which could then be compared and cross-referenced with other crimes. New York State had created an additional section, called Homicide Assessment Lead Tracking, with another thirty-nine lines of information. Using HALT-VICAP, an investigator looking for leads in a given case could search out possible links between his case and similar crimes, criminals, M.O.s, or victims from records nationwide.

He pulled a search request form from his file drawer, looked it over, slapped it back onto the desk. Ordinarily, he'd fill out the forms and send them to Albany, where the HALT information would be processed, and then HALT would forward the rest to the VICAP people in Quantico. Results could take days or weeks. Not good enough.

Mo flipped his Rolodex, dialed a number at FBI headquarters at Quantico. Jane and he had met at a VICAP conference in Washington, had gone out looking for a decent meal and gotten soaked by a thunderstorm, and had ended up in bed at his hotel room. Just the once, they'd both agreed afterward: She was married. They'd agreed to forget all about it, but that small, secret, nostalgic tenderness still remained in their rare professional contacts. They did each other work favors now and again.

Mo expected to leave a message on her voice mail but wasn't really surprised when she answered in person: Jane was working late again, a habit that Mo had decided reflected equally on her professional commitment and the health of her marriage. Without going into details, he explained his need to expedite a VICAP search request.

"Just how expeditiously do you want me to handle this, roughly?"

"Roughly, to run it through and fax it to me tonight."

"Like I've got nothing else to do, right?" Jane said. "Must be a good one. I think I can do that, Mo. But don't tell anyone I do favors, okay?" The smile in her voice served as a faint reminder of their shared secret. Janie was a good kid.

"This one is simple," Mo told her. "We'll just do sections six, seven, and

eight. Skip the rest." The sections he listed were titled "Offense M.O.,"
"Condition of Victim When Found," and "Cause of Death or Trauma." Mo
looked over the form he'd filled out and read out the boxes he'd checked as
Jane made out a duplicate form at her end, naming descriptors that he
hoped to match with other crimes: extreme violence, dismemberment, indications of extreme force, perpetrators with great physical strength.

"Jesus, Mo! I thought they already caught King Kong. What've you got
going up there?"

"Janie, if I knew I wouldn't be bothering you with this."

"Okay. I'll get to work. As long as you're sufficiently appreciative."

"You know I am," he said, meaning it in the same several ways she intended the question. Though she'd said little about her marriage, the bony,
sweet, shy, sexy woman he'd spent that lunch hour with had needed affirmation more than gratification. Much as he had.

As if they'd both revealed too much, their good-bye felt a little awkward,
its cadences uneven.

Mo got himself dinner from the vending machines in the hall, micro-
waved a plastic-wrapped meatball sandwich, worked on some other projects, then gave up and paced and watched the fax machine. At last it
shrilled and began to spit out pages.

At his request, Jane had sent him reports on just eastern region cases, a
couple of dozen records of crimes that had matches with the line descrip-
tions he'd given her. The first he looked at was a sordid account of a son's
chainsaw attack on his father in Strafford, Vermont. The attack had been
witnessed by neighbors, the case closed by the arrest of the son. From the
narrative section, he was able to determine from the medical jargon that
the chainsaw left a unique "signature" on the bones and flesh of the victim.
Did a vehicle leave such a signature—an *unmistakable* signature? Mo made
a note on a scratch pad, *Ask M.E. about automotive signature.*

It made for a gory night's reading, but in all the reports where extreme
violence or dismemberment had occurred, the weapon or means was clear,
and most were closed by arrest. After automobiles, it was elevators, die-
stamping machinery, and farm equipment that seemed to be the most
popular means for deliberately inflicting massive injuries upon someone
you didn't like. An industrial bandsaw was the weapon of choice in one incident at a factory in New Jersey; there was even a multiple-victim *steam-
roller* situation in North Carolina. None had even the remotest possible
bearing on Richard Mason or the business at Highwood.

The best Mo could do was a report of a detached human thigh that had
been found in the woods near Highway 102 outside of Ridgefield, Connecticut, a few weeks earlier. No identifying marks; victim unknown but
indicated by lab tests to be female and around age thirty; thigh *ripped* off

the body, and lower leg separated, by means unknown. A search of the surrounding area by police and civilian volunteers had not turned up anything, and no thirtyish female from the area was known to be missing. In his notebook, Mo jotted down the file numbers and the name of the agent in charge.

It was almost eleven by the time he got back to his apartment, feeling baked, beat, fried. He fumbled with the keys and had swung the door open before he noticed the note that was taped on it at eye-level. He flicked on the lights, wincing at the unflattering illumination of his bare apartment, and opened the folded paper.

It was a short note from Alice, his neighbor downstairs, inviting him to drop by for some wine if he felt like it, don't worry if it's late. Alice had been making her interest clear since he'd moved in. Mo swore she had a radar that could spot a single man, could pick up that single man's lonelier and more vulnerable moods. Or maybe it was just that her apartment was directly below his, allowing her to hear his footsteps, and that Mo could generally be counted on to be in a lonely and vulnerable mood.

She was in her late thirties, divorced twice, a sweet kid, and not Mo's type at all. Mo had run into her on the street a couple of times, once accompanying her to the deli to grab a sandwich. She'd talked at him fast and loud, office gossip from the travel agency where she worked. Overdone black hair piled and frizzed and sprayed into place, a plain face that she tried to dramatize with too-bright lipstick and eyeshadow, and a good figure kept trim from aerobics classes at Mt. Kisco Athletic Club, where Mo also worked out occasionally. In fact, it was the recollection of meeting Alice in the lobby of the club—smiling, sweating, and for once scrubbed clean of the too-much makeup, wearing a red-and-white-striped leotard and white tights—that now bothered Mo. Damned good legs, trim stomach, broad hip bones. Aerobics-firmed arms and shoulders. Downstairs right now with a bottle of Chardonnay.

Why not? Mo got a beer from the refrigerator and slumped in his chair. Why the hell not? Partly because nothing came without a price, and if the price was at some point in days or weeks having to tell her it wasn't going to work out, then it was too steep. She was just doing what he was doing, keeping the loneliness at bay however she could, and she didn't need any more disappointments. Anyway, the image of Alice in her tights had quickly given way to the memory of Lia McLean, the sun slanting onto her dark honey-colored hair, her clear, alert eyes, the sweet perfection of her legs in her jeans as she sat in the wing chair at Highwood—

Mo swigged down the beer, took off his shoulder holster and draped it over the chair at the head of his bed. If he were smart, he would probably go see a shrink or join some self-esteem group or men's drumming circle or whatever crap you did nowadays, to figure out his thing with women. The hell with it. He hoped he'd be able to get some sleep. He cut the light and got into bed.

39

On Friday, Mo made a point of stopping in Tommy Mack's cubicle first thing. It was wise to catch the Lewisboro barrack's lone Narco investigator early in the day, before the day's stress and overwork and frustration had melted down his circuits. Tommy should have burnt out long ago, but some incredibly durable part of his constitution kept him coming back at it day after day, year after year, like an Irish pub brawler with an iron jaw. In the mornings, before the day got away from him, he was generally clear-headed and not unfriendly. Tommy was too harried to give Mo's past any concern; probably, if put to a choice, he'd be one of those to come down in Mo's favor for having put those neat clusters of holes in the mutts in White Plains—especially given that it was a drug-related thing, Tommy's specialty.

"Yo, Tomas," Mo said.

"Oy," Tommy returned, not looking up.

"You were in here pretty late last night. I thought I smelled something cooking—you must have some pot about to boil over."

"Ahh." Tommy looked disgusted. "That was the smell of burning insulation." He tapped the side of his head meaningfully. Tommy saw himself as a David, facing every day the Goliath of entrenched state and federal bureaucracies and the tangled morass of the laws he was expected to enforce, the bumbling incompetence of police and civilian administrations. It wasn't a good idea to get him started.

"Got a question for you. Have you got anything going with this place, Highwood, over on the Lewisboro Reservoir Road? I need to look into some things there, but I don't want to step on anybody's toes."

"Huh?" A blank look.

"You using uniform help on a marijuana case in that area?"

"Uniform help like who?"

"Pete Rizal."

"Rizal?" Tommy made a face like he'd bitten into something rotten, then caught himself. "No," he said. "Not using Rizal on anything."

"Well, let me ask you this: If there was anything going on in Lewisboro, maybe out of another jurisdiction or something, you'd know about it, right?"

Tommy smiled evilly. "Who, me? Hey, I'd be the last to know. I'm just the Narco officer in charge here, that's all. Why would anybody let me know what the fuck they were doing?" He laughed sourly. "Seriously, what kind of thing? If it's something really big or something imported, Customs or the DEA might take the lead, I might not know first off. But they sure as hell wouldn't be asking for uniform support at the barracks level if that's what it was."

"What I heard was, it concerned somebody bringing home-grown marijuana down from Vermont."

Tommy shook his head *no.* "Then we'd get it first. Lewisboro, North Salem, they'd call us in right away. It'd be ours. We've got nothing like that going right now."

Mo thanked him and went back to his own office. So Paul was right—Rizal had some other ax to grind. How did he tie in?

He left a message at the office of Bennett Quinn, the agent in charge of the Ridgefield case of the human thigh, asking for a call back, then did the same with Dr. Mathewson, the medical examiner who had done the autopsy on Richard Mason, at the Vallhalla M.E.'s office. His telephone luck wasn't running good and Mo decided to give it a rest.

Back at his computer, Mo did some more routine work, looking up Royce Hoffmann. As he'd suspected, there was nothing. The petty vandalism Royce had committed back when, "criminal mischief," wouldn't ever have made it past the police blotter to a permanent file. As for more serious juvenile crimes, it was likely that Royce or his mother had gotten the record scrubbed—asked for a sealing order that permanently expunged any record of criminal activity from police files. Very common for juvenile offenders.

Mo sat with his notebook in front of him, thinking about what he'd learned and looking over his checklist. The sticky one was Rizal. It looked as if Rizal had motives of his own for his visits to Highwood. His main goal, if he had one, seemed to be to get Paul to leave the job. Why? The problem was that looking into a fellow New York State Police employee wasn't easy to do, especially when half the system had doubts about Mo's own conduct. Without bringing a charge of malfeasance or conduct unbecoming, he didn't have any right to suspect Rizal of anything. He was willing to bend rules, but this was serious stuff, enough to ruin Rizal's career or his own. He'd have to give the matter some thought.

Next he ran a search for Salvador Falcone, who according to Paul Skoglund had been a gardener at Highwood. Paul had said that his aunt suspected Falcone because they'd had some kind of altercation long ago. NYSPIN showed that a Salvador Falcone, of Purdys, had been charged twice with assault and battery, with one conviction resulting in a short jail sentence, in the mid-eighties. Mo jotted down Falcone's address and telephone number.

What he needed was some local perspective on Falcone. Mo thumbed through his Rolodex until he came up with a name Wild Bill had suggested as a resource in North Salem, Sam Lombardino, who for the last twenty years had run a dry cleaning business by day and worked as one of North Salem township's handful of police constables by night. Sam had lived in the area all his life and would know about Falcone if there was anything to know about.

Risking the phone again, he called the dry cleaner's number, and the woman put him through to her boss.

"Mr. Lombardino? This is Mo Ford, State Police BCI in Lewisboro. Have you got a minute?"

"I got about that," Lombardino answered. He had a gruff, harried voice. "Everything's gone haywire down here, I got repairmen all over the place."

"Okay, this won't take long. I'm looking into a case, I can't disclose the specifics just yet, but the name Salvador Falcone came up. Lives in Purdys. You know him?"

"Yeah, Salli. Family's been in the area forever."

"You know much about him? Ever have any trouble with him?"

Mo heard the sound of the phone being covered with a palm and Lombardino's muffled voice, barking at his repairmen or whoever. Then: "Sorry. I got a mess down here. Salli's got a wife and four kids, drinks a little too much and gets mad too easily. I had to arrest him once, for beating the stuffing out of a couple of guys outside the liquor store here. Salli's a big guy, not someone you want to get physical with—I was a little nervous when my partner and I went over there. But I got him into the car okay. I knew his father a little bit, twenty, thirty years ago. When he saw it was me, he calmed down."

"He the type to hold a grudge?"

"I'd have to say no, I'd think he gets it out of his system pretty fast. In fact, I wish he'd hold his grudges a little better. And his booze."

"Do you know where he works?"

"Well, I saw him at the butcher counter in Croton Falls for a while, but I think he moves around, job to job, quite a bit." Through the phone, Mo heard a loud *clunk!*, followed by a gabble of voices. "Son of a—listen, I gotta go now. I don't know anything that'll help you anyway."

After saying good-bye to Lombardino, Mo checked his watch, then put on his coat. It was nearly lunchtime, and he thought he'd visit the grocery store in Croton Falls, see if he could get a look at the Great Beast Falcone.

Falcone had left his job at the grocery store, but the manager said he'd heard he went to work at Jason's Gym in Danbury. The manager hadn't fired him; he'd quit.

"The gym job's perfect for Salli," the manager said. "He was there half the time anyway, training for these bodybuilder competitions." With his hands spread, he made a gesture around his own bony chest, signifying bulging muscles.

Driving toward Danbury, Mo began to realize that if Falcone had worked at Highwood in the early sixties, he'd now have to be the world's oldest competing bodybuilder. He wished he'd looked more closely at the records generated by his computer. Something didn't figure.

At Jason's Gym Mo followed his nose to the workout rooms and spotted Falcone immediately. There were only a few people inside—a pair of women pedaling stationary bicycles, a lean older man on the rowing machine, a handful of others. But directly in front of Mo was a broad, muscled back shaped like a shield, glistening with sweat. Falcone was seated on the bench of a Universal machine, wearing small purple briefs, a sleeveless T-shirt and training shoes, no socks. As Mo watched, he raised the bar and lifted an incredible column of stacked iron weights. The muscles of his shoulders swelled and striated as he did eight repetitions, breathing in rhythm, then dropped the bar. The floor shook with the pile-driver impact.

Falcone groped for a towel and wiped his body down, then turned to dry off the vinyl seat. An impressive specimen, Mo admitted. His thighs and arms were wadded with muscle, his sweat-soaked T-shirt clung to a stomach sectioned into sharply defined squares, his calves were swollen spheres gripped by branching blue veins. Black hair, heavy brows, a square face. He put the towel over his shoulder and approached Mo.

"Help you?" he asked.

"Are you Mr. Falcone?"

"Yeah. What d'you need?"

"I'm Morgan Ford. I'm an investigator with the New York State Police. I was hoping I could talk to you." Mo flipped open his ID.

Falcone glanced around the room. "What the hell? I just started working here. I don't need any trouble." He took a black sweatshirt from a hook and pulled it over his huge torso. It was a hooded sweatshirt, but the sleeves had been cut out of it to reveal Falcone's knotted arms. With his face shadowed by the hood, arms bare, Falcone looked to Mo like a medieval executioner.

"There won't be any trouble if you answer some of my questions." Mo tipped his head toward the free-weight room, which was empty now. "We could go in there to talk. If your boss asks what it's about, tell him I'm thinking of becoming a club member."

In the free-weight room, Falcone sat on a tall stool while Mo leaned against the wall, facing him. "I don't know nothing about nothing," Falcone said. "Whatever it is, you got the wrong guy."

"Maybe so. You're not who I thought I was going to be talking to. Your father's name is Salvador too, right?" Mo had figured his stupid mistake the moment he saw Falcone's unlined face. He couldn't be any older than thirty-five, if that.

"That's right."

"Where's your father now? Maybe he's the one I should be talking to."

Falcone gestured with both hands, as if throwing something into the air, Italian for *it's a moot point.* "He's dead. We think he's dead. He disappeared a long time ago."

"Why do you think he's dead? Maybe he just—"

Falcone thrust the idea back at Mo with a pushing gesture of his huge right arm. "You never heard of family pride? You don't know me, you don't know my father, you don't know my family. So don't insult. My father wouldn't have left my mother and us kids."

"I respect that," Mo said. "No insult intended." So family pride was a big issue with Falcone. Having already put his foot in it, Mo decided he might as well tough it out for the duration. "Listen, Mr. Falcone, tell me about Highwood. About Vivien Hoffmann." At the sudden change of tack, the bodybuilder's head jerked minutely toward Mo, eyes suddenly wary.

"I don't know anything about them."

"Yeah, you do. You got a grudge going, Mr. Falcone? You mad at somebody?"

"I never been up there in my life."

"Oh? So who's smashing the place up?"

"The fuck should I know? I wouldn't set foot up there."

"Why's that?"

Falcone got off his stool and lifted it with one hand, holding it near the end of one metal leg and swinging it up and down, using just his wrist and the bunching muscles of his forearm. "Because the bitch that owns the place, the Hoffmann bitch, is the one that screwed my father."

"How'd she do that?"

"She got him set up. When he worked there as a gardener. She called the police on him, said that he'd stolen things and wrecked some valuable stuff. It was all bullshit. But she was rich and he was a dirt laborer. Who was the judge going to believe? And when he got out of jail, he couldn't get a decent fucking job around here. My mother had to support us. He was home for a few years and then he disappeared. Personally, I think he was ashamed he couldn't support his family and went off and killed himself. She fucked him up. She fucked up my whole family."

"So you want to pay her back."

Falcone set the stool down, closer to Mo, and sat on it again. He was breathing hard, out of proportion to his exertion, and Mo was aware of the power and mass of his body, like a throbbing diesel engine. "She could die for all I care," he muttered.

"You want to help her along, maybe?"

"I haven't *thought* about the bitch for maybe five or ten years. For all I know, until you come in here today, maybe she's already dead."

"Why would she do that to your father?"

Falcone's eyes were bitter. "You want to know? My brother told me why, when I was a little older, I could understand shit like that. You know what my brother said? Because he wouldn't fuck her. See? My father had a build'd make me look like a faggot, he had nine inches where it counts. Face like Mastroianni. She's up there alone on the hill, divorced, he looks pretty good to her. Only she can't understand maybe he's got a wife he likes, maybe he's a good Catholic. Just maybe he's got some goddamned pride. So she's gonna make him hurt."

Falcone glared at him defiantly, and while Mo thought about where to go with it, the two women from the stationary bicycles came in and started working out with tiny dumbbells. They were both skinny and dressed in neon Spandex that made Mo's eyes ache.

"And now I got work to do," Falcone said. He got up and walked away from Mo, back into the main workout room. Mo did a few curls with a forty-pound barbell, trying to decide whether to push Falcone a little harder this time, or wait. Finally he decided he'd probably done all he could for now. When Mo passed Falcone on his way out, the bodybuilder was doing some paperwork at a small desk near the door.

"You've been a lot of help," Mo said. "This is my card. I'll want to talk to you again."

"Anytime," Falcone said flatly.

It was two-thirty by the time Mo made it back to his office. He checked his messages and found only one, a short, harried-sounding message from Bennett Quinn: "On the thigh, we've got nothing, nobody, and no leads yet. Lot of help, huh? We're having a little task force meeting in a few days, and the thigh's on the agenda. I'll keep you informed."

He sat at his desk and jotted a few notes. Beyond establishing that Falcone was a tank and had some anger in him, the interview hadn't revealed anything definitive—if what Paul and Lia had told him was true, a lot of people had something against Mrs. Hoffmann. On the other hand, he'd accomplished one of his objectives: He'd given the bodybuilder fair warning that he was under some suspicion. If Falcone had been taking out his anger by smashing up Highwood, he'd think twice about returning. Lia and Paul would maybe be a little safer. If Falcone got nervous and tried to disappear, Mo would have a suspect.

He was about to go get a cup of coffee when the telephone rang.

"Detective Ford? Dr. Mathewson from the lab in Vallhalla. I'm returning your call." The doctor's voice was breathy, thin, an unhealthy sound. Mo hadn't met him, but he had his suspicions of anyone who wanted to make a career of forensic pathology. His voice didn't help: Mo had to overcome his mental picture of him as hunched, pale, bug-eyed.

"I won't take much of your time," Mo said, "but I'm hoping you might be able to help me. I'm working on a case that may have connections with a hit-and-run from this area. I understand you did the autopsy. A Richard Mason, killed August sixth, in Lewisboro. Young man hit by two separate cars? Your report mentions 117 bone fractures—"

"Oh, yes. I remember that one fairly well. You don't often see such a, uh, such an extreme case."

"Let me start by asking a general question. Is there a signature to vehicle-inflicted injuries? I mean, can you tell *for sure* an injury is caused by a vehicle?"

"That's a very good question. The range of vehicle injuries is very broad—penetrating injuries, crushing, acceleration-deceleration injuries, secondary-impact injuries, flying-object injuries. The forces are tremendous and unpredictable. Someone can be effectively *kneaded*, like dough. So it's hard to say. When I get a body, the coroner has already made a determination of cause of death, after looking at the scene and a preliminary medical report. I'm looking for specifics. Unless I find something that directly contradicts the coroner's report, his determination stands."

Mo made a note on his pad: *forces unpredictable, wide range injuries.* "If someone had brought you this boy and not told you it was vehicular, what would you have said? Based only on the condition of the corpse?"

"Vehicle," the doctor said unhesitatingly. "That or an accident involving industrial machinery. I'd prefer the latter, actually, but then the death would have had to happen elsewhere and the body get transported. But if that were the case, there wouldn't have been so much blood at the scene. I seem to recall that all the blood was accounted for."

Mo made a note on his pad, *poss. industrial machinery,* then scratched his head, beginning to feel like an idiot. His idea was too far-fetched, science fiction. No wonder Barrett didn't trust him. "One more question,

Doctor. Can you think of any other way that level of damage could have occurred to a strong, healthy young man?"

Mathewson said nothing for a moment. Mo could hear his breathing, close to the telephone mouthpiece. "Sure," the doctor said at last. "He picked a fight with the Incredible Hulk. Or maybe Superman." He wheezed a breathy laugh. "Sorry. Not a subject to joke about. Really, I can't think of anything at all. Is there anything else I can help you with, Detective?"

Mo made a note on the pad, said good-bye, and hung up. Then he sat for a long time, thinking, staring at what he'd just written: *Superman.*

40

Paul kicked open the kitchen door as the phone rang again. Two A.M., Saturday morning. He'd had it with riddles and mysteries. If someone wanted to hassle them, they'd better be ready to get hassled back. He crossed the ravaged kitchen and yanked the receiver off the hook.

"Hello?" he barked.

There was silence at the other end.

"Hello, who is this?"

"Dad?" a small voice asked.

"Mark! Where are you? Is everything all right?"

"Yeah, everything's okay. I'm home. You sounded mad when you answered."

"Well, I didn't know who it was. I thought it might be some weirdo or something, calling so late. What are you doing up at this ungodly hour?"

"I snuck down to call you." Mark was almost whispering.

There were so many questions to ask all at once. "Snuck? You can call me anytime, you know that."

"Oh, I don't know. Mom doesn't like me to talk to you."

"Did she say that?"

"No. I can just tell."

"Well, you call me anyway. You call me any time, day or night. I mean it."

"Yeah."

"Mark," Paul said softly, "was that you who called before? Late, like this?"

"Yeah."

"So it must be something important, to sneak downstairs and call me in the middle of the night."

"I just needed to talk to you. I miss you."

"I miss you too. Really badly. I'm sorry I've had to be down here."

Mark took a breath. "Mom doesn't understand me very well."

"You mean in general, or you mean the problem?"

"I guess mainly the problem. Both. I don't know."

"Has it been bad recently?"

"It's like it's always there, I have to fight it off. I want you to come back. I get scared I can't fight it off all the time. I feel like there's, like an *animal* in my head. I get scared that there's something the matter with me that can't be fixed. That something bad will happen to me."

The small, tired voice coming over the line broke Paul's heart. "Mark, nothing bad is going to happen to you. I'll come back tomorrow. Will that help?"

"Yes."

"In the meantime, you tell Mom about what you're feeling. I think she'll understand better than you think. Mom is very smart, and she loves you just as much as I do. Promise you'll tell her what you told me. I guarantee you'll feel better."

Mark hesitated, as if thinking it over. "Okay. But only if you promise you won't tell Mom I called you."

"Why shouldn't I tell her?"

"She'll be mad that I snuck down."

"She'll get over it," Paul said, more harshly than he intended.

Mark paused. "But her feelings will be hurt. That I said she doesn't know how to help as well as you do. That I thought I had to sneak. You have to promise me you won't tell her."

As worried as he was, he was still trying to protect his mother's well-being, *her* confidence, *her* security. It was this concern for Janet that lay behind the midnight calls: *Mark didn't want to worry her.* Paul loved his son almost intolerably at that moment. The distance between them was agony.

"All right, I promise. I won't tell her." Paul said. "Okay? Now you go to bed. Just be sure to talk to Mom, and keep on fighting it, and tell yourself that everything's going to be all right. Because it is. And I'll be back to see you soon."

He stumped back to the carriage house. *Everything's going to be all right,* he sang to himself. *Everything's all right. Right.*

Lia got into the Subaru and started it, then rolled down the window and looked up at him in the dull light. "Can I ask a favor?" she said. Saturday morning: She was on her way back to Vermont. During the night, the clear weather had given way to an overcast that threatened snow or, worse, freezing rain, and she wanted to get on the road before driving conditions got dangerous.

"Could I ever refuse you anything?"

"*You,*" she said, "you have this marvelous, histrionic way of turning everything into a struggle of, of positively *earth-shaking* scope. It's good versus evil, light versus dark, reason versus whatever. You seem to like to, I don't know, *distill* everything to some essential question of values. And this is part of what makes you such a good person, and I love it about you." She stopped, reached up and cupped his cheek in her warm palm. "But I wish for once you could see things more the way I do. For me, the situation here or with Mark and so on, they're just specific and pragmatic problems and opportunities. They can be handled if you take them one at a time and don't blow them up into bigger issues. Taking on evil itself is a pretty big job, but dealing firmly and successfully with, say, Janet, is more manageable. Right? This is one of the most important things I've learned from scaring the shit out of myself, Paul. Just focus on the job at hand, on your equipment, on conditions, on your own preparedness. Don't go all abstract and grandiose. Otherwise it *will* kill you."

She looked at him very seriously, and he wondered just what level of favor this was. Was this just good advice from your loved one, a gesture of support? Or was it a more dire species of communication, a help-save-our-relationship request? He pushed the idea away.

"Okay," was all he could say.

Paul watched her pull away, wishing that there was time to talk, wishing they could drive together, concerned for her safety. The clouds had lowered until the tops of the bare trees up slope were being erased by trailing strands of mist, and now a fine rain drifted down, freezing on the ground, promising tricky driving. Not wanting to scrape later, he took the precaution of backing the MG into the carriage house's garage bay and shutting the doors. If Albert Martin didn't come to install the gate this morning, he'd have to get a temporary chain to string between the pillars while he went back to Vermont. The situation with Janet and Mark couldn't wait.

On Friday they'd spent an hour digging in the biggest drifts of debris, looking for the frozen corpses that on Thursday night they'd been convinced filled the house. There'd been some relief in not finding any, and they'd all put in a hard day's work, Dempsey coming and going with the windows, Cohen and his nephew working like miners in the basement. A productive day: They'd begun to see progress in the library. Paul had explained to the crew that he and Lia would need to return to Vermont, himself until Tuesday, Lia a day longer, and they made arrangements for Dempsey and Cohen to get a key from Albert if he did manage to install the gate. Lia and he stayed up until after midnight, working until their eyes blurred. Then Mark's phone call.

After putting away the MG, Paul made a call to Albert Martin's garage to see if he was still on track with the gate. Albert answered breathlessly on the first ring.

"I'm pinned down here at the station," Albert said. "Pump attendant called in sick on me. Still hoping to get there today. Do the best I can—maybe by two, three o'clock. Sorry!"

By noon he'd sorted four more boxes of papers. After a quick lunch of canned beans, he filled another box and took it to the warmth of the smoking room. The first page he picked up, a wrinkled onionskin half-covered with single-spaced typing, was a letter from Ben to Vivien, signed in fading blue fountain pen with Ben's confident, looping signature. He pawed quickly through the rest of the box. At a glance, he could see that there were many pages of similarly typed text among the jumbled papers.

He read several. One early letter concerned Ben's work on his Jefferson biography, the ups and downs of his research. One referred to another dinner they'd had together, with profuse thanks. Another discussed Philippine history, the role of the United States at the turn of the century.

There was a vividness to Ben's letters, a vitality: Ben Skoglund, professor of history, student of philosophy, and amateur rock climber, biographer of Jefferson and champion of the Enlightenment, of Reason, of Humanism. Of facing into it. His confidence, if you could forget the way he ended, was inspiring.

Paul put the handful of letters aside, a little special file, and rummaged again in the box.

Dearest Vivien,

Not to burden you with my worries . . . but I don't feel I can trouble Aster any more than I already have. Perhaps because you have confided in me, I feel I can confess my worries about Paulie.

He is an exceptionally bright boy, with a rare and precious instrument in that little head of his. And yet this fine intelligence is held in check by one terrible obstruction after another. Just when we have begun to get control of his first problem, some new, equally mysterious demon has reared its head. And as before the quacks cannot agree on a name for it, a cause or a cure. I say hang them all for the charlatans they are.

My outrage this evening is directed at the most recent specialist I consulted, highly recommended, who has at last issued his august diagnosis: congenital choreoathetosis. Congenital choreoathetosis! When I challenged this opinion, he looked quite offended. "Are you a medical doctor, sir?" he asked me. Naturally, I've refused to pay his fee. He can have me to court if he wishes.

So, yet another in the ongoing series of idiotic misdiagnoses. I remain more convinced than ever that the solution to this mystery falls to me, to my own ingenuity and research. In the meantime, Paulie is becoming conscious that he is an "oddball." He has been returning home from

*school with bruises, the result of schoolyard fights caused by his strange-
ness. I worry that this will shape his sense of himself in unfortunate
ways. My dear, difficult, marvelous, strange son.*

    *In any case, I take some comfort that you are familiar with how
painfully concerned a parent can be. There are times when I fear I will
be overcome with anguish—if anything could strike me down, it is this.
I'm more grateful than you know for your understanding.*

    My love to you,

Ben

Paul felt a familiar stab in his own heart. *Ben really did know that feeling.*
Ben really cared about his son. As he cared about Mark. He felt the building pressure behind his eyes, the overflowing well of sorrow, ancient guilt
and pain and confusion. Ben hovered in his memory, taking on dimension.

He had just reached for the box again when he heard a muffled thump
from the direction of the kitchen. Ice tingled in his veins. Immediately another noise came, closer, something cracking or crunching in the main
room. As of a piece of china underfoot.

Someone was in the house.

Not Albert—he'd been at the garage less than ten minutes ago, he
couldn't possibly have gotten to Highwood from Somers in that time. Paul
listened anxiously, ears straining against the rush of blood hissing in his
ears, and thought he heard small rustles or scrapes, fading away. Without
thinking, he looked around the room in the inky light for a weapon. A primal impulse: find something heavy for the hands to wield. He backed
toward the hearth and silently lifted the poker from the rack of fireplace
tools. It had a good weight to it, a solid iron point and hook.

Akatheeesia! his brain screamed. He bit his tongue to keep it silent.

He walked stealthily to the door, listened, then slowly swung it open. His
heart was pounding so hard that his body shook. The big hall was dimly lit,
and through the door opposite the smoking room he could see through the
dining room all the way into the kitchen. Where the outside door stood
open, a blue rectangle of forest hanging in the dark.

No one was in the big room. He was disappointed. Part of him had
hoped it might be Dempsey, come back for a tool he'd forgotten. *Or,* he
thought, suddenly certain, *for whatever other purpose Dempsey had going.*

Holding the poker in both hands, he walked quietly into the middle of
the room, staying in the lane he'd shoveled clear of debris. For a time he
stood near Dempsey's work table, listening, hearing nothing. Then he
heard another muffled thump, a small cracking noise. From upstairs.

Paul bit his tongue harder, shrugged to loosen the clench of tension in
his shoulders, and walked carefully up the littered stairs. At the top, he

paused on the balcony to listen again. A rustling came from across the big open space—from Vivien's room. He walked swiftly around the balcony, the poker ready, watching the doorway to the bedroom. The first shaky rush of adrenaline had worn off, replaced by a state of taut alertness, cautious yet purposeful. And, surprisingly, a feeling of elation, almost of joy, in the clarity and simplicity of it: *Don't fuck with me.*

As he came along the cluttered south-side balcony, his foot grazed a tall silver cup, a trophy of some sort, which spun away and clattered against the balcony railing. He stopped and waited, his heart jarring against his ribs.

No more noise from Vivien's bedroom.

And then a shape leapt out of the doorway, a looming black silhouette against the muted light from the window. Paul drew back the poker, and instantly the broad-shouldered shape did the same thing, pulling back a bat-size leg of some piece of furniture.

It was Royce.

"Good Christ, cousin. You look like you're ready to kill someone. Who in hell were you expecting?" Royce lowered his weapon.

"I didn't hear anyone come up," Paul said. Royce must have arrived while he'd been in the library, gathering another box of papers.

"Drove right up. Car's right out front. Would have knocked, but it didn't seem as if anyone was here." Royce tossed down his club, dusted his hands against each other.

"What are you doing here?"

Royce came toward him, smiling. "Thank you for the hospitable greeting, Paulie. Quite the welcome home for the prodigal son." He clapped Paul on one shoulder, and then gently pushed the point of the poker toward the floor. "I don't think that's necessary, do you?"

"What do you want here, Royce?"

"I grew up here, remember? I was in the area, visiting some old acquaintances. Thought I'd stop by, seeing as how you didn't give me the courtesy of a return call, to finish our discussion. Which you told me you'd think about. Also to take a look at the old homestead. After what you told me, I was curious."

"I thought you were flying to Europe."

Royce put his hands on the railing and looked out over the incredible chaos of the big room. "And here I thought you were exaggerating! This verges on the downright fabulous, doesn't it? In a morbid sort of way. How intriguing." Royce spat over the railing, watched his spit drop, then turned to face Paul. "Indeed I am leaving. First thing tomorrow. Time, as they say, is therefore of the essence regarding my proposal."

"I can't do the work at your apartment. I'm committed here."

"Certainly there's enough here to keep you busy." Royce turned back to the railing. "Well. It does something to one to see the old place like this, doesn't it? One's boyhood memories and all."

"Who did it, Royce? You?"

Royce jerked his head slightly, as if he'd started to turn toward Paul again, but kept looking out over the room. "I'm not, as you've gathered, *fond* of my mother," he said. He sighed and began to walk around the balcony. Paul followed, still gripping the poker. "But I assure you, cousin, if I wanted to revenge myself upon her I would think of more effective means than this."

"Such as?"

"Such as the one thing she absolutely cannot endure: ignore her. If you understood her better, you'd see that. For me to spend this much time and energy, even to strike out at her, would constitute nothing less than an effusive gesture of affection." Royce laughed, a harsh bark that echoed in the cold, still room. "And I would never give her that satisfaction."

Downstairs, Royce picked his way across the big room to the bedroom that had been his. He stopped just inside, surveying the rubble: drifts of shattered pieces of wood mixed with bedding, clothes, papers, tangled cords of lamps, ripped canvas and splintered frames of paintings. A section of the paneled wood ceiling had been ripped open, leaving a dark cavity where the joists and subfloor of the room above could just be seen, a loop of sagging wiring hanging from the gap. The exposed piano harp leaned against one wall, trailing a snarl of broken strings. The skin and head of a polar bear, its jaw broken and ripped impossibly wide, seemed to writhe in the rubble. Over all of it lay a haze of goose down, from some shredded pillow or comforter, drifting lazily in the drafts their entrance had caused.

Royce prodded the stiff raccoon corpse with his toe. "Too bad. I always liked raccoons," he said. "Well. My mother didn't exactly preserve my room as a shrine to her dear boy, did she?" He stooped to pick up a brass claw foot, its talons clenched around a glass glide. "You know what this is? The earthly remains of my piano stool. One of those three-legged ones, the kind you spin on to adjust higher or lower. Used to have a good time making myself sick, spinning around on it." Royce held the foot to his eye, peered through the glass for a moment, then slipped it into his coat pocket. "A little souvenir. I'd prefer my old polar bear rug, actually. But I suspect you'd object."

"Personally, I don't care. But my employer might."

Royce kicked at the debris absently, roiling the feathers. "All I can remember of my adolescence is the joy of discovering masturbation. In those days, you couldn't just pick up girlie magazines in every grocery store. I'd sneak across to the library, bring back a volume of the *Encyclopaedia Britannica* and open it to 'Greece.' The pictures of Greek sculpture. Gave myself what you might call a classical education. Inadvertently picked up the principles of aesthetics and proportion, caught a glimpse of some decent architecture whenever I thumbed past the Parthenon on my way to the nudes. Pity kids nowadays." A wry smiled played on his lopsided mouth. "Of course, when I came of age it took me years to get used to women having arms. Well. Nothing comes without a price."

Hunched in his overcoat, hands in his pockets, Royce looked pensive. "Cold as a bitch in here," he said at last.

"I've got a heater set up in the smoking room. You're welcome to come in to warm up," Paul said, "before you leave."

"Yes, yes. Which of course I'm expected to do shortly. Well, warming up sounds delightful. Lead the way."

They went into the smoking room and stood next to the heater, turning their hands in the rising heat. After a few moments, Paul lit the lantern.

With the room better lit, Royce scanned the labeled boxes of papers and turned aside to shuffle through some of the photos Paul and Lia had spread out on the broad leather-topped game table: "I suppose my mother has evidence of my own sordid adventures salted away here somewhere. Quite the little bastard, wasn't I? Mind if I look at some of it?"

"Yes, I mind. Among other things, Vivien asked me, quite emphatically, to maintain her privacy."

"And you're being a dutiful guardian of it."

"She's paying me for the job, and that's part of our agreement. And I'd just as soon not get caught in a conflict between you and Vivien." Paul stood across from him, knuckles of both hands on the table, making it obvious it was time for him to leave.

Royce flipped through a few more of the photos. "So, Paulie," he said, scrutinizing one closely, "there's nothing I can say to persuade you to change your mind? I should think you'd be overjoyed to get away from this museum of horrors."

"We've been through this. I said no. I've got a contract here."

"Your loyalty is admirable. But has it ever occurred to you that Vivien may not be so very deserving of your loyalty? That she isn't, shall I say, entirely forthcoming with you?"

"Unlike Royce, who is totally aboveboard."

Royce's cheek twitched, but he kept his eyes on the photos, fanning them like cards. "Yes, you are very wise to want to avoid getting caught in a cross fire between my mother and myself. That could get awfully unpleasant. But has it occurred to you that you already have?"

"Is that a threat?"

"God, no. A simple observation." But the look he gave Paul was dark, as if his anger were building. He cleared his throat, raised his chin to straighten his tie, and buttoned his coat. "In any case. On the assumption that your homegrown naïveté is genuine, let me make an observation: You're neck-deep now. Do you really want to find out how much deeper it gets?"

"Try me."

"I don't think you're up to it, cousin." Royce's uneven smile flickered.

Push back. "How about telling me what you were looking for in Vivien's room?"

"Actually, what I was looking for was this—or something like this. I wanted to see if she'd kept . . . such things." Royce picked out one of the photos and flicked it spinning across the table toward Paul. It was the shot of Vivien with the two children, Royce the baby in her arms, and the other, the toddler. "Tell me," Royce said. "Who do you think this is?"

"Vivien. You. I don't know the other kid. Why the riddles, Royce?"

"And this—your father, whom we all admired so greatly." Royce shoved across one of several photos of Ben that Paul had found. He was seated in a wide-backed wicker chair, looking up from reading a book, his shirt sleeves rolled up to reveal strong forearms. "Who do you think *he* is, Paulie? What made him tick? Ever wonder what made him—"

"Don't push your luck," Paul said.

"Wasn't it you who just said, 'Try me'?" Royce shrugged. "Just obliging you. Perhaps these are things you might want to look into. Good-bye, Paulie." At the door, he turned to look at Paul, a surprisingly open look of appraisal. Then he shut the door, and Paul heard his footsteps fading away. Paul looked at the photos, the wide-faced strange boy, the smiling Ben. After a few moments, he heard Royce's car start up and scatter gravel as it pulled out.

By the time Paul put the pedal down and spun the MG onto 684, it was just getting dark. Heading north, the open highway—he was glad to leave Highwood behind for a few days. And he was relieved that Albert had actually arrived to put up the gate. But there was still no shortage of things to worry about. Who was the strange boy in the photo Royce had tossed at him? Seeing Albert again had reminded him of the old woman, Albert's grandmother. *Those two kids,* she'd said. *One just a baby, the other not right in his head.* Senile rambling, or had his mention of Highwood triggered something in her memory? *Living alone up there. Very wealthy. No husband.*

And Royce. Beyond all the disturbing questions Royce's visit had raised, what stayed in Paul's mind was the first moment he had encountered him, on the balcony in front of Vivien's room. The queer elation of confronting a concrete, material enemy. The strength that came with the resolution to fight back.

As he thought about it, he kept returning to the image of Royce's dark silhouette as he'd leapt out of the doorway, landing with his feet well apart, the table leg held ready. He'd shown remarkable agility for a man his size.

41

Mo came home from work Friday night feeling pissed off, sick of an endlessly ramifying case and of having Superman breathing down his neck. How many NYSP investigators had to deal with crap like *that*? Unable to sleep, he turned on the computer and dicked around trying to construct a graphic model of the case, factoring in every variable that he thought might bear upon it.

He sat in the glow of the computer monitor, scowling. Everything about the case bothered him. The level of destruction at the house, for example. He couldn't think of any other description beyond what he'd told Paul and Lia: *pathological.* Not that there wasn't plenty of room for more conventional modes of vandalism; no doubt, in addition to whatever else had happened, local teenagers had come and gone many times. But kids alone couldn't account for it. Not that level of strength and persistence and *intensity.*

If he could safely assume that there was a pathological aspect to the whole thing, certain other assumptions might follow. When he had first started taking forensic science courses, the psychology textbooks talked about there being two general categories of violence: what they called "emotional" and "instrumental." Instrumental violence was violence intended to achieve a particular goal or reward—money, status, territory, etc. A terrorist bombing or an armed robbery, for example. Emotional violence, on the other hand, stemmed from feelings of rage, anger, hate, fear, frustration, jealousy, et cetera—the jealous husband killing his wife's lover, the coke dealer who offed somebody who'd dissed him.

Then there was an emerging third category. In recent years, neurological and biochemical theories had become increasingly influential in the study of violence. A lot of violence was now thought to stem from medical problems such as temporal lobe epilepsy, schizophrenia, depression, paranoia, cranial trauma. Often these neurological conditions amplified emotional triggers, increasing the likelihood of feelings spilling over into violent actions.

And increasingly the law accepted such considerations as factors mitigating guilt. Neurological conditions could result in *automatism,* defined in both medicine and law as a state in which a person "though capable of action, is not conscious of what he is doing." Hell, even variations in your blood sugar level could make you violent. Or at least let you get away with murder: Look at Dan White, who shot to death the mayor of San Francisco and an alderman but got off because he'd eaten a Hostess Twinkie an hour before. The Twinkie Defense. It was enough to make you sick.

Mo swiveled in his chair from the computer screen to his bookshelf and leafed idly through a couple of criminology texts, eyes not focused, as if he could pick up ideas from the blur of pages. Aristotle and the other ancient Greeks talked about *catharsis,* the purging or release of emotion, an idea refined by people like Freud and Lorenz into what some psychologists called the "hydraulic" principle of violence. That is, violent impulses built up until they reached an intolerable level and demanded an outlet, like steam in a boiler. Healthy people, so this reasoning went, let off steam bit by bit, or chose harmless objects for their anger; violence-prone people let the steam build up until they had to explode.

Somebody had exploded at Highwood.

A cop saw evidence for the hydraulic theory every day. People harbored hatred or anger or repressed sex drives—sometimes consciously, sometimes not—and it eventually burst out. Wife beaters, serial killers, tavern brawlers, abuse victims who finally turned the tables, rapists, violent school kids. The whole zoo. For some it took a lifetime to get to the point of explosion, for others it took only days or weeks.

The problem with accepting the "hydraulic" theory was that it inevitably suggested an unpleasant answer for the ancient argument over whether mankind was inherently violent and aggressive. You couldn't help but conclude that the secret soul of man contained an ever-filling well of poison.

Mo tossed the books onto the floor, making a thump that he immediately regretted, thinking he'd either bother Alice downstairs or prompt another invitation he'd have to decline. This was what happened when you pondered weighty issues late at night after a long work week in an apartment that was stark and underfurnished, in the general aftermath of a divorce, et cetera. Over the centuries, better minds than his had pondered such issues and hadn't come up with squat. No sense in wasting time dealing with gargantuan abstractions or pondering the poor savage soul of mankind, which in any case Mo Ford was unlikely to miraculously fix. He'd do better to keep his agenda manageable. Maybe that's one reason you became a cop in the first place: It was a way to break off one piece of the world's problems at a time and do your bit to contain the damage. Sometimes you succeeded, sometimes you didn't. In any case, you had specific tools and techniques and rules you could use: the law, the forensic sciences.

Okay. So what the science of criminology clearly demonstrated was that violent behavior tended to be periodic. Cyclical. Studies showed that the cycles could be connected to almost anything—the moon, the tides, rising sex urges, mood disorders, medication cycles, drug availability, the arrival of welfare checks or paychecks, school semesters, menstruation. Serial killers almost always killed at regular intervals, getting their jollies and then chilling out for a while as the well of poison filled and the urge became overpowering again.

Assuming the Highwood thing was connected to the missing kids at all, could it be something like that—a serial killer at work? Is that what Heather Mason had figured out when she'd sent him the letter? *It's going to happen again. Probably before Christmas.*

But she'd also said, with that fiendish, innocent certainty, *See, you think it's just a detective story, but it's much much more than that.* What'd she say then? *It's about when we think we know what's real and then find out we didn't know. How people can do things nobody ever imagined they could.* Then she'd gone on like King Lear, *ever, ever, never, never,* and so on. What exactly had she seen somebody do?

Mo shut Heather out of his thoughts with difficulty. Assuming for a moment that there was a cycle here, what was it? He tapped the keyboard to call up the calendar he'd constructed. Richard Mason died and Essie Howrigan disappeared on August 6, Dub Gilmore and possibly Steve Rubio disappeared on September 19. Forty-four days, a little over six weeks apart. If you factored it forward at cycles of forty-four days, you'd get another blowout of whatever psychopathology around November 2, and another—he clicked ahead—about December 16. Before Christmas, like Heather said. Coming right up. How nice.

Of course, he only had two real dates, and two dates didn't add up to anything. You needed at least three to triangulate. And he had nothing to plug into the November slot.

Mo backed out of the program and switched off the computer. It was all bullshit, flailing around in the dark because he had so little to go on. It was too late at night for this crap. He cut the lights and groped his way to bed.

His resolution to spend the weekend relaxing, resting his brain cells, broadening his personal horizons, lasted only until Saturday afternoon, when the phone rang and he picked it up to hear Lia's voice.

"Is this Mo?" she asked.

"Yes. Lia?"

"Hi. Did I call at a bad time?"

Mo realized he must have sounded startled. "No—this is fine. It's great."

"Well, I'm glad I caught you. I should have called before I left, but I didn't have time, so I'm calling from Vermont. We couldn't remember if we'd told you we'd be back up here this weekend."

"No."

"I drove up this morning. I guess the guy is supposed to put up the driveway gate today, then Paul's driving up too. We wanted you to know our number up here, in case you needed to reach us. Do you have a pencil?"

"Yep." Mo jotted the number.

"We'll be up for a few days. Paul's coming back down on Tuesday, I'll need to stay until Wednesday."

"Okay." He felt knocked off balance at hearing the sound of her voice here in his apartment where he'd suffered through two mostly sleepless nights trying not to think about her. He found himself listening closely, yet not hearing what she'd actually said, tuning in instead to the music of her voice and the nuances it might contain. Did she seem a little shy too? *Yes,* he decided.

"Anyway," Lia said, "I should go." She hesitated, then seemed to choose her words carefully: "I was thinking about you on the drive up, and I just wanted to tell you that it was a pleasure to meet you, and that I'm very glad to have you helping us with whatever it is that's happening up at the lodge. We both think you're a great guy. So, anyway—thanks."

"I'm glad," Mo said. "Yeah, well, it was great to meet you, you two. I'm looking forward to next time."

"Okay. *Ciao,*" she said brightly.

Then he was just sitting there holding a telephone receiver in his hands.

He realized he'd said maybe ten words to her during the whole call. Was there anything in the call besides what she'd said? *I was thinking about you on the drive up.* Hard to tell what she'd said and what he was reading into it. He suppressed a feeling of elation that wanted to burst into bloom in his chest.

Her call set his thoughts percolating again, to the point where he abandoned his resolution, decided to make a few phone calls, weekend or not. It was December 3—if Heather was right, if there was any truth to the idea of cycles, he'd better crack this son of a bitch soon.

First he failed to reach Mrs. Mason, with whom he was planning to plead for another interview with Heather, and then failed to reach a highly regarded professor of Asian studies at NYU who he hoped might give him some ideas about a possible Philippine connection to Highwood. He left messages on both answering machines, debated whether he should bother with another call given that his luck was running so bad, then gave it a try anyway. To his surprise, he managed to reach Rick LePlante, a reporter for the *Times* who often wrote about events in Westchester and Putnam counties and made a hobby out of local history. They chatted for a time, then Mo asked him for information on Ku Klux Klan activities in Westchester County. Rick couldn't recall any major incidents but promised to look into it and call Mo back.

Mo hung up, put a check next to Rick's name on his call list, and went back to his notes, still thinking about his conversation with Lia. *I was thinking about you on the drive up. I'm very glad to have you with us on this thing.* Could mean anything.

But one thing was for certain: She was a very smart woman. She put things together fast. It hadn't escaped him that she'd said "whatever *is* happening" up at the lodge. Present tense. A continuing situation.

42

It was almost eight o'clock by the time Paul reached the Hanover-Norwich exit. He'd been driving in the dark for over three hours, but instead of feeling drained and hypnotized from the drive and the long day, he felt oddly energized. Part of it was the anticipation of seeing Mark tomorrow. Part of it was the decision he'd made to fight back—starting with a little research. Rather than turning left on 10A, toward home, he swung right, crossed the river into New Hampshire, and went to Hanover.

The Dana Medical Library had closed, but the huge Baker Library was still open. Paul showed the reference librarian his on-line database access authorization and found an empty terminal at the center table. He'd occasionally used the electronic reference resources at Dartmouth to research current information about education, but more often had made use of the medical database MedLine while pursuing various ideas about Mark's condition. The service provided listings and abstracts of articles from 2,500 medical journals from around the world. If there was any serious, current information on hyperkinesis or hyperdynamism, he'd find it here.

The reference room was long and narrow, two stories tall, with a balcony running around three sides. After a week in the wreckage of Highwood, he found the pervasive order and cleanliness especially soothing. Reassuring. What had Ben always said? "A library is a temple to Reason."

The MedLine screen told him that 332 entries were on file for hyperkinesis, and showed the titles and authors of the first eight. He read the first screen of titles, then moved ahead one screen, then another. As he'd anticipated, the articles he found dealt with hyperkinesis as a side effect of diseases, brain injuries, or drugs. The majority dealt with hyperkinesis as an aspect of pediatric pathologies, notably hyperactivity and attention deficit disorder.

After half an hour, just as he had begun to despair of finding anything relevant, he got his first hit.

Record No.:   94284930
Author: Stropes, M.
Address: Roosevelt Medical Research Institute, New York
Title: From the anecdotal to the empirical: a case for research
                of hyperkinesis/hyperdynamism.
Source: Kin Disord, 1992, Nov. 8, (4): 352–377
Abstract: Study of human hyperkinetic and hyperdynamic potentials has been prejudiced by limiting research to known physio- or
psychopathologies. Despite a wealth of anecdotal evidence attesting
to spontaneous displays of vastly accelerated metabolic/kinetic activity and increased muscular strength in humans, clinical observation and analysis of such phenomena have been limited. Based on a
new assessment of historical data and a hypothetical model for the
mechanisms of the phenomenon, Dr. Stropes argues for systematic
research into hyperkinesis/hyperdynamism.

To suggest likely mechanisms, Stropes cites the case of a 27-year-
old Florida woman in whom regional cerebral glucose consumption
was measured shortly after hyperkinetic/hyperdynamic movements
subsided. While cerebellar and cortical glucose consumption was
near normal, hypothalamic, lentiform and caudate glucose consumption was significantly increased in both hemispheres . . .

Despite Stropes's assertion that hyperkinesis and hyperdynamism needn't
be associated with illness, the list of cross-references at the end of the abstract was ominous: *aggression, epilepsy, hysteria, movement disorders, rage,*
stress, trauma, violent psychopathologies.

Paul found another relevent title almost immediately, this time a highly
clinical piece by a Dr. J. Horowitz. Reading between the lines of tongue-
twisting medical terminology, he was able to deduce that the article reported on electrical activity and regional glucose concentrations in the
brain of an emotionally traumatized but otherwise healthy twenty-four-
year-old man. The subject had demonstrated a period of extreme strength
after witnessing his younger sister being hit by a car. He was apprehended
while ripping parking meters out of the sidewalk with his bare hands.

Paul's hands rang the invisible bell and he suppressed a series of little
barks. If a person could rip up parking meters, he could also rip sinks out
and shove them through walls, or throw bureaus through windows, or tear
the doors off refrigerators. Or knock bowling ball–size finials off their
posts hard enough to dent walls fifty feet away.

He scanned several more screens before finding another article by
M. Stropes, entitled "Evidence of hypothalamic and pituitary hypertro-
phy in subjects demonstrating hysterical hyperkinesis/hyperdynamism."

Stropes had added the term *hysterical* to indicate a prolonged state of supernormal strength and activity induced by extreme emotions, usually of mortal fear or protective concern for loved ones. He argued that one basis for the phenomenon was a great increase of the brain's ability to produce the fight-or-flight chemicals that allowed the body to respond to threats. Stropes pointed to evidence that the main structures of the limbic system in hyperdynamic individuals were larger than normal or had structural anomalies.

He found only one more relevant entry: an abstract of a review of Dr. Stropes's article. The opinion of the reviewer, Dr. I. Barrington, a bigwig at some neurological research institute, was that Stropes's methodologies and interpretations were suspect. The abstract quoted Barrington's conclusion verbatim: "Dr. Stropes has failed to make a convincing transition from folktales of supermen to clinical demonstration. Until the phenomenon can reliably be repeated and observed under laboratory conditions, it will and should remain suspect and unsuitable for serious consideration by the medical community."

Screw I. Barrington, Paul thought. If there was one thing to be learned from the history of the establishment's view of Tourette's, one thing he'd learned the hard way while working on Mark's problem, it was that the old guard of the medical establishment would defend its orthodoxies regardless of how much evidence was presented to the contrary.

Paul thought of quitting for the night, but instead exited MedLine and selected MediaList, a database that provided word searches for thirteen thousand mainstream newspapers and periodicals. One of the advantages of the database was that it carried the entire article on-line—if he managed to find anything, he'd be able to read the whole piece or print it out immediately. Punching in *hyperdynamism* here, he was rewarded with only a handful of entries, but a quick glance at the titles showed him that he'd hit the jackpot.

The first article, from a newspaper in Oklahoma, was headlined "Big John in Real Life": A seventh-grade English teacher had rescued his class from a school devastated by a tornado. Using superhuman strength, the teacher had lifted the main roof-support I-beam, bearing thousands of pounds of weight, and kept the roof from crushing his students. The people in Tannersville, where the incident happened, had taken to calling the teacher Big John after the old popular song in which a miner saves his fellows after a mining cave-in.

Paul could feel the shape of the melody in his fingers. Jimmy Dean, 1961.

After the highly technical medical journal abstracts, regular journalistic prose sounded sensational: "Man Lifts Car Off Mother of Two," "Miracle on 3rd Avenue," "Superman Lives in Indianapolis." The Superman article concerned an Indianapolis construction worker who had used his arms like the fabled Jaws of Life to free a fellow worker who had gotten trapped when a section of an office building under construction had collapsed. Witnesses claimed the hero had momentarily been able to rip corrugated sheet-steel and bend rebar with his bare hands. The article quoted the same Dr. Michael Stropes who had written the articles in the medical journals, describing him as "the leading authority on hyperdynamism" and head of the Metabolic Disorders Research Unit of Roosevelt Institute.

Dr. Barrington's opinions notwithstanding, Paul decided his next step would be to try to talk to Dr. Stropes.

Paul leaned back in his chair, exhaustion beginning to wrap him in its fuzzy bear hug.

One nagging problem: Lia. While he couldn't wait to tell her the results of his research, he didn't look forward to the skepticism he expected from her. *It's tabloid stuff, Paul,* she'd say. *More of your neurological bias, neurochemical chauvinism.* Or worse, she'd believe it, and the implicit danger would snag her. He'd never persuade her to leave Highwood, if it came to that, until she'd satisfied her curiosity, her hunger, her peptide addiction. Maybe he'd postpone telling her.

His fingers twitched and a tune teased him: "Big Bad John." How long would that stay with him? The articles he'd come across suggested as many questions as they answered. The second article, for example, the one about the young man who had watched his sister get run over: *Just how do you "apprehend" someone who can rip up parking meters with his bare hands?*

He guided the MG through the beautiful Vermont night, oblivious to its charms. Outside, stars shone above the bare woods and lightless houses of the serene countryside. Inside the MG it was a different kind of darkness. What had Royce said? *Reality is subjective. It's whatever you make it.* All too true.

If only he'd quit while he was ahead, feeling hopeful that he'd found a key to the Highwood business. But he hadn't quit. After looking up hyperdynamism, he'd done just one more piece of research, idly, offhandedly. This time he'd punched in *KKK.*

There'd been thousands of article titles to scan, but several had jumped out at him immediately. The first he pulled up was called "The Other KKK: Turn-of-the-Century Terror in the Philippines."

Forget the Ku Klux Klan. KKK stood for *Kataastaasang Kagalanggalang Katipunan ng mga Ank ng Bayan,* Tagalog for "The Exalted and Most Honorable Society of the Sons of the People." It was a secret society, part religious cult, part political party, part crime syndicate, operating in the Philippines during the islands' revolt against Spain, and, later, against U.S. colonialism. Like similar cults throughout the Orient, the KKK used mystic rituals, blood pacts, covert names, esoteric martial arts techniques, and special codes and languages as it carried on a terrorist war against the Spanish colonialists. Members wore *anting-antings,* traditional amulets they believed gave them superpowers in battle. Founder Andres Bonifacio and his followers were outraged by atrocities against their people and declared war against Spain in August, 1896. They'd make a raid, assassinate some Spaniard, and scrawl KKK on or over the corpse, in Roman letters. For foreigners in the Philippines at the turn of the century, KKK was synonymous with terror.

There can't be a connection, Paul thought. *That was a hundred years ago, half a world away.* But then he remembered the first of Ben's letters they found: Wasn't Bonifacio one of the names Ben had mentioned—someone Hoffmann Senior had known?

The MG's headlights made a small, wan circle of light in the deep backroad night, and the dashboard lights flickered slightly, making Paul wonder if some new wiring problem were starting to crop up. The least of his worries. What worried him was the wiring in his head: He'd been at a quarter of his old haloperidol dosage for five days now, and his neurochemistry was changing. His own thought processes were becoming unfamiliar to him, untrustworthy.

In his mind he saw a band of KKK members, still operating in secret all these years, bursting into Highwood for revenge or to recover something that they'd lost a long time ago, maybe something the original Hoffmann stole from them. With superpowers derived from their *anting-antings.* Performing esoteric rites, chanting, ripping the place apart in a trance-induced frenzy.

The problem was that he couldn't quite disbelieve it. It seemed no less likely than any other scenario. *Reality is subjective. It's whatever you make it.*

Equally real yet impossible was the idea that had been growing quietly in his mind: the secret child, the secret sibling. You couldn't look at the photos of the strange child without feeling they were family portraits, mother and sons. What—Vivien had another child that nobody knew about, nobody talked about? But the Skoglunds had been up at the lodge once or twice a week for years. There'd never been any indication of another kid, nothing at all. Impossible. Surely Royce would have loved to reveal tantalizing tidbits, dropped hints, back then. A secret only enhances your status if someone knows you have it.

Paul gripped the wheel tightly. Isn't that what Royce had just done? *"Who do you think this is?"*

So maybe there was a secret sibling. Mentally or physically defective, unacceptable in the Hoffmanns' stratum of society, not a good scion for the Hoffmann lineage. So they hid him away, like in the old days. The Hunchback of Highwood Lodge.

Paul felt a chill come over him: *The strange room off Vivien's bedroom. Like a vault. You could keep a kid in there. Nobody'd ever hear a thing.*

The scenario played out in his mind, a perfectly conceived image, detailed, absolutely convincing: *Vivien's other child, kept in that room all those years. Cooped up because he was prone to violent, episodic dyscontrol, maybe deformed. Huge, pale, monstrous, pathetic. Growing older and stronger and at some point breaking loose, full of hatred for the mother who'd imprisoned him so long.*

Just a flight of morbid ideation, he told himself. But the thoughts kept coming. *If it was designed as a vault, why are there air vents? Why are the ceiling lights recessed and behind steel grates? Not a darkroom—not without plumbing or electrical sockets. Not with the light switches in Vivien's bedroom.*

He could imagine Lia's skepticism: "Isn't that a bit *too* Victorian Gothic?" And ordinarily he'd have agreed. But after only a few days at Highwood, anything seemed possible.

Which brought up the question of Lia again: to talk to Lia about these things, or not? Why did the prospect of talking to her about this stuff make him feel so uneasy?

Because he didn't trust himself, his own thought processes, anymore. He couldn't deny it any longer. It had now been ten days since he'd reduced his haloperidol dosage, and in that time he had been changing. Things seemed clearer, their patterns or systems more apparent. Surprisingly, his tics had not gotten any worse. But the disturbing dream or memory images were getting clearer, and the trancelike calm came upon him more often as he was thinking through something, following down the branching of thoughts. And of course the flights of morbid ideation.

The problem was he couldn't tell a reasonable idea from a morbid fantasy. Hysterical hyperdynamism, the KKK, the secret sibling: A little factual support and a lot of vague, morbid intuition, and the images were as real as the night road rushing toward him in the headlights.

No, he couldn't talk to Lia about any of it just yet. Not without more tangible evidence. She'd be skeptical, she'd be concerned for his mental well-being—a concern that wasn't entirely unjustified.

He didn't like the idea of a wedge opening up between them, especially now. Why was he feeling so sensitive to nuances of their relationship right now? Face it: He was holding back from telling her things because he didn't want to look stupid, nuts, overly credulous, naïve—especially not since Detective Mo Ford had come into the picture, with his decisiveness and professionalism. The aura of competence and security around him. Lia's obvious attraction to him.

Pulling into the farm driveway, he reaffirmed his decision to wait on talking to her. It was all too tenuous. He'd write to Dr. Stropes first, learn more about hyperdynamism; for the KKK and the secret sibling, he'd try to garner more clues from Vivien's papers, maybe talk to Vivien. Lia was high enough on the whole scenario. No sense in adding more fuel to the fire. Most important, he'd wait until he had some kind of a handle on his changing brain, his changing thoughts. In the long run, that was what mattered most.

43

Mo rolled out of bed and winced at the glare of the sun off the waxed floors in the living room, reminding him that he didn't own a rug of any kind. Maybe he ought to go out and spend a few bucks to make the place presentable. He made some coffee and drank it slowly, scalding hot, as he looked out the window at the street. After the dismal weather of Saturday, the bright sky seemed encouraging, beckoning, and the heat of the coffee radiated pleasantly from his belly.

Sunday morning—maybe he'd take a walk in the country. True, during their meeting on Friday, Barrett had told him that he'd gotten a call from Vivien Hoffmann, who had mentioned Mo's request for a consent search. "She emphatically reiterated that she will gladly comply with a court-ordered search, and that until such time as such a warrant is issued she wants nobody nosing around," Barrett said, glowering at him. "I told her, 'Of course, Mrs. Hoffmann, absolutely, Mrs. Hoffmann.'" Barrett looked like he'd had a bad night. "End of discussion. I'm not going to remind you that I don't want your problems working with your superior officers to surface here."

But it would be a shame to waste a nice day like this. Mo put on jeans and hiking boots, pocketed a tape measure and a magnifying loupe, strapped on his shoulder holster, and drove up to Golden's Bridge. He cruised slowly along Route 138, over the top of the Lewisboro Reservoir, until he came to the pullover where Richard Mason had parked the night he was killed. Mo locked his car and stood shivering in the unexpectedly chill breeze, looking through a thin screen of bare trees at the blue-gray water. On the far shore, the land rose, a dark hump of forest. The lodge at Highwood would be just about straight across, at the top of the swell of land. Five months after the fact, he had no expectation of finding anything specific here. He was just getting a feeling for the place. An intuitive understanding.

Mo walked east on 138, the route Richard Mason had taken, probably with Essie, the night he died. Forest framed the road on both sides, the reservoir showing through the trees on the right, a rock-strewn slope rising on the left. The occasional houses he passed were well up in the woods to his left. All had security system warning signs out front, with company logos on them—a way of letting serious burglars know exactly what system they were dealing with, Mo thought cynically, what techniques they'd need to get past it.

About a half a mile from the car, the woods closed in. At the middle of the curve, no signs of habitation were visible, and the trees almost met overhead. Mo matched the scene with his memory of the accident-scene photos, placed the first point of impact, then the second. Then he kept walking east.

At the eastern end of the reservoir, he turned onto Marsh Road, which would connect with the old reservoir road. The trees here were big-boled willows, some still holding their leaves, dried and bleached pale. The area felt remote, at least to a city boy; only one car passed in the time it took him to walk three quarters of a mile to the driveway of Highwood.

Standing at the stone pillars, Mo checked his watch. It had taken him thirty minutes to walk the distance from his car to the bottom of the drive, but that included some backtracking and standing around. Walking without pausing, you could do it in fifteen minutes.

A new gate closed off the bottom of the driveway, painted in gray primer, and Mo leaned against it as he double-checked his conscience. Paul and Lia were in Vermont. The house was up there, unattended, and Mo really wanted another, slower look through the place, without the distraction of Paul and, especially, Lia there. But he had no legal right to enter the property, he'd made a deal with Paul about respecting his aunt's privacy, Barrett had warned him, et cetera.

Inspecting his conscience took all of ten seconds. If it didn't hurt anyone, if no one even knew about it, if it contributed a little to the Good Fight, do it. He turned and jogged quickly up and around the first bend in the drive.

Mo was blowing hard by the time he reached the crest of the driveway and looked down slightly at the circular drive and the lodge. In the diluted sunshine, the house looked forlorn. All around the lodge, bare tree branches tossed in the breeze, like an agitated but eerily silent crowd with arms raised. Uphill, the headless statues stood or lay, looking as if they'd been caught at some odd game and had frozen just as he came over the hill.

He started by walking around the outside of the house, skirting various appliances and furnishings that, judging from the way they'd broken or embedded themselves in the soil, had been tossed from the windows. On the south side, Mo paced off the distance from a shattered bureau to the wall of the house and came up with thirty-five feet. Quite a throw. Could even a bull like Falcone accomplish it? Maybe—if he'd taken a good hit of methedrine beforehand. Maybe there was something to think about there.

Mo used his Swiss Army knife to slide the latch on the new kitchen door. Inside, things weren't much different from when he'd last seen the house. He scanned the wreckage as he passed slowly through it. Looking for what? Signs of a struggle, for Christ's sake? The place was a disaster area. *But maybe hair. Blood.* Or anything that would let him open this up for the full-scale investigation it required.

Here and there, as he'd noticed during his first visit, suggestive dark splashes and stains marked a few of the walls. After quick inventory, he took out his jackknife and scraped off some of the discolored surface into a little envelope he fashioned from a teller's receipt he found in his wallet. It might be soup, for all he knew. Or blood from some animal, like the un-lucky raccoon he had noticed in one of the bedrooms. He'd bring it to Hel-mut Pierce, one of the forensic chemists at the Valhalla lab, for analysis, ask him to keep his request unofficial.

Cycles. Was there a way of determining whether this was the result of just one psychopathic incident, one incident and a number of lesser visits by local teenagers, or several main incidents? In the downstairs bedroom, Mo knelt to look closely at the heaped mash of debris. Conceivably, there'd be stratification—the rubble would be layered and differentiated by type or condition in a way that would indicate the sequence of events. One by one, he began peeling back items from the heap, inspecting each closely. Blue terry-cloth robe: mouse droppings in the folds. A splayed *Psychology Today* magazine, January 1994 issue: faint variation of ink hue at open pages, sug-gestive of fading from exposure to light. Rags of white cotton cloth, as from shirts, mixed with splinters of wood: mildew stains, smell of urine, proba-bly mouse piss. A flattened wire-and-fabric lamp shade, age-yellowed, dusty, mildewed. Shards of a heavy ceramic object, elaborately decorated on one surface, as of an Oriental vase. More magazines. A tangle of wicker, as of a chair seat.

He worked through the knee-deep debris all the way to the floor with-out finding anything definitive. The best observation he could make dealt with strata of mouse droppings, scattered like rice at a wedding: There was the top layer, then another heavier concentration about midway down in the heap, and another near the floor, suggesting that those levels had been exposed at one time and later covered by a successive layer of debris. Paper gave good clues too: Pages left exposed turned yellow and puckered, their ink faded.

Totally involved, he conducted another dig nearer the southeast corner, with similar results. The most suggestive object was a ripped New York City white pages, which lay open below the corner window on the east wall.

Phone book paper was infamously poor in quality, moisture-absorbent, prone to yellowing. From the condition of the paper and the places the book fell open, he couldn't help but feel it had lain open at three places, maybe four, during the last few months. Along with the strata of mouse droppings, a vague and inconclusive suggestion of three or four periods of disturbance.

He stood up, knees aching and hamstrings stiff. For the moment, short of a comprehensive workover with high-tech forensic support, he couldn't think of anything else to do. He'd neglected to eat breakfast, and it was after noon. The comfortable glow the coffee had made in his stomach earlier had worn off, leaving an empty, acidic hollow. Time to head down the hill.

Mo was picking his way across the big room when a dull *whump!* echoed through the house. Immediately, adrenaline flooded his body, his hands tingled, glass dust in his blood. After several seconds, another thump and a faint crash. The sound seemed to come through the floor: Someone must be breaking into the downhill basement door or windows.

He moved quickly across the room to squat behind the remains of a large couch. The position gave him a view of the whole north wall and the doors from the library and the kitchen. If someone came up from the basement or in through the kitchen door, they'd have to come through one of those doors. *Don't you want to know what happens to the detective?* Heather Mason had asked. He was surprised to look down at his own arms and hands, the pistol that had materialized there, leveled at the kitchen door in a two-handed grip.

He waited, breathing only minutely despite his pounding heart. For a time he heard only a few very faint sounds, someone's progress through the basement. Then silence. Then a loud thump and a crash. Someone had thrown something breakable against the wall in the kitchen. Too chilly only a moment ago, Mo felt a drop of sweat roll down his temple, into the collar of his shirt. Fear sweat.

It wasn't the intruder he was afraid of. It was Mo Ford and the gun he held in his hands. It was the lesson of White Plains. Inside him, almost with a life of its own, was a lethal, mindless thing which would strike like a snake, reflexively, unless he could control it.

Take it slow. Hold off. Mo made his arms bend, brought up the barrel of the gun. He made himself breathe slowly and steadily. *Keep the finger on the trigger guard. Take a good look. You'll have plenty of time.* The important thing was to stay conscious, deliberate.

Then there was another crash from the kitchen, something heavy, and the light shifted in the dining room as someone filled the doorway and then there was a shape moving into the main room. Mo's arms straightened and his finger slipped into the curve of the trigger and the sight on the barrel effortlessly tracked the left ear of the person as he took two steps and stopped. And then with a conscious effort Mo bunched his biceps and pulled the gun up again.

"Stop right there," he said.

The boy's jaw dropped. He started to bolt, then froze.

"What the fuck you think you're doing?" Mo said. He stood up from behind the couch.

The kid's face was a mask of fear. He was about sixteen, dark longish hair, wearing an expensive leather aviator's jacket. He couldn't say a word.

Another shape emerged from the dining room door, a girl. "What?" she said, then "Oh!" when she saw Mo. She put her hands up in the air, just like in the movies. She had a pretty face framed by long, golden, perfectly straight hair that fell in two smooth curves onto the shoulders of her jacket.

"We didn't know anybody was here," the boy said.

"This your house? Does it matter if somebody's here?" Mo walked toward the pair. His approach caused them to move their limbs with considerable restlessness, as if their arms and legs would run off without permission if they could. He realized he must look like a demon of sorts, gun in hand, panting slightly, sweating. "Put your goddamned hands down."

The girl's hands flew down to her sides. "We're sorry, we didn't know anybody lived here anymore."

"You didn't notice the nice new gate at the bottom of the driveway?"

Again it was the girl who spoke. "We didn't come up that way. We came through the woods—there's a sort of a path. To where we live."

"You can call my dad," the boy volunteered. Mo felt embarrassed for him: Moments ago, he'd no doubt been a real cowboy hotdog daredevil. Now he was a cringing piece-of-shit juvenile.

"You're trespassing. What were you doing in there, throwing things?"

"I'm sorry," the boy said. He looked more frightened than the girl. "Everything was like this already." He gestured around at the chaos, guiltily, as if Mo wouldn't believe him. "Are you going to arrest us?"

Mo couldn't help himself. The little shits deserved it: "What makes you think I'm a policeman?" he asked, smiling evilly.

Their eyes widened as a new gust of fear blew into them.

"Relax," Mo said, putting his gun away. "You're in luck. I'm with the New York State Police. No, I'm not going to arrest you. But I want your full names and addresses, and your parents' names."

He wrote down the information. They lived in the new yuppie development down the hill toward Golden's Bridge. Mo felt sorry enough for the boy that he decided to spare him the embarrassment of asking what they had come to Highwood for. She was a pretty girl, doe-eyed, sweet sixteen. No point in rubbing the boy's nose in shit in front of her.

"How often have you kids come up here?"

They looked quickly at each other. "We never did before," the boy said.

"Yeah? Then how come you thought nobody lived here anymore? How'd you know it was already like this?"

"It's just, we live not far away," the girl said. "In Briar Estates. All the kids know."

"Fine. So, how often have you come here before?"

They looked at each other again. "Once or twice."

"Which is it? Once? Or twice?"

"Just once," the girl said decisively.

"When was that?"

"I guess September," the boy said.

"We just started going together in September," the girl explained. She was looking for sympathy. A smart kid. Knew her resources well.

"Was it like this when you were here before?"

They looked around the room. "Yeah," the boy said. He shrugged. "Maybe. Yeah."

"I think it's worse now," the girl said. She flipped her golden hair up and back, seeming to gain confidence. "Are you trying to figure out who did it?"

Mo didn't answer but continued probing them for a few minutes more. They didn't know, or didn't reveal, anything else useful. They just wanted to look around. Other kids at school knew about it. Who? Everybody. Nobody in particular.

He was escorting them outside, around the house toward their path, when the girl gave him something to think about.

"Are you the same policeman who was up here the other time?" she asked.

Mo stopped walking. "What other time? The one time you were here?"

The boy rolled his eyes, exasperated with her, but the girl didn't miss a beat. "One other time we were going to come up, up the driveway, but we didn't because we saw the police car there. At the bottom."

"When was this?"

They thought about it. "Like a week or so after Halloween," she said.

Rizal? Mo questioned them some more but got nothing. No, they hadn't seen the policeman, he wasn't in the car. Yes, maybe it was a State Police car, but it might have been a Town of Lewisboro police car. The boy had gone mum, the girl was willing to talk all day even if she had nothing to say. At last he walked them to the edge of the woods, where they headed down a small ravine.

"I told you we shouldn't have, you idiot," the girl said in a loud whisper as they moved into the trees. She must have thought she was out of Mo's hearing.

Mo waited for a moment, then walked to the top of the driveway. The tension had left him, and now he felt drained. Conclusions, none. Maybes, two. Maybe three cycles of damage. Maybe Rizal had been up before, maybe around the time of the hypothetical third cycle, in early November.

Not worth it, considering how close he'd come to the ultimate fuck-up. He'd come within one motor nerve impulse, a tiny shock of electricity down his arm, of blowing two kids away. That would have been fun to try to explain to Barrett and the Inspection boys in Albany.

"Fuck," he said out loud. He kicked at the gravel. He told himself he'd managed to master the impulse, he'd made progress, he should feel good. Instead, he felt like shit. The Rizal thing was a major headache. Also, the girl had been very pretty. Her confidence had come back as she'd recognized something in Mo. Disgusted with himself, he spat and started walking down.

44

"**Janet**, it's Paul. I'm here at the farm. I want to see Mark today." It was eight-thirty Sunday morning.

"I thought you wouldn't make it back until tonight."

"Yeah. Well, I was able to leave earlier than I expected."

"Well, fine. But not knowing the whimsy of your schedule, we've already made plans for the day. Mark has Tommy Clarke coming over at ten to play."

"Okay. So give me a time this afternoon when I should pick him up."

"I never agreed that you were going to see him at all."

Fight back, Paul reminded himself. "I'll be there at two. Have Mark ready to come back to the farm with me."

"And if I disagree?"

"You and I have a prior and established verbal agreement about the disposition of Mark." Paul was bluffing, trying to invent some plausible legalese, as if he knew what he was talking about. "Until such time as a court decides otherwise, that agreement stands. If you prevent me from seeing him, I will call the police and claim you've abducted him."

"They won't believe you."

"Oh? I'll have them ask Mark if he'd like to see me. If he routinely does see me. In any case, I don't think having an abduction charge pending will help your custody action, or whatever it is you're planning. Have him ready at two."

His heart was thudding, hands shaking, when he hung up. He was pouring himself a cup of coffee, spilling some on the counter, when Lia came into the kitchen. Her eyes were still puffy from sleep.

"What was all that about?" she asked sleepily.

"No more Mr. Nice Guy." Paul sipped his coffee and bared his teeth at the heat of it.

"Oh—you were talking to Janet," she said. "Got a cup for me?"

They sat at the kitchen table, drinking coffee and planning the next few days, their calendars open on the checked tablecloth. Lia's work at school would take most of her time. Paul's priority would be to sort out things with Janet, consult a lawyer if necessary, and spend time with Mark. He also had a lot of calls to make: Kay, Aster, Vivien. Especially Vivien. He jotted notes to himself, then remembered an additional errand: *Call M. Stropes.*

"Kay, this will sound weird, but bear with me, okay? Royce was an only child, right?"

"Of course! Why would you think otherwise?"

Paul had caught her up on events at Highwood, ending with Royce's visit, and now he debated how much to tell her. He decided on a compromise: "We keep running into pictures of Vivien with two kids. There's a family resemblance."

"Maybe some cousin? I seem to remember there were a few other branches of the Hoffmanns around."

"Do you know any of them?"

"No. Never did. Especially after the divorce there wouldn't have been much contact. What does it matter?"

"Royce handed me one of the photos, implied it was in my best interest to find out who the other kid was."

"That's just Royce, jerking your chain. Trying to put you off balance."

"Maybe. But he seemed sincerely, if that's a word one can apply to Royce, pissed off when he said it. He'd lost his cool a bit."

"Good work Paulie!"

"I've got another question for you. Do you remember a room that opened into Vivien's bedroom? No windows?"

"Can't recall. I remember wondering what was in there—that whole wall of the balcony. I guess I figured Vivien had a suite. It wouldn't surprise me if that house had lots of hidden closets and nooks, though. Why?"

"It's just an odd room. Just very strange."

"Paulie." Kay's voice took on her warning tone. "Are you getting into something you shouldn't?"

"Like what?"

"Like trying to unravel the Hoffmanns and their family problems and intrigues? Because, talk about Hercules and the Augean stables, there's no end to it. Tar-baby city. Of course the Hoffmanns would love to get you entangled."

"Why would either of them *want* me to get entangled?"

"Are you kidding? Never underestimate the power of sheer narcissism.

It's a kind of an exhibitionistic thing: 'Aren't my knots and tangles just so scandalous and fascinating?' You make a great audience."

"I'll bear it in mind," he said. "But I have a couple of other questions for you."

"Go ahead. Not that you'll listen to what I say."

"Vivien—if she's as conniving and rotten as everyone says she is, why were she and Mother and Ben such good friends? There's got to be more to her than just the Leona Helmsley side."

"Oh, of course there is. She's human. More or less. I think she's a very smart woman, with strong and interesting perspectives on things. I think that's the side Ben liked, a challenging intellectual companion. But I remember other sides of her too. I don't think she was always such a calculating, manipulative, imperious person. I think that came later. I think there's a powerfully sentimental person there too. Deep personal loyalties. Or there *was,* anyway."

"What changed her?"

"Several things, I'd say. I think Hoffmann's leaving her was a crushing blow. She was only about eighteen when she married him, and I think she was really in love with the son of a bitch. Practically a child bride, the only man she'd ever loved, right? Big disillusionment. After the divorce, around 1952, her world started collapsing. First the divorce, then Freda's death, then Royce being such a pain. And then all those years of solitude. So she started getting hard. It's as if she had to become as calculating and cynical as she had been innocent and hopeful. If she wanted to survive. Ben's death probably didn't help, either—they were pretty close."

"Which brings up another question. Kay, why do you think Ben did it? Why'd he kill himself?" He didn't mean to sound so morose.

She whistled quietly. "Boy, you *are* getting put through the wringer by this Highwood job, aren't you?" There was sympathy in her voice. "Listen, Paulie. If you feel you've got to work through this, fine. But don't ask Mother any of these questions, okay? Don't dredge it all up for her. She seems particularly fragile now. Will you promise?"

He had a moment of trepidation as he knocked at the door of Janet's modern duplex, keying "No Reply" on his lapel as his abdomen clenched spasmodically. Anticipation was always the worst for bringing on the tics. He dropped his hands as Janet opened the door.

She was wearing faded jeans and a heavy blue-checked sweater, bare feet. She had her hair cut in a new style, a chin-length, straight cut that was very chic.

"Hi," he said. It was always unsettling, seeing Janet or Mark here: the wall-to-wall carpeting that she'd once claimed she hated, the too-prominent television, the coordinated furniture. Mark wasn't in the living room.

She shut the door behind him. "I tried to call my attorney, but of course I couldn't reach him on a Sunday. I take it you were bluffing me with that legal vernacular."

"Looks like you'll have to wait until Monday to find out, doesn't it? Where's Mark?"

"In his room."

Paul felt a flood of relief just knowing he was nearby. "I brought you something from New York. A little place in Chinatown," he said, putting the box on the table. He rustled in the tissue wrappings and took out the Chinese teapot he'd bought. "I remembered Mark had broken yours last month. When I told the man who ran the store it was going to be a gift, he told me that in China you always offer a gift with both hands. It signifies that it is a gift of value, testament to the esteem in which the receiver is held by the giver."

It was a risky gambit, too virtuous, one that could easily backfire, but he cradled the delicate porcelain pot in two hands and held it out to her. For a moment he saw her resistance start to build, the spark of fury kindling in her eyes. He made himself hold her gaze, and to his surprise he saw the anger in her face give way to a brief indecisiveness and then a split second of softness.

She took the pot from him, two hands. "Thank you," she said simply. There was a lot of elegance in her gesture. For a moment a kind of grace held between them as she admired the teapot, stroking its flawless surface, and he admired her. Then the moment passed, and when she spoke again her voice was flat, all business. "It's very pretty, and you're right, I need a teapot. But you can't bribe me."

"Don't I know it. I have more respect for you than to try." He unpacked the cups that went with the pot and set them on the table beside it. "And you can't threaten me. Not when it comes to my son. How about a truce? How about talking to me about what's going on?"

"Mark," she called in the direction of the hallway, "your father's here."

Back at the farm, they went for a walk, catching the remains of the afternoon sun. In the woods above the high field, both were thrilled to find a recent trail of moose prints, matched pairs of crescents, bigger around than a saucer. Nearby they found a tree that the moose had eaten from, its trunk stripped of bark in a long slash that clearly showed the marks of the scraping front teeth. They decided it had been a bull moose, a big one: The top of the slash began three feet above the highest point Paul could reach.

The sun was going down as they headed back to the house. Mark seemed thoughtful. "What if we saw the moose?" he asked.

"That would be great, wouldn't it?"

"No—I mean, what would we do? So he wouldn't get us."

"He wouldn't want to 'get' us. They're pretty friendly guys, I gather. The only time you have to worry about them is in rutting season, when they get territorial."

"What's rutting season?"

"Well. That's when they mate. The males sometimes butt heads, lock horns, deciding who gets to be with the female moose." He laughed. "It's not so different from when humans are in love—they just lock horns in different ways."

Mark had a stick and was systematically slapping every tree they passed with it. "How come everything, people and animals, fight when they love each other? Like you and Mom. Or in stories and movies. It's almost like loving and fighting *always* have to go together."

Mark was always catching him by surprise, the sudden lateral step, the innocent wisdom. *You always hurt the one you love*—who sang that? The Coasters? No, Clarence "Frogman" Henry. It was true: love and war, love and hate, even love and death, forever paired. Who didn't wish for just love, without its dark twin? Love had its *shadow*.

"You're a pretty smart kid," Paul said. "Seriously. You ask terrific questions, ones that need long answers. There's a lot of truth in what you just pointed out. But it's not always all that gloomy, I assure you."

Mark didn't seem to hear the compliment. "Like Mom says negative things about you, usually when something else is making her feel bad. I think maybe when she's missing you."

"What kind of negative things?"

"Today she said you were a quitter. That you always run away from things, you're good at starting things but never finishing them. She said you'd quit the job you have in New York now, you'd give up before you were finished."

Paul struggled with the anger that reared up. He didn't care what Janet thought about him. But she had no right to make Mark distrust his father. The kid was entitled to the security of feeling that Paul was going to be there and was competent to protect him, guide him, instruct him.

"I have no intention of quitting that job. And what she said just isn't true, I don't quit things."

"You quit from being married to Mom." *Whack-whack:* Mark hit another tree.

There didn't seem to be an adequate response. The explanations could take a lifetime. "Well," Paul said, trying to keep his tone conversational, "that's another subject that deserves a long answer. But the most important thing, right now, is that you know—I mean *know,* for sure—that I'm not quitting being your father, ever. Do you know that?"

Mark didn't answer. They came out of the woods and stood for a minute on the hill overlooking the farm. The direct sunlight was gone, but the landscape still glowed with a faint lavender tint, as if giving off the sunset colors it had absorbed. Paul found himself holding his breath, watching Mark covertly. Then they started down the hill. He was relieved when Mark took his hand and held it as they walked, but wasn't sure whether Mark was taking, or offering, comfort.

45

After a Monday morning talk with Barrett in which the basset-faced senior investigator made it clear that Mo was expected to have found his sea-legs by now, and that he wanted some reports on various other cases, Mo worked on everything but Highwood. To his surprise, he found that looking at the other cases was refreshingly easy, uncomplicated, real-world. The whole tangle of missing kids and pathological violence and big old empty houses and schizophrenic girls had created an aura of weirdness around the Highwood case, aggravating his superstitious tendencies. It was good to come back to Earth.

On Tuesday, when he finally took a few hours to run down a couple of details on Highwood, he found his outlook much improved. Dealing with good old, straightforward greed and dishonesty had reminded him of some useful truths. At bottom, he decided, he was a traditionalist who believed in the meat and potatoes of investigation: motive, opportunity, means. Give him MOM every time. Mostly people did things because they wanted the green stuff. Money. So who stood to gain from the destruction at Highwood?

At the Mt. Kisco library, he found a copy of *Hoover's Handbook of World Business* and looked up Royce Hoffmann. Hoffmann was listed in association with two corporations: the Pacific Development Corporation, which apparently lent money to other companies with interests in Asia and the Pacific Rim, and Star Technologies, an outfit with offices in Europe and Malaysia that produced high-tech components of one kind or another. He wondered how many others Royce might be involved with.

Remember MOM, he told himself. Money: Star Technologies made a lot of it, sales around $750 million. On the other hand, Star had several thousand employees. Pacific Development was possibly as lucrative or more so: Being a lender, its sales were not listed, but it had to be substantial to warrant a listing. And it had only twenty-three employees.

Of course, it added up to nothing.

Mo thought back to his meeting with Lia and Paul. Something Paul said had struck him. "I just keep feeling it's connected to the *past*," he'd said. "To something when I was a kid. A gut feeling." It was the way he said it, the kind of groping, inward-looking, troubled yet somehow certain pronouncement Mo had learned to value in interviews. And the idea was backed up, possibly, by the photos Lia had shown him, the KKK photos. Clearly some sort of major violence had happened at the lodge years ago. Mo put the photos at thirty years old. Had Vivien called the police back then, as she had on Falcone, the gardener? Was there a way to find records that old?

An angle occurred to him, a way to find out about the earlier cycle of violence, if that's what it was. Despite the absence of current records, there might still be a way to sniff back into the past. Every call to either state or local police was entered into the dispatcher's blotter—an actual ledger, hand-written moment-by-moment to record complaints or requests for assistance, and the office's response. Local State Police barracks kept blotters around for five years, then either put them in storage or destroyed them. Handling of old blotters by township police departments varied town by town.

The Lewisboro and North Salem police claimed they kept their blotters at the station level for fifteen years but then incinerated them. But Wild Bill had told him that in fact many old blotters from regional departments had survived.

"There're these little old ladies in the Putnam-Westchester Historical Society who like to save everything," Bill had said. "I mean *everything*. I know because my wife is one of them. They've got feed orders from when the circuses were in the area, a hundred fifty years ago. Playbills from the turn of the century, phone books from when you only needed five numbers. For a long time, they even collected the old blotters when the police were ready to get rid of them, put them in their attic. I guess they think of themselves as a sort of a time capsule, although who's going to want any of that crap I couldn't tell you."

The museum was a handsome cube of a brick building, late eighteenth century, near Lake Lincolndale: two stories of brick surmounted by a slate mansard roof with small white-trimmed round windows in it. Inside, Mo found an immaculate foyer with glowing wood floors and white walls, surrounded by glass-fronted cases displaying books, monocles, inkwells, quill pens. The air smelled agreeably of furniture polish. A gray-haired woman glanced up, startled, from the desk opposite the front door.

"Can I help you?" she asked. She looked as if she expected a stickup.

"Well, I hope so," Mo said, smiling. "I'm doing some research, and everybody tells me that this is the place to find what I'm after." He looked around the room appreciatively. "I can see they must be right."

The flattery seemed to work. "Oh yes. We have a very unusual collection. Is there a particular area—?"

"I understand you keep police blotters."

"Yes we do. Just since 1950, though." The request seemed to disappoint her.

"That's perfect for me, actually. I'm really interested in the period of, say, 1960 to around 1965."

"You don't know the particular year?"

"No. I'd hoped I could, you know, browse through a few years' worth."

"Because I'm afraid some of our collection isn't very well organized. We have only so much display space. Documents of that sort, you see, we keep in the attic, and they're not very accessible. I'd be happy to get you down a volume, but you'd have to tell me which one."

"Oh, I wouldn't think of it, Mrs., uh—"

"Otis. Dorothy Otis."

"Pleased to meet you." Mo extended his hand and shook hers, a narrow bundle of bones that was lost in his palm. "I'm Morgan Ford. Mrs. Otis, I wouldn't think of bothering you to find the books for me. If you'll just show me where they're kept, I'll be happy to look through them myself."

"Just a minute, please," Mrs. Otis said. She went through a door into an office, where she consulted another old woman who was standing on a footstool to sort papers in the top drawer of a file cabinet. The other woman tilted her head to look over her half-lens glasses at him.

"Don't you know who that is?" she whispered loudly to Mrs. Otis. "That's *Norman Mailer*!" Mrs. Otis turned a startled gaze upon Mo. Mo turned away, smiling. Only a faint resemblance, to book jacket photos of thirty years ago.

When Mrs. Otis returned, she smiled at him conspiratorially. "Come right this way, Mr. 'Ford.' I'll take you upstairs myself."

Mo followed her up a broad stairway with a beautifully carved banister, and then up a narrower stairs to the attic. She opened a last door to reveal a large bare-raftered room, lit by rows of fluorescent lights and by the round windows Mo had seen from the outside. Along the walls, and in two rows down the middle, were tables and shelves laden with books, stacks of papers, and cardboard boxes.

"I'm sorry, it's just a bit chilly up here," Mrs. Otis told him. She drew her sweater around her bony frame, then led him to the right, scanning the shelves as she went, and finally stopped in front of a series of wooden shelves that bore hundreds of identical canvas-bound volumes. "Here you are. Lewisboro, Somers, North Salem blotters. The dates are on the spines. You can use this table. Now, if you get too chilled, you must come down for a cup of coffee. I'll start a fresh pot."

Mo decided to start looking at the Lewisboro blotters from 1960 and work forward from there. He pulled several, brought them to the table, and sat on the wooden stool provided. The blotters were meticulously dated, the hour and minute specified. He scanned rapidly, looking for names of people or places that sounded familiar. An hour later, after a couple of volumes, he got lucky and encountered the name Hoffmann: In July 1962, Mrs. Vivien Hoffmann of Highwood Lodge had called in with a complaint against her gardener, who she alleged had stolen some things and done some damage to her property. The date supported what Paul and Lia had told him and corroborated what he'd heard from Falcone.

There was no more about the Hoffmanns or Highwood in that volume. He set it aside and opened the next, scanned through the pages. Here was the secret history of the area, he realized, the sad, sordid underbelly of the county. Car accidents, thefts, burglaries, fires, trees fallen across roadways, heart attacks, drownings, biting dogs, marital arguments, truant kids, drunkenness, violent assaults, petty mischief, noise complaints, smelly trash fires. All the mean and unpleasant stuff, distilled to an essence of pure misfortune, despair, squalor. You had to have a certain bent to be a cop, a cast-iron stomach for this stuff. Mo wasn't sure he had it.

By three o'clock he'd only gotten through 1963 and hadn't found anything on the Hoffmanns since his first lucky break. He was freezing to fucking death, about ready to call it a day. Clearly the good luck had passed on by again. He'd give it one more volume and then quit, try again some other time.

But then he got lucky again. *Very* lucky. This was better than he'd hoped. Much, much better. It explained a lot. For the first time, he felt he was maybe beginning to get a handle on the case.

Mo stood on the museum's broad granite steps for just a moment, breathing deep and letting his eyes adapt to the brighter light of the day. He wasn't yet sure what to do with what he'd found, but he would think of something. It would be a pleasure to tell Lia and Paul. Lia would think he was hot shit for thinking of the old blotters.

He'd found reference to the arrest of three teenaged boys, all under driving age, who had stolen a car and driven it around for a few hours until smashing it up on Route 100. The boys were brought into the station and held until their parents could come in to get them and sort things out with the owner of the car. One of the boys was Royce Hoffmann. One was a boy from Purdys, a name Mo had already forgotten; the other was that lifelong resident and local hero of Golden's Bridge, Pete Rizal.

46

While Mark was at school on Monday, Paul accomplished five things. The first was to leave the bottle of haloperidol pills on the medicine-cabinet shelf, unopened. His first full day without any at all since that day in the woods so long ago. No big thing, no damned ceremony. Just no pills.

The second was more prosaic. The MG had been missing on a couple of cylinders, giving him the jitters about driving it as far as Westchester again. He cleaned the points and plugs and reset the timing, and was pleased that the motor ran smoothly again.

The third was a call to Charlie Gold, a friend who maintained a single-practitioner law office in Norwich. He was a lousy guitar player and a mediocre lawyer and a good person who had chosen his low-key way of life wisely. Charlie had a healthy distrust and dislike of lawyers.

"I need some legal advice," Paul told him.

"Uh-huh. Shouting obscenities in public? That sort of thing?"

"Not exactly. This is serious, Chaz." Paul explained the situation with Mark, Janet's recent threatening talk.

"I'm not the guy for this, Paul," Charlie said at last. "Way out of my league. I do real estate, little civil stuff. Knowing Janet, she's probably seeing some high-priced friend of her old man's—Brown and Caslick or some-body. Hired killers who'd chop you and me both to pieces. You'd be advised to retain somebody like that yourself."

"Any suggestions?"

"If you can't get Brown and Caslick, I'd say Perry Associates. High fees. But when it's your *kid*—" Paul sensed Charlie's shrug: *What else you gonna do?*

Paul jotted the name. "Any general advice?"

"Sure. Custody courts are conservative. Typical advice is, walk the straight and narrow. Get employed if you're not, stay employed if you are. Get a good, conservative suit to wear to court, one that says 'reliable' and 'upwardly mobile.' Not that you've got long hair, but get a haircut anyway. Shacking up? Get married. If you've got a copy of *Playboy* in the house, even the swimsuit issue of *Sports Illustrated*, burn it. Drive at or below the speed limit. Brush and floss after every meal. You think I'm fucking kidding? I'm not."

Paul thanked him, promised to get together when his schedule eased up, then said good-bye. He got in a call to Jason Perry's office and was told by the secretary that Perry would return his call when he had the time. Her snooty tone made it sound like the custody business was booming, a bull market for those who'd bought in early. *Sign of the times,* Paul thought.

Afterward, he agonized for a while and then accomplished his fourth deed of the day. He went into the bathroom, opened the medicine cabinet, and took one milligram—half the dosage he'd been on for the last week. It was a compromise, the best he could do. Somewhere in between Charlie's straight and narrow and Damon's wild and woolly.

The fifth accomplishment took only a few minutes. He called New York City information and got a number for Roosevelt Medical Research Institute. Paul dialed the number and got patched through to Stropes's line, where he left a message on the voice mail. He had a moment of indecision about what to say. *I'm into something big, ugly, and strange, and I think maybe you can help me.* No. *I have reason to believe—*

He settled on stating his general interest in HHK/HHD, and leaving his numbers at the farm and at Highwood. As an afterthought, he left Dempsey's number and address.

He held back the tics until he got off the line. "Big Bad John," he said, basso. The odd thing was, despite his misgivings, he couldn't deny that there *was* something morbidly intriguing about the whole idea: a power that lived in you, that broke through all conscious constraint and—what? What did it do with its freedom? Vivien had said it perfectly: *How do you know what you're capable of?* It might be nice to know.

"Big Bad John," he said again, almost getting it right.

"You sound . . . troubled, nephew," Vivien said.

"Yeah, well. It's been a rough day." Paul stared at the wallpaper over the telephone desk in the farm's kitchen, wondering why he'd called her. Lia was upstairs, probably asleep. Mark was back at Janet's. Paul was exhausted, drained, demoralized, as he always was after one of Mark's episodes. He'd been kicking himself for hours, feeling he should have seen it coming, could have prevented it.

"Are you having problems with the house?"

"No. We're pretty well on schedule. Actually, I'm at home—I've been in Vermont for the last couple of days."

"Aha." Vivien gave that a moment. "I take it that means you're wrestling with some of the . . . issues . . . that came up when we last spoke."

"My son had another of his seizures. It's always hard for me." Paul was surprised at himself. He'd told himself he was calling to ask Vivien some questions about the vandalism—about the KKK photos, at least. But he was too exhausted to muster any challenge to her. Anyway, he realized he'd called her for another reason entirely: that somehow Vivien was the sounding board he needed. Somehow at this point the Dragon Lady was the one person who might understand. Maybe it was her connection to Ben. Right now he felt lost in the job of being a father.

"Tell me," Vivien said sympathetically.

He told her: Monday afternoon, Paul had picked up Mark from school and they'd returned to the farm. Paul had sent him to his room to pack up his things, preparatory to returning to Janet's. Lia would be at Dartmouth until late, and he planned to have dinner and some relaxed time with Mark, just the two of them, before Janet came to pick up Mark.

That was the plan, anyway.

When Mark returned to the kitchen, Paul talked casually as he cooked dinner, not noticing Mark's immobility until it was too late. Then he'd tried desperately, the usual pointless *shit*, to get Mark out of it. It was an unusual episode in that Mark went through the catatonic phase and into the violent phase in less than an hour. As he told Vivien about it, Paul winced at the memory of holding Mark's writhing, kicking body from behind. In the bruised muscles of his chest and stomach, he could still feel Mark's wrenching, convulsive movements, the struggles of the *thing*, not human, that Mark had become.

By the time Janet arrived, the fit was easing off. She came into the kitchen to see Paul sitting on the floor among the toppled chairs, spilled food, broken dishes, holding Mark in a bear hug from behind. Mark came out of it crying heartbreakingly.

"You have my deepest sympathy," Vivien said. "It is a terrible thing to see a loved one in such distress. I know your father often spoke of his similar . . . concern . . . for you."

Paul said nothing for a moment. When Mark was leaving, he had burst into tears again and refused to let go of Paul: "Please, don't be away so long. It's scarier when you're not around." He was looking at Janet as he said it, as if he knew the real obstacle to being with his father was now her resistance.

Paul and Janet had locked eyes. "I've got to stay down there now, until the job is done," Paul told Mark, told Janet. "I've made a commitment, I've spent most of my advance money. But you can come visit me there, stay at Dempsey's house. Would you like that?"

"Yes."

"If your mother agrees." Paul held her eyes until he knew she'd relented. Under the circumstances, she had little choice. Only when they settled on Mark coming down the following weekend did he let go of Paul.

When he walked them out to the car, Paul said good-bye to Mark and then walked around to Janet's window. "Janet," he'd said quietly. "Honor Mark's desire to see me. Don't change our plans for next week."

"I promised my son, Paul," she'd hissed. "*I* keep my promises."

Paul came back from the memory. Vivien was saying something: "Paulie, tell me this," she said. Her voice had dropped, intensified. "How is Mark's physical health, generally?"

"He's prone to colds, little infections. Nothing serious."

"A lot of them? Is there a pattern to his getting sick? What I'm driving at is this: Is there any relation between his episodes and his minor illnesses? Frequency, intensity, duration?"

Paul thought back. He couldn't really remember, but it seemed like a possibility. He was too tired to concentrate well. But Mark's physician's records and his journal would reveal a pattern if there were one. "I'm not sure. Maybe. Why?"

"Just look into it. I have another request. Remind me of what diagnostic work you have done."

"We've done EEGs, CAT scans, MRIs. Nothing shows up."

"No PETs, no 18E fluorooxyglucose? How about SPECT?"

"No." These were new cranial imaging technologies, prohibitively expensive.

"What about blood work?"

"Standard full-spectrum tests, many times over. His blood is good."

"You checked for high levels of plasma tryptophan?"

Paul thought for a moment, remembering. "I believe so. As I recall, it was normal. You're asking about IED, intermittent explosive disorder, aren't you? We've ruled it out."

"Very impressive, nephew! You do know your physiology, don't you?" Vivien's voice took on a hushed intensity, almost a whisper. "I have another suggestion, then: The next time Mark has an episode, get him in to draw some blood. Have them look for CRF levels. Look for ACTH levels. It's imperative you do it *while* he's having the seizure, or very soon after."

Corticotropic releasing factor was a "messenger" secreted by the hypothalamus that stimulated the pituitary gland to produce adrenocorticoptropic hormone. ACTH in turn caused cortisol to be released into the bloodstream. Both were reactions to environmental stimulation or stress, producing a variety of bodily responses from rage to panic to sexual arousal.

"Right." Paul wrote down the words. "Why those?" He came close to asking her something else: *Is that something you learned from your own secret son, Vivien?*

"I've been thinking about what you've told me. Just a theory of mine. I could be wrong, but it can't hurt to try, can it? *Do it,* Paulie. And let me know what they find."

Why not? He was reluctant to subject Mark to any more clinical work, but anything would be better than what he'd witnessed tonight. Anything. It had been a relief to tell it all to Vivien, and there was even a glint of hope in her ideas, her theory. Maybe it was the grasping of a drowning man, but he needed to have hope that *something* would help.

Paul hung up, turned out the downstairs lights, trudged upstairs, too exhausted to think anymore. If he were to ask the gods for one favor, he'd wish he could forget the sound of Mark's grating teeth, creaking and screeching in his skull as he'd writhed in Paul's arms four hours ago.

47

"Okay, to summarize," Mo was saying, "we've got a number of possibilities of varying likelihood. The problem now is to follow down each one to see what's real and what isn't. That's what these sessions are for."

They were in the smoking room. It was mid-afternoon, a dull day outside. Paul turned on the lights just to cheer things up. Once Cohen had declared the wiring safe, he'd ordered electrical service reconnected and had bought a couple of clamp lamps at the hardware store. It would still be a while before the new furnaces could be installed, but having electric lights meant that they could work longer hours after sunset. Dempsey was working in the main room, at last able to use an electric soldering gun to reassemble lead mullions in the badly damaged windows. Now they'd see some real progress.

Paul had been surprised when Mo suggested the three of them hold a skull session, not imagining such a term would be vernacular in the Bureau of Criminal Investigation. Mo said that BCI staff often put together skull sessions, where the agent in charge of a case, his supervisors, various forensics experts, maybe some fresh ears and eyes, all sat down and brainstormed about where to go with a case that had stalled out.

"Anything goes," Mo had told them. "No matter how far out. A skull session is when you let whatever's in there"—he tapped his head—"rattle around, recombine, come out in whatever form it takes. If an idea rings bells in somebody else's head, jibes with something in their files, then you toss it around. If it doesn't strike any sparks, it probably doesn't hold water. Sorry about the mixed metaphors." His apologetic grin was directed to Lia.

Mo had brought them up to date on his meeting with the man who turned out to be the son of the original Falcone, Vivien's gardener. He'd also done some homework on Royce's finances but hadn't really gotten anywhere with it. To his knowledge, he admitted, Rizal had indeed been bullshitting Paul with his talk about a drug investigation involving Highwood. Paul had to credit him with a sense of the dramatic: He'd wound up with the story of his visit to the historical society until last, building the suspense until he revealed that Royce and Rizal had been juvenile partners in crime.

"Leaving us with the question of whether they are still 'collaborating' on any little schemes," Lia said. "Like trying to scare us or tempt us or otherwise get us away from fixing up Highwood."

Lia seemed impressed with Mo's ingenuity. And he did have a kind of heat as he stalked back and forth, lost in his story, his smart, tough talk. He rolled his shoulders as if loosening up for a fight.

When no one had any more to offer, Paul told Mo about Royce's visit, the sense of threat in his comments. Mo took notes.

"Making me more sure than ever your cousin ties in," Mo said. "Just how or why, we don't know, but we'll get there. Anything else? No matter how wild?"

Again, Paul debated mentioning his other ideas, his intuitions. *Tell them now*, his mind screamed, *the door's open*. But he found he couldn't. He couldn't match Mo's certainty or Lia's enthusiasm. His thoughts had become too personal, somehow, too revealing: *Weird medical conditions that give people super strength, secret societies from a hundred years ago, violent psychopaths imprisoned in windowless rooms. Paul's gone nuts, gone morbid. He's got a neurological condition, so he thinks of everything in those terms. He's got a son with mental problems, so he projects that predicament onto everyone. He's letting this place get to him.*

Mo had been watching him closely. "Why do I get the feeling that you're not happy about where we're going with this?"

Paul thought for a moment about how to phrase it. "I keep feeling that we're ignoring what we see here at the house. Maybe we can answer the *why* and the *who* if we can just answer the *how*." He grabbed a handful of air in frustration.

To Paul's surprise, the question seemed to pierce Mo. For a time the detective seemed to be looking inward, frowning slightly. "Duly noted," he said simply. "We should give it more thought."

"Something that's been bothering me since you told us about Falcone," Lia said. "That Falcone Senior disappeared. His son thinks he's dead because his family pride makes him need to see it that way. Or he claims to think that, to throw you off. But what if the elder Falcone isn't dead?"

"Right," Paul said, glad the attention had shifted from him, "and he's living around here, in the woods like the Leather Man. And he's still got a grudge."

"Leather Man?" The reference was lost on Mo.

"A famous eccentric who roamed this area, sort of a wild man. A hundred years ago."

Mo rolled his eyes, an elbow-in-the-ribs gesture intended for Lia. "Stranger things have happened."

"What about you, Mo?" Lia asked.

"Me?" Mo walked away from them again, turned, the restless energy of a panther in a cage. "I keep coming back to the son, Royce. A very old-fashioned motive: He's got something to gain by your aunt's leaving the house. Either he lays hands on something here, or something else. He wants her gone, that's why he doesn't want you to fix the place up for her."

"How would that tie in with your missing kids?"

Mo looked bothered by the question. "Maybe no connection. And maybe the kids got hurt because they happened to be in the wrong place at the wrong time. Or maybe the psychopathology that did all this manifests in other ways as well. Like serial killing."

They mulled it over for a time. Paul felt tics building. A mournful tune was playing in his head, infuriating him: "Ringo's Theme," The Beatles, 1964. "That bo-oy took my love away." He played the rhythm with his tongue on the roof of his mouth, angry at himself. Pathetic. But Lia and Mo looked great together, they had some of the same, what, *aura,* the same *juice.* The fact certainly hadn't escaped Mo's notice.

Plus there were the things he couldn't bring himself to mention, skull session or not. Dempsey's strange behavior: In a flash, he saw Dempsey, harboring some ancient grudge against Vivien, coming up and ripping the place apart. The old fighter still had banded muscles in his working man's arms, the deep chest of an athlete. The image played like a movie in his head, and he shivered involuntarily. Not just the brutality of it, the deception. Dempsey, the one person he'd always counted on. But who could you trust? Could you really trust anyone? Paul bit his tongue. He was beginning to sound like Vivien. He was right to hold back—there seemed to be no end to his paranoia.

They spent the next fifteen minutes thinking up practical steps to take. Mo would look into Royce some more, see if there was anything else to be found on Falcone, explore the Royce-Rizal connection. He'd make another attempt to talk to Heather Mason. Paul and Lia would keep on with the papers, looking for anything else on the Philippine connection. Paul would talk to Vivien.

And, Paul thought, *try to meet with Stropes. And make Dempsey talk.*

"I've got a question for you, Mo," Lia was saying. She beckoned him to turn, and when he did so she pointed to his gun. "Do you always carry that?"

Mo smiled, looking flattered by her attention. "Not when I'm in the shower."

"Do you ever have to use it?"

The detective lost his smile. "On occasion, yes."

"Can I see it? Is it some special kind? My father likes a Walther 9-millimeter."

"It's a good sidearm. Glock 17, also a 9-millimeter. What, uh, occasions your interest?" Mo had gotten stiff, lost his insouciance, Paul thought. He made no offer to show the gun to Lia.

"We brought a gun with us," Lia said. She brought out the box containing Ted's revolver and opened it. "Smith and Wesson .38. Any advice? I'm assuming you're an expert."

Mo lifted the gun out, flipped the cylinder and inspected the weapon. "This has been well taken care of."

"My brother-in-law's an ex-cop," Paul said. "It's his gun."

"You want advice? I'll give you some: Don't take it out of the box again. Guns seem to beget shooting. Shooting seems to beget serious mistakes."

"You say that like you know what you're talking about," Lia said.

Mo ignored the prompting. "Another suggestion: Don't use it to frighten somebody. Don't think it'll accomplish anything by waving it around. It's not a fucking magic wand. If you show it, use it."

"Not a magic wand—I think Paul and I can grasp that, conceptually." Lia smiled at Mo, gently mocking his sudden seriousness, and it seemed to work: He came back out of whatever mood had taken him.

"Okay," Mo said. "Sorry. I don't like guns. A necessary evil. But I do have a suggestion for you. If you're going to load it, use the hollow points. It looks like your brother-in-law put a box of them in there."

"What's the difference?" Paul asked.

Mo tilted his head toward the door. "I'll show you. We'll let off a couple of rounds. Not SOP for a New York State Police employee, but who gives a fuck? Excuse my French."

They went out to the driveway. Under Mo's supervision, Paul found a suitable target, a three-foot length of rough-cut two-by-eight lumber from the carriage house. Paul propped the board upright at the top of the retaining wall at the curve of the driveway, a slope of soft earth behind it. Mo walked them back twenty paces, loaded the .38 with bullets from one of the boxes of ammunition Ted had provided.

"Go ahead," he said. "Take a few pops."

Lia offered the gun to Paul, but he shook his head. With the look of focus on her, face set, somehow streamlined, eyes alive, she checked the cylinder, closed it, slipped the safety. *Beauty and the beast,* Paul thought, although it didn't look foreign in her hands. She took a stance and with both hands aimed at the board. The explosion made him jump. The board didn't move.

"Out of practice," Lia said.

"Excellent form, though," Mo said. Then he looked embarrassed.

Lia aimed and fired again, missed, held her stance, fired twice more, knocking the board over with her last shot.

They went to inspect the board. A hole the diameter of a pencil had appeared near its upper right edge. Where the bullet emerged, it had flipped off a chip of wood the size of a postage stamp, but otherwise the hole it had burrowed stayed the same width all the way through two inches of pine. Paul set up the board again.

"Okay. So that's solid point," Mo said. He ejected the spent shells, then loaded the .38 with one bullet from the other box. "This is a hollow point—what we call jacketed controlled-expansion bullets. Basically a cute technical euphemism that Albany decided would be better PR—especially since their use against humans was outlawed by the Geneva Convention."

They paced back and Mo turned, fired. The board did a back flip. The frozen black earth behind it was now littered with chunks and chips of yellow wood.

Mo walked back and leapt easily up the retaining wall to retrieve the board. When he brought it back down and showed it to them, they could see that the bullet had gone in small and come out in a ragged, fist-sized crater.

"That's hollow nose," Mo said. "In flesh they're like little bombs. Somebody's coming at you, you even tip him and he'll lose a handful of tissue. Hamburger on the wall. He'll lose interest in you, fast."

Lia watched Mo with one eyebrow raised. "I take it you've had some experience."

Mo looked away.

"Show us, Mo."

Mo started to protest, then shrugged. They walked back with him to the middle of the drive and turned. Paul didn't see him draw, but suddenly his Glock was in his hands and without a pause he was firing. The first shot flipped the board up, and Mo's successive shots kept it walking, flipping end over end, uphill. He fired five times in no more than two seconds. When he was done, the board had traveled twenty feet uphill. Wood chips littered the slope.

Lia's jaw had dropped. "That's . . . uh, impressive, I guess you could say," she said at last.

Mo put his gun away. "Thanks," he said. He shrugged again, straightened his jacket lapels, checked his watch.

After Mo had gone and they went back inside, Lia appeared thoughtful.

"Our friend Mo," Paul prompted, "is a remarkable fellow."

Lia nodded.

"I take it that's good shooting."

"It's supernatural shooting," Lia said. Being out in the cold had brought color to her face, a blush high on her cheekbones, the kind movie stars paid fortunes to makeup artists to achieve. She picked up a sheaf of papers, started going through them—rather listlessly, he thought.

Mo certainly did have a showman's instinct. The effortless leap up the retaining wall, the marksmanship, the nonchalance, the understatement. How much of it was conscious, a show to impress Lia? It was hard to tell. And Lia: Did her idea of risk include risking their relationship? Even a month ago, he'd have said no. But clearly her risk-taking compulsion was growing, permeating all parts of her life. Now, about Mo, he couldn't be sure. One of many uncertainties. Was it just his changing neurochemistry, or was there something there he should worry about?

Lia interrupted his musings. "I just thought of something."

"What's that?"

"Rizal. The name. It's been nagging at my memory since last week. I can't quite remember the context, but I think I've come across it in Vivien's papers." Lia looked thoughtful for a moment. "Stupid of me. But I'll try to dig it up again. Don't let me forget to tell Mo—I should probably call him," she said, brightening.

48

After the session with Paul and Lia, Mo returned to his office feeling like he'd been riding a roller-coaster. His heart had flown up like a lark in springtime at the sight of Lia. He'd had to muster all his self-control to keep their discussion focused and purposeful. God, she was everything he'd ever wanted. No one had ever clicked like this. Being around her that long had been at once ecstatic and painful.

But then Paul kept asking *How?*, and Mo kept thinking, *Superman. Superman did it.* Thinking about it in that wrecked house, Mo had felt momentarily sick all over. A strange feeling, a dark déjà vu. *Don't you want to know what happens to the detective?* Roller-coaster down.

But then Lia had given him the perfect excuse to show off, and he'd gone out to the driveway and had just let his gun do what it did so easily. And he'd felt Lia's eyes go keener, more attentive. He'd fucking *basked* in it. God, to see that again. And to see her shooting, legs wide, a trim sweater showing her perfect waist, the athletic grace and competence of her shooting form. Roller-coaster up.

And yet, driving away, he'd felt more than a little remorse. Paul had caught the whole thing. And Paul was a good guy. He had some nervous disorder, Mo was certain, that made him start to say things and stifle himself, or make an odd gesture now and then. But otherwise he seemed an admirable guy. He had the kind of build Mo had always wanted—rangy, tall, well-muscled—and that open, square face. Honest. A person who went by his conscience, always. A noble look, a face that had seen a large measure of sorrow and had found something to sustain himself with despite it, and kept a sense of humor into the bargain. Kind of the way King Arthur was always portrayed in the movies. Right—and Lia was Guinevere, leaving Mo to be Lancelot, the king's most trusted friend, and his betrayer. Roller-coaster down again.

Then, stopping at home briefly on the way back to the barracks, he'd found her voice on his answering machine, telling him thanks, telling him it was good to see him again, and oh, by the way, Rizal was a Philippine

name and Rizal had apparently helped Royce feed razor blades to some
show dogs in the distant past. There was an excited, confiding tone in her
voice, the timbre of a comrade-in-arms. What else was she telling him? His
neck veins pulsed as he replayed her message. His instincts were screaming
at him: *Go for it. For once in your life, reach for what you really want. Respect
yourself enough to believe it can be reciprocal. It's too bad about Paul, but it's
nobody's fault, all's fair in love and war. She knows herself, she makes her own
choices.* Roller-coaster way up.

It was almost four o'clock by the time he made it back to the barracks, just
enough time to follow up on a couple of small details. He picked up a
handful of mail from his box, checked his phone messages, and filed some
notes on other cases. Then he dialed Helmut Pierce's number at the Valhalla lab to see about the scrapings he had taken from the walls at Highwood. Dr. Pierce wasn't available, the secretary said, but he had left a
message with her in case Detective Ford called.

"The samples you gave him definitely include blood," she said. Mo's
hopes leapt. He'd finesse a way to have come by the samples legally, open
Highwood up for a real forensic investigation. "Blood of a *Procyon lotor,* he
says."

"What's a *Procyon lotor?*"

"I asked him. He always does this, thinks everyone knows everything he
does. It's the Latin name for a raccoon. It's raccoon blood."

Roller-coaster down. One of those days, start to finish.

But his pulse rose abruptly when, sorting his mail, he came across another monogrammed, lavender-tinted letter. His hands shook as he slit the
envelope.

Dear Detective Ford,

*In my story, what happened was I got tired of waiting in the car and
went down the road. It was so dark I couldn't see very well. Then I heard
someone coming, running, and I got off the road and hid in the bushes.
It was Richard, and behind him someone else. The first part was bad,
when he got folded in half backward and I could hear the sound in his
back like someone cracking their knuckles, and then he got turned almost inside out with that sucking kind of noise. But the worst part was
right afterward, when there was just this wheezing from him, I think his
lungs were still going even though they weren't connected anymore, like
Richard was just this meat machine that didn't know yet it was broken
and its parts were still trying stupidly to work. It humped on the ground
for a few seconds and I couldn't stop looking at it.*

Probably the same thing happened to Essie, but I didn't see that. Probably it happened to those other kids too—I heard you talking to my mother about them.

Is this what you wanted me to tell you?

The question that keeps bothering me is about what Richard was, right afterward. Was he just that meat machine, breaking down because the Richard part of him was gone, and it was still going, automatically, for a second or two? Or were the noises it made really Richard, still in there and trying to talk or move but unable to because his meat machine had been so completely screwed up? Which one am I? Which is worse? You can see why I say it's only "sort of " a detective story.

But I've decided on a title for the story. I call it "Five Things Worse Than Dying," because the schizophrenic girl keeps thinking of things and she makes a list. Here's the list:

1. Being just a meat machine, almost like you're trapped inside of it, it does what it does whether you want it to or not.

2. Losing your sense of what a human being is, what they're capable of, what the word human *even really means, and so not having any idea what you are or where you belong.*

3. Living life but not being able to feel it, because it's either not enough or it's too much.

4. Being so alone, you're not sure other people are real.

5. Going through life not ever sure what's inside your mind or what's in the world outside you.

Mo rocked back in his chair, feeling Heather's words as if they were blows, battering him remorselessly. After a stunned moment, he quickly folded the letter and covered it with his notebook to shield himself from the anguish it expressed. On the heels of his shock came anger, a bone-deep hatred for whoever or whatever had done this to the poor kid. *Somebody was going to have to pay.*

For half a minute he labored to calm himself, then dialed the Masons' number, only to get the answering machine again. He left another pleading message and hung up, suddenly feeling the fatigue come over him, a sense of the impossibility of taking this on. He knew what a shrink would say about the letter: a plea for attention, a cry for help. But was it only that? The five things, that was pretty inarguable, but the part about what happened to Richard—had she really seen something? Was what she wrote real or delusion, as she herself seemed to ask, or a third, more devious possibility that she didn't mention: fucking with Mo's head? Just jerking his chain, a complex, troubled child's idea of a joke, of kidding around?

He was debating what to do next when the phone rang. It was Bennett

Quinn, agent in charge of the case of the human thigh in Ridgefield, Connecticut.

"Sorry it's taken me so long to get back to you," Quinn said. He had an agreeable, tired-sounding voice, a New Jersey accent. "We've had some action on the severed thigh. I don't know what you're after, but maybe this will help. It's a little unusual."

"I'm after something unusual."

"Good. See, here these kids are playing around in the woods near Highway 35 and they find this human thigh, but nobody seems to be missing one, right? It's obviously been around for a while, hard to tell, maybe a month or more, right? Some animal tooth marks, it's been partly eaten, dogs, raccoons. For a while we check out the idea that maybe it's from a grave, but no embalming chemicals show up in the tests, so that's out. You can see why we were stuck."

"So what happened?"

"Well, several things broke at once. First we find the rest of the body—remains are unrecognizable, but from dental records we find out it's a Priscilla Zeichner, twenty-four years old, lived in Waterbury. The reason we didn't locate the rest of her right away is she was found in the bushes next to some railroad tracks near here. It's a dedicated track, about three miles long, runs from the Lanier Company plant to the main trunk freight line. Lanier's a big employer over here—they build these huge container tanks for like gasoline tanker trucks and milk trucks? The only time their track gets used is when they have an order being shipped out, flatcars full of stainless-steel tanks, like to the truck company that's going to assemble them. Wooded area, no houses nearby, no traffic on the line for anyone to notice Ms. Zeichner's remains, until the crew on the next shipment out found her. Five days ago."

Mo's hands were tingling. "I take it she was . . . in pretty bad shape?"

"Oh yeah. Missing more than her thigh, I'll tell you that. Couldn't have identified her without the lab work. We're figuring she got hit by the Lanier train that went out on November second. The thigh, we don't know how it got four miles away except some dogs carried it. But the date we've pinned down tight—once we ID'd her, we found that ties in with when she was last seen, according to her friends."

"What was she doing over in Ridgefield? On the Lanier train tracks?"

"Well, that's what we wanted to know. We started looking for friends, neighbors, asking around. You know. Apparently the boyfriend's from over your way, but what they might've been doing at this end of the state we don't know yet."

"So how're you looking at it? Accident or—"

"Let's say we're keeping our minds open. Could be accident, sure—

you've got to figure nationwide there's two hundred fifty–some train-pedestrian deaths a year, right? Happens. But we're real interested in the whereabouts of the boyfriend, Eddy."

"I'll bet. Any leads?"

"Hey, this just broke open for us," Quinn said, laughing good-naturedly. "I figure we've done pretty good so far."

After they hung up, Mo checked his regional atlas, which showed the Lanier tracks running from the plant, about five miles east of the New York border, southeast into Ridgefield. Less than ten miles, as the crow flies, from Highwood.

He brought up the computer file he'd started, the calendar he'd built for the missing kid case. *Cycles.* Calculating on a projected cycle of about forty-four days, he'd figured that a third cycle of violence would have had to happen in early November. And there it was: November 2nd, the date Priscilla Zeichner disappeared, plugged right into the projection. Which left December 16th, give or take a few days, as the next one. Eight days away.

So no matter how he kept trying to stay clear on familiar turf like financial motives and so on, there was a big ugly scary that kept popping out at him. The general drift of it was that somebody was chopping people to pieces, by means unknown, at fairly regular intervals, in upper Westchester County. How many people? Two at least, and maybe Essie Howrigan, and Priscilla Zeichner's boyfriend, and maybe Dub Gilmore and Steve Rubio, and maybe more. So where were the others? They could be buried, they could be lying along some other seldom-used railroad track. The woods could be full of body parts. How would it work? The perp or perps did the deed and bagged up the remains and put them someplace, like the road, like the tracks, that would make the whole thing look like a somewhat bizarre but ultimately believable accident. If John Wayne Gacy could keep twenty-seven corpses secret in the crawl space of a ranch house in suburban Milwaukee, somebody could stash an army of them in the woods of upper Westchester.

And somehow, if that wasn't bad enough, into that you had to fit a crazy kid who claimed fucking Superman did it and who brought up existential questions best left unasked, and a big house all wrecked up, high school kids talking about Satanic rituals, Paul and Lia only half kidding around about Falcone Senior gone wild and living in the woods.

And hard-boiled, pragmatic Mo Ford, try as he might, couldn't quite disbelieve any of it. It was truly the shits.

49

"**You** sound rather taken aback," Vivien said. "Of course I will need to review the progress you've made so far before proceeding to the next phase. And of course I ought to take another look at my lonely fortress before deciding if I have the . . . endurance . . . to live there again."

"I expected you would come east sooner or later. I just want to be sure it's all in order when you arrive."

"I have perfect faith in you. And you needn't worry about my well-being. I'll rent a car and reserve a hotel room in the city. I'll be no trouble at all."

Paul sat on the motel bed with the phone while Lia splashed in the tub, poaching herself in water hotter than Paul could have believed possible. They'd splurged on a night in a nearby motel as a respite from the chaos of Highwood.

Yes, his discomfort level had risen abruptly when Vivien casually informed him that she would be flying east in just over a week. The work was behind schedule—he'd really have to haul ass to abide by his end of the contract. There was Mo's investigation to think of too, which he'd concealed from her. And Dempsey's working at the lodge, which he hadn't yet mentioned.

"I do enjoy our conversations, nephew," Vivien was saying. "And do you know, I believe you do also. Quite against your will, I'm sure, quite against your better judgment, but nonetheless. . . ." She trailed off, letting him see it for himself.

It was true, if hard to admit. Paul couldn't decide just how talking to Vivien fit into the scheme of his life. He still distrusted her, still disliked her contempt for her inferiors—a category that seemed to include almost everyone—but nevertheless he couldn't deny the paradoxical need to talk with her, the pleasure it had begun to give him.

Maybe it was just the sheer intellectual stimulus. In the course of a fifteen-minute telephone call, they had discussed the repairs at Highwood and then digressed to Festinger's dissonance theory, then gone on to

Aristotle's *heart* versus Plato's *mind* as the defining characteristic of human beings: "Not such outdated concerns as we post-postmoderns would like to think, nephew." Vivien had talked about the usefulness of other "quaint" terms, such as the German *Gemut,* meaning a person's nature, *Seele,* the psyche or soul, and *Geist,* the spirit or ghost, and was pleased when Paul responded with the parallels between those concepts and the ancient Egyptian *ba* and *ka.* No question: His mind was hungrier now, more awake. He was able to enjoy the interplay of ideas more, follow the branching of thoughts better, than at any time he could remember.

But there was more to it than that. None of the concepts they discussed were abstractions to Vivien: They were real to her, even urgent. Her obvious emotional investment in such ideas, her hushed, urgent tone of voice, gave their conversations a curiously intimate quality.

"I am curious to hear about your son," she was saying. "Have you had the opportunity to look into those . . . issues I suggested last time we spoke?"

"As far as the blood tests go, he hasn't had another seizure, so we haven't done any new diagnostics. I did figure out that, yes, there is a correspondence between his seizures and minor illnesses. Less than a one-to-one parallel, but a clear general pattern. We hadn't noticed. It's a good point."

"Have you any idea why that would be the case?" Her interest level had intensified and was beginning to feel intrusive.

"Sure. The episodes are draining, stressful. Exhausting for Mark. He'd naturally be more prone to infections."

Vivien cackled. "Yes," she said, "that sounds like a very sensible conclusion."

They talked some more about Mark, but Paul couldn't concentrate on what she was saying. Her condescension irritated him. Anyway, he had promised Mo and Lia to probe her about the house. Her sardonic amusement seemed to grow until, abruptly, he'd had enough. "Vivien, not to change the subject, but I've got a question for you. Tell me about KKK. Tell me how it bears on what happened here."

"Aha. Doing some detective work among my papers, apparently." There was acid in her voice.

"We're sorting them, as you requested. I'm curious about two old photos that showed some damage up here, and the graffiti. I know about the Philippine secret society."

"Good heavens! You *have* been doing your research!" Then her voice changed again, darkening with anger. "And what about my concern for privacy? Have you ever considered that your detective games are an intrusion that I don't care for?"

"You're dodging me."

That brought her back. She laughed again. "Oh, Paulie. Oh, my! Who's got the kleig lights and truncheons now? You are so much more assertive lately! Well, I don't see any harm in a revelation or two, especially since it is not at all as interesting as you apparently have fantasized. Royce, of course. He had such a flair for the dramatic as a boy. I'm certain he'd read every last swashbuckling tale of Oriental pirates and cults and oddities then in print. Or perhaps he got the idea from his vicious little friend, Peter Rizal. The son of a Filipino family nearby. I've always maintained it was dear Peter who gave Royce the idea to do in those St. Bernards in that particularly ... gruesome way." She snorted indignantly. "I swear Royce befriended Peter just to irritate me. That boy was positively *steeped* in every sort of nonsense from his ancestral islands: secret societies, native superstitions, the injured self-righteousness of the victims of colonialism—"

"What happened in the library?"

Vivien chuckled again. "My dear son's idea of a prank, Paulie—tear apart the library, smash a few things, leave the blood-chilling signature of the Katipunan. Presumably I was supposed to be terrified—some vengeance due the Hoffmanns, I imagine, catching up at last. However, in his enthusiasm, Royce quite forgot that I would recognize his handwriting. One of those incidents that so *endeared* Royce to me."

"Who did the damage this time? Was it Royce?"

"You asked me that once before. I take it you have entirely discarded my answer then—the ghosts?"

They were sparring again, and Paul was suddenly impatient with it. "Do you really mean *Geist*? Or perhaps you mean *Gemut*, or *Seele*?"

Vivien paused. "Lovely," she said sincerely. "Quite lovely, nephew, truly. An elegant challenge and provocation. You are changing, aren't you? Does this mean you are doing something different with your medication? You remind me more and more of your father."

"You're evading me. I asked if you thought your son had done this. Is that why you don't want the police in? Are you protecting him?"

"My son," she said. Her voice had gone flat—dry, unyielding, filled with world-weariness. "No, I assure you I am not protecting Royce. But you appear to have been giving this a great deal of thought, Paulie."

"You've asked me many questions about *my* son. I thought I'd reciprocate."

"And it's a fascinating topic, one deserving of more time than either of us has at the moment. Perhaps we'll have the opportunity to continue this conversation when we see each other."

She'd deflected him again, but he was tiring of their fencing. "I will hold you to that, Vivien."

"Now, I will be arriving early on Saturday, the seventeenth, staying at a hotel in Manhattan. I intend to rent a car and see you that afternoon. You needn't worry about transporting me. I'm sure you'll have other things to occupy you."

"Yes." Eight days. Not long enough to get everything done. Yet in so many ways not soon enough, either.

She chuckled, a cynical half-laugh. "And if you have any other fantastic theories to grill me about, you can wait until I arrive."

"I'll make a list," he said dryly.

"Paulie." Her voice had changed again, husky and full of insinuation, almost sensual. "Our recent . . . *association* has come to mean more to me than you could possibly know. I am so looking forward to seeing you again, Paulie."

Right, Paul thought as he hung up the phone. The tone of her good-bye stayed with him. Amazingly, he believed she meant it—that in her loneliness and isolation and strangeness these thorny conversations meant a lot to her. Maybe he was more like Ben than he knew.

Over the granite spine of the ridge beneath the big trees, ducking beneath vines, beneath a huge fallen trunk that leans against a boulder. Then the crows rise up like ashes, making just a tingle of being afraid, but going on because an explorer doesn't let himself be afraid, he's always more curious than afraid, Father says.

Farther down, deep in the folded woods: The dog hears it first, the strange noise, the knife-sharpening noise. Then the shadowy ledge of rock, and something moving on the other side.

Then seeing them, the pink shapes. The tree jerks like something dying, helpless. The man's pink-brown back, arching, and the black triangle between the woman's legs and the jerking way she moves. How wrong their naked skin is in the woods, how out of place and shocking, and the red parts, and the dirt on their skin. And the fast in-out rough noise.

The dog bolts, running tuck-tailed away. Starting to turn, tripping over the thing on the ground and getting up and the fear strikes like lightning, painful fear, being too afraid to look, afraid to look back, and knowing you're not supposed to see or tell ever, and running away, and then the pain of skinned hands and shins and the tangled woods snatching.

"Paul!" Lia shook him, drops of moisture falling onto his face from her hair. "Paul! Wake up!"

He sat up, lost. "What's the matter?"

"*You* are! You were moaning and thrashing around. Are you okay?"

Lia had come out of her scalding bath and stood before him naked, bright red, her skin radiating heat and humidity, hair tangled and dark from the water.

"I guess I fell asleep," Paul said lamely.

After the images of his memory, or dream, the sight of Lia was like a life preserver in a stormy ocean. He put his arms around her waist and drew her to him, inhaling her smell with gratitude. She massaged his head, tugging at his hair, not speaking. There was nothing he could say, nothing he could explain. Gradually, the terror began to evaporate.

The memory was clearer now, he realized, his ability to recall images better, the power to hold them in his mind's eye. Maybe it was the circuits reawakening, he thought, his neurochemistry changing. Maybe it was just being at Highwood, the saturation of his mind with images from the past.

Or maybe he was going crazy.

Lia pushed him back, held him at arm's length, looking searchingly into his eyes. "Your turn for the tub," she said at last. "It'll make you feel better. You've been under a lot of stress."

She smoothed his hair, still nailing him with her eyes—a look of wary concern, almost of accusation.

50

Mo made a point of coming in late and taking a seat far back in the bleachers. The White Plains High School gym echoed with the voices of five hundred excited kids and parents. For this event, the basketball backboards had been cranked up into the girdered ceiling, light green mats laid over the court floor. Mo had grudgingly paid five dollars to a smiling PTA-type mother at the entrance of the gym, doing his bit to benefit the school's sports teams. It was Saturday morning, but he thought of himself as very definitely on duty.

On Friday he'd gone on to the Lewisboro town hall and gotten lucky looking through the property and tax records. Very lucky. Another piece of the puzzle had fallen into place. One more and he could go to Lia and Paul with a pretty complete picture.

On cue, a team of men and women bounded out of the locker room and into the center of the gym, taking wide-legged stances in neat rows. All had bare feet and were dressed in baggy black or white martial-arts outfits, belted at the waist with black belts. As the audience quieted, they began their warm-up exercises, thrusting mean-looking punches, left-right, perfectly synchronized. Their explosions of breath with each punch shook the big room. Mo looked for Rizal and found him in the first row, throwing truly nasty jabs, enjoying himself.

Rizal loved to show off. He'd put up posters for the demonstration at the barracks and had talked it up. Mo had overheard a couple of the younger troopers talking about Rizal's various black belts. Apparently he was to be one of the stars of this show.

The showmaster for the event was a portly man in a black martial arts suit and incongruous brown oxfords, maybe the principal of the school, who dragged a microphone with him as he turned to the bleachers and back again to the fighters, reading from a sheet of paper. The audience had a real treat in store for them today, courtesy of the Southern New York State Martial Arts Association, which had assembled this production to benefit high school sports and to enhance the citizenry's awareness and appreciation of the martial arts. The audience could look forward to dazzling displays of karate, savate, judo, tae kwon do, tai chi, by various regional and national champions. To top it off, they'd be among the first in the United States to witness some more esoteric forms: ba chi, the top-secret fighting art from China, some secret ninja killing arts, and displays of the incredible fighting techniques of the famous warrior monks of Shaolin monastery in China. Big-time gratitude and rounds of applause were in order for the various martial arts clubs, diverse financial sponsors, and of course the terrific kids of White Plains Central High.

After the warm-ups came bouts between combatants in various disciplines. Down on the mats, a Japanese man leapt with both feet at the head of his opponent, his body fully five feet off the ground, only to be swept down by a scything circular kick. Yet he landed well, somersaulted, and landed a vicious kick of his own as he came upright. It was incredible what the human body was capable of, Mo thought. The audience screamed its appreciation.

Rizal came on against a bigger, blond guy. The bastard was good, Mo admitted. Too fast. Like a snake. A couple of times when Rizal made contact, the other guy was genuinely hurt, giving Rizal a look like, *Hey, this is a demonstration, pull the contact.* When the other guy opened up a little himself, scoring a hard hit to Rizal's temple, Rizal was all over him instantly. When it was over, the blond fighter's smile looked forced. The bows he gave to the audience looked painfully stiff.

Then the hand-to-hand phase came to an end and the more exotic demonstrations began. Which apparently would feature Rizal, who stood at the sidelines, now stripped to the waist, tying on a black headband. The master of ceremonies announced a demonstration of ninjitsu, and a man dressed theatrically in black, complete with black tabis and black face mask, came out with nunchuks whistling around him, behind his neck, between his legs, the two short sticks a blur at the end of their chain. After the nunchuks, he demonstrated hand-to-hand with short and long spears, whirling and jabbing, and ended by pitching shuriken, the ninja's six-pointed steel throwing stars. He held the first one aloft to show the audience his two-fingered grip on the palm-size star. Then with a series of flicks he sent one after another in flat streaks to a man-shaped cutout propped against the rear wall.

Then it was Rizal's turn. He came out bare-chested, the overhead lights cutting the muscles of his torso into sharp shadows. He raised his hands above his head, relishing the crowd's approval, flexing a bit. He didn't weigh over 155, Mo guessed, but he had zero body fat. The perfectly delineated muscles of his chest and striated shoulders looked as if they'd been carved with a chisel. *His whole body's a weapon,* Mo thought, *he's tried to make himself into metal. Man of steel. Superman?* Rizal made a show of preparing for his next feat by taking sharp, convulsive breaths that puffed his cheeks as the air burst from his mouth.

Rizal had apparently specialized in some classic karate showmanship, breaking first two-inch wooden planks, and then stacks of two, three, and four concrete blocks, with sharp blows from the edge of his hands. His focus was fiendish.

You've got my attention, Pete, Mo thought.

"Next," the M.C. announced, reading from his script, "Trooper Rizal will demonstrate some of the techniques of the legendary fighting monks of Shaolin monastery. Over the centuries, these reclusive monks have developed fighting skills unknown anywhere else in the world. The Shaolin tradition includes the discipline of turning common household items into lethal weapons. As Trooper Rizal will show you."

Rizal's helpers brought out various pieces of furniture: a table, a chair, a squat wooden footstool, an iron frying pan, a short garden spade. Rizal began with the spade, sending it spinning around his bare waist, twirling it like a baton, under his armpits and over his shoulders, between his legs. Incredible reflexes, Mo thought. Unbelievable hand speed. The muscles of his chest and back looked as if they were made of cut crystal.

Rizal showed off some elaborate moves with the chair, then took a break from the furniture for some Shaolin hand-to-hand fighting.

The announcer gave a spiel about the miraculous powers of the Shaolin monks. "This next technique has never before been mastered outside the ancient walls of Shaolin," he said. "I need to request your silence to allow Trooper Rizal to concentrate fully. He is actually risking serious injury to demonstrate for you the incredible mental and physical state required for this astonishing defensive technique." The audience leaned forward. *Why not some snare drums while we're at it,* Mo thought. He wondered if Rizal had written the script.

Rizal stood, arms crossed, legs slightly spread, jaw clenched. The Japanese fighter came out, bowed to him, and abruptly delivered a hard upward kick to Rizal's crotch. The force of the kick lifted Rizal off the ground, yet he retained his posture, landed taut and ready. The crowd gasped. The Japanese repeated the kick five or six times, Rizal turning so that the whole crowd could get an optimum view. People were shaking their heads, amazed.

"Don't, I repeat, *do not* try this one at home, ladies and gentlemen," the M.C. quipped.

Rizal's final act was with the stool, which he whirled around him in a blur, spun at shin height, over his head, between his legs, using both hands and arms to wield it in a dazzling variety of swipes, jabs, spins. At last he brought it out of an overhead spin and unexpectedly brought it down on the wooden table with a crash that forced a collective gasp from the crowd. The table buckled and broke in half, scattering splinters across the gym floor.

Mo got up to leave. He'd gotten what he'd come for. Anyway, he thought, you didn't want to get caught in the crush in the parking lot. Watching Rizal eat up the applause was enough to give you gas. On the bright side, it had been an engrossing spectacle, and he'd avoided thinking about Heather Mason or pining after Lia for fully ten, fifteen minutes at a stretch. Definitely worth five bucks.

Half an hour later, Mo sat in his car outside the Burger King, finishing off a Whopper and fries, thinking. Rizal could be an answer to Paul's concern about the *how* of it. He certainly knew how to bust up furniture. And probably, if you used that stuff on a human body, if you really had a lot of pressure to let off, anger to vent, you could probably manage 117 bone fractures, or dismember somebody.

His mind recoiled from the idea: *Rizal's a State Police trooper!* On the other hand, Rizal seemed pretty well capable of anything. The next question, the one that would help him unravel the case, was *why?* There were obviously some deep motives at work, and while Rizal was lethal as a pit viper, he didn't seem to have anything to gain from the destruction of Highwood. And he wasn't smart enough to concoct anything complex—if he had any real brains, he wouldn't have tipped his hand by overtly threatening Paul. Therefore the motives and the brains were elsewhere. Which was where Royce came in. Put Royce and Rizal together, buddies since childhood—

Mo looked up from his fries to see Rizal walking toward him, dressed now in black Levi's and a black leather jacket. He was grinning, the big star after his show, probably still pumped up on adrenaline. Mo rolled down his window.

"I was driving home when I thought I saw a pile of shit in a car," Rizal said. "I couldn't believe my eyes, so I stopped to verify."

"You were right. Anything else I can do for you?"

"You were at the show just now. I never imagined you were such a big fan." Rizal felt in his element, wanted to gloat. "Like it?"

"It was amazing, I have to admit," Mo said. "I especially liked the one where the guy kicked you in the balls."

Still flushed with the thrill of performing, Rizal took an instant to hear it right. His face changed from a smug smile to a quick frown and back to the smile in less than a second. "Takes balls of steel," he said. "Balls of brass, Ford."

It wasn't a bad recovery. Mo nodded, trying to look first impressed, then a little concerned. "That, or no balls at all, I suppose."

Rizal's face took it with a flash of anger. Then he shook his head sadly. "Very funny, asshole. You are a regular Jerry Lewis, so help me. Or at least one of Jerry's Kids. You know what I think? I think you'd be a pushover in a fight, Ford, I think you'd piss your pants. That's something maybe you should think about—what you would do if somebody who knew what he was doing came at you."

Mo dutifully thought about it, letting his face take on a troubled expression. "Like that Japanese guy? Like you? Shit," he said, shrugging, "I guess I'd have to shoot him."

He looked at Rizal deadpan, kept his eyes on Rizal's snake eyes. You could always see a move coming in the eyes. He put another french fry in his mouth.

51

"I should have known I wouldn't be able to carry it off," Dempsey said. "Does it help that I thought it was for your own good? I thought I'd spare you that disillusionment, or whatever you want to call it."

Paul had considered various ways to catch Dempsey in the act as he searched through papers, but as it turned out no subterfuge was necessary. Sorting the next box of papers, he found what he needed to put it together— Dempsey's sneaking around, his inability to meet Paul's eyes.

"How long were Ben and Vivien having an affair?" Paul asked.

Dempsey shrugged. "Maybe a year? I was never sure when it started."

"How'd it end?"

"Your father jumped off a goddamned cliff, that's how." Dempsey turned a circle on the rug. "Actually, I don't know. Things he told me, toward the end, it sounded like he was beginning to want out of it but didn't know how. I think he was afraid she'd tell your mother. After Hoffmann, Vivien had this thing about rejection. She was dying for company, for closeness. Everything she did, it was . . . larger than life. Big appetites, big hungers, big hurts. Big grudges. I have no doubt she could do something lousy to Ben if he blew her off."

"What about Aster? *Did* Vivien tell her? Did Ben? Is that why the two sisters split apart after he died?"

"I don't know. And you can't ask your mother, can you? Lose-lose situation. If she knows, you revive the humiliation and anger and so on. And if it's news to her—"

A complicated tic twisted Paul's head on his neck and caused his arm to writhe out, his hand seeming to grip and turn an invisible doorknob. The motor tics were changing, he noted, less frequent but more severe, complex and prolonged.

In frustration he swatted the sheaf of letters he'd found, some of them clearly referring to trysts Ben and Vivien had managed to conceal from everybody. Probably Dempsey was telling the truth when he said Ben had wanted to call if off. In one of the later letters, written near the end of his life, Ben talked about Vivien's "yearning for companionship." "You must face the fact that to know another human being, in the way that you so hunger for, may not be possible. I doubt that I am capable of offering you that kind and degree of companionship." Ben went on about loneliness: "The lot of all human beings, ultimately . . . take solace in our unique-ness . . . try to cherish our splendid solitude." It could easily be the prepara-tory rhetoric for a parting of the ways.

"You have to put it in perspective," Dempsey said. "Here's somebody Ben is really close to, a very remarkable person, and she's dying of loneli-ness. Waiting for her ex-husband to come back to her for twelve years or so while her youth was fading. Not to sound like Zorba the Greek, but here's a beautiful woman, going to waste. I meant that about the chivalry stuff, and your father was a perfect candidate for the white-knight syndrome. It probably started out of sympathy, or compassion—"

"Spare me, huh?" Paul said.

"I mean it."

"Dempsey, do me a favor."

"I'll try."

Paul slammed his fist on the table, and the old fighter startled. "No! I want you to do better than *try*! I want you, Dempsey Corrigan, never to lie to me again. Never to try to protect my goddamned respect for Ben again. If you want to honor Ben, or me, or yourself, then you've got to tell me how it really was."

"Probably that's right, yeah."

"I want to know if there's anything else you're not telling me. Anything else you know about this house or this mess."

"Like what?"

"Like, did you do this?"

"What, to get myself some furniture repair work? Hey, I'm poor, but I'm not that desperate."

"Why do you think Ben killed himself?"

"You're acting like you've got me up against the ropes, like you can throw anything at me you want because I said I'd be straight with you. Watch out, Paulie. The guy on the ropes may have a surprise punch waiting for you." Paul had never seen Dempsey angry. It was intimidating. "You think I haven't searched my soul, wondering why? This man was like a brother to me. Maybe if Vivien told Aster, as I said. Only a couple of other possibilities occur to me."

"Such as?"

"You really want it, don't you?" The old man turned away again, flung up his hands. "I was afraid of something else you might find in his letters. Maybe you still will, if you haven't read them all, so I'll throw it out now.

It could be maybe he was feeling bad about his son—his beautiful, brilliant son, with all the neurological problems. Who'd started this new drug therapy that helped his symptoms but shut him down, turned off the music, killed the spark, put him half to sleep. I didn't want you to run across something like that." Dempsey watched Paul's face as he took it, a gut punch. "You asked me for it, damn it," he said softly.

Dempsey had confirmed the lurking fear, the ever-present guilt: *He did it because of me. I let him down.* Of course. It would explain a lot: the thousand odd looks from Aster, her unwillingness to talk about it. Kay's insistence on leaving the past behind. Paul felt like he couldn't breathe.

"I'm not saying that's what happened," Dempsey said. "I'm saying that might be what somebody'd think—"

"What was the other possibility?"

"That he didn't in fact commit suicide." Dempsey's face was working, and he was starting to sweat. With jerky movements, he unbuttoned his heavy wool shirt. "People *saw* Ben jump off—observant, conscientious people. I met them, I believe them. Fine. But I *knew* Ben, and I know suicide wasn't his style, or his mood."

They were quiet for a moment. Like two fighters, wearying in the late rounds, Paul thought. And yet he felt better. You had to trust somebody. You could trust Dempsey.

"Another question," Paul said after a time. "What do you know about the room upstairs? The one off Vivien's bedroom?"

"I built it. That's how I got to know Vivien in the first place. They'd been here about a year, your mother recommended me. This would have been around 1950, somewhere in there. I closed off the windows, reinforced the walls—four inches of additional insulation, interior walls and ceiling sheathed in quarter-inch steel plate, then paneled in two-inch oak. I poured a three-inch, reinforced concrete floor, covered it with the maple that you see now."

"A lot of work. What for?"

"A vault. She had furs, clothes that cost a fortune, jewels, artworks, antiques. It made sense to me they'd want a vault, out here in the sticks. They were in the habit of traveling a lot when they first came here."

"Why the recessed light fixtures on the ceiling? Why'd she want that steel grid over them? *Inside* the vault?"

"Never occurred to me to wonder. She'd had some architect draw up the plan. I just followed the blueprint. What's this got to do with anything?"

"One last question. Did you ever see or hear anything that suggested Vivien had another son besides Royce?"

Dempsey looked at him strangely. "This is nuts."

"Please, just think about it. Think back."

Dempsey rubbed his grizzled chin, stared off into space. He shook his head. "I'd have to say no. It was a long time ago." The old man looked weary, and Paul felt a pang of sympathy: This wasn't easy for him, either. "A long time ago," Dempsey repeated sadly.

They stood around for another minute. Then Dempsey went to the door and outside, and Paul followed. The sun had come out and though it was a cool day the dark slate of the terrace gave off some of the heat it had soaked up, a comfortable warmth. They sat on the steps, surveying the driveway, their two cars, the wrecked garden, the sky.

Dempsey fished in his shirt, pulled out a package of chewing gum, offered a stick to Paul, peeled one for himself.

Paul unwrapped the gum slowly, the images coming to his mind unbidden: *the man's broad, arching back, the woman's jerking movements, the triangle of pubic hair. Ben and Vivien? The brutal aspect of sex, its mindless, animal movements, inexplicable and horrifying to a six-year-old. The shock of recognition, the intuitive understanding of betrayal, upheaval in the family.* Maybe. Possibly.

"Vivien and Ben," Paul said, fitting pieces together. "That's why you stopped working for her?"

Dempsey peeled another stick of gum, flicked the balled-up foil into the drive. "Not that it was any more her fault than Ben's. Nobody's 'fault.' I just . . . after Ben's death, I couldn't look at her. I don't know. The thought that maybe she'd threatened to talk to Aster. Added the straw that broke the camel's back." A dark spark pulsed in his eye. "Couldn't stand to look at her."

Good point, Paul thought. How would it be, talking to Vivien the next time? She must have known he'd find these letters. She had been manipulating him. What else did she have planned?

One thing for certain, though, Paul realized in another leap of understanding—his neurological state was changing. For both better and worse. Every time he found the disturbing memory, he was slipping into a shallow doze, a preoccupied trance, some sort of hypnogogic state. A lot like Mark's trance, the one that preceded his seizures. A lot like Paul's own early problems.

"I still say you're nuts about her having another kid," Dempsey growled.

"How can you be so sure?"

Dempsey chuckled grimly, sucked his teeth. "Self-restraint, you could safely say, was never Royce's forte. No kid could have survived long with him as a brother."

Very good point, Paul thought.

52

Lia yanked the car to the shoulder and they looked up at the cliffs, the broken walls of rock and scrub on their right. On their left, just as Paul remembered it, the Hudson took a wide bend; on the west bank, the towering palisade fell dramatically into slate-colored water. It was a glorious day, sun mixed with a few clouds, not too cold, and at Lia's insistence, they'd started out on a drive "just to get a break from Highwood." She'd driven them along Highway 35 to Peekskill, where they stopped for gas, ate an early lunch at a diner. He should have guessed what she was doing when she headed north, up 9D along the river. It was the first time Paul had been back to Break Neck since he'd climbed it with Ben, that summer before Ben's suicide.

"This is a shitty idea," Paul said. He was in a black mood after Dempsey's revelations. Everything seemed devalued, tawdry, seamy, cheap. Life was unlivable. "I don't have time for an outing. I've got my old bitch aunt coming in seven days and I'm behind schedule on the fucking job. And you know what else? I've had it up to here with your controlled-risk, face-your-fear shit."

Lia didn't blink, her certainty didn't waver. "That's not what this is about, Paul," she said firmly. "This is my gift to you. Now come with me or I'll go up by myself and you'll have to worry about me, won't you?"

She got out of the car and began walking quickly back toward the trail head, above the old water station. Paul swore to the empty car, then got out and followed her.

He'd talked late into the night with Lia, telling her about Ben's letters to Vivien, about his showdown with Dempsey. Ben and Vivien, Dempsey's comment about Royce, his speculation about reasons for Ben's suicide.

Lia had listened raptly throughout, absolutely unmoving. "You really think, you really believe for one moment, that *you* could have been the reason Ben jumped?"

"How the fuck should I know?" Paul was in the blackest funk he could remember. "It's as good as any other theory. Whenever Mark starts to get worse, I can believe a father would want to. Not a fuck of a lot I can do about it now in any case, is there?"

Lia had looked at him hard then, the arch of eyebrows telling him her wheels were turning.

Now they were on the steep trail at the base of Break Neck. The Hudson opened below as they climbed, its slate-blue curves disappearing in the distance, colossal cliffs rising on the other side. Above and ahead of him, Lia picked her way wisely. She seemed to be enjoying herself. Paul just felt angry. No, sad. No, scared—but not of the height, exactly. The height was just there, available if Death needed it.

Death lived here.

After fifteen minutes, Lia paused at a level outthrust boulder, turned to catch her breath, facing out over the valley. "This is *gorgeous*," she said. Already she'd tied her windbreaker around her waist, and her breasts pushed up against her sweater as she inhaled and threw back her shoulders. "God, it's beautiful. We're lucky to have such a fine day."

"Yeah," Paul said.

Lia sat and patted the rock next to her. "I've got a couple of candy bars. Want one? Keep your blood sugar up."

Paul sat. "My blood sugar's fine."

"Well, I'm going to have half of one." She unwrapped a bar of chocolate and broke off several sections. Then she opened up a small map. "I found this at the gas station. Trail map of Break Neck."

"Terrific. Exploit the place. Put up hotdog stands. Thank God we're here out of season." In fact, they were the only ones on the cliff. It *was* past the season—most climbers preferred warmer weather. There could be ice in tricky spots. Paul's body was warm from exertion, but his hands were cold, fingers stiff and red from the breeze that rose up against the highlands.

"Have you noticed something about yourself recently? Your Tourette's, I mean. You don't seem to have as many tics."

"Yeah."

"And yet you've been cutting back on medication. And you've been under a lot of stress, which should exacerbate symptoms."

"Periods of full or partial remission are not unknown. Symptoms often abate as you get older. Maybe it's fading out." Right now he felt resentment toward her. He wasn't going to confide that as of this morning he'd stopped haloperidol completely.

Lia nibbled her chocolate thoughtfully for a time, then wrapped the remainder neatly and put it in her pocket. "Paul, do you know, can you remember, where your father jumped?"

"The Chute," he answered without thinking. The memory surprised him. He hadn't known he knew. Lia's catching him by surprise renewed his irritation. "What is this little exercise you've got planned, Lia?"

"You've got to trust somebody, Paul," she said. One quick bolt from her eye. "The way you do that is, you start close to home. With yourself. You've got to trust yourself. After that, you move on to the people closest to you." She continued up the trail.

Paul gave her a head start, then reluctantly followed.

The climb got harder and steeper. Behind them the huge valley of the Hudson gaped, the sky opened up. The slope rose more and more steeply until they were climbing, using all fours now as much as walking. Sparking silver in the bright sun, a commuter train inched along the line of tracks, a millipede lost in the vastness of river and rock. South, where the river widened after the landbreak, a tug pushed a pair of barges, cutting a neat V in the water. Farther up, the edge cut closer to the trail. On their right, they looked down on a valley that angled up from the river, a mix of steep, forested slopes and jumbled rock. The big empty mass of air seemed to exert a pull, a spacious vacuum wanting to be filled.

"I think this is the Chute," Paul said dully.

"It tops off just above," Lia said, pointing. The steep walls of the cliff culminated in a shelf fifty feet above them. Beyond the shelf, the slope softened, the narrowed chute ended. Paul remembered Ben, urging him along: "C'mon, Lazybones, just a little farther. It gets easier after that little plateau."

"Let's just go up there," Lia insisted. "Then we can head back down if you want."

The trail wound away from the steep precipice, zigging and zagging among boulders and sculpted rock faces. Then they came out of the last switchback and onto the shelf, a nearly level patch of solid rock the size of a large living room. A scattering of stunted trees shared the shelf with a litter of fallen rock from above. The view was breathtaking.

"What do you want here, Lia? Goddamn it, this isn't fun for me."

Lia had gone to the edge, the very top of the famous Chute. She leaned, peering over, then jerked back, got down on all fours and crawled to the edge. "Wow!" she said. "Come look, Paul. Christ! Scary as hell."

Paul crawled to her side and felt a lurch of vertigo. Immediately below them the Chute began, a sheer gash in the side of the mountain, dropping almost straight to the floor of the valley. Far down at the base of the cliff was a jumble of boulders and fallen tree trunks. It wasn't perfectly vertical—you'd probably bounce at least twice before you hit. This was just right for Ben, the perfect ending: beautiful, dramatic, final.

"Okay," Paul said, pulling back from the edge. "Can we go back down now?"

"No."

"What do you want from me, Lia? Good Jesus." He lay with his cheek against the stone, still feeling the whispered tug of the chasm. He was empty of emotions, but he sensed the heat of tears at the corners of his eyes.

"Jump off, Paul. I want you to jump the fuck off. You're so goddamned depressed about Ben, about Mark, about yourself. It's hopeless. Jump off. Finish it. Do it with dignity."

"Fuck you."

Lia sat up, tugged Paul upright by his shirt. She manhandled him back from the edge to the undercut wall, thirty feet from the edge. *A good running start,* Paul thought.

"Go ahead," Lia said. Her face was hard, her skin pale in the cold.

Paul shook free of her grip, squared his shoulders, looked at the short, easy run in front of him, the blue-hazed abyss beyond pulling him, the tangle of barbed wire and broken glass inside him. *Jump, Paul.* Lia stood back.

After a few moments, he took her hand and they sat down side by side in the little shelter of the overhang.

"Okay," he said. "Okay. Do we always have to do things the hard way?"

"Sometimes the hard way is the only way."

"Okay. So he didn't kill himself because of me." He hadn't had a conscious thought, but it had percolated up. "The logic's not right. I know because I have Mark. Sometimes I despair he'll ever be okay—talk about the dark night of the soul, yeah, it could make you jump off a cliff. But if it's my concern for his future that gives me the pain, then I couldn't . . . do something like that . . . to him. Because if anything would hurt him, wreck his future, that would. See?"

"Yes," she said simply.

Paul sat, feeling the sun-warmed rock against his back, the gentle heat of Lia's thigh along his own.

"Which is why you contrived this whole scenario. Your gift to me."

"Yeah."

He gave it some space so she'd know he meant it: "Thanks," he told her. He sat for another moment, safely back from whatever edge he'd been near. "How'd you know I wouldn't do it?"

"At first I was sure you wouldn't. Down below. Once we got up here, I wasn't sure at all. But I couldn't seem to give you any wiggle room. I'm very glad I was right."

. . .

They headed down the switchbacks below the top of the Chute, and paused again at the turn below the shelf.

"Leaving one to wonder, still," Paul said, "why he did do it."

Lia gazed upward. "*If* he did. Because if this was where those other people saw him jump, the ones in the newspaper article, they couldn't see everything. And this had to be the spot—you can't see the shelf from the trail anywhere below or above this point. They'd see him at the edge, then backing out of view, then rushing off the edge. They wouldn't see whether he really got a running start. Or whether there was someone else on the shelf, back against the overhang."

Paul could picture it: Ben at the edge, looking down. He backs up. He'd be out of view from below by the time he was two paces back from the edge. What then? Somebody gives him a powerful shove? Who?

An idea clicked into his head. What had Royce meant when he'd alluded to Ben's photograph? *Who do you think he was, Paulie? Ever wonder what made him . . .* It had seemed threatening, a provocation. Maybe Royce knew about Ben and Vivien. A sociopathic kid, deeply angry at what he perceives as Vivien's betrayal of his father, Erik Hoffmann. That and Oedipal jealousy. He knows Ben likes to go to Break Neck, so one day he follows him—

But what then? In 1965 Royce would have been only fifteen. And Ben wouldn't be taken by surprise, he was strong and fit, he'd fight. Even pushed, he'd be struggling for balance, flailing, something that would have been evident to the Melchers and the rest of the witnesses. Assuming, that is, he didn't want to go over.

"Leaving one to wonder," Paul said again.

53

Mo dialed the Manhattan number, got Grisbach's answering machine, a short, wheezy announcement: "Leave a message."

"Mo Ford," Mo said. It was easy to be terse and concise around Grisbach. "Call me, I need you." He hung up.

When Mo had first begun as an investigator, Gus Grisbach had already been part of the secret lore of New York law enforcement for a decade. His name, how to get access to him, were closely guarded secrets, off the record, handed down from investigator to investigator. As Mo pieced the story together, Gus had been a New York City detective until he'd taken two bullets in his head, then retired on disability allowance. His affection for criminals had never been great, and it hadn't been enhanced by getting injured. After retirement, he'd set himself up to continue law enforcement work. Sort of going freelance.

They'd been able to get the bullets out of his brain, and Gus's ability to think hadn't been impaired. But they'd never managed to rewire him just right. Supposedly he'd once been a charming guy, but the bullets had killed that part of him, whatever part of the brain gave a person social sensitivity, warmth, interest in others, all the checks and balances that kept a person human. Mo had heard the human brain described as having three main layers, added as the organism had evolved—the reptile, the mammal, and the human. The functions of the reptile brain could be summed up as the four Fs: *fight, flight, food,* and *fuck.* The mammal brain, so went this schematic, added a fifth F: *family,* the need and the ability to bond, to protect and nurture, to engage in complex social interactions. The most recent addition, belonging to *Homo sapiens* alone, did something that didn't begin with an F and so destroyed the neatness of the scheme: *abstract and associative thinking.* Gus's abstract thinking had survived just fine, but what had died in him, Mo felt, what had taken the bullet, was that fifth F.

After losing parts of his neural equipment, and especially after being removed from police work, Gus had become impossible to be around, bitter, hostile, unstable. He'd have been dangerous to keep on the streets. He had also gotten hugely fat. It was said he never left his apartment now. Mo had never met him in person, but he could picture him, lurking in dim rooms lit only by computer monitors, nursing his insane anger. A spider at the center of his web of myriad computer connections, filaments linking him to information all over the world.

Mo got the call, as he expected, after midnight. Maybe Gus had some image of himself as a sort of Cyber Batman and liked the idea of secret, midnight intrigues against the global criminal conspiracy. Maybe he just didn't know what time of day it was, or didn't care.

"Mo Ford," Gus croaked. He spoke with the fat man's deep and wheezy voice, with a little bubble at the back of his throat that made Mo want to clear his own. "You need my help."

"Gus, thanks for calling. Two things. Status of a couple of companies—a Pacific Development Corporation and a Star Technologies. Both with connections to Asia. I need to know if they're legit, if they're doing all right, if there's any scuttlebutt in the markets about them—if they're in trouble, if they're trying something aggressive, anything fishy about them, whatever. I'm looking for reasons somebody would need money. Head honcho is a Royce Hoffmann, New York and Amsterdam addresses."

Mo could hear the clatter of a computer keyboard as he talked, Gus taking notes.

"What else?" Gus asked.

"The whereabouts of this Royce Hoffmann. Supposedly was leaving the country from New York on or around December fifth. I'd like to know where he is, what his travel plans are in the near future. In fact, see if you can figure out where he has been during the last year. Could use commercial flights, but might go by corporate or private planes—the best way might be to check customs, when his passport has been in or out."

"Tell me what you want, skip the advice."

"Sorry. If you can put together a profile on his lifestyle—where he stays when he travels, how much he spends, what kind of personal loans he's got out, that'd be great. He's supposed to be rich as shit. I'd like to know for sure. Especially if there've been any changes in his spending habits in the last year or so."

"What else?"

"Look into this guy Gus Grisbach for me. Supposed to be a computer wizard somewhere in Manhattan. Completely crazy, but a legend in his own time. Let me know how he's doing, how he's feeling, how's his health. That kind of thing."

"Fuck you, Ford," Grisbach said.

The line went dead. Gus didn't ask when Mo needed the info. If you'd resorted to calling Gus, ASAP was a given.

54

"I think it's beginning to come together," Mo said. "We're no longer chasing wild geese. The ends are starting to tie up, the lines converge. You are going to love this." His last comment seemed directed to Lia.

They were in the smoking room, Paul and Lia sitting in the big wingback chairs, Mo pacing back and forth. He had that light about him, Paul decided, the same as Lia's when she got excited about something. The hunter on the trail. Lia watched him, captivated by his intensity. From the basement they could hear muffled hammering as Becker's crew dismantled the old furnaces. Through the smoking room window, Paul could see Becker's van and a huge pickup truck in the driveway.

"I've made a lot of progress since we last talked. Starting with a big day Friday. I went down to the Lewisboro town offices, then the courthouse in White Plains. Did some research into this property. Turns out your aunt isn't the owner of Highwood, Paul."

"What!"

"That's right. Your cousin is. Transmitted to Royce Hoffmann earlier this year from the Hoffmann Trust, which got it from Erik Hoffmann II at his death in 1985, subject to provisions of divorce proceedings, *Hoffmann* v. *Hoffmann*, 1952."

"So how does Vivien live here?" Lia asked. "Under what auspices?"

"Aha." Mo was clearly enjoying his tale, the timing of the hints he dropped. "Your aunt lives here as the result of a property division resulting from the divorce settlement. She apparently got a chunk of money and generous alimony. But the property ownership stayed with Hoffmann. Vivien got what they call a life estate—the right to live here for the rest of her life. It must have been a hell of a divorce, every inch of ground fought over, because her life estate was restricted by certain provisos."

Lia turned to Paul. "He's really enjoying this, isn't he? Keep us in suspense, feed us tidbits one by one." She grinned at Mo. "That's my cue to ask what kind of provisos, right?"

"Yep." Mo returned her smile. "And the answer is, continuous occupancy. Hoffmann was a canny old buzzard. If Vivien should retain the right to continue to live at Highwood because of a 'deep emotional attachment' to the premises, as she claimed in her settlement arguments, then she'd have to continue to demonstrate that attachment. Vacations, normal short-term absences would be fine, but if she leaves here and establishes a primary residence elsewhere for a period of six months, she loses her right to live here."

Mo waited, letting the ramifications of that settle in.

"And of course if the place is really beat to shit, she can't live here," Paul said. "And if she doesn't live here for that time, she loses it. Presumably the property would go to Royce."

"Beautiful," Lia said. "Royce wanting the place for himself would explain two things we've wondered about. One, why such extreme damage? Answer: because he'd need to guarantee that it would be uninhabitable for a long enough time to trigger the continuous occupancy clause. Two, why not just burn the place down? Answer: because if Royce is doing this to get his hands on the money value of the place, he doesn't want to destroy the house. It's got to be worth a couple of million—intact. Also why Royce would try so hard to bribe Paul away from the job. And any other contractor would have fallen for it. Royce wasn't counting on a family member, somebody who'd stick by his commitments, contracting to do the work here."

"Which Vivien may have anticipated," Mo said. "Possibly the reason she initiated the contact with Paul in the first place. This whole thing could be part of an old, old chess match between mother and son."

Paul thought about it. "Royce mentioned to me that he often wheels and deals well beyond his own liquidity. Maybe he's pressed for cash now—he'd like to sell this property, but he can't do it with Vivien's life estate in place. And I'll bet there's a clause specifying that nobody can borrow against the equity value of the estate as long as Vivien is in possession."

Mo nodded, impressed. "Correct. Because default on a loan against the property would endanger a prior contract—Vivien's life estate—neither Royce nor his father were allowed to borrow against it while she was in residence. Well, you both get an A in deduction—I came to the same conclusions."

"Thanks, teacher." Lia reached out a foot to kick him softly in the calf, smiling. Mo obviously savored the gesture.

"But what was the Hoffmann Trust?" Paul asked. "If ownership was going to come just to Royce anyway, why did Hoffmann Senior bother with the intermediary entity—the trust?"

Mo shrugged. "Keeps it out of Royce's hands until he's of a certain age? Tax dodge? If you really think it matters, I can look into it." He took another turn on the rug and stopped, facing them. "But I've got another juicy one for you. I've been saving the best for last."

Lia shot a glance at Paul. "Let's not encourage him," she said.

"Paul, I took your question seriously—the question of *how*." Mo said. "Frankly, it's been bugging me too. So I went to see Rizal at a martial arts demonstration. He's into some very exotic Eastern fighting techniques, and he's good, Paul. He's one of these guys who breaks boards with their bare hands, bricks with their heads. Probably there's nothing here he couldn't have done. Suppose he works for his millionaire friend Royce in his off hours."

"I propose a toast," Lia said. "Mo, you're a genius. You're a great detective and you're a great storyteller. You oughta be on Broadway." She raised her coffee cup in salute.

Mo turned his head away, Paul noticed, to hide his pleasure. *He's doing this for Lia,* he realized. *This is the cop equivalent of bringing her a bouquet.*

Lia and Mo chattered on excitedly, but Paul tuned them out, his thoughts spiraling in on what he'd learned. Rizal was into Eastern martial arts. Was there more to it than Mo knew—maybe a tie to the KKK, the Katipunan, after all? But why wreck Highwood? *That boy was positively steeped in every sort of nonsense from his ancestral islands—secret societies, native superstitions, the injured self-righteousness of the victims of colonialism,* Vivien had said. Maybe it wasn't all nonsense.

And Vivien: When had she gone to California? And how did her impending return tie in with the continuous occupancy clause? It had to be nearly six months ago that she'd left Highwood—if she wanted to keep the place, she had to be getting nervous by now. Which upped the pressure on Paul to get the repairs done. Would she pay him the rest of his fee if he fell behind schedule and cost her the lodge? Fat fucking chance.

And the Hoffmann Trust. When Hoffmann died, Royce would have been thirty-five—why not just leave it to Royce? Why create the trust, which was the owner of record for nine years after Hoffmann's death? Was the Hoffmann Trust Royce alone, or Royce and someone else? And what had caused the trust to revert entirely to Royce?

Patterns: Mo had found a pretty neat case against Royce. Paul realized he'd felt the shape of a pattern emerging too, even before Mo came, big pieces of the puzzle shifting, aligning. Their discussion this afternoon held parts of the puzzle, if he could just sort them out. It also confirmed what he'd been suspecting for several days: that his own ability to track patterns had been changing since he quit haloperidol. There was a clarity, an ability to assimilate details and connect the dots, that he only vaguely remembered. Yes, the parts had begun to fit. Paul could almost *see* it, *feel* it. The only problem was, it didn't look anything like the pattern Mo had assembled. Or maybe Mo's was part of it—part of a bigger picture, bigger and stranger.

It was something like the discovery of the planet Pluto, Paul thought. Long before the planet was seen through telescopes, scientists were puzzling over disturbances in the orbits of Uranus and Neptune. *Something* was out there, a hidden presence, an invisible force, in the scheme of the solar system. Once astronomers had calculated the inexplicable quirks in the other planets' orbits, they knew where to look, and sure enough, there was the dark ninth planet, almost invisible yet affecting space around it. That's how this situation felt. A hidden player. Something they could *sense,* could *feel,* but couldn't see. Not just yet, anyway.

55

Monday afternoon Mo continued down his checklist, feeling energized after his meeting with Paul and Lia. It was only three o'clock, and a worn-out-looking janitor was polishing the hall floors with a noisy, shopping cart–size machine that stank up the air with cleaning solvent fumes, like a goddamned bus station. You had to wonder why they couldn't wait until after hours. Typical mismanagement, he thought, then realized he was starting to think like Tommy Mack. He got up and shut the door to cut the noise.

Feeling a familiar trepidation, he dialed the Masons' number. As usual, the phone rang four times and was answered by the machine: "You have reached the Mason residence. I'm sorry, but . . ."

"This is Morgan Ford, calling again from—" Mo began when he heard the beep. He was cut off when the machine squealed suddenly and clicked off.

"Hello, Mr. Ford."

"Mrs. Mason, thank you for answering. I'm sorry to be calling again, but—"

"Yes, I'm sorry you're calling again too." Her voice was flat, empty of emotion.

"Listen, Mrs. Mason. You know why I'm calling. I need your help. I need Heather's help."

"Yes, I know exactly why you're calling. And no, we can't help you, Mr. Ford." Her voice was absolutely toneless. It was hard to imagine such a voice coming from the deep-eyed, sincere woman he'd met.

"But—"

"You can go to *hell!*" she cried suddenly. "You can go to *hell* and leave us alone!" In the background, Mo heard a man's solicitous, cautioning voice: *"Honey . . ."* "You can stop calling us now. Because you'll never talk to Heather. You *can't* talk to her. Because my daughter is *dead*, Mr. Ford. Is that good enough? Are you satisfied?" She was suddenly crying, keening.

"What happened, Mrs. Mason?"

"My daughter committed suicide. My only child left, my beautiful daughter cut open her wrists and let her life run out of her and down the tub drain like water, like *sewage*. Oh, *God!* Leave us alone!"

Mo sat down, almost missing the edge of his chair.

"Mr. Ford?" The husband's voice, a man struggling to maintain any control at all. "My wife can't talk to you now. I can't. We've ... it's all we can. . . . Don't call us again. Please."

Mo listened to the dial tone for half a minute. *Five things worse than dying.* Then he fumbled the receiver back onto its cradle.

It took him a few minutes before he'd recovered enough to ask around about Heather Mason's death. One of the risks of being out of the office so much, dodging your colleagues and superior officer: You got left out of the loop.

He got the details from Joe Matarini, who'd gotten the case. Matarini was clean-cut, smart, an experienced investigator. Suicide, nothing but. Heather's shrink, Dr. Kurtz, had sorrowfully agreed it was entirely in line with her mental state. Mrs. Mason had found her on Sunday afternoon in the tub in the bathroom of her suite, naked, her inner thighs and wrists slashed. A single-edged razor blade was still in her hand, and the M.E.'s report stated that it was compatible with the many shallow, clean cuts, drawn deftly along the length of her arteries. She hadn't left a note other than the inch-thick sheaf of lined paper, torn from spiral notebooks, covered with meaningless squiggles, lines of waves and loops, which sat undisturbed on the edge of the dry tub. Her story. With the title that explained everything.

Mo thought: *This job is the pits. The absolute pits.* Numb, he got his mail and headed back to his private utility closet.

Where, looking through the assorted letters and junk mail, he got another shock. With a Jewish mother, Jewish aunts and uncles and cousins, he hadn't been brought up with a lot of faith in the idea of resurrection. Even if their household had embraced his father's lapsed Catholicism, Mo's own philosophical inclinations were that when you died you were dead, gone, gone, gone and probably glad of it. But in his hand was a feminine, lavender-tinted envelope addressed to him in ball-point pen. From Heather Mason.

There was a single piece of lined paper inside, a ragged-edged page from Heather's spiral notebook. Checking quickly, he found that the envelope was postmarked Saturday, the day before she died. He'd have to give a copy to Matarini, part of the file on Heather, the story of her ending that would get closed and submerged in a sea of other wretched paperwork in an obscure cubbyhole somewhere, the exhaustively chronicled history of misery in Westchester County, and everywhere.

I wasn't kidding, she'd written. *Do you believe me now?*

56

"I know about you and Ben, Vivien," Paul said. "I know you were lovers." She didn't say anything for several breaths. When she still didn't speak, his anger rose. "Vivien? Did you hear me?"

"What is it, exactly," she said, "that you want me to say? How, precisely, do you wish me to respond?"

It was a fair question. What had he hoped for? Denial? Apology? Against her weariness and resignation, his anger seemed suddenly trivial. Paul stood in the cold kitchen at Highwood, not knowing where to go with it. Lia was in the carriage house, cleaning herself up before they took a couple of hours off to go to dinner at the Corrigans'. After the revelations of the last few days, he'd felt a growing pressure inside: Vivien had a lot of explaining to do. He'd called her impulsively, determined to put an end to the mystery.

When he didn't answer, she rallied. "So you have discovered some of your father's letters. And you're angry with me. What would you have had me do, Paulie? Announce it to you beforehand?"

"Did you ever tell Aster?"

"Don't be absurd! What—I went to her on the eve of her husband's suicide and told her that he'd not only killed himself, he'd betrayed her? Do you know, I believe you are asking me something else entirely. You want to know if my telling Aster, or threatening to, drove him over the cliff. It sounds to me as if you are looking for a scapegoat for your mother's, your family's unhappiness. Well, for that I will accept no blame. To my knowledge, she never knew. She and I both had enough to suffer with."

Her insightfulness stopped him. Yes, it would have been nice to pin the blame neatly on someone. Vivien, or anyone.

"There's something else, Vivien. I know you don't own Highwood. I know about Royce, that you've got a life estate and that he comes into ownership if you don't move back in here soon. Why didn't you tell me that?"

She was wordless again. He heard her breath come erratically, as if she were struggling with her feelings. At last she spoke: "Would it have made any difference? Must I trumpet everything to all and sundry? No, I am not proud that my residence in the house I have lived in for forty-five years is contingent upon conditions and strictures and the whims of others. No, I do not like to recall the very, very difficult period of my separation from my husband. And yes, though I am sometimes ambivalent as to whether I ought to resume residence, yes, I am concerned that I will lose my home if I do not return. I'd have preferred to make my personal choices without duress." Her voice had been rising, her breath coming harsh and fast. "But is this another confession I was somehow *obligated* to make to Paulie Skoglund because I hired him to repair my house? Have I *no right* to keep anything at all to myself, just because my house has been destroyed? Having been violated once, must I therefore be violated again? Frankly, your intrusion offends me. If I were not, as you *so* tactfully pointed out, rather desperate at this time, I'd fire you."

He couldn't find a reason to contradict her. If he were in her shoes, he'd react the same way. In comparison to the injuries she'd suffered, his earlier pique seemed petty.

He made one last sally: "I only ask because the destruction of the house seems to implicate Royce. If he's doing this to force you out of here, why don't you want to do something about it? Why not accuse Royce?"

"You're assuming I agree with you—that Royce was responsible."

"Why don't you think so?"

She got quiet, as if searching for an answer that would make sense to him. "I have no doubt that Royce would be quite happy to come into possession of Highwood. And I know that there is nothing Royce wouldn't do to accomplish his ends—nothing. But he would never be so overt. He would never let his desires be so obvious. I would of course see his hand in things and be, frankly, rather flattered by his attention. And I assure you he would never permit *that*. So," she went on witheringly, "I am afraid you will have to look elsewhere in your little detective games."

Just as Royce had said: *For me to spend this much time and energy, even to strike out at her, would constitute nothing less than an effusive gesture of affection.* How well the two of them understood each other.

To his surprise, her contempt seemed to have vanished. When she spoke again, it was in the husky, hushed tone she took on when the hunger for intimacy came upon her. "You have learned some very private things about me, Paulie. My weakness, my vulnerability. Do you know, you are the only living person who knows these things about me? And, I am astonished to admit, I find I don't mind."

"Look—"

"Tell me something private in return, Paulie. You have changed your medication, haven't you? I would like to know how you are finding it—sailing forth into the unknown waters of your own mind. So much promise there, yes, Paulie? And so many perils."

"I've made a habit of not discussing my—"

"Then break your habits! What are you afraid of?"

He was relieved when Lia came into the kitchen, dressed in clean blue jeans, her hair brushed and tied back. She gestured with her thumb: *time to go.*

"I've got to go now. It'll have to wait until you come out, Vivien."

"I'll look forward to it, then," she said. Her voice was full of insinuation, as if they'd agreed to a lot more than Paul intended.

57

"Oh, before I forget," Dempsey said. "I got this in the mail for you." He handed Paul a manila envelope, a question in his eyes. The envelope was from Roosevelt Medical Research Institute.

"Thanks. Just doing some neurological research. You know." Paul tapped the side of his head, and Dempsey nodded understandingly. It wasn't entirely a lie, Paul told himself.

With only five days before Vivien's arrival, Paul had only grudgingly taken time away from Highwood to have dinner with the Corrigans, and had explained he'd have to cut it short, get back to another late night of work—after talking with Vivien, he was more anxious than ever to finish the house on time, get the hell away. They'd eaten another of Elaine's excellent meals, and the Corrigans had insisted the three of them stay at the house when Lia returned with Mark. Paul had gratefully accepted the invitation.

Dempsey launched into one of his fascinating narratives about the history of the area, but Paul couldn't make himself focus on it. The letter from Stropes burned in his hand, and it occurred to him that he'd have no chance to read it later, at the carriage house, without Lia observing him. Willing the preoccupation from his face, he tucked the envelope casually under his arm and realized that for the first time in his life he was concealing things. Not a comfortable feeling, not a wise idea for a Touretter. *You bottle up, you blow up*, was the way Damon put it. But this couldn't wait, and he wasn't sure it was something he wanted Lia to know about. Not just yet.

After a few minutes, he excused himself, went to the cedar-paneled bathroom, locked the door, and ripped open the envelope.

Dear Mr. Skoglund:

I received with interest your message concerning hyperkinesis and hyperdynamism. I am sorry I haven't had the time to return your call, but my free time during daylight hours has been very limited. Rather than disturb you with a late-night call, I am taking a few moments after hours to address your inquiry by mail.

By way of a disclaimer, I must tell you that my own field is the regulatory mechanisms of human autonomic functions, which bears only peripherally on HK/HD phenomena, and that while my interest is enthusiastic, I have not been able to devote the research time the subject deserves. Because reports of extraordinary physical speed or strength tend to have a hyperbolic quality, and because the state cannot be reproduced in laboratory situations, the topic is often regarded with skepticism in the medical/scientific community. The phenomenon has therefore not attracted the serious attention it warrants.

To my knowledge the only two exceptions to the above are experiments in deliberately induced HK/HD carried out by German military intelligence during WWII, and the joint Army Intelligence–CIA project during the Vietnam War, both intended to produce men who could fight with "superhuman" strength, speed, and ferocity. The latter effort has received some attention in the press, but the details are shrouded in secrecy. We know little about the German effort beyond the fact that one by-product of their research was the synthesis of a compound related to methedrine, which the Reich gave to soldiers in a few theaters of war, with mixed results.

However, despite secrecy and skepticism, there is abundant evidence that under certain circumstances humans can move at speeds and with muscular force vastly greater than the norm.

HK is characterized by hyperactivity and extreme rapidity of motion. That even the average person is capable of motion much faster than we consciously use is demonstrated by a common reflexive response to everyday mishaps. Perhaps you have had the experience of tipping a glass off the dinner table and catching it before it hit the floor. Commonplace, but bear in mind the glass is falling at 32 feet per second—from a 30-inch-high tabletop, therefore, leaving you about 1/13th of a second to notice the glass, calculate its arc, and move hand and arm in response.

This example of our latent reflexive potentials provides proof that the average human being has neuromuscular capabilities far beyond the needs of daily usage. It also illustrates the difficulty of subjecting these latent capacities to clinical testing. Our normal reflexive responses, not to mention the "altered states" of HK/HD, seem resistant to conscious activation. The inability of researchers to duplicate HK/HD activity in laboratory settings has understandably contributed to the medical establishment's skepticism.

Nevertheless, there is a large body of evidence that substantiates the existence of the phenomenon. The most well-known, probably, is the case of William Anderby, which was written up in Life *magazine in 1946. Anderby was serving on a destroyer attached to a convoy in the North Atlantic during World War II. The Germans ran a bomb and torpedo attack against them, during which Seaman Anderby witnessed the destruction of several nearby ships. When a large bomb fell onto the forward deck of his ship and failed to explode, Anderby picked it up, carried it rapidly to the railing and threw it overboard.*

Anderby was 5'7" tall and weighed 152 pounds, according to his enlistment records. The bomb was a naval armor-piercing bomb, weighing 610 pounds. If we additionally take into account that he had to wrest it free from the crease it had made in the deck armor, and that (as witnesses swore before the admiralty board) he carried it "effortlessly," "ran" to the railing, and "flung" it overboard, we must acknowledge a demonstration of muscular strength far beyond that of a normal man— at least that of a normal man in a normal state.

This episode illustrates a typical feature of the HK/HD phenomenon: that HK/HD behavior is brought on by a specific "trigger"—a psychological catalyst. Seaman Anderby reacted as he did out of fear for his own life and concern for the lives of his shipmates. Precisely what the range of triggering emotions is, I can't say, but extreme emotional stress, often of imminent mortal danger or protective concern for loved ones, is the common denominator in most cases.

Displays of hyperkinesis and hyperdynamism seem to fall into two general categories. The most common is what I call reflexive *HK or HD—that is, a momentary single act of supranormal strength, speed, or agility, brought on by a reflexive response to mortal peril or extreme emotional shock. Catching the falling dinner glass, though it hardly qualifies as HK, could be viewed as a very minor demonstration, brought on by a tiny "spike" of subconscious urgency.*

Rarer, and more interesting, are the prolonged or sustained displays, which I refer to as hysterical *HK or HD. It is during these incidents that the most astonishing feats are reported. HHK/HHD is usually induced by anger, mortal peril, protective concern, etc., but there are also reports of the trigger being emotions of a more long-term and seemingly less urgent sort. One case I have researched appears to have as its stimulus a long-held, pathologically intense sibling jealousy.*

I owe much to the research done by Dr. Frederick Simpson Wilkes, an English physician born in 1881. Before his death in 1949, Wilkes recorded scores of incidents of "superdynamism," and did clinical work with about a dozen people who had displayed various degrees of HK/HD and HHK/HHD. His science is somewhat dated, but his meticulous description of the incidents and his investigation into the family histories of HK/HD "carriers" are very helpful. (He demonstrated convincingly that there is an inherited trait, a propensity or tendency, in people who display HK/HD, and that there are specific indications in childhood for HK/HD–prone individuals.)

He was fortunate enough to have interviewed several individuals shortly after reported hyperdynamic activity, and so could assess their physical and psychological conditions. His reports leave the reader with unforgettable images. One elderly gentleman ran through the wall of his house to lift away a farm tractor which had tipped over onto his adult son, who had been driving it. In a grief-stricken rage, the old farmer also dismantled the tractor with his hands, flinging away its wheels and engine, when he found his son dead beneath it.

According to Dr. Wilkes, HK/HD activity appears to be an inherited tendency, most common (if still very rare) in people of Scandinavian/ Germanic descent. In his book, A Study of Superdynamism, *he cites the well-documented tradition of the* berserkers *of Viking lore, who entered a state of irresistible killing frenzy during battle. The berserkers were used as elite bodyguards for Norse chieftains, or point men for attacks; to cast fear into their enemies, they wore the furs and skulls of bears (thus the appellation "bear-shirts") and wolves.*

Norse sagas refer to the berserkers' "fire-rimmed eyes" and the "rage-stink" of their bodies, statements that give us excellent clues to their metabolic states—the bloodshot eyes suggesting radical increase in blood circulation, their odor suggesting the overload of arousal hormones in their bodies. They wielded weapons the average man couldn't even carry, many favoring battle-axes with which they would cleave armored enemy warriors in two halves, top to bottom. Or they dismembered them with their bare hands. Berserkers were usually isolated from their own comrades-in-arms because when the state was upon them they apparently didn't distinguish between allies or enemies.

My own research is more technical than Wilkes's. While I do catalog new incidents as they are reported to me, and conduct limited investigation into these reports, my foremost effort has been to look into the physiological processes that would permit such extraordinary feats. Such expenditures of energy require appropriate biochemical and neuro-muscular activities, and these I can project fairly well with computer models.

Without getting too technical here, I believe that the triggering sequence involves a form of epilepsy. Triggered by emotional stress, the seizure sends an extraordinarily powerful signal to the HPA (hypothal-amic-pituitary-adrenal) axis. A cascade of neurochemical processes ensues, producing vastly altered activity levels. In HHK/HHD-prone individuals, I believe, these responses are greatly exaggerated by a rare combination of unusual electrical activity in the brain—the initial seizure—and neuro-anatomical abnormalities that greatly amplify the response. The HHK/HHD is sustained for as long as the combination of chemical and neurological conditions lasts, and its degree depends upon a wide range of variables.

My guess is that this theory will eventually find general acceptance. However, the simple structural limitations of human anatomy are important to consider. Flesh is simply not as strong as wood or metal. I remain skeptical of many hyperbolic reports, because to believe them would be to deny the known material limits of our organism, requiring a "supernatural" explanation.

I hope the above has been of some assistance, and I thank you for indulging my own infatuation with this esoteric topic. Your letter gave me no specifics regarding the reasons for your interest; however, if you know of an incident of HK/HD, I would be grateful for information concerning your experience, for my files.

> Sincerely,
> Michael Stropes, M.D., Ph.D.

Paul shifted his position on the closed toilet seat in the Corrigans' bathroom, and stood achingly, searching for the energy he'd need to put in another long night of work.

"Submit to the dahk side of The Fawce," he intoned. Other than his obvious enthusiasm for his hobby, Stropes didn't sound at all like a crackpot. *No such luck.* It would be imperative to meet with him.

58

Tuesday morning, Mo awoke a little hungover. He'd come home Monday night feeling alternately high on Lia, Lia, Lia, and crazy fucked-up about Heather Mason. He'd found that he couldn't stand his apartment and went out to Paradise, a down-at-heels bar around the corner, where he drank three double screwdrivers before he thought to put on the brakes. He stumbled home, lay down on the bed in his clothes, woke up with a headache.

Getting drunk wasn't a habit you wanted to cultivate, but it hadn't been a total loss. Somewhere in there, he'd more or less banished the double guilts that had come over him. It was nuts to think he was responsible for Heather's suicide, even if her mother implied that Mo's questioning of her had dredged up her grief over her brother's death. It just wasn't so. She'd been a deeply troubled kid. If anything had driven her to her death, it was the memory of what she'd seen that night in August. Which Mo was trying to do something about.

And as far as Paul was concerned, Paul didn't own Lia. Lia could and certainly would make up her own mind about things. You had to believe that matters of the heart worked out the way they were supposed to, that if Paul and Lia didn't fully satisfy each other, then in the long run Paul would be better off with someone else. Anyway, what were you supposed to do if you were Mo Ford, thirty-four and single and lonesome as hell? If you wanted to be with someone exceptional like Lia, of course she'd have previous involvements of one kind or another. Of course somebody would have to get left out. Paul was a great guy. He'd find someone else in no time.

It seemed a little thin, but he was determined not to probe his conscience too deeply.

He took a long shower to clear his head and get rid of the boozy sweat on his skin and the cigarette stink left in his hair from the bar. When he came out, still dripping, he saw the red light blinking on the answering machine. It was a message from Lia: She had some things she wanted to talk with him about, very important, she didn't feel good leaving details on the machine, but could he call or stop in? "Actually, it'd be great if you stopped up here—we're always happy to see you." She sounded like she had a lot more to say. He called Highwood immediately, but no one picked up the phone.

He dressed, called the barracks for his messages, then spent a few hours making calls from his own phone. By one o'clock, no breakfast yet and no lunch, his stomach was a high school chemistry experiment gone awry. He walked downtown to grab some lunch in a place with some fellow human beings in it.

The streets were so busy Mo wondered if some event were taking place, the president in town or something, then realized it was just Christmas shopping. His nose had been to the grindstone so hard he hadn't looked up to remember the date: December 13th. He was musing cynically on rampant commercialism when Alice appeared next to him and took his arm.

"Mr. Morgan Ford! I thought that was you!" Alice had a pair of shiny shopping bags over one arm, a red fake-leather purse the size of a gym bag. In the sunshine, her piled-up black hair and makeup looked theatrically cheap. She wore a short red corduroy coat that showed off her killer legs in black tights and small, high-heeled boots. Alice, Mo thought, knew enough to underscore her strong features. Right now her big face was beaming with pleasure at running into him.

"Hi, Alice," Mo said. "Beautiful day, huh? Looks like you've been shopping. Beating the rush?"

"You don't call this a rush?" She fell into step beside him, still holding his arm. "Let me tell you."

"Haven't seen you at the club recently."

"I been there—it's you who's been someplace else."

"Ahhh," Mo growled. "Work's been eating me up. No time."

"Must be something exciting, Mr. Detective Ford. Sure it's work, not a lady friend?"

Mo laughed. "Just work, I assure you," he said. Then he regretted saying it: She might hear it as some kind of an invitation.

She looked pleased. "Listen, you had lunch yet? I'm starving. About to drop onto the street and embarrass us both. Let's stop in and get a sandwich. You wanna take one of these for me?"

Mo accepted a gigantic string-handled shopping bag, let her steer him into a glass-fronted cafe with lots of green plants in the window. They stood for a moment behind a couple of other customers waiting for tables.

Alice had gotten onto telling him about her mother, who lived in New Jersey with her third husband, who made good money but who needed bypass surgery. Mo was beginning to tune it out and was feeling his hangover return with a faint throbbing in his temples, when the woman in front of them turned around.

It was Lia. Mo's gut lurched.

"Mo!" she said. Her whole face brightened. "God, amazing! I was just in town to get some supplies for up on the hill and thought I'd treat myself to some lunch." Lia's eyes flicked almost imperceptibly, taking in Alice's arm, still through Mo's elbow, the shopping bags they both carried. "Hi," she said to Alice, "I'm Lia." She started to offer a handshake but then laughed at herself. "Guess you've got your hands full."

"Lia, Alice, Alice, Lia," Mo mumbled.

"Hi," Alice said.

A waiter appeared. "Table for three?" he asked.

"Are you up for company?" Lia asked. "Or, I don't at all mean to intrude, if—"

"Three," Mo told the waiter. Alice disengaged her arm.

They sat at a table beneath a fountain of fern hung from the ceiling. Mo made a point of taking the chair farthest from the seat Alice had taken, his back to the window. Lunch with Lia, alone, would be heaven. Looking at the two women, he couldn't believe the contrast: Lia with her heart-shaped face, her fine cheekbones, her mobile lips and brows, her clarity and confidence. Her hair blown crazily and perfectly around her face. Alice with her unfortunate, powdered, plain face, hair piled and sprayed. The worst of it was that Alice was sharp enough to know when she was outclassed. She looked miserable.

"What brings you two downtown?" Lia asked.

"Shopping, lunch, you know," Alice said.

"You got my message?" Lia asked Mo. "There are some . . . developments we've got to talk about."

"Great," he said. He couldn't take his eyes off her. The light from the window fell on her so that she seemed to glow, more animate and clear than her surroundings.

"I'm sorry, Alice. Maybe I shouldn't assume Mo has told you about this, uh, situation at Highwood," Lia said.

"Yes, he's very close-mouthed about his work," Alice said guardedly. "Confidentiality and all."

"Lia is a real whiz as an investigator herself," Mo found himself saying. "Makes me feel like an idiot. Put a few like her in the BCI, we'd clean up the whole state in no time."

Lia put her hand on Mo's arm, just an offhand, momentary touch. "I wish it were true," she said to Alice, smiling, "but I don't mind the compliment." Mo couldn't believe himself. He had jerked, literally his whole body had moved, when she touched him. He was going nuts.

His reaction hadn't escaped Alice. She sipped from her water glass, brown eyes watching Mo, assessing him, then quickly scanning Lia one more time. Then she set down her glass and gave a small nod, to herself, as if she'd decided something.

"Actually," Alice said, "you know what? I just remembered I've got an appointment in"—she checked her watch—"oh my God, in five minutes." She gathered her bags and purse, stood up. "It's been just lovely. Enjoyed meeting you, have a great lunch."

She walked out. They watched her pass the window, heading quickly back the way they'd come.

"I assume Alice wasn't keen on company for lunch," Lia said.

"Apparently not."

"I'm sorry, I really didn't mean to—"

"Alice is my neighbor. She's not my wife and she's not my girlfriend."

"You don't have to explain anything, Mo," Lia said, still wearing a slight frown of concern for Alice. "Whatever she is or isn't, she obviously has some hopes in your direction."

"Yeah, she's made that pretty clear."

"I commend her good taste. Well. I assume you'll sort it out with her, won't you?" Lia said. Then her frown went away, and she smiled slightly, conspiratorially. "It's awful of me, she seems like a sweet person, but my first thought was, 'Oh no, this can't be, she's not right for Mo at all.' Isn't that horrible?"

"Only a little horrible. I agree."

The waiter returned: "Just two after all?"

"Just two after all," Mo affirmed. It felt good to say. They ordered sandwiches.

"And the fact is," Lia said, "I don't mind the idea of lunch with you. I mean without someone else here."

"I was thinking the same thing." Her words dazed him. *Here's a million bucks, Mo, you just won the lottery.* He felt himself at the top of something, holding just back of the edge, nearing a sweet fall, something he hadn't felt since the night Dara and he first admitted their love and went to bed together. The wonderful letting go, the release of the secret of longing. Lia was coming toward him, they were coming toward each other. His every instinct was screaming, *go, go, go to her.*

"What was it you wanted to discuss with me?"

She looked thoughtful, as if wondering where to start. "Several things. First, I don't think Paul remembered to tell you that his aunt is returning here soon—this Saturday. It seems like your investigation at Highwood is getting going, but it'll be hard to keep up our meetings and so on once she's here. I thought you should know. On the bright side, maybe you can approach her about a consent search again, in person."

"Thanks—I'm glad you told me."

"Another thing is, I'll be heading back to Vermont for a few days—I'm leaving tomorrow and I'll be back Saturday with Paul's son. It's bad timing in terms of the house getting done and Vivien's arrival, but Mark's coming down can't wait and I have end-of-semester obligations at Dartmouth I can't get out of. I thought that before I left, maybe you and I should talk."

"Okay."

She grabbed his forearm across the table, squeezed it hard, then looked away, having difficulty saying what she intended. "It has to do with Paul, actually."

His heart was pounding. There was a time to think and hold back, and there was a time when you mustn't think, when you had to let go. You couldn't think *this* dance through. You let go, found the moves as you went. Your brain was too stupid. You let other parts of you take over.

"Yes. I want to know about you and Paul," Mo said.

"What about us?"

"I mean where do you stand. Married? What's happening? What does *he* think is happening?"

"Not married. Paul and I live together in Vermont."

"So where does that leave you and me, Lia?"

She rocked back in her seat, green eyes drilling him. Then she put a hand to her chin, looked out the window, thinking for a moment before she turned back to him. "You're an amazing man, do you know that, Mo? I knew from the moment I first saw you. Sexy as hell. Incredibly observant. Smart. And you and I have a lot in common. We think so much alike it sometimes scares me."

"Me too. I look at you and I say, God, she, she *fits,* she's perfect. So help me, I've never felt like this. Lia, what's going to happen here?"

She continued as if he hadn't said anything. "You like danger, and I do too. You make decisions like I do. And you make me laugh, and I think I make you laugh too."

"Yeah. Yes."

Lia took his hand, working her thumb across the back of it, still holding his eyes. "And you need to be absolutely clear that I am in love with Paul Skoglund. He's a lot of things you and I are not, and that's one thing I love about him. That's why I keep learning things from him, why I need to be with him. I like you immensely, Paul does too, I could love you like my brother. You're so . . . so competent, so in charge of yourself, I'd trust you with my life. I mean that. But Paul—I trust him with my *whole* life. Do you see the difference? I'm with him for the duration. I'm not available, Mo. I am terribly, terribly sorry if anything I've done or said gave you the idea it could be otherwise."

Mo sat. Neither of them said anything for a full minute.

"I meant that about sexy," Lia said.

"Don't."

"Okay." She grinned ruefully.

The waiter returned with their sandwiches, and they each took a bite in silence. Mo breathed in and out, chewing but not tasting the food. He kept his eyes on his plate: Lia was too beautiful to look at. She'd handled it with a lot of class, he'd give her that. Of course she had.

So much for trusting your instincts. How many times do you have to get the same lesson? *Don't shoot yet, asshole.* Don't shoot your mouth off, dick-brain. Show a little restraint, hotshot.

He sighed. "Okay," he said. "I'm clear. I'm clear on that."

"I'm sorry, Mo."

Mo reached into his pocket, feeling suddenly weary. Chronic fatigue syndrome again, or something. He got his notebook out, flipped it open, clicked his pen. "So tell me what's on your mind."

59

There are parts of a woman's body, Paul thought, that are perfection. Lia stood in the middle of the room, shaking out her hair, brushing it. After she'd come back from her supply run to Mt. Kisco, she hadn't said much all afternoon and evening. Something was on her mind. Now, with the gas heater in the carriage house front room turned on, she was wearing only her blue jeans, her shirt off, her feet bare. Paul lay with his arms behind his head, watching her.

Draw a line from the bottom of a woman's jean pocket in back, around the outside of her thigh to the double seamed crotch: that circle, if there's the right strength and fullness and delicacy, it's inexpressible. No poets have ever gotten it. That circle of thigh didn't just awaken desire, although that was certainly there, so much as a nameless feeling of tenderness. Maybe *reverence* was the better word for it. Something you couldn't really tell anyone about.

That line on Lia was perfect.

And then there was the line of the breast, the slope from her collarbone, forward and outward, trim and yet somehow generous, beckoning, offering. Culminating in her two different nipples and then tucking back in the sweet, soft, shadowed undercurve. Suggesting nurture and compassion as much as erotic possibility. The softest and warmest place in a hard, cold world. Worshipful grace.

Too bad the current climate of gender relations discouraged talking or even thinking about that beauty, that grace, the real feelings it awakened. You couldn't even explain to one woman how beautiful she was: These feelings didn't fit in short phrases, even making love wasn't enough. The only way was to let her know it over a long period of time, let a thousand gestures and words add up until she knew. Over many years. Maybe if you were lucky she'd feel some female equivalent toward you.

Lia finished her hair and sat down on the bed next to him. Her breasts swung slightly. "I ran into Mo in Mt. Kisco today," she said. "We had lunch together."

"Great. How was he?" Something was coming. Lia wasn't smiling.

"Pretty good. We talked about things."

She was stalling. Paul gave her time.

"Among . . . other things . . . we talked about you," she said quietly. "I told him I was worried about you. That you're exhausted and you're getting into this thing at Highwood in ways I'm not sure are good for you. That I feel there are a lot of things you're not talking to me about. That some of the papers we've been finding indicate some history of violent pathology in the past of this place, which you have studiously avoided talking about with me. Mainly that you've been different, and I'm not sure I feel good leaving you here alone for the next three days."

"Oh, for God's sake! What, you wanted Mo to take care of me? I can look out for myself. Christ!"

"You're getting secretive and morbid and paranoid, Paul."

"I thought our hero Mo had it all figured out, anyway—Royce, Rizal, Vivien's continuous occupancy, a neat package."

"But you don't believe it. What do you believe?"

He looked at her and away. "I've got a few things I need to work through. Give me a couple more days."

She nodded and was quiet for a time. "I guess there's something else you should know," she said at last. "Concerning Mo."

So here it was. They'd made more progress, faster, than he'd have imagined. The sharp, sensitive-tough detective, and brilliant, beautiful Lia, Lia of the perfect line of thigh. He felt impaled on a spear of pain.

"He basically told me he was in love with me."

"I know. I've been watching him. Can't blame him. I am too."

Lia knelt on the bed, facing him, still tense. "I told him I liked him a lot, that you did too. Then I told him I wasn't available."

Paul couldn't look at her. "Why not? He's good-looking, employed, doesn't have Tourette's syndrome. He's got a nice, high-risk job—"

"He isn't Paul Skoglund."

"My point exactly."

"Paul, you look at me, right now. Stop this! I told him I am in love with you, and that I valued our relationship beyond anything I—"

"So? All the better. I'd think you'd like the element of risk. You value it, you risk it, you get off on the tension there, right?"

Lia jumped forward, straddling him, pinning his arms down with incredible strength. She blazed at him: "You cut that out! Don't you fucking dare, Paul! I'm telling you something." She was shouting, on the verge of crying. "That wouldn't be risky, that'd be just stupid. I'm not stupid, Paul!" Then she did let the tears come, lowering himself against him, wrapping around him.

She had released his arms, and he stroked her sobbing back, loving the feel of her.

"Sunday? At Break Neck? The only reason I was right about why you wouldn't jump off, why you'd think it through better, was that *you* showed *me* about those feelings in the first place—the way you feel about Mark. I don't have a kid of my own to love that much. When I was caught on that rock in the cave, and afterward, when we made love, I realized, these risks, it's not just *me* I'm risking. If all I cared about was me, it wouldn't matter so much if something happened, if I got killed, but it's—there's *you* too. And I, I wouldn't—you're the only person I've ever loved that much."

There didn't seem to be any adequate response, so he didn't answer. He tried hard to believe it, to believe he was enough for her, to believe he could draw all of her, even her dark places, to him. But despite the sincerity and elegance of what she said, the worm still squirmed in his soul: He couldn't quite open himself and accept her love. He'd been Plodding Paul, Predictable Paul, Play It Safe Paul too long. Pathetic.

As if she saw it in him, Lia pressed herself against him so forcefully he could hardly breathe, as if she wanted to rub away their skin and merge their flesh and bones.

60

Lia's leaving on Wednesday morning left a hole in Paul, as if his heart had been wrenched from his chest. *It's not forever, she'll be back Saturday,* he kept reminding himself. *Only three days, she'll bring back Mark, it'll be wonderful to see them both. The people you love most, under the same roof again, at last.* He turned to look at the lodge. *But not under this roof, thanks.* The three of them would stay at Dempsey and Elaine's for the final few days as he finished the job. Vivien would come, they'd work out some closure, and good-bye. The sooner he was done with this place, the better.

With the library papers done at last, the books stacked, the floor swept, he went to Vivien's bedroom and began digging through the rubble, scanning papers, setting some aside. It took less than an hour for him to realize that this was the gold mine. *She'd kept these papers close to her. Of course: here in her always-locked room.* By noon he took what he'd culled to the smoking room to go over in detail.

These papers were in worse shape than the papers in the library, as if like everything else in her bedroom a particularly intense frenzy or rage had been directed at them. Many were ripped, wrinkled, stained. Rain had been blowing in the blasted windows and ruining everything for months. No document was complete. But what he found was enough.

Paul set the stack of papers on the game table, then went to the library and returned with several volumes they'd found when sorting the books, a medical dictionary, a *Physician's Desk Reference*, a beat-up *DSM IV*. He should have seen it before: that Vivien possessed several editions of the *Diagnostic and Statistical Manual* was in itself suggestive. In the *Manual*, the American Psychiatric Association listed and described in detail 187 psychological disorders. *So many ways to go crazy,* Paul thought. *So much that can go wrong.*

He was familiar with the *DSM*, having referred to it many times in his quest for anything that would help him solve Mark's problems. Now he needed it to help decipher some of the tattered papers he'd found in Vivien's bedroom. Most of these were disordered pages of psychiatric diagnoses, using a lot of technical medical and psychological terms. Letters from doctors, dealing with psychological diagnoses. Bills for services and payment receipts.

Just the range of diagnostic records, what remained of them, was full of implications. Paul recognized several tests: the Reiss Screen for Maladaptive Behavior, the Psychopathology Inventory for Mentally Retarded Adults, the Apperceptive Personality Test. Not evaluatory procedures administered to just anybody.

Poor Vivien. Everyone had a different answer, another name for it, didn't they? And none of them helped at all.

Turning back to the *DSM IV*, he looked up the diagnostic requirements for Intermittent Explosive Disorder. Criteria for IED included multiple episodes of uncontrolled aggressive impulses "resulting in serious assaultive acts or destruction of property," "behavior that is grossly out of proportion to any provocation or precipitating psychosocial stressor." The listing went on to note that the "spells" or "attacks" of explosive behavior were "preceded by a sense of tension or arousal" and were "followed immediately by a sense of relief."

Close but no cigar. Another letter spoke of Psychotic Trigger Reaction. PTR was a lot like IED, with the twist that while a specific stimulus may trigger the violence, the violence may be directed toward inoffensive persons "at which time the aggressor is apparently reliving past experiences."

Almost, Paul thought. Any one of these could describe part of the condition, but none grasped the whole picture.

Ultimately, it was one of the bills that gave him what he needed. For a long time, he stared at the two photos of the strange child, which he'd set out on the table. Then he put down the papers and went into the kitchen to call Morgan Ford. He and Mo had some unfinished business anyway.

"His name was Erik Hoffmann III," Paul told Mo. "He was my aunt's first child, Royce's older brother. I suspect he was born in the Philippines when they lived there, probably around 1949. Maybe good medical care wasn't readily available in the islands then, maybe there were problems with the delivery. I say this because the type of neurological problems he suffered from often result from oxygen deprivation or other birth trauma."

"Exactly how would you describe his, uh, condition? His problems?" The detective was looking over the array of tattered papers Paul had assembled. With Lia gone, the issue of her hanging between them, Mo seemed tense, uncomfortable, stiff. Paul thought of bringing it out into the open, getting it out of the way, then decided that it was Mo's job to bring it up. He could sweat a little until he did.

"I can only piece it together from fragments," Paul answered. "Sounds like a combination of conditions. He was able to do basic things for himself, like go to the bathroom, wash himself, and eat, had basic verbal skills, but was profoundly asocial, was never expected to live on his own. Most important, he had periodic outbursts of explosive violence. That he was extremely, unmanageably violent I can deduce from the level of supervision they assigned him, the occasional use of isolation and restraints—they obviously considered him a risk for his caretakers or other patients. Then there are the drugs they gave him: metoprolol, for example. Basically blocks the body's ability to use adrenaline. Physically and mentally, you can't get cranked up with that stuff in your veins."

Mo looked up. "How come you know so much about this stuff?"

"My own son has had some . . . problems," Paul said, turning away. "I've got a neurological problem myself—Tourette's syndrome. Done a lot of reading."

"Tourette's—I've heard of that." The focus in Mo's eyes sharpened with unabashed interest. "Fascinating. I've never met . . . one of you before."

" 'We' are a pretty diverse bunch," Paul said stiffly. "I can't claim to be representative."

Mo cracked a grin. "Okay. No stereotyping." He picked up some other papers, the bills from several long-term psychiatric care facilities, which Paul had arranged in chronological order. "These—obviously he was institutionalized. It looks like they moved him several times. Any idea why?"

"There could be a lot of reasons, but I have a theory, sure."

"Which is?"

"Personally, I don't think he was safe around his brother, Royce. I think we'll find that the Hoffmann Trust consisted of Erik III and Royce. Maybe their father was old-fashioned, traditional—he couldn't stand to disinherit his oldest son, even if he was mentally incompetent. If Erik had periods of comparative normality, his father may have held out hope he'd recover." *Like the rest of us.* "So Hoffmann set up the trust in both of their names. It would make sense anyway, a way to provide for Erik III's medical care."

"Which must have added up. What—forty, fifty thou a year? Over twenty, thirty years—" Mo scratched his head, calculating. "Erik III was spending a lot of trust money. And as long as he was alive, he stood between Royce and a lot more. Is that what you're saying?"

"If I'm right that Erik III was the other beneficiary of the trust, yes," Paul said. "One other consideration. If Erik was legally mentally incompetent, my aunt as custodial parent would probably retain his power of attorney. And that would give her at least some influence over the trust."

"Which, if I'm understanding the, uh, family dynamics, your cousin probably wasn't thrilled about." Mo chuckled at his own understatement.

"I tried to call my aunt today, to ask her about Erik III, but she didn't pick up the phone. I'm pissed because she's keeping things from me. Whenever I've confronted her on this stuff, she feeds me just enough to appear to be answering my questions, but never gives me the whole picture. I'd like to know why. I'll try her again later, but I'm not confident she'll tell me anything."

"So what's next? Where do you want to take it?"

"I want to know where Erik is. Whether she feels like telling me or not."

"I can see," Mo said, "how that would be nice to know."

"While we're at it, we should also figure out why the trust reverted to Royce alone."

"An excellent point, Inspector," Mo said.

"I mean," Paul went on, "what are the options? A timetable built into the trust from the beginning. Or a successful legal challenge by Royce, based on something like technical failings in Hoffmann's will or the way the trust was set up, or maybe on Erik III's mental competence. Or Erik died. Can you think of any others?"

They both considered it briefly. Outside, the bushes and trees above the garden shivered in the wind, full of nervous energy. As if the silence of the house reminded them both of Lia's absence, the tension grew between them. Mo fidgeted, picking up and discarding the handful of interesting trinkets Paul had found in the big room and left on the table along with the photographs. A ball of amber with a small dragonfly trapped inside, a queer earring consisting of a silver skull backed by a small red-and-green feather, a pewter paperweight in the form of a miniature steam locomotive. The detective's fingers returned several times to the earring.

"A weird piece, isn't it? My aunt has strange tastes," Paul said, feeling awkward.

Mo dropped it distractedly back onto the table, shrugged. They were both stalling, Paul realized.

For a moment, Paul felt the old tics building, the itching inside. To cover the bell-ringing gesture, he stretched and stood up. "You want some coffee?" Paul asked.

"Coffee'd be good."

Paul turned to the table and poured coffee into Styrofoam cups. "Black okay? We've got powdered white stuff if you want it."

"Black's fine."

"I've been drinking a lot of this shit the last few days. I don't know if I told you, my aunt's supposed to come out this weekend. I'd like to be further along. I'm trying to catch up—a lot of late nights."

"Yeah, Lia mentioned she was coming back." The detective's eyebrows jumped involuntarily as he realized he'd backed into the issue. "She, uh, told you we had lunch the other day?"

"Yes, she did."

Mo nodded. "I figured she would."

Paul didn't answer.

"I've been working too hard," Mo said. "One of the kids I've been talking to about this whole thing killed herself, it kind of bent me out of shape. So I got drunk the night before, I was a little off when I ran into Lia. I guess you could say I, uh, came on to her. I don't mean anything physical, but—she told you this?"

Paul nodded.

Mo looked at his hands. Then he seemed to get over his need to apologize. "The hell with excuses. I fell for her like a ton of bricks. She's an exceptional person. You are a very, very fortunate son of a bitch."

"You're divorced, aren't you?" Paul said mildly. "Sometime within the last year or so?"

"I tell you that earlier?"

"Let's just say I recognize the state of mind. From first-hand experience." Mo had handled it well, humbling himself only so far and no further, paying some dues but not more. You had to like him. "Mo, if I met Lia now, I'd go for her like crazy, I'd try for her, no matter who she was with. I don't blame you."

He sat back down, facing Mo. They drank coffee in silence.

"Anyway," Mo said, calmer.

"So where do we go from here? I'd like to figure things out up here, but I can't go running any outside research. I don't have the time, I'm scrambling to get this job done, with my aunt coming. I want to finish my job, get the rest of my pay, and get the *fuck* out of here. Can you look into Erik III for me?"

"It's on my agenda. I'll start with the last place we know he was—this Westford Center in Schenectady." Mo slapped the wrinkled papers.

"This is Michael Stropes." The voice was deep, cultured. Not a crackpot's voice.

"Dr. Stropes, this is Paul Skoglund. I wrote to you recently about hyperdynamism."

"Oh, yes, Mr. Skoglund. Did you get my letter?"

"Yes, I did. I wanted to thank you for taking the time, and also to ask if there was any chance you and I could meet. Preferably sometime soon. I'll gladly accommodate your schedule if you can spare me the time."

Stropes was quiet for a moment, and Paul wondered if the doctor had noticed the urgency in his request. "As a matter of fact, I do have an unexpected window coming up—Thursday afternoon has suddenly opened up for me. A cancellation. Not that there hasn't been a rush to fill the vacuum, but I'll gladly set aside some time to see you, if you can make it tomorrow."

They settled on one o'clock, at Stropes's office in Manhattan.

After talking to Stropes, Paul tried Vivien in San Francisco, and again she didn't answer. He hung up, feeling speedy, impatient, full of energy, full of pressure. Through the kitchen windows, he could see that the weather had darkened and seemed to be mirroring his internal state: The trees and undergrowth jerked as if something were scurrying among them. Without really thinking about it, he brought Ted's .38 upstairs when he went back to work in Vivien's bedroom. The feel of the gun tucked under his waistband wasn't too bad, he decided.

He filled bag after bag with shattered things, putting valuables or reparable items into boxes he stacked along one wall. The longer he worked, the more he saw the details, the more the damage level registered. Here was a solid rosewood drawer-front, folded in thirds as if it were cardboard. The heavy, lathed ebony legs of what had once apparently been a canopy bed, broken and *twisted*. What finally stopped him was a crushed, grapefruit-size sphere of brass, elaborately etched with Arabic designs. The sphere was hollow, with threaded holes at both ends, and from the shred of electrical wiring running through it Paul deduced that whatever its original function it had served in Vivien's house as the base of a lamp. Turning the heavy thing in his hands, he could see that the brass was over half an inch thick, yet had apparently been squeezed almost flat by some incalculable pressure. Looking closely, he saw a familiar pattern in the four evenly spaced parallel dents that marred one side. He slid his fingers into them, and found it a perfect fit. On the other side, the rounded dent of a thumb.

Yes, it had to be. A handprint.

61

Thursday morning, Mo sat at his desk, looking over his notes, reviewing his conversation with Paul Skoglund. There was something different about him, Mo decided, beyond just the bloodshot eyes of overwork. Some quality of assertiveness or alertness. He had seemed to take charge of their conversation, leading, deciding, anticipating.

All in all, their talk about Lia had gone better than Mo had any right to expect. He found himself appreciating Paul more than ever. Part of it was the way he'd smiled when they talked about it. There wasn't any pity or condescension or one-upmanship in it. Just a moment of understanding, an *ain't life a bitch* smile. A way of saying he knew all about the ache of a lonely heart. A good guy.

He wasn't sure how the sudden appearance of another Hoffmann son altered the picture. Paul thought it was important, and the history of violent pathology might connect to the business at Highwood, the dismembered and missing kids, or it might not. What did Paul think, he was living up there in the woods or something? Was Erik III, in his violent rages, Heather's Superman? It was asking too much. Mo still couldn't escape the feeling that Paul wasn't telling him everything.

The problem in tracking Erik Hoffmann III was that the last institution he'd been committed to, or at least that they'd found the papers for, no longer existed. None of the directories in the library reference section showed a Westford Psychiatric Treatment Center licensed in New York, and the Schenectady phone directory did not list a number. Westford must have gone out of business since 1983. Presumably its patients had been transferred to other institutions, and patient records would no doubt have traveled with them. What about other records of a defunct mental facility? Some would be found in various files maintained by the state—licensed care providers, registered corporations. But would they offer information on transfers of patients? And would Mo be able to get at those records, given the rules of confidentiality? There had to be a way to narrow the field of where to look.

Okay. Treatment or long-term care for somebody like Erik Hoffmann III would have to be a specialized thing. You wouldn't want him in a bed next to a sweet grandmother with advanced senility, and you'd want staff trained to deal with violent behaviors. Plus Vivien would no doubt have looked for top experts in the field.

Mo thumbed through his phone book, dialed a number in Albany. He got routed through several departments before finding the right person in the records department and identifying himself. "I'm in a rush on an important investigation," he told the secretary. "Perhaps you could do me a favor? I need information on the Westford Psychiatric Treatment Center, in Schenectady. I believe it is now out of operation but was still in business in 1983."

"We maintain annual directories from prior years, sir. Yes, I have it here."

"I need the name of the director of the facility. Also of the chief of psychiatric services."

"Okay." Mo could hear her lips moving as she scanned the page. "Oh, here. Dr. Bernard B. Andrews, executive director, Dr. Mona D. Wright-Kerson, managing director, Dr. Morris K. Gunderson, director of psychiatric services."

"Perfect," Mo said encouragingly, jotting the names. "Now do those things have indexes? Are they cross-referenced by staff?"

"Let me see. Yes, it has a staff index."

"Fabulous. Can you do me one more favor? Get a copy of the current directory. Tell me where those people are now?"

Mo waited, listening to the air on the other end of the phone. "Looking in this year's edition, sir, I don't see a listing for Dr. Bernard Andrews. I've got the other two, though."

"Okay. Where do they work now?"

He heard the flipping of pages, and she read off the names of two facilities.

Mo asked for Mona Wright-Kerson and was told in clipped tones that Dr. Wright wasn't available, but that he could leave a message. He wondered if Dr. Mona had gotten divorced since 1983. *Welcome to the club, Mona.* Dr. Gunderson was now director of the Isaac P. Cohen Center in Syracuse. Mo dialed and asked for the doctor and was shocked to find himself on the line with the man within moments.

"Dr. Gunderson, this is Morgan Ford, I'm an investigator with the New York State Police BCI. I'm sorry to take your time this afternoon, but I'm hoping you can provide me with some information."

Dr. Gunderson had a deep voice and spoke like a man accustomed to authority. "First of all, Mr. Ford, because of the nature of our facility, we need to be cautious about issues of legal authority and medical confidentiality. I can't promise I'll provide you with what you want."

"I'm trying to locate a person who may be associated with a series of violent crimes in upper Westchester County. Specifically, I am looking for an individual who was under your nominal care at Westford, around ten years ago. I want to know where he is now."

"That's correct, I was chief of psychiatric services there. But as to where a given patient is—"

"His name is Erik Hoffmann III. Mother and legal guardian is Vivien Hoffmann, from Lewisboro—"

"As to where a given patient is," Gunderson went on, "I can't and won't tell you. The laws of medical confidentiality prevent me from even acknowledging whether a person is or is not currently a patient at this or any other institution. Without proper authorization."

Gunderson's implacable tone made it clear he wasn't going to be shaken. Mo's heart sank. This could be a major runaround, weeks of paperwork or risky ploys, and probably all for nothing anyway.

"But frankly, Mr. Ford," Gunderson went on, "I don't know why you're asking me this. Your department should know all about it already."

"How so?"

"Because we sent you Erik Hoffmann's complete medical records. When he disappeared. For the missing persons investigation."

Mo rocked back in his chair. "I'm sorry. Please explain."

"The only patient I've ever lost that way. The only patient ever to be lost from this facility. And the only reason I'm telling you this much is that confidentiality was waived a long time ago. When he disappeared, his mother authorized giving your agency his records, to help trace him. I suggest, Detective, that you do your homework before wasting your own time and other people's. I'm sure the State Police still have the records. Now, if there's nothing else—"

"When was this?"

"Six years ago. I remember it well because it nearly wrecked my professional career—the patient's mother certainly did her best to see that it did." Gunderson's voice had some venom in it, barely concealed. "I'd ask what brings it up again, but, frankly, I'd just as soon not involve myself or this institution in any way. Good-bye, Detective."

62

"I appreciate your seeing me today," Paul told Dr. Stropes. "And for your letter. For someone with a very busy schedule, you've been generous with your time."

"The pleasure is mine," Stropes said affably. "You've given me an excuse to expound on my favorite subject. And my so-called 'free' time today we both owe to the fact that a video conference we'd planned for this time had to be rescheduled."

They stood at the security desk in the polished marble lobby as the guard filled out a temporary visitor's authorization for Paul.

Stropes was a tall man, not much older than Paul, with slightly stooped, narrow shoulders, intelligent eyes behind wire-rimmed glasses. He had skin the color of dark chocolate, with the shining, scrubbed look Paul invariably associated with medical people. He was dressed in dark slacks, a starched blue shirt with its sleeves rolled up, a boldly striped tie.

Paul followed him through a pair of glass doors that Stropes opened by putting an identification card into a slot, then down a hall to another pair of doors.

Stropes's office on the third floor was large and well-lit, separated from the hall by glass walls. Inside, the office was furnished in tasteful natural woods and textured fabrics. A counter ran the length of one wall, holding two oversized computer monitors, keyboards, a pair of printers, stacks of paper and manila folders. A floor-to-ceiling window let in light from a small internal courtyard.

Stropes gestured for Paul to sit in one of the chairs in front of the counter and took a seat himself. "Only so much of my work is actually done in the lab. A lot of it is done here—the data entry, statistical analysis, graphic development, projections, computer modeling. I can access files from all over the country. One of the side benefits for me, of course, is that I can use the hardware for some of my personal projects. If I may ask, what prompts your interest in the arcane field of HD/HK?"

Paul had anticipated the question but still wasn't sure how he'd answer it. "I'm in education," he improvised, "and I'm fascinated by the study of cognition. I think I stumbled across a piece you wrote when I was doing some neurological research in the MedLine database. I was thinking I'd write an article about the topic sometime."

"So you've come to the horse's mouth. Be forewarned, my work in this area is not—what's a nice euphemism?—'enthusiastically embraced' by many of my colleagues." He clapped his hands on his thighs. "But I'll tell you what I can. Let me start by asking a question: Are you pretty good with computers?"

"I'd say I have basic computer literacy," Paul said.

"Well, these stations are connected to a mainframe Cray, which will handle pretty well anything. So in my spare moments, I get to play with some very powerful applications." Stropes slapped a key on the keyboard in front of him. "You've heard of Virtual Jack?"

"Virtual, as in virtual reality, I'm familiar with. What's Virtual Jack?"

"Well, Virtual Jack is a sort of a, a cyberspace robot, a computer program of a human form in three dimensions that will operate on the screen in a way that's almost exactly anatomically correct. The original was developed by a friend of mine, Norm Badler, at the University of Pennsylvania. Jack is quite an amazing fellow." Stropes moved the mouse and clicked it several times, opening up a succession of brightly colored windows on the screen. "In the medical field, a number of variations of Virtual Jack have been developed for specific purposes. What I've done is borrowed some ideas, invented a few new twists. This is my masterpiece, so far. I call him Hyper Jack." Stropes's grin broadened, a shy smile of pride. Paul guessed that in the skeptical confines of the research center, he didn't show his masterpiece to many.

An outline of a human figure appeared in neon blue against the almost black background of the screen. Within seconds, a tracery of lines filled in the outline, until the figure appeared to Paul as a three-dimensional wire sculpture of a man, made of polygons like a geodesic dome. He stood on a checkerboard floor that tapered away into the distance.

"What's valuable about this simulacrum is that he is subject to all the same constraints of motion as a real person. Each line of the grid he's made of is mathematically quantifiable. If he lifts his leg or bends his arm, it's within the real limits of skeletal arc and muscular contraction or extension that human beings are stuck with. He has virtual weight and mass. The forces that Jack can bring to bear are all accurate models of a living human and available for me to visualize and measure."

Stropes's enthusiasm grew as he talked: "As I said, each line, and each area enclosed by the lines, is a quantifiable unit. That means I can get a true measure of what any movement means. I can see it in graphic form on the body of Jack, or I can see it in a numerical readout up here. For example, when he bends his arm, say like this, the biceps must contract to lever up the forearm. I can visualize the amount of contraction by looking at Jack's arm, shortening here, thickening here and here, or I can see on the readout that in moving the arm through a 135-degree arc the biceps shortens from ten inches to seven-point-two inches. I can do this with every muscle system in the body. The program can also calculate the speeds of movement caused by any amount of muscular contraction, and the foot-pounds of force required to produce any speed."

On the screen, Jack did knee-bends, jumping jacks, squat thrusts. Flashing figures in a column of boxes at the right of the screen analyzed the movements of each muscle group.

"This is the skeletomuscular Jack, but there are several other views of him. First is the internal Jack—his organs. Not only his organs, but the biochemical processes occurring within the organs."

As Paul watched, the hollow interior of the blue image filled with colored structures. He recognized lungs, heart and circulatory system, spinal cord and peripheral nerves, other organs. The heart pulsed regularly, the lungs expanded and contracted.

"For me, the important part is what each anatomical system does. Let me give you an example. Jack is right now an adult human male, five feet eleven, 175 pounds, he's in his mid-twenties and is fit and active. Let's look at him in two different modes of activity." Stropes touched the mouse and the screen split in two, with an identical version of Jack on each side. Now, inside the neon blue outline of his body, his heart, organs, brain, and muscles showed in varying intensities of blood red.

"I'm going to look at his blood flow patterns. On the left is Jack at rest. You can see that his heart and lungs are pulsing slowly—about seventy heartbeats and ten breaths per minute. You can also see by the intensity of the color of his organs and muscles where his blood is going. The figures over here tell the exact story: At rest, he's pumping about 5,900 milliliters of blood per minute. About 750 go to his brain, 250 to the heart, 650 to his muscles, 500 to his skin. The biggest recipient of his at-rest blood flow is his internal organs, which are getting 3,100 milliliters a minute."

Stropes tapped the mouse again, and the Jack on the right-hand screen changed. He did a quick round of calisthenics, then began to run at a good clip, arms pumping, the floor scrolling behind him as if he were on a gigantic treadmill. His heart fluttered, the lungs squeezed faster. The organs dimmed, while the large muscles just beneath the tracery of lines that marked his skin exploded with crimson.

"On the right side, now, you've got a normal human being at maximum exertion. Heart rate increases to 184 per minute, breathing increases proportionately. Blood flow has skyrocketed to more than four times resting rate—to 24,000 milliliters per minute. But what's really fascinating is *where the blood is going*. The heart muscle is receiving four times what it was at rest, 1,000 milliliters. The organs are receiving far *less* than they were at rest—only 600, about a fifth. But the muscles have gone from 650 to 20,900 milliliters."

The Jack on the right side of the screen, pulsating with motion, was almost painful to watch.

"But blood flow is only part of it. I can graphically illustrate the level of glucose or oxygen consumption at different levels of exertion. Also the levels and locations of adenosine triphosphate, creatine phosphate, glycogen—each of the major 'fuels', you might say, of muscular exertion. And then I can go a step further: I can project what Jack's body would *have to do* if it were to go hyperkinetic or hyperdynamic. To throw a 200-pound sofa across the room requires specific brain and body chemistry. I program this system to show me what that activity level would look like in a variety of ways."

Stropes had gotten himself worked up as he spoke, moving around in his chair, gesturing dramatically. Paul couldn't help catching some of his excitement. "So have you got a program of Jack in a hyper mode?" he asked.

"I do. It's not a pretty sight, if you find regular Jack a little nerve-racking, but it's instructive. Here." Stropes entered several commands, and again the screen unified so that there was only one Jack on it. "Here we go. Heart rate 260. Breathing rate 140. Blood flow twice the normal maximum at 50,000 milliliters. Internal organs receiving the barest maintenance flow, about 300, skin losing a little. Heart muscle gaining big. And muscles exploding with blood, oxygen, glycogen, ATP, getting 45,000 milliliters. I can calculate the power and speed of every muscle, every limb. The figures are staggering. But those are the figures you'd need to have the strength and speed indicated by hundreds of well-documented reports."

The Jack on the screen was a seething blur of crimson as he ran on the flowing treadmill of the computer desert. There was a desperate, tormented quality to his motion. Frenetic. *Hysterical.* The endless empty plane of Jack's universe poured away behind him as he struggled, going nowhere. It was as if he were striving to break out of the screen, out of the confines of his digital self, into a more real world. Paul had to look away.

"Somethin', ain't it?" Stropes hit another key and Hyper Jack started doing jumping jacks and squat thrusts with a hideous, fanatical intensity. "I can show you what he'd look like in other activities, lifting something heavy, throwing things—"

"No. No thanks." Paul shook his head. "I get the picture." He found his own pulse racing, his breath hard to catch. Why was Hyper Jack so disturbing? There was something about his isolation on that geometric desert under that black, empty, computer sky, the futility of his simulated exertions. Jack looked like he had terminal Rimbaud's disease, Paul thought, was flailing to get out of his bleak world. A tic built in him. He started to reach out, twist the invisible doorknob, then suppressed it, only to be surprised by a facial tic that tugged his cheek uncomfortably.

Stropes was looking at him with concern, and Paul struggled to clear his head. "Is this possible? Wouldn't his heart fail? Could the circulatory system really handle that much blood flow?"

"Those are just the questions I've had to ask. The answer is a provisional yes—under very rare, very particular circumstances. Let me show you one more Hyper Jack—that'll help me explain." Again he worked the keyboard with practiced strokes. In place of the full figure of Jack, the screen filled with a close-up of Jack's head, a hollow shape created by a three-dimensional grid of neon-blue lines. "Here's Jack's head. Now I'll fill in his brain. I gather you're fairly familiar with the anatomy of the brain?"

"I've done a bit of reading, certainly."

"Okay. So we've got the main structures: in green here the brain stem, in purple the cerebellum, in blue the cerebrum, and so on. One of my primary concerns is the HPA axis."

"The hypothalamic-pituitary-adrenal axis. Fight or flight."

"Exactly. The basic process of alarm looks like this. This red, walnut-shaped thing is the hypothalamus. When the senses tell it that there's a threat or a source of challenge or stress, a cascade of neurochemical processes begins. First, an electrical signal is sent to the hypothalamus, which squirts out CRF—corticotropin-releasing factor. This travels by a private blood supply straight to the pituitary gland, often called the master gland because it tells the other glands throughout the body what to do." On the screen, a series of tiny, brilliant white dots left the hypothalamus and traveled forward in Jack's cranium to a peanut-size gland. "The CRF kicks in the pituitary, which secretes ACTH, adrenocorticotropic hormone, into the bloodstream. Within a second, this reaches the adrenal glands, which pump out cortisol. Cortisol converts the neurotransmitter norepinephrine into the hormone epinephrine, and the body enters its fight-or-flight response.

"It's a very ancient survival mechanism that kicks the organism into overdrive. The heart pumps much harder and faster, the lungs take in more oxygen, the liver releases more sugar, the muscles become more active, the pupils dilate, the body begins to sweat."

"But everything you've described is the normal process of arousal," Paul said. He tapped the monitor, where Jack was becoming stimulated by the digital chemicals in his bloodstream. "What happens in the hyper mode?"

"Okay. We know the level of arousal is dependent upon the intensity of the threat or challenge input that's given. Obviously, if kitty knocks a flowerpot off the windowsill and startles you, your heart beats a bit faster. If three large guys come at you with lead pipes, your body really gets cranked. So if you've gone into hyper mode and you're peeling back steel plate with your bare hands, it's going to require a measurable amount of strength. I've calculated backward from what Jack's muscles and lungs and heart *have* to do to make him hyper, and calculated the level of excitement of each part of the HPA axis. What I've found is that a normal brain can't do it—can't produce the intensity of electrical stimulus and the quantity of arousal chemicals needed. But let's assume a few minor, entirely possible, deviations from normal anatomy. First, let's add a variant of epilepsy that, triggered by emotional stress, shoots a drastically increased electrical charge to the HPA axis in the brain. Second, slightly change the size and shape of the HPA components and the glycogen storage capacity of the liver. The necessary combination of factors would occur only very rarely in any given human population. Probably, as Wilkes said, the needed variations in brain activity and structure are inherited."

"Ah," Paul said. *Of course. Like so much else.*

"Now, even the *normal* HPA axis is in many ways an independent, almost enclosed, mechanism. Its parts are closely linked, have dedicated blood supply, and so on. In the hyperdynamic individual—in my opinion—the hypothalamus and crew act even more as an independent entity. It's like, like a separate, very primitive but very vital being that lives within us. For some period of time, however long it remains aroused, it's in total control."

Paul felt vaguely sickened by this.

Stropes stood up and paced to the window, where he stared out at the courtyard briefly, biting his lower lip. "Of course, the fight-or-flight aspect of it is only one angle. As complex as it is, in some ways it's the easiest aspect of the phenomenon to deal with. In my letter, did I mention the U.S. Army Intelligence research on HHK/HHD?"

"You said you'd tried to look into it but got nowhere. Concerns for secrecy."

Stropes nodded again, a mild frown on his brow, and returned to his chair. "Actually, it's not quite that simple. I don't know much about their science, but I know they're doing something, and that they keep their antennae up for data on the subject."

"How do you know?"

"I was very indirectly, very discreetly asked to come work for them. I declined. Made it clear my priorities didn't include helping to create invincible killers." Stropes's brown eyes met Paul's, apparently saw the agreement there. "The little I know I got when I met a biochemist who was connected with the project, at a convention in L.A. This was in the hotel bar. Even drunk, he was pretty close-mouthed, but he told me a little. It was typical military stuff, very heavy-handed: all chemically induced fight-or-flight, designed to induce mortal fear. Some interesting physiological results, apparently, but the drug couldn't be used as a tactical tool because the soldiers they tested the drug on indiscriminately attacked any source of fear or anxiety. Including each other."

"Sounds grisly."

"Oh, they ripped each other to shreds—literally *disemboweled* each other with their bare hands. You can see why I say screw the AI and CIA. Also, compared to the incidents I catalog and Wilkes talked about, the HHK/HHD their subjects displayed was fairly low-level. I believe that the army didn't know that specific neuroanatomical characteristics give some individuals greater potentials than others. You can't turn just anybody into a human juggernaut. Plus, I'm convinced there are other factors too, more difficult to explain."

"Like the range of triggering phenomena," Paul suggested. "Most of the examples you've cited seem to have an almost, I guess you'd have to call it *altruistic* emotional trigger. People acting out of concern for the well-being of others—their kids or spouses."

"Exactly!" Stropes's face came alive again, and he looked at Paul piercingly. "You've put your finger on one of the most important points I've been dealing with—what I call the altruistic paradigm. There are cases in which the trigger seems to have been rage or mortal fear, but the most powerful examples of HHK/HHD stem from what we're calling an altruistic or protective impulse. That, or a related emotion, the *frustration* of the protective impulse—the grief or anger resultant from deep loss."

"So aggression or competitive impulses or rage aren't adequate emotional triggers?"

"Oh, sure. You can get extremely violent behaviors from those. But the real thing? Sustained, let's face it, *superpowers*? No. Not just from an aggressive or hostile impulse."

"Why would that be?"

"This gave me a hard time at first too. But if you think about it, to be an aggressor, to *choose* to be an aggressor, is to have already presumed an *advantage*."

"The presumption of advantage means that it's not a life-or-death emergency. Your system won't be kicked into overdrive."

"Right! In behavioral terms, it's a matter of *control*. It's been well-established that control has a role in how an organism responds to stressors. Thinking that you have control is sufficient to suppress the biochemical responses to a threat. There's another possibility—that the ultimate HHK/HHD response is triggered not only in the old 'reptile' brain, but also needs the boost of more refined, but still very powerful, emotional responses. Parental protectiveness, sibling or spousal bonding, and so on. I believe it may *require* the involvement of those parts of the brain relating to social or familial instincts—the more of the central nervous system that's 'on line,' available to support the HK/HD response, the more powerful that response. I have to admit to a bias in favor of this hypothesis. Perhaps because it affirms my hope that, at bottom, humans are *good*. That our good instincts are ultimately more powerful than our—I was going to say 'evil,' but that's hardly a scientific term, is it?—than our more selfish or aggressive ones." Stropes chuckled at himself. "But I'm sure you didn't come here to get my opinions on issues like that."

Paul was thinking about Highwood. The damage would have required many hours, longer than any mortal panic could be sustained. Nor was it believable that ripping up the house could have come from an altruistic impulse. Anyway, you didn't slash hot-air ducts or bend stove knob shafts on the basis of those emotions. So that left catharsis. Maybe. But for what emotion? None of it quite fit.

A thought occurred to him: "But what about the examples you gave of the berserkers? Weren't they aggressors? How did they achieve states of HHK/HHD?"

Stropes glanced with irritation at his desk telephone, which had begun to flash demandingly. "Good point. The deliberate arousal of HK/HD poses problems for the altruistic paradigm. I guess I'd have to answer with several qualifications. It may be that berserkers can best be described as deliberately putting themselves in a situation where mortal desperation is likely to occur. Fear of the enemy, or grief over the death of friends and relatives in the battle. Conceivably the response could be cultivated. Also, it may be that the level achieved by the average berserker—there's an idea for you, the 'average' berserker!—was only a small percentage of real capacity. For all their ferocity, their displays of strength can't compare with, say, a 107-pound housewife picking up and throwing a burning gas range through the wall of a house to save her kids."

Paul digested this briefly. "Another question: injury. You don't mention wounds to the person demonstrating HHK/HHD. You've sold me that people can have the strength to run through a wall, bend steel, lift a burning stove. But wouldn't they be hurt? No cuts, bruises, burns, bone injury?"

Stropes sighed. "This is the area that's given me the hardest time with my colleagues. Damage to skin, flesh, or bone doesn't seem to happen to a person in the HHK/HHD state. Frankly, I try not to bring it up, because I can't explain it." He scowled and went on in a quiet, urgent voice, as if afraid he'd be overheard. "*Why? How?* There's precedent for the idea of invulnerability—fire walking, yogis sitting on nails, people eating glass, enduring incredible voltages of electricity. But I'm having a hard enough time convincing the skeptics as it is. I've got a tidy theory that gently stretches our sense of what's real, playing by all the biochemical and anatomical rules. These areas—we'd have to change our fundamental ideas about the nature of reality, the laws of nature. I'm not up for the fight."

Stropes pulled back a sleeve and checked his watch. "I have one other thought that might bear upon the berserker riddle. It may be a conditioned response—that is, maybe going hyperdynamic and hyperkinetic *feels good.* Maybe it could become a 'high.' Literally, an addiction."

"A *high*? I'd think that the trauma required for the trigger would constitute a form of negative conditioning!"

"Aha! But I can give you three arguments for the idea of positive conditioning, of HK/HD conditioning. One, there's the satisfaction of catharsis—for those incidents where cathartic release of grief or anger is the trigger. Two, assuming that a form of seizure, an intense electrical burst within the brain, is part of the trigger, some individuals find seizures 'ecstatic.' Dostoyevsky wrote volumes about the joy, the ecstasy of his seizures—doesn't sound too bad, right? Third, you've got the huge release of endorphins that *must* accompany the HHK/HHD state. Normal high exertion, like jogging, fills your body with endorphins, the natural painkillers your body manufactures whenever it exerts itself or is injured—the runner's high. If you're amplifying your exertion by 300 percent, you're going to get a 300 percent increase of endorphins. You're not going to feel any pain at all while in the state, and you're going to be a very, very happy camper afterward, when you slow down enough to notice. They're chemically very similar to morphine. And just as addicting."

"So someone could become positively conditioned to enter the HK state. Could someone *choose* to enter it?"

"With practice, yes. It would help explain the berserker phenomenon, certainly." Stropes stood up and began to sort through some papers.

Paul stood too. "Doctor, I know you have to go, but I'd like to ask you one more question, if I may."

"As long as I can get upstairs in exactly four minutes, sure."

"In your reading, in your case studies, have you ever encountered evidence of periodicity of HHK/HHD episodes? Cycles?"

Stropes laid his perfect hands on his desk and looked at Paul with a new interest in his eyes. "Either you've been doing research, or you know some things you aren't telling me."

"I don't know anything."

Stropes looked skeptical, but humored him. "Wilkes documented several cases of periodic HHK/HHD. Some of the most extreme cases too."

"But it seems incongruous with the idea of triggering phenomena—the cases you've mentioned to me all seem the spontaneous result of an unanticipated, shocking event—a sudden emergency."

"Right. The idea of periodicity bothered me at first, for the same reason. But then I found a small percentage of cyclical cases in my own research. It's very rare, but it's really not so hard to explain. First of all, all seizure activity has cycles of 'kindling' and 'quenching.' So do other neurological or personality disorders, like bipolar disorder. As I think I mentioned in my letter, some HHK/HHD results from profound, long-held emotions, or from trauma that is relived when 'retriggered' by some event. It may also be that, if your body is producing the huge quantity of excitor chemicals needed, the pressure builds until release is inevitable. Whatever the mechanism, there's no question that it can be a periodic phenomenon."

Stropes gave Paul another penetrating glance, then began stuffing manila folders into a large briefcase. "I know I can't make you tell me," he said quietly. "But I wish you would."

Paul shook his head. "Sorry. There's nothing to tell."

"Okay. But if you ever *do*—" Stropes let it hang, snapped his briefcase shut.

They went to the door together, then out into the hall, where they stood side by side at the elevator.

"I hope you won't mind if I don't see you out," Stropes said. "I've got to see Dr. Assad in her office and then get up to the fifth floor. Good-bye— and seriously, please keep in touch."

Stropes waved and started down the hall. He'd only taken a few steps when he snapped his fingers and spun on his heel to face Paul again. "I just remembered something else I meant to mention. You're from upper Westchester, right?"

"Born there, but I live in Vermont. As it happens, I've got a job near Golden's Bridge now."

"That's right—the return address you gave me was in Golden's Bridge. That's what brought it to mind."

"What's that?" The elevator chimed and its doors slid open, waiting. Paul put his hand on the rubber buffer.

"There's another aficionado up that way. In Lewisboro. Haven't heard from her in a while, but I corresponded with her for several years. Very smart woman, seemed very knowledgeable. I thought maybe you'd like to meet her—a Mrs. Hoffmann. Lewisboro address. Probably in the phone book."

"Okay," Paul said. "Thanks." He stepped into the elevator, and the doors slid shut noiselessly. "Thanks a lot," he repeated to the empty elevator. He clapped his hands, relieved to let them play the kinetic tune they'd been itching to. "Thanks so very much," he said. He was surprised at how unsurprising Stropes's news was.

63

On the bright side, Mo thought cynically, after embarrassing himself with Lia, after closing off the little dream he'd been living in for a couple of weeks, he was better focused on his work than he'd been in years. Nothing like a nice slap in the face to wake you up. He attacked his work with a vengeance, mad at himself and at everything that stood in his way, ripping and bullying and bluffing his way through red tape, incompetent or overly rule-oriented underlings, confidentiality concerns. Time to wrap this fucker up.

It was also Thursday, December 15th: If there was a cyclical pattern to the violence, something could happen at any time. An aspect of the situation he had neglected to mention to Lia and Paul.

He sat at his desk and opened a series of manila file folders, went down the checklist he'd assembled for each lead.

Rizal. A tricky aspect of the case. It made sense that Rizal might help out his old buddy Royce by smashing up Highwood in the aunt's absence, and by trying to discourage Paul from finishing the job so that she'd stay out and lose possession. But was he the killer? *Was* there really a killer? Rizal had the means and the opportunity, but what was the motive? Something to do with the Philippine connection? Some kind of psychotic revenge on healthy teenagers because his own kid was crippled? It didn't sit right. Anyway, looking into a State Police trooper was a sensitive task. You could make enemies even feeling it out. If you had a history with the organization like Mo's, you couldn't count on a lot of favors from your fellow cops or your superiors anywhere along the chain of command. Maybe go straight to Inspection in Albany. But there again, Mo's own dubious reputation would precede him. And all he had was a case so tenuous it hadn't even gotten local approval for a homicide investigation.

Falcone. Mo called the gym in Danbury, asked for Salvador Falcone. Just a moment, please, I'll get him. Mo hung up. So Falcone hadn't bolted.

Then he called Sam Lombardino at his North Salem dry cleaning business.

"This is Mo Ford. Sorry to bother you again, but I've got one more question about Salli Falcone. He's got two assaults on record. You told me about one, where you picked him up. Know anything about the other?"

"Ah shit," Lombardino said, as if he wished he didn't have to talk about it. "I know a little. It's bullshit. He beat up on somebody in a store in Manhattan."

"Yeah? What was he doing down there?"

"Bullshit, like I said. The D.A. there tried to make out it was part of something else, not just Salli's temper. It's enough to make you join the Sons of Italy Anti-Defamation League. Falcone broke this guy's arms, Falcone's Italian, so the D.A. down there wants to say it's organized crime. Says there's evidence Salli's been hired to hurt people by a large Italian family wholesale grocery business. Maybe it's just because I'm a Guinea myself, but I couldn't see it that way. Anyway, the D.A. never got anywhere with that angle—all Salli got was simple assault, no conspiracy. No weapons involved."

"Pretend I'm a Guinea too," Mo said flatly. "What do you really think?"

"Hey, court said it was simple assault, that's what it was." Lombardino paused. "Of course, it could also be Salli was looking for work, tried it once, was too stupid to avoid getting caught. Or maybe he had too much of an attitude. So afterward he's not a good candidate for full-time permanent work. He's been a pretty good boy ever since."

Mo thanked Lombardino and got off. So maybe Falcone had some connection with organized crime in Manhattan. Terrific. There were a thousand possibilities there. Just what kind of "groceries" did this family business wholesale? Might Royce, with his import/export business, tie in— some Far East commodities needing a distribution network in Manhattan? A Royce-Falcone connection. Why not? There was already a connection: Salli Senior had been gardener up there.

Mo set the file aside. He'd stew on that one for a while too.

Which brought him to Royce. Grisbach had called back late Tuesday night while Mo was tossing and turning in bed, reliving his conversation with Lia in excruciating clarity.

"I've got some shit for you," Grisbach wheezed.

"Terrific. I need all the shit I can get."

"The companies look legit and more or less in the black. Nothing jumps out—your guy makes lots of bucks, owns big percentages of his companies, has a big portfolio in other firms, very diverse. He has high-roller spending habits that haven't changed in the last two years. Doesn't mean he doesn't need money, but he doesn't act like he's hurting."

"Real estate?"

Grisbach coughed right into the phone, a wet, rich, bubbling cough.

"Residential property in Westchester County, apartments in Manhattan and Amsterdam. Nothing overtly suspicious."

"Debts?"

"Some. More than he should have, probably. In other words, just another rich guy, not that different from a hundred others I've looked at. Which means he's about eighty-five percent legit, fifteen percent bent. Guy like this is always hungry for more, Ford. Don't waste your time looking for a specific reason he might be hungrier than usual. He wouldn't need one."

"Okay. What about travel?"

"He gets around. Flies Lufthansa and SwissAir once in a while, or goes on company planes. He's been in and out of the U.S. twice this year that I can track. Came over from Amsterdam, commercial flight, July twentieth, spent the night in New York, then went on to San Diego. Spent August ninth in New York again, left to Amsterdam on August tenth."

"Great." Mo jotted notes.

"Left the country, New York to London to Amsterdam, on December fourth. He's still over there. Lufthansa has Royce Hoffmann listed as a passenger, Amsterdam to New York, on December sixteenth, evening arrival. Tomorrow night."

Royce had told Paul he'd be out of the country for longer. A deliberate lie or just a change of plans? How convenient that he was returning just at the end of Vivien Hoffmann's absence from Highwood, just about when the continuous occupancy clause would be triggered if she didn't move back in. Just when another cycle was due. And how interesting that one of Royce's prior visits coincided with the destruction of Richard Mason and the disappearance of Essie Howrigan. Too many coincidences.

But why would Royce need to be on hand for the fun? Rizal, or another hired man, could go up to the lodge whether Royce was in the U.S. or in Timbuktu. Unless, as Lia had said, there was something in the house that Royce wanted to find—something only he could recognize, or something he didn't want Rizal to know about. With friends like Rizal, you didn't need enemies.

He was getting close, but not close enough. He'd stew over Royce a little longer too.

On Friday morning, Mo sat in his car, smoothing the real estate map of Briar Estates on the seat beside him. The winding road of the development began about a mile and a half from Highwood, at the western end of the reservoir. It was one of the neighborhoods recently carved out of the thick woods, with large new houses in a Tudor style, straining at ostentation but showing signs of budget-consciousness. Faux upscale. At the far end of the development he came to several incomplete houses, big balloons of plywood in mud lots, with grading equipment parked here and there. Innumerable smaller roads, not yet paved, branched off the main artery and disappeared into the woods, driveways for houses not yet started. At the farthest uphill point, the road made a loop back on itself. Mo parked and looked at the woods. If he guessed correctly, this would be the closest point to the lodge, maybe a bit less than a mile.

Mo found what looked like a path at the bottom of a dry ravine and began walking up. It had turned uncomfortably cold, with a buffeting, erratic wind that drove down the collar of his coat. The dead leaves on the old oaks shivered, making a noise like rattlesnakes.

Several times he chose forks that petered out, and he had to retrace his steps, but after a while he caught a glimpse of shingled siding above him, and soon the lodge materialized among the trees. It was a longer walk than going up the driveway, but not as steep. A good route for anyone who had business up there they'd rather nobody knew about: Park your car at the end of one of the dirt drives, walk up overland. Nobody around to notice.

He lifted the heavy iron knocker on the smoking room door, dropped it several times. Paul opened the door.

"I'm sorry you had to walk up," Paul said. "It just occurred to me that I should go down and open the gate for you."

"Actually, I came up through the woods," Mo said. "I wanted to see how someone could get up here unnoticed. Anyway, I needed the exercise."

Paul did look different, Mo decided. Older, leaner. Stripped down, as if he'd been up late a lot recently, looking straight at some tough stuff. And yet he also seemed more alert, sharper. There was an intensity about him now, almost like Lia's.

"On the phone you sounded like you had something urgent to discuss," Paul said. "I take it you've had good hunting." Without asking, he handed Mo a cup of black coffee.

Mo took the cup and sat in one of the wingback chairs, glad for the heat in the room, the scalding cup in his hands. "I had good hunting, yeah, although I don't know if I got answers or just came up with more questions. But yes, I think it could be urgent."

"How so?"

"I've got a feeling maybe this is coming to a head in the next couple of days."

Paul took this in, nodding thoughtfully. "Why do you think so?"

"Number one, I was able to track your cousin. He went to Europe, all right, not long after you saw him. But he's not staying over there—he's due back from Amsterdam tonight. He was lying to you. How safe do you think your aunt is? I'd say not very. She should be warned."

Mo got up to pace. "Number two, something I don't know if I've mentioned to you, I think there's a cycle with the missing kids thing. Every forty-four days. Periodicity is a typical feature of serial violence. So I charted the intervals. If I did it right, we're due for another round sometime very soon—as soon as, well, tomorrow. I wasn't sure, but just in the last few days there's been some, uh, other corroboration of a cycle."

Paul smiled, a sour sort of grin, nodding again. "What kind of corroboration?"

He told Paul about the dismemberment of Priscilla Zeichner on the railroad tracks, only a few miles away, which nailed down the third cycle, November 2nd. Again Paul took it in stride, nodding his head thoughtfully.

"Most people would get a little nervous hearing something like that," Mo said. "Let me ask you something, Paul. What's your stake in this? Why do you care what happened here? Why do you stick it out?"

Paul drew a slow breath, a guy with a lot on his mind. "This'll sound old-fashioned, but I guess it's that I need to *understand*. I'd have preferred not to get involved in anything like this, but I did, so. . . . Anyway, you can't spend your life running from everything that looks scary." He chuckled unhappily. "Christ, I'm sounding like my father. The other thing here is, this is my family. There's a lot I'd like to know about who my people are, why they . . . did the things they did. Maybe it'll help me figure out who I am. A long story. I'll tell it to you sometime."

Mo nodded, letting him go on as needed. After another moment Paul looked at him sharply. "And why are *you* so involved in this, Mo?"

"Me? It's my job. I get paid for it."

"The hell it is. You've been basically told hands off by your supervisor. Not that I disagree with anything you've said, but your whole theory is based on very little hard evidence, some pretty tenuous theories. I get the feeling it's more than a job for you."

"It shows, huh?" Mo had to laugh. "Maybe so. I'm pissed off. I think whoever did this, whoever offed the kids, should get paid back. I hate the thought of that prick Rizal getting away with anything. But mainly—like you said, this is old-fashioned too—mainly I guess I want to 'do good.' Not that I always know what 'good' is. But at the very least it has something to do with preventing other people from getting hurt."

"I guess we've got several things in common, then," Paul said. "Besides falling for the same woman. We both want to understand. And to do good." The way he said the two words put quotation marks around them, as if to point out how fickle and subjective such ideas were. Paul looked at Mo

with a disarming directness, and Mo felt that they'd each confided something important to each other. *We're a pair of fucked-up idealists,* Paul's
look said, *what're you gonna do?* Mo liked him a great deal.

Mo found the skull earring in his hands again, and for the first time
looked at it closely. It was dirty with the skin-oil residue of an often-worn
piece, but was well sculpted, probably expensive. "Where'd you get this?" he
asked.

"Out in the rubble. The big room, I think. I don't know why I brought it
in here. Just a curiosity, I guess."

"Unusual, don't you think?"

Paul shrugged. "My aunt is a person of peculiar tastes. Why?"

It was Mo's turn to shrug. No real reason. He made himself put it back
down, focus on business. "So I did some work on the whereabouts of Erik
Hoffmann III. You'll never guess what happened." Mo told him what he'd
learned from Dr. Gunderson. "After he disappeared, the State Police did a
missing persons investigation, considering him an adult at risk, but he
never showed up. This was five, six years ago."

Paul just grunted, almost as if he'd been expecting to hear it. "So how do
you think he ties in?" Paul asked. It was interesting, Mo thought, that Paul
was doing the interviewing here. It was as if he had some overview, were
fitting pieces into his own construction.

"I don't think he does," Mo said.

"Why not?"

"Because then I went to look up the trust. You were right—the Hoffmann Trust consisted of Royce and Erik III. But it reverted to Royce because Erik was declared legally dead earlier this year. On June twentieth, to
be exact."

"Legally dead?"

"Happens fairly often. Husband disappears while out sailing, wife wants
to collect life insurance, company won't pay unless they see a corpse that
nobody'll ever find, wife files for legal declaration of death. There's a time
factor. In New York State you have to wait five years before the court will
declare a missing person dead."

"Which means he could be dead, or might not be."

"I'd say so, except that my guess is that he disappeared because his
brother killed him, or had him killed. The way I see it, like you said, that's
why your aunt transferred Erik III so many times—to keep Royce from locating him. But Royce succeeds in finding him, offs him, waits five years for
the legal declaration of death, this June twentieth. First thing he does when
the trust passes exclusively to him is fuck up this house, that's on around
June twenty-second or twenty-third. His mother knows he's going to try
something like that, gets scared, runs away to California." To Mo's frustra-

tion, Paul didn't react, just kept staring thoughtfully into the distance. "Personally, that's what I think we're dealing with here. But it looks to me like maybe you're not so sure."

"I've got a few problems with the scenario you describe, yes. One, you talk about cycles of violence. But that's emotional violence, resulting from rhythms in the psychological or neurological states of the perpetrator. At the same time, you're trying to pin this whole thing on a strictly deliberate, thought-out, long-term plot by Royce—instrumental violence."

The inconsistency was so obvious that Mo felt stupid. Completely inconsistent psychological profiles. Some of the air went out of his theory. Suddenly depressed, he poured himself another cup of coffee, swished it through his teeth as if he could suck some immediate stimulus out of it.

"Okay," he said. "I agree, I don't have all the answers. But let me tell you one other little piece of research I did. I wanted to know when your aunt left here, exactly when, right? So I called the Royale Hotel in San Francisco, said I was your aunt's accountant in New York. Told the clerk I needed her date of arrival at the hotel so I could put some numbers together for tax purposes. She checked in on June twenty-fourth, Paul, which not only ties in with the declaration of death but which also means she's got exactly one week to resume residence here. And don't think Royce doesn't know it—if I could get the date that easily, so could he. And the hotel records provide all the paperwork he'd need to prove she was gone."

No reaction. It was hard to tell if Paul was even listening.

"So let me tell you where I went with it," Mo went on, beginning to feel desperate. "I came here wanting to ask your help. See, I've got several problems here. Not only figuring out who did what, but how you catch and convict a guy like Royce. He's rich, I've got little or no concrete evidence against him, he's no doubt got a lot of pull. Or Rizal—how do I go about accusing a police officer? Plus, my investigation is pretty unofficial. How do I apprehend these guys?"

"I can see that would be tricky, yes."

"But the plan I have might help us there. Assume for a moment I'm right and Royce wants this place, or the money he could get for it. And he's not sleeping nights because his plan is maybe not going to happen because his cousin Paul has come out of nowhere to be a monkey wrench in the works. He's invested a lot in keeping his mother out of here. The deadline's coming up. What's he got to do?"

"He's got to mess the place up again. And he doesn't have much time. So what are you proposing?"

It was time for the hard sell. Mo laid it all out: how Paul and he would jointly approach Vivien, soonest, Saturday, tell her they knew what was going on, make clear the extent of the risk to her if she tried to return. Tell her that opening the place up for a forensic investigation would be a way to protect her. If she still refuses, Paul and Mo go to Barrett, insist there's evidence that crimes have been committed at the lodge. Paul as a relative, as a person intimate with the current condition of the house. And Paul goes with Mo to Inspection in Albany, about Rizal. Barrett agrees to throw it open for investigation, Inspection goes after Rizal, Rizal and Royce are frozen out of it, maybe the investigation turns up something to pin them with.

But the distant look had come over Paul again.

"I'm not sure, Mo," Paul said at last. "My situation is complicated too. This is my family. My aunt insisted I preserve her privacy, and I agreed. Plus, I've got some problems with my ex-wife, some child-custody shit coming up—I have to finish this job so I can get the rest of the money my aunt owes me. If you're wrong, it'll cost me."

"Cost you? Hey, if what I'm saying is right, and these guys are willing to kill people if they need to, why shouldn't they just take *you* out too? In fact, that's an important part of what we need to tell my supervisor about—that a major crime is likely to be committed unless some action is taken."

Paul stared through the wall again, then shook his head minutely. "I can't decide right this minute, Mo."

"You can't wait forever, either. Royce and Rizal've only got a few days. You can bet they're not going to wait."

"Give me until tomorrow morning. I'll make up my mind by then."

Mo was frustrated, but it was better than nothing. They agreed that Mo would meet Paul at the lodge at ten in the morning, and they'd take it from there. Mo inspected the skull earring again, then put it down, wondering why it bothered him. He swigged the last of his coffee. Paul offered to drive him back to his car, but Mo declined, wanting one more look at the path to Briar Estates.

He walked down the hill, learning the path backward. The wind was still picking up and some heavier clouds were moving in. Mo moved in and out of the shadow of boulders, the tangle of fallen trees and tented vines. He slid on some loose rock and wished again he'd thought to wear the appropriate shoes. Something strange was working inside Paul, for sure. But he was a good guy—hopefully as of ten tomorrow they'd start breaking this thing open.

64

Paul stared at the wall of Dempsey's guest bedroom, numb from fatigue. Friday night. Vivien was no doubt already somewhere in New York. Dempsey and Elaine had sent him to bed, cleared the dishes, and now the house was quiet except for the faint sound of wind in the eaves. He'd gone to the Corrigans' for what was intended as a quick, late dinner but had nearly fallen asleep at the table. In his exhaustion, he'd been unable to contain a set of mimetic tics that aped Dempsey's hand gestures unflatteringly, and was relieved when Dempsey gave him a wink of understanding.

"Stay here tonight, Paul," Elaine had said. "A comfortable bed, a hot shower. I'll cook you a great breakfast."

"No. Got to get more work done tonight." Paul groaned, tried to rouse himself. His back ached from hours of stooping, of carrying pieces of furniture to the terrace railing and tossing them into the Dumpster he'd had brought up, of boxing up salvageable stuff.

Dempsey shook his head. "Paul, face it—you're beat. The amount of work you'd get done tonight won't make much of a difference with Vivien. Better you should be rested when you meet her and sit down with her to figure out what you need to do to finish up. You'll need a clear head more than another square yard of floor cleaned up. Think of Mark too—he doesn't need a father who's a smoldering hulk. Stay here."

Paul's elbow had slipped off the dinner table, bringing his head with it, startling him awake. Dempsey had stood him up and herded him into the bedroom. "No arguments," Elaine said firmly.

And now, paradoxically, he couldn't quite sleep. Despite his exhaustion, a current of anxiety ran through him, a relentless nervous energy.

On the bright side, he tried to remind himself, he'd made almost enough progress. When Vivien came, the lodge would have electricity, and glass in the windows. And maybe even heat: Becker had agreed to work Saturday and thought he'd be able to get the new furnaces running. The house would have intact plumbing, with running water in the kitchen and one functional toilet. Her papers would be sorted into file boxes. The downstairs rooms would be mostly cleared and swept, the salvageable stuff sorted for repair or disposal. The upstairs rooms would be still heaped with rubble, but that wasn't so bad: It would give her a better idea of what he'd been up against. Vivien would pay him what she owed him, and he'd be gone. He'd let her find someone else to do the rest of the work.

Dimly visible outside the windows, the trees swayed in a rising wind, and a fine windblown sleet hissed against the glass. Paul stood up, paced in a circle in the little room, his thoughts spinning. Lia and Mark. Got to tell them not to come down from Vermont. *Lia,* he'd say, *Royce is returning, there's a cycle here and it's coming around, there's a window of a few days for Royce to act to keep Vivien out of here, Mo's convinced people are getting killed over this. There's a weird neurological condition that—* No. Keep it simple: *I don't want you or Mark anywhere near Highwood.*

Paul left the bedroom, walked through the darkened house to the phone on the kitchen counter, dialed the number of the farm, got a busy signal, hung up.

Still pacing, he went to the hallway, thumbed the rheostat switch for the ceiling lights, bringing them up to a dim glow, just enough to look over Dempsey's little gallery of fight posters and handbills. Young Dempsey with the sloped, muscle-corded shoulders, the banded long muscles in his thighs, the lethal eye. He'd been one tough customer, a brawling Irish kid with a famous right hand. *The secret to a good punch is* converting, Dempsey had told him once. *At the last instant you put the entire weight and strength of your body into it, from your toes on up you're rigid as a plank of wood at the microsecond of contact. Boom, your guy goes down, every time. One of the great lessons I learned from fighting, applies to any project: Learn to focus all your mental or physical energy into a single point, into the job at hand.*

Good advice, Paul thought, wondering how he could bring to bear his own mental energy. There was a pattern in it all, if he could just see the whole picture. At times it seemed close to resolving, all the pieces settling into place. So close. And it had nothing to do with the scenario Mo believed in. That's why he'd had to stall Mo. That's why the solutions Mo envisioned wouldn't work. That's why Paul couldn't just walk away from it.

Farther down the hall, he stopped in front of a little collection of framed photos. Most were of the very early days, Dempsey building his house, Dempsey and Ben and Aster, Dempsey and Elaine with other people Paul didn't recognize. There was even a small portrait of Paul and Kay.

Paul stared at the ones of Ben, searching the face of his father, looking for whatever insight might be found in his level gaze, his square chin, the lines of his mouth. One photo showed Ben and Dempsey standing proudly on a massive tree trunk they'd just felled. Ben smiled a cocky grin and held one end of a seven-foot two-man saw.

Paul cut the lights and tried Lia again. Still busy.

The problem of the nature of the violence was that Mo's theory relied on two completely different motivational forces. Royce did it, or instigated it, because he's got plans for the estate. Yet there was a rhythm to the intervals of violence, a serial or cyclical pattern such as would result from a psychopathology. Royce's coming back right on schedule reinforces the serial theory; the serial theory, in turn, implicates Royce because he's returning just when another cycle is due.

No. It wasn't just bad psychology. It was bad logic, a tautology: Proposition A is proven by proposition B, which is proven by proposition A.

No anyway. His gut told him otherwise.

Paul debated taking a couple of aspirin. He needed to sleep, but his thoughts festered and gnawed and wouldn't quit. Severe akathisia. Maybe it was the coffee he'd been drinking. His nerves were jangled. He needed to do something physical, yet he was too tired, it was almost midnight. He paced in circles in the living room, rotating his shoulders, trying to get the tension out of them.

Why couldn't he quite choke down Mo's theory about Royce's motives, despite the apparent evidence for it? Because Paul's instincts told him unequivocally that the root of it all lay in personality. The Hoffmanns were too wealthy and too complex to bother being involved in anything for purely material reasons. They were connoisseurs of mind games, of the kind of warfare of attrition and subterfuge that only families waged. Whatever or whomever this game involved, the key was to be found in the psychology of the players.

And how did Erik III fit into the equation? Did he? Was he dead, as the law had officially declared, as Mo believed, or was he . . . what? *Out in the woods. Half wild, living like the Leather Man, hugely strong, deeply angry, frustrated, full of raging sorrows like the wind outside now, prone to explosive violence. To HHK/HHD. When his cycle came around, coming down to the lodge like a winter-starved bear, ripping and rending.* Paul's neck hairs rose at the thought. It would explain a lot—Vivien's interest in neurology, her desire to draw Paul into her affairs, her curiosity about Mark, her contact with Stropes. Her willingness to stick it out year after year at the lodge. Yes, and her resistance to bringing the police in: still trying to protect her beloved but demented first son.

And Ben. Was the mystery of Ben's suicide connected? Had Royce killed Ben—was that what he'd been hinting? Unlikely: Royce would be too smart to let something like that come out. More likely it was just Royce's sadistic, manipulative impulse of the moment, finding what he knew would be a sensitive nerve in Paul. Or wanting to expose the tip of Vivien's affair with Ben, turn Paul against her.

Abruptly too tired to stand, he went back to the bedroom, sat on the bed again, listening to the wind noise rising in the trees, the thousand tiny creaks and groans of the house shifting minutely under the pressure of moving air.

The issue of instrumental versus emotional violence: Was the damage at Highwood the aftermath of the periodic explosions of some violent psychotic, or the carefully devised plan of someone who wanted the house or something in it? The question wasn't necessarily that simple. There was a precedent for the two combining, he realized with a flash of lucidity. He'd just been talking about it with Dr. Stropes: the riddle of the berserkers. The same problem applied. Berserkers could plan to be in a battle, knew in advance how they'd respond, could enter their hyperkinetic, hyperdynamic killing mode at will. They'd put on their pelts, they'd stare crazily through the eyeholes of a bear skull, and they'd chop anyone who resisted them into squirming guts and chunks of bone.

Yes. And with that came several inferences. In his mind's eye he held up the possibilities and examined each one. He followed out his meandering thoughts until he jerked suddenly upright, aware that he'd started to fall asleep, had crossed the vague line between reflection and dreaming.

He stood and went back to the telephone, clumsily punched the number of the farm, got the busy signal once more. Maybe the lines were screwed up in some way, he was thinking, and suddenly he realized he'd been listening to the signal for a full minute or more. Too tired to stay up any longer. He'd call her first thing in the morning, tell her not to come down. It would be better then anyway: He'd be better able to explain when he wasn't so exhausted.

Back in the bedroom, he turned out the lights, lay back on the pillow, feeling his own weight pulling him down, irresistible. *August 6th,* he thought, *September 19th, November 2nd.* Yes. A clotted warm darkness began to blossom inside him, consuming his mind, blotting out the swirling thoughts.

His last thought had to do with railroads. What was her name? Priscilla something. *Train tracks. Getting hit by a train. That was one of the keys.* And then he was asleep.

65

MO checked the gate and found it locked. He got back into the car, parked it to one side of the driveway, and began the walk up to the lodge. There'd been wind and some sleet for a while during the night, but it had warmed up and just rained, leaving the ground wet. Now it was just a gray, raw, lousy day. The weather reports had yammered about the early winter storm hitting New England, but it had pretty well fizzled out by the time it got this far south. It was typical of the times, he thought morosely, that even the weatherman had to sensationalize the headlines. A whole society with jaded senses, no way to reach them but the extremes.

Against his chest he could feel the slight pressure of the photograph he'd slid into his inner jacket pocket before leaving, the one he'd confront Vivien Hoffmann with. He'd gone home from his last meeting with Paul and found that, despite all the other urgent aspects of Highwood, what he kept thinking about was the unusual skull-feather earring Paul had picked out of the rubble and left on the table in the smoking room. The earring that had teased him every time he'd seen it.

Late last night, on the verge of sleep, he'd found the nagging memory that had evaded him for almost a week, sat up suddenly, slapped on the lights, went to the case files he'd brought home with him. Not Essie, not Richard, not Steve—flipping through the photos in the files, he found the school portrait of Dub Gilmore, who along with Steve Rubio had disappeared in September. A plain-faced kid, small nose, brown hair just slightly punked-out. And one pierced ear, with a small but unusual earring in it. A silver skull and small bright feather, some tropical bird's feather.

Afterward, he couldn't sleep. *Mrs. Hoffmann, I want to show you something,* he rehearsed. *Your nephew found this earring here at the house. This is a photo of a kid I'm looking for. Same earring, right? Either the kid took yours from this house, or he left his here. In either case, he was up here. I want to know where he is now. I need to come in here with a forensic team.* If she didn't come around, he'd get a judge to give him a warrant on the basis of the earring. Period.

He should be pumped up with the find, feeling lucky, but instead all he felt was a peculiar resignation, a lot like the suspension of caring you went through when you went into a possibly dangerous arrest or stakeout, but with an added melancholy. It had to do with women, he decided. With Lia. For the past few weeks he'd been living with Lia always at the back of his mind, always in his heart. She'd been like the sun rising on a clear and perfect day. Without the prospect of her somehow coming into his life, his horizons seemed bare and stark. He'd have to get deliberate about meeting women—hanging out in bars, joining clubs, whatever. It was a depressing prospect. He marched, mad at himself for feeling crushed because some completely unfounded fantasies, fucking *hallucinations* really, hadn't materialized.

One thing was clear: It was time to finish this up, get on with something else, begin to forget.

Mo tugged his parka collar up against the cold. Maybe Paul hadn't forgotten to leave the gate open, but had gotten nervous about unexpected visitors and relocked it. Mo's talk about an imminent repeat of the violence had probably gotten him on edge. Good.

He came over the crest of the drive to find that Paul's car was nowhere to be seen. So Paul was late. Terrific. He half-heartedly tried the smoking room door and found it locked, as he'd expected—leaving him with the choice of hanging out and freezing until Paul showed, or walking all the way down the driveway again to wait in the car. His luck didn't seem to be running good.

Killing time, trying to keep warm, he walked around the lodge, getting an idea of approaches, hiding places, lines of sight. The woods were a dense tangle, even with the leaves gone: wrist-thick, ropy vines hanging from the big oaks, jagged points of granite ledge breaking through, a snarl of fallen trees and branches. Good killing ground. No one would ever know.

Mo came out on the uphill side of the house, near the kitchen door. He tried the knob and found to his surprise that the door was unlocked. In his exhaustion, Paul was forgetting things. Still, he was glad to be inside. He made his way across the main room and into the smoking room, where he followed the instructions on the kerosene heater and got it lit.

Another reason for his feeling low, despite the imminent resolution of this case, was that the nature of its closure wasn't quite satisfying. Sure, maybe he'd slam the door on Rizal and Royce, and after months or years of paperwork and trials *maybe*, long shot, manage to get a conviction. But part of him longed for something more certain, decisive, dramatic. Let that fucker Rizal and Royce or whoever come up, catch them in the act, blow them away. Somebody deserved payback for what had happened to Richard Mason, and Heather, and who knows how many others.

On the other hand, you couldn't just shoot people all the time. It was difficult to explain. Also, if they'd killed before to protect their plan, they'd no doubt try to kill Mo. It was always unpleasant to have people trying to kill you.

Mo listened to the silent house, warming his backside against the heater, holding the earring and matching it to the photograph of Dub. No mistake: either the same earring or one that was identical.

Where was Paul? They'd arranged to meet a half hour ago. Paul would have to be anxious to get the work done before his aunt got here. Anyway, he didn't seem the type to keep someone waiting.

Mo put away the photo, took a turn on the rug. The room was getting warm now. He could picture Lia sitting in the wingback chair, one leg over the arm, the band of sunlight falling across her face and hair. Remembering the joy of being around her, the *inspiration* of her, he abruptly felt lonely, empty, hollow. When was he going to feel that warmth again, the closeness? What if it was never? Guys got routed away from all that, there was nothing you could do about it, the tracks of your life could just be laid in that direction and you wouldn't know until you woke up to find you're in your mid-thirties, divorced, not up for anything short of the right thing. And before you know it you wake up to find you're mid-forties or fifties, living in hotel rooms. The elbows of your suits got shiny, you ate dinner at bars—burgers and pickled eggs and booze. You wouldn't recognize the right thing if you tripped over her, and she wouldn't know you either. It happened a lot to career cops.

The thought made him breathless for an instant. The old feeling of exhaustion came over him, and he wished he'd taken the time to eat breakfast.

When the sound came from the far end of the house, it was not what he'd been expecting, and yet there was an odd familiarity about it. A heavy thump and clatter, and a sound like a bunch of kids scampering, lots of little footsteps. It wasn't Paul, who would have seen Mo's car at the bottom and would have come in through the smoking room door, or called out when he first entered.

Mo's heartbeat quickened, and he felt the weight of his gun against his ribs, warm, heavy, insistent. After due deliberation, he took out the pistol. *Stay intentional,* he reminded himself. *There's no hurry. Stay calm. You'll have the time.* The old fear came up in him, of the lethal reflexive thing that lived inside him and made his gun a perfect extension of its will.

He opened the smoking room door a crack and listened. The pattering noise was louder in the big room, and now he heard another noise that he couldn't place. *Shicka-shicka-shicka,* like someone sawing wood, or filing something, only much faster. There was an almost metallic edge to the sound, like his father sharpening the knife before carving the roast, strop- ping it first down one side of the steel and then down the other. Only this was impossibly fast.

In one motion, Mo shoved the door all the way open and stepped into the big room, legs spread, elbows bent, the gun pointed toward the ceiling. The scampering was louder, heavier now. The floor seemed to vibrate slightly. And the other noise, coming closer.

The light shifted in the dining room doorway, someone momentarily blocking the light from the kitchen windows. *Hold back, hold off, stay delib- erate,* Mo screamed at himself. *Stay conscious, keep control, don't go reflex- ive, no mistakes.* The gun's grip was wet with sweat from his hands.

Then there was someone in the doorway, coming into the room faster than Mo would have thought possible. He held off the impulse to fire for an instant, commanding his hand to wait, and immediately realized he'd made a mistake, he'd lost his one chance because now the utterly impossi- ble being was moving in the big space, too fast to track, and now it was coming his way. He fired and fired again, knowing as he did that he was too slow, he was way behind it, he didn't have a chance.

Mo started to dodge sideways but then felt the first colossal impact, and then without any transition he was facing the wrong way, a view of the cor- ner of the ceiling when only an instant ago he was looking across the big room. There was a feeling like pain but impossibly large, an everywhere sensation too big to feel. Then as if there'd been an earthquake the view shifted again and he was staring across the room, eyes level with the floor, and the *shicka-shicka* was all around him. A blurred pair of dancing feet moved across his sight and the sound drifted farther away. *Bare* feet. That seemed particularly horrible and terrifying.

So this is where my tracks lead, he thought dreamily. There was some- thing very sad about it. And yet a relief too. *You're always dying, all your life, only you don't recognize it.* It was good to let go and stop fighting it. He wished Lia were nearby, one more glimpse of that wonder, then realized she would be back soon and would be killed too unless Paul could do something, maybe Paul had it figured out by now and would know what to do. Not that there was much anyone could do. Abruptly he wished his mother was there, not the little dried-up white-haired way she was now but how she was a long time ago. He felt the shape of her name on his lips, *Mama,* although no sound came.

How ironic. First you let go, you let yourself go on automatic and that's what fucks you up. So you learn to hold back and the next time you hold back and that's what fucks you up. It was almost funny. Paul should know.

There was something sad and strange in his field of view, and he focused on it with all the effort he could make. A familiar shape, two shapes, but different than he'd ever seen them. After a moment he recognized the objects as his own legs, his own lower body really, lying on the floor with the legs still in their pants and still joined at the hip, one foot with a shoe on and the other off like the nursery rhyme "My Son John," only the legs were too far away, and there was a trail of red and white slimy fat strings from the top of the waist toward where he lay. *Five things worse than dying,* he thought. *Only five, Heather?* Then he thought: *No, nothing's worse.* It was a funny way to see your own legs, your bottom half, and wasn't it appropriate that he'd finally been made into two totally separate parts, Paul would appreciate the ironies of it, wouldn't Paul be amazed by the whole thing, and it was sad because the legs were so pitifully awkward and motionless.

He looked at them as if they were old friends he'd miss terribly, and then they disappeared along with everything else.

66

Paul jerked out of the dream to find himself sitting up, panting and blinking in the too-bright light of mid-morning. He vaguely remembered waking up earlier, then pausing as he sat on the edge of the bed, mustering the energy to get up for the day. He'd begun thinking about the situation at Highwood, closely examining the buckle on the band of his watch, turning it in the sunlight, fascinated. The trancelike state had come over him again, deeper this time. Just like when he was kid.

The unforgettable image stayed in his mind's eye:

Seeing the sapling thrash, the pink shapes moving, ears filled with the sawing sound. Dropping the handkerchief with the snack in it, turning to go, mindless, and tripping over something in the path. Looking back to see a head, *a man's grimacing head, staring stupidly at the ground, red-streaked tongue too far out the mouth, neck a ragged, torn stump, the ground beneath glistening red-black. Scrambling upright, running away, seared into a white empty panic by the sight: a head without a body, on the ground.*

Paul felt his stomach start to turn. It couldn't be a real memory. It was an anxiety-inspired dream, an exhaustion dream. Any psychologist would tell him the same thing: "Tripping over your head" was such a perfect symbol of his own lifelong dilemma. He'd been tripping over his head all his life: his early neurological problems, then the Tourette's. Tripping over his fucking mind, his intellect, second-guessing his every move, reasoning the joy and spontaneity out of everything he did. Plodding away with his systematic but sluggish haloperidol-saturated brain.

But maybe that wasn't all there was to it. The image was too real, too detailed: blood-streaked extended tongue, lightless eyes, white knuckly glint of spinal column—

Abruptly he was wide awake, energy surging through him as if an internal switch had been thrown. *Railroad tracks. Forty-four days.* Mo forgot one thing, looking forward from his two dates for the third cycle. What happens when you count back—for an *earlier* cycle? Yes, the parts connected, the pattern took shape. Yes, it made sense of Mo's convergences of dates, deaths, comings and goings. The mandala of cause and effect around the hidden mover, the hidden gravity well, the spiral of light that surrounds the invisible black hole. *Who could you trust?* Yes, the blood tells.

How long had he been sitting? From the windows he could see that the storm had come and gone during the night, leaving the land wet, with only a few small pockets of sleet still on the ground. The sun was too high. He turned over the watch, still in his hands: 11:30. He must have been sitting staring at the watchband buckle, upright but unconscious, for over four hours.

He got quickly out of bed, stood up into his jeans. He'd agreed to meet Mo at the lodge at ten. It was vital to meet with Mo, let him know what he was getting into. But first: Lia. Paul ran to the telephone in the kitchen, dialed, and, half-expecting to get a busy signal again, was relieved when it rang. Then the line was picked up and he heard his own voice: "We can't come to the phone right now, but if you leave a message when you hear the sound of stampeding elephants. . . ."

He waited impatiently for the message to finish, astonished that he'd ever lived a life that indulged the dull, innocent, formulaic humor of telephone machine greetings. "Lia, it's me," he barked at last. "Listen, some things have come up. It's important that you don't, *do not,* come down today after all. I don't have time to explain right this minute, but call me tonight here at Corrigans'. I'll call Janet and explain that our plans for Mark have to change."

There was a note from Elaine on the counter: *You'll probably be cross with us, but we haven't heard a peep out of you this morning and we decided to let you sleep in. You deserve it. We're out running errands and shopping so we'll have lots of goodies for Mark. Help yourself to anything in the icebox. Good luck with the Dragon Lady. We'll be back around one o'c. If M. and L. come before then, just have them come on in.*

He balled up the note, dialed Janet's number. "Janet, it's Paul," he said breathlessly.

"I'm on my way out the door. It's not a good time to get into anything complicated."

"This isn't complicated. I can't seem to reach Lia. I need you to tell her something when she calls or comes by for Mark. There's been a change of plans. Tell her not to bring Mark this weekend. It's very important."

"Number one, Paul, I don't appreciate your lack of respect for other people's schedules, especially when it concerns your son, who is very, very much looking forward to seeing his father, as we planned. Number two, I'm not going to start being personal secretary for your girlfriends. Number three," she said with satisfaction, "you're too late. They left, what, over three hours ago."

Paul couldn't say anything.

"Lia said she was having difficulty reaching you. She said she tried to reach you this morning but didn't get an answer. I thought she left you a message."

For the first time, Paul noticed the blinking light on the answering machine. No doubt she'd called the lodge, then called Corrigans', left the message. Dempsey and Elaine must have already left the house, he'd been sitting in his trance. "They left?" he croaked.

"She came to pick him up at nine." Janet paused, and her tone of gratified annoyance changed to one of suspicion. "What's this about, Paul?"

Time to be careful of Janet. He had to avoid giving her anything she might use against him in the future. She had already convinced herself he was unstable, erratic. Don't bolster her case.

He tried to calm himself, modulate his voice. "Nothing to be concerned about. Janet, do me a favor, will you? If you happen to hear from Lia or Mark while they're en route today, please tell them to come straight to the Corrigans'. Will you do that for me?"

As he'd hoped, the request brought back enough of her hostility to override her suspicion. She agreed curtly.

He reversed the answering machine tape and listened to Lia's voice: "Hi everybody! Paul, if you're hearing this, I tried to reach you at the lodge, but no luck. Everything's gone like clockwork here. I got lucky and finished my errands yesterday, so Mark and I are going to get an early start today. I miss you horribly, and I can't wait to see you and Mark together. Look for us noonish, maybe early afternoon. Dempsey and Elaine, we'll swing by the lodge to see Paul on the way in, I want Mark to see what an amazing job his father has done, and see you later this aft. Bye!"

Empty of thoughts, Paul yanked on his boots and his down jacket, threw open the door. Outside, the air hovered just above freezing. The big winds had plastered wet oak leaves over the MG's red finish, making it look as if it had sat in the driveway for years. Paul wiped the windshield clear, then slid behind the wheel. To his relief, the motor started readily. He let it warm up for a few seconds and pulled out.

The relief lasted only until the first bend of Dempsey's driveway, where the car sputtered and died, rolled to a dead stop. He tried the ignition only twice, not wanting to run down the battery. *Distributor cap,* he thought. The important thing now was not to let things unravel. Moisture must have blown into the engine compartment, condensed in the cap. Easy enough to fix.

Paul jogged back to the house, where he yanked off a wad of paper towels from the roll in the kitchen. He grabbed a screwdriver from the counter on the way out, then ran back to the car. He opened the hood, dried the spark plug wires, and pulled off the cap. It didn't look bad, but you couldn't always tell. He dried it carefully and screwed it on again, then did a routine check of the electrics, blotting up any moisture he found as he went. *Coil wire okay,* he told himself, mentally checking off each part to preserve his sense of control. *Spark plug wires okay. Condenser wire okay. No need to panic. Might not be today. Please, God. Mo's probably up there—he'd have waited, to meet with Vivien, to protect us all. Voltage regulator dry and probably okay. Lia and Mark might not have gotten down yet, maybe they stopped for lunch. Ground wire okay. Mo's a supernatural shooter. Battery terminals okay.*

He finished the check, slid inside and turned the key again. The starter turned the motor listlessly. No combustion.

He resumed his checklist, trying to keep the rising tension in check. *Fuel okay. Too warm for fuel line icing.* Nothing enlightening on the instrument panel. He went back to the trunk, found the tool kit and returned to the engine compartment, where he went down the list of possibilities. Fingers stiffening in the raw air, he fumbled with the screwdriver and dropped a screw in the wet gravel of the drive. *The boot, the bonnet, my ass. The fucking Brits.*

Fuses appeared okay but he replaced them all anyway from the spares he kept in the glove box. He tested the spark at every juncture and found the circuitry intact. When he was done, he got back inside and turned the key. The car refused to start.

He cleaned the breaker points with a piece of emery cloth. When the car wouldn't start for the third time, he realized his fingers were too stiff for any further fine work, and he returned to the house.

It was a quarter past noon. He worked his fingers, trying to get feeling back into them. Trying to think.

He scrawled a note to Lia and tacked it to the front door: *Lia, please come in, call me at the lodge. DO NOT come to Highwood today. I'll explain later.* On the off chance she'd come here first. He wished he hadn't given her a key to the driveway gate.

Then he went out to the garage. The Corrigans had two cars, Dempsey's Buick and a little Toyota, and as he'd expected the big old Buick was still in the garage, gray and solid as a piece of military equipment. He'd look for a key for five minutes, he decided. Then he'd hotwire the car.

He rummaged hurriedly through the interior. No key in the ashtray or over the visor or under the mat. He felt beneath the seat, then got out and checked the garage, looking for pegs or convenient hiding places. No key. He realized he was throwing things, starting to lose control.

He returned to the house and began rummaging in the kitchen: hooks, drawers, cubbies. House keys, padlock keys. Didn't Dempsey use a key ring? Did he take it with him when they left? Where might he keep a spare car key?

He found the cluttered ring on a bureau in the Corrigans' big bedroom, the Buick's long stiletto key prominent. He charged outside again, ran to the garage, remembered, ran back to the MG. *One more little detail.* He unlocked the glove compartment and took out the box containing Ted's .38, which he'd made a point of keeping with him, not wanting it to fall into the hands of some kid visiting the lodge on the sly.

He opened the gun as Lia had shown him, quickly familiarized himself with its features. He released the cylinder and rolled it out to the left, verified that it was empty, then swung it back into place. He practiced sliding the sharply knurled safety button back and forth with his thumb, and pulled the trigger. The gun smelled of oil, the scent of fine machinery. It was heavy and cold to the touch, its plastic grips shaped perfectly to his hand, every feature purposeful and full of deadly logic.

Just a tool, Paul thought. Just a well-made hand tool like so many others he'd mastered. He could make do with it if he had to.

The Buick rumbled to life with a cloud of blue smoke. *Not yet one o'clock. They're probably not there yet. I'll be there in ten minutes. Mo may still be there. They'll be okay.* At the thought of Mo with his alert eyes, his smooth competence, his gun, he felt a wave of gratitude, affection. *When this is all over,* Paul thought, *we'll be friends.*

He clunked the lever into drive and peeled out of the garage only to realize he couldn't get around the MG. The driveway was raised, with a drop on the right side, too narrow for two cars to pass. *The hell with it.* Suddenly he hated the little red car, and without slowing he brought the Buick's bumper up against its back end. The Buick lurched, the MG lunged forward. It was a bad match, and he could see the trunk lid crumple. The MG rolled a few feet and he hit it again, keeping the pressure on as it swung left and right and finally went off the low end of the driveway. It bobbed abruptly down the embankment and stopped hard against a clump of saplings. Their tops thrashed once, and suddenly Paul could see the memory image again, the tortured sapling jerking, the loathsome head on the ground. He spun out of the driveway and floored the car toward the lodge.

The first thing he saw was Mo's Chevy, pulled over to the side of the driveway. The gate was open, and a pair of tire tracks were faintly visible against the rain-wet ground. Mo must have arrived at ten, found the gate locked, walked up. He'd found a way inside, waited for Paul, determined to meet Vivien today. Then Lia and Mark must have come, probably only moments ago, opened the gate, driven up. Paul shifted into low and blew on up the winding drive.

At the top he was surprised to find only the furnace crew's van, pulled up at the far end of the terrace. *Of course.* He'd forgotten that he'd given Becker keys too, forgotten Becker had planned to come by today. Why wasn't he more relieved? He pulled up behind the van and got quickly out of the Buick, bringing the gun box with him, trotted up the steps, fumbled with the key ring on his belt for the smoking room door key. Through the windows he could see the well-ordered room, the stacks of file boxes against the wall. Lia and Mark hadn't arrived, he should be feeling some relief, some calming, but his nerves wouldn't stop screaming. *Akathisia.* He knocked at the door, expecting Mo to open it, but no one came.

He unlocked the door, stepped inside. His first impression was that the room was fully warm; someone had gotten the heater going a good while ago, Mo no doubt. His second was that the smell was wrong, a faint salty-sweet odor that eluded a name until he remembered the most recent time he'd smelled it, only a few days ago. It was when Mo was showing off for Lia, demonstrating the effect of hollow-nose bullets. The smell of gun-powder. And the house was completely quiet, only the faint hiss of the heater drawing air. There should be muffled noises of work in the basement, some conversation. Something was wrong.

Suddenly he felt sick, shaking with anxiety. *Lia. Mark. They could arrive at any moment.* Leaving the door open, he put the box on the table with the photos, quickly took out the gun. *Load the hollow-nose.* As he fumbled six ugly gray bullets into the chambers, he scanned the photos spread out on the table: Vivien and the two children. Royce in some junior-high class photo. Ben looking up from his reading. Aster and Vivien, smiles, summer dresses, martinis. Dempsey and little Paulie and Kay, waving tiny American flags. Vivien standing with a group of unsmiling, impeccably dressed Filipino men.

It was all different now. The past had changed. It had all been ordered around a huge hidden force, all those lives shaped by something they knew nothing about. No one could have imagined what they were dealing with. Except the one, the berserker.

Time to face it, at last. Face into it. Paul swung the .38's cylinder shut and thumbed off the safety.

The door to the main room was slightly ajar. He didn't see Mo until he'd stepped all the way into the cooler air of the big space. The sight caused his abdomen to clench so hard that the breath was forced out of him. Mo had been torn in two at the waist. His upper half, the broad shoulders and chest and arms, lay on its right side, supported by the outflung arms. A few feet away was his lower half, legs looking as if they were running, connected to the abdomen only by a string of tangled guts. The floor was red-black with viscous, thickening blood. There was another smell here, a meat and shit smell. Mo's natty suit had soaked up blood. His head was tilted so that it rested against the floor, his face staring across at his own distant legs, eyes half-lidded, a wistful, innocent face Paul had never seen Mo allow himself.

He stifled the gag reflex, scanned the room. The berserker had obviously come through the kitchen door, which swung open to the woods, and had taken out a three-foot chunk of the door frame between the main room and the dining room. Splinters of oak and chunks of plaster had blown inward, scattering across the broad floor he'd swept clean only two days before. No need to wonder about the fate of Becker and his crew.

His heart had begun to pound so that his body shook with each beat. He could feel sweat start on his skin. He had to get away from the smell of Mo, Mo who had been turned into a pile of butcher's leavings.

There was a trail of sorts, wreckage that marked the wake of violent passage. On the stairs leading to the balcony, several of the newel posts, fourteen inches square of solid oak, had been ripped out of the superstructure of the staircase and lay strewn among the neat piles he'd left. The five-foot posts, each with its pinecone finial, looked like bowling pins, scattered by impact with an impossible force. Banister and balustrades lay splintered, strewn like hay.

There was a crossroads here, he was dimly aware. He could run out of the house, get down the driveway, stop Lia and Mark, get away, call the police. But that wouldn't help. It wouldn't end unless he stayed. *The blood tells.* It was a family matter, wasn't it. Anyway, some part of him had already made a different choice. His feet seemed to lead him, and he silently began to climb the stairs.

He had reached the landing when he first heard the noise, a quiet, rhythmic sound that had been concealed by the drum of his own accelerating heart and the jet-engine hiss of blood in his ears. A sharp, regular sound, almost metallic, echoing in the big room. He turned his head, trying to orient toward the source. It sounded like a saber being slid into and out of its scabbard, but fast, faster than anyone could have drawn a long blade.

Paul turned and squatted on the landing, back to the wall, facing the stairs. From here he could see all of the balcony and most of the downstairs floor, with only the side of the room directly below him out of view. If lead time were what he wanted, there was no better vantage point. Below him and across the room, the wreckage of Mo lay in its blackening pool of blood.

The *shicka-shicka-shicka* grew louder, then faded, then began to swell again. He remembered it now: from the memory, the incident in the woods, thirty years ago. *Shicka-shicka-shicka.* Filing, sawing, a blade in and out of its sheath. Abruptly he knew what it was. Stropes had shown him. Of course: To sustain the hyperkinetic-hyperdynamic state, the aerobic metabolism needed its basic fuel, oxygen. The berserker needed to gulp air like a ramjet engine. The noise was the shriek of air in its throat, the sound of its frenzied breathing.

The thought brought back an image of Hyper Jack convulsing on Stropes's computer screen, and listening to the sound, visualizing the processes required, suddenly made Paul sick. The berserker was no longer human, no longer even animal. It was more of a machine, an engine driven by a sustained biochemical explosion, ruthless, mindless, unstoppable.

A rending crash came from the area of the library downstairs, cutting through the aural fog he was in, causing the floor to pulse. Afterward he couldn't seem to hear the berserker's breathing for a moment. He shook his head, straining to hear. His ears seemed stuffed with cotton, deafened by the roar of his own bloodstream.

He crouched, clenching the gun in front of him in his right hand, steadying his wrist with the other hand as he'd seen Mo do. He was startled when a new sound penetrated his deafness: a creaking screech, small but intense, like some insect. As he waited, listening, it came again, tiny, a grating squeal. Nearby.

Suddenly he realized what the noise was. Of course. Every piece fit perfectly, as if inevitable, as if preordained.

Downstairs the berserker was making crashing noises again, shaking the house, but Paul ignored it. He was staring in fascination at the gun in his right hand. The gun was the source of the new noise. As he watched, it creaked again. It was the force of his hand on the plastic grips. They were moving minutely against the steel, under enormous pressure. *Amazing.* In his hand, the gun was deforming slightly, screaming like a suffering thing. *Oh, yes, the blood tells. Every time.*

The house shook again and suddenly a shotgun blast of debris sprayed into the big room, followed by a cloud of plaster dust. The berserker had burst through the wall of the library, out of view beneath the near end of the balcony.

His conscious thoughts were small and fleeting, birds tossed and scattering in a rising internal whirlwind. He held against the state, part of him wanting it, yearning for the release, but at the same time afraid of how deep it might go. He had to stay conscious, deliberate, intentional, if there was any chance he could keep Lia and Mark alive. With the state fully on him, would he know them? Would he be able to stop the juggernaut inside him? *The soldiers in the Army Intelligence experiments had disemboweled each other.*

He could just do it, he realized, he could just hold himself in. And the only reason was that he'd had thirty years of practice. *In a way it's just another tic, a huge big seductive all-consuming rabid killer-whale big-bang of a tic. I can keep it down for a while. Thank you, Ben, curse you, you never could have guessed how your most difficult lesson has affected my life.* A lifetime of holding back.

The berserker state would be there if he relaxed his guard, if he got pushed too far. He'd be fighting on two fronts, the war with the creature in his head and the war with the monster loose in the house. Which was more dangerous? For a moment his control wavered and he felt a wave of hate for both of them. Abruptly the gun's grip deformed in his hand like clay. He loosened his fingers and set the .38 carefully down on the floor.

He got control again, stood up, and stepped toward the stairs. *Come on. Try me, try to take me apart. Only this time you'll be up against one of your own kind. Up against another berserker.* Another thought occurred to him. For only for an instant he was surprised at it, and then knew it with certainty: *Which is exactly what you've wanted all along.*

67

The berserker came out from under the balcony and into the room, just a blur, leaving a trail of bare footprints in the powdering of plaster dust. Things scattered from its line of motion, ricocheting away from the wild feet. Its skin was dusted white, streaks of brilliant pink showing where sweat had run and washed it clean again. Its clothes were ragged, torn away by its exertions. It slowed as it came into the center of the big space, looking around with a face like a grimacing demon mask. Dancing in place, pulsating with its breathing, it turned, as if searching for something. *For me,* Paul knew.

Stropes forgot about one characteristic of the HHK/HHD state, he realized. *The heat.* Even this far away, he could feel the radiant glow the berserker gave off, like an out of control woodstove. *A by-product of all that glucose oxidation, all that metabolic activity: body heat.* His conscious thoughts floated on the surface of the chaos inside him, like a thin crust of ice over turbulent water.

"Here I am," he said. It came out hugely loud, a single explosive exhalation. The berserker spun to face him, *clicked* to face him, no visible intervening motion. "Here I am, Vivien. What now?"

Her exertion-contorted face drew back in a grin that stretched her face until Paul was sure the skin would rip. Her big, half-naked body was in constant motion: chest convulsing with breath, spine rippling, limbs moving, as if she were full of separate struggling living things, snakes under the skin.

For a moment, with all the control he could manage, he held back the bursting energies inside him. Then a spike of fear came, his thoughts stuttered, and the tiny conscious part of him recognized the seizures, the HHK/HHD seizures, sending voltages into his hypothalamus. He tried to fight it, but his control slipped and without thought he was running across the room toward her. She didn't move until the last second, and then she was gone from his view. Something hit his back and he accelerated, rocketing headfirst into the far wall. The painted surface loomed in his vision and exploded and then he was through the wall, lying with half his body in the dark of one of the downstairs closets, tangled in broken lathe and chunks of plaster. He shook off the encumbering debris and stood up. The wall seemed to have the texture of a reed mat, palpable but eerily insubstantial.

He turned. The berserker was back in the middle of the room, full of motion, grotesque, the embodiment of everything fearful. Just as terrifying was the presence he sensed in his body, in his skull: He could feel *it* in there, as if a cobra reared erect, ready to strike, its swollen hood arched taut over his brain. Hate and terror overwhelmed him, and he rushed at her once more. This time he found himself pivoted onto his back, driven into the floor by a blow he hadn't even seen. The room shook. He disengaged his shoulders from the broken floorboards and stood again.

Vivien's blood-gorged eyes seemed to snap like a camera shutter, seeing all of him instantly and utterly, assessing his metabolic state in a microsecond. As if she'd seen his internal resistance, a ghost of disappointment passed quickly across her face, replaced instantly by rage. The heaving of her chest accelerated, her breathing shrieked, and she was moving toward him. He leapt sideways, but one of her flailing arms caught him in the cheek and lashed his head backward. His whole body spun and he lost balance again, smashing face first into the oak plank stairs. The sudden pain, even through the haze of endorphins, affronted him, stirred his rising fear.

Without thinking he grabbed one of the fallen newel posts and thrust it at her, a hundred pounds of solid oak, oddly weightless in his hands. She batted it away, hit him with the side of her arm and the room blurred and exploded.

Paul sat up out of the plaster dust, scrambled on all fours along the wall. He had just tasted it that time, the edge of complete release. It was bottomless, a rage that knew no limits. He had to avoid it at all costs.

Vivien had gone to Mo's body and was brutalizing it, screaming in frustration and shaking the torso so that it came to pieces in her hands. She threw it down, then turned to Paul and rushed at him again, scything the air with her arms and legs with the noise of a sword being swung.

He grabbed another newel post, pitched it at her. She swatted at it and it burst into splinters around her. Then a blur came toward him and though he ducked he was far too slow and the room tumbled as his body cartwheeled into the wall. Vivien followed through, coming against him with her whole body and for an instant he felt it iron-hard and burning hot against him, the one solid thing in the dreamlike insubstantiality of the house. Her breath stank, a sharp chemical smell as the flood of epinephrine and other arousal chemicals in her bloodstream outgassed. Abruptly she pivoted and then it seemed as if the house fell on him. Great weight, brutal impact, the chaos of noise and motion and pain suddenly fading, going distant. The world contracted to a pinpoint of light surrounded by blackness.

And then roared back. He struggled up from the verge of unconsciousness to find himself lying against the great hearth. Reflexively he jerked upright to see Vivien, her whole body throbbing like a tortured heart, watching him from a dozen feet away. His legs gave way and he fell to the floor again, tried to rise, fell, waited.

Vivien's breathing slowed markedly, and the sight paradoxically terrified him. Her sentient self struggled briefly for control, face contorting with the effort as for an instant the machine resisted, then became by degrees at least a parody of his aunt. For the first time, Paul realized what he was up against: *She'd had thirty years of practice commanding her neurological state too.* The true berserker, learning her own triggers, willing the state to come on, learning over the years to kindle and to quench it, coming to know its preposterous freedoms.

Her first words came out in staccato bursts, then slowed as her metabolism calmed. "I won't let you off the hook that easily," she rasped. "Because you've made such a promising start. That would have killed anyone else, you know. But it's only a start. Wake up, Paulie! Do you know how long I have wanted to dance with an equal? With one who knew this, who had any idea of this power and ecstasy? You will dance with me, or I'll kill you. I won't be denied!"

"Why?" he croaked. Meaning all of it.

She spat like a cat, disgusted with him. "The question *why* is not your basic impulse. That's a *mental* question, the lightest froth on a much deeper sea. The real you, the whole you, doesn't want to *know* anything. You are full of anger and fear and hate. When you ask *why,* in a way you're lying, aren't you? An old self-deceiving habit. Base your actions on your real urges, Paulie, then you'll have some power. Power to affect things, to affect the outcome. And isn't that what you really want? Really, what you want is to hurt me, isn't it? Take me apart, kill me?"

When he couldn't answer, her mouth drew into a taunting sneer. "You're soft, nephew, you're *flaccid,* you're nowhere near it yet. You're still in your straitjacket!" She was goading him, he realized. Groping for his triggers. Trying to get him to join her, her endless desperate search for companionship. *Dance with me.*

"This is what you did with my father." He'd spoken the words before he was aware of the realization. "You were there with him at Break Neck."

Vivien's face writhed, sorrow wrestling with her manic excitement. "You are a very perceptive boy, aren't you?"

"You killed him."

She spun away. "I *loved* your father. I tried to *awaken* Ben, Paulie. I tried to give him *life.* I had told him about this, I believed it was what he wanted, what he of all people could have the hunger for."

"So you threw him over."

"He wasn't coming around. I thought if his life was really at peril we could share . . . this." Vivien seemed to falter slightly. "This was before I knew about the hereditary factors. I thought everyone could . . . awaken. But now I know better."

There had to be a way to stop her. If she could try to control his neuro-chemistry, arouse him, maybe he could do the same for her: awaken her conscious mind, damp the berserker reflex. Keep her talking, keep her thinking. She was highly intelligent—that part of her had to have some power too. Maybe there was a chink in the berserker's armor. He was twenty-five years younger, heavier, more muscular—surely if he were to fight her in a normal state he could overwhelm her. He'd have to take her by surprise, incapacitate her immediately, before the reflex kicked in. The first step was to keep her talking, reasoning.

"You're full of shit," he said. "That's what you've been telling yourself, but it's a lie. You went up there and Ben told you it was over between you two, didn't he? And that's when you conveniently thought to test him. How handy for you. And you've been lying to yourself ever since."

For an instant her face registered agony, but then the anger and pride reasserted itself. "You have no idea what it is like to be a singularity! To be the only one of your kind in a world of sleepwalkers, anesthetized by their reasoning minds. Shitting little hamsters in their wire cages. A world of *ghosts,* no more substantial than a cloud of gnats!" Her arrogance returned. *Good,* Paul thought. Another step toward her humanity. Toward her vulnerability.

"Do you know how I know you're lying to yourself? Because you tried the same thing with your gardener, with Falcone, two years before you killed Ben. Because I saw you that day, in the woods. I tripped on his fuck-ing *head* while you were busy turning him into pork chops."

She looked at him in astonishment. "Oh, my fabulous nephew. I often wondered whether you had seen—you were so traumatized by your walk in the woods. And you've never spoken about it? Yes, the raging bull came back to harangue me, to threaten me, after his stay in prison. Such a beau-tiful body. Such a good lover the first times, before his Catholic guilt caught up with him. Yes, I became very angry with him. Very." She grimaced, as if her face could not decide whether to frown or smile. "Yes, I killed my lover! Yes, I felt entitled to love and affection and sex, as deserving as my mouse of a sister."

Keep her talking, Paul thought, standing slowly upright. *Quench the re-flex.* "So by the time you went up there with Ben, you knew from firsthand experience that not everyone could do it—just a threat wouldn't awaken it in everybody. A rare combination of neurological and anatomical characteristics. One in a million. You had to know. You killed my father because he rejected you, you were angry, you lost control." *Where were Mark and Lia?* "You killed your lover like a black widow spider."

Her face twitched again, and he realized he'd made a mistake. *Her triggers.* Her chest started pumping again. She moaned, a keen of grief. "Don't you see? I had no choice! I would have lost Ben whether he went down that mountain still a sleepwalker, going back to his wife, or fell and died! Oh, Ben!" Her jaw dropped, mouth opening wide as a soul-deep anguish stretched her whole face. "There's a place in all of us," she panted, "where no one dares to go. Where it is too dangerous to go because there's a storm compressed inside it. *I go there,* Paulie. I *live* there! Yes, I went to Break Neck that day with your father. Yes, I regretted it, yes I hated the loneliness after I lost Ben. For years afterward I tried not to need so much, tried not indulge the hunger. That's how much I loved him. But who hasn't felt what I felt when rejected by a lover? Shall I be blamed because I have a unique capacity to act upon feelings *every* human being feels?"

She quelled her rising agitation, and a cunning light came into her eyes. "Yes, I killed your father. I betrayed your mother by seducing him. I killed your friend the detective. I'm going to kill you. Surely you're entitled to hate me for all that. Now, don't I deserve to die? Don't you want to kill me?"

Yes, he thought, that's there. A hard, dense thing in him, like a piece of plutonium, a bomb, waiting, close to critical mass. And yet he couldn't let it. *She's trying for my triggers, looking for the thing that will set me off.*

"And what else?" Vivien was saying. "Look at yourself. Neurological problems all your life, not just one but two different conditions. Money problems. A son crippled by a neurological disorder he inherited from you. An angry ex-wife who is scheming to get him away from you. Don't you wish you could strike out, vent the anger and frustration?" She held his head between her hands, bathing him in her chemical breath. "What about all that wasted potential, Paulie? Such a bright child, such a fizzled adulthood. Look at you: You're thirty-eight, you've got a fine mind, a master's degree, and yet you were overjoyed to get a couple of weeks of manual labor, picking up my house! Doesn't that make you angry?" She watched him closely, calmer, searching for the effects of her goading. "Can't you feel it in you?" she asked, knowing he could.

With all his strength he struck at her. Before his fist connected the air hissed into her lungs, she had his arm and was swinging him, flinging him across the room and out into the middle of the floor. Her mouth made a popping sound like an engine kicking over, cheeks puffing out and slapping against her teeth as her lungs pumped explosively. And he knew that he'd failed. *The state was upon her instantly.* Before he could recover, she was on him again, tumbling him over and over, toward the far corner of the room. When she came at him again he resisted briefly before being thrown through the wall, on into Royce's bedroom. The impact dizzied him. As he tried to get up, his legs failed him, and he sat down on the floor again. Vivien loomed over him, clutched his head against her shuddering iron-hard stomach, and as she squeezed he heard the bones shift in his skull.

Only one way to survive. He opened himself wide to the reflex, willed it upon himself, felt the snake rise, the hood of the cobra spreading in his brain, its body stiffening in his spinal cord. His breathing accelerated again, tiny stutters of seizure rippled his thoughts, and the anger loosened in him, the desire to lash out, to strike at her face, to shake loose of her controlling grip. *His own controlling grip.* He swung his arms up and managed to bat her hands loose, then got his legs under him and drove his shoulder into her stomach.

She fell away from him, but within an instant came back, impossibly fast. Paul felt himself driven backward through the wall, into the big room again, saw the pieces of wall float slowly away. Already she was hunched over him, starting to shake his shoulders, and in desperation he gave himself to the hatred of her, the fear.

And it wasn't enough. It wasn't there. It wouldn't come. The voice of his conscious mind, though shrill and small, wouldn't cease. He couldn't let go all the way, couldn't match her. Her grip crushed the bones of his shoulders and pain shrieked in his nerves and his prying and flailing hands did nothing to stop her. She was killing him.

Abruptly she tossed him aside and walked away, spat, disgusted. Again her motions slowed as she mastered her neurochemistry.

"That's it? That's all your self-preservation instincts are good for?" She screamed with frustration, swiped at the wall and with one clawed hand carved out a gash, spewing splinters across the room. She grabbed the flesh of her own face and tortured it, pulling her cheeks, shrieking. Then she regulated herself further, breathing subsiding again, motions slowing. She leaned back against the wall, facing him.

"You really aren't going to, are you?" A hollow voice, sepulchral. "Such a disappointment. Such a deep disappointment. You, my last, best hope."

It took him a moment to find his voice. "You knew I had inherited the capacity."

She indulged him. "Not when you were a child. Later I learned it's hereditary, deduced that if I had the gene, your mother probably carried it too. With your early neurological history, with what I heard from Kay about Mark, I knew to a virtual certainty. And you . . . showed potential . . . when you dealt with that pathetic mugger in San Francisco." Her voice took on a weary tone, the familiar weltschmerz. "But of course there are degrees. And varying levels of superego suppression—you appear to be a true champion at that. So much like your father. I should have known."

Paul's thoughts scurried. *One other possibility: the gun. Vivien didn't know about the gun. If he could get to the top of the stairs, if he could keep her in this quiescent state for a few minutes—*

"I'm sorry I've disappointed you," he said. "So what now?" He stood up painfully, started to move away from her. A patch of sun slanting through the windows fell on the separate parts that had been Mo Ford.

"I'll have to kill you, of course. Can't have loose ends." Bottomless weariness and disappointment.

Paul took another step, limping, trying to appear vanquished, without hope. "Is that why you killed the teenagers? I take it the furnace men were 'loose ends' too?"

"There it is again: *Why?* How could you understand, Paulie, until you have had the *experience?* You couldn't possibly."

"Was it cathartic for you? Killing people who had done nothing to you?"

"I take it that's why your friend the detective was here?" Vivien stopped and turned to face him, and Paul stopped too, not willing to get too close to her or reveal his destination. "Yes, the hapless furnace men are dead, down in the basement. Let us say that they were a sort of collateral damage. The first two children were collateral damage too. I had come back and they were here, invading my house, indulging themselves, showing a complete want of respect. The big boy I chased down the road at midnight, letting him get far enough away and then catching him. Wouldn't do to have suspicious occurrences here at the house."

"What about the girl he was with?" Another apparently aimless step.

Vivien snorted. "In the woods between here and the road. She ended up spread out over rather a large area. I rather resented her taking physical pleasure in my fortress of loneliness." Her breathing quickened slightly. "And yes, there were others. Two teenaged boys, who felt they could come into my house, break my things. One young woman and her boyfriend, whom I ran through the woods for several miles for the pleasure of it. I left the girl's remains on the train tracks—a convenient explanation of her condition." Despite her contempt for reasons, justifications, she seemed to enjoy confessing it all to him. Revelation, self-exposure, a desperate simulacrum of closeness.

"You see," she went on, confidingly, "for a long time I held back. After Ben, I swore never again. But I was not always successful. There were times when memory came back too forcibly, when my prison grew too confining, and I would dance alone in this house, or outside, in the garden or the woods. Isolated incidents—I could have the house repaired. Later, it seemed to me I had restrained myself long enough. What does your generation say? 'Let it all hang out.' I did. I'm much more complete now, Paulie. As I told you, I have found some pleasures to sustain me."

Vivien's eyes flashed. "For a time the house alone was enough. But after my first visit back, after the first boy and girl, just accidents, I found that there were . . . rewards in exacting some punishment from others. Oh, God, yes, I loved dismantling them, the ultimate shattering of every taboo, the sense of *freedom,* Paulie, the raw *intimacy* of it, the sheer undeniable *reality* of it. And yes they deserved it, *someone* did!" Her voice had risen to a joyful certainty, but fell back into the dry, bitter tone Paul knew so well. "But even that became insufficient. After the third time it all became . . . unreal. That's when I decided to seek you out. Which plan almost succeeded but not quite. Ben trained you too well. Dear *bastard* Ben!"

Two steps, as if off balance. "But you had other relatives—I'm not the only one. What about Freda? What about your sons?" Too late, Paul realized that he'd made a mistake. The memory kindled the blaze in her eyes again. Vivien's head twitched on her neck, tiny seizure tremors, and the bellows of her lungs picked up their tempo.

"Oh, yes, my other relatives. My mother, unaware of the trait that ran in my father's genes. I assure you it was unintentional. Those were hard years, Paulie! She was my *mother.* I *loved* her. But one day, I was crying my heart out to her. My husband had left me, I was beginning to realize he was never coming back. And I knew my sons were lost to me. And as I wept and as my old mother comforted me, I felt it for the first time, rising in me. And when I . . . came out of the state, I was bathed in her blood! Can you even imagine the horror and the remorse? I doubt it."

Vivien was kindling again, gesturing, pacing in a big circle in the room. He saw it now: *Everything triggered her.* There was no part of her mind or memory free of grief and pain and loneliness and rage, no corner of the world that didn't remind her. Her voice was rising, coming in shorter and shorter bursts as her breathing accelerated, and Paul slid another step toward the stairs. He was halfway across the room now. Once he got to the bottom of the stairs he'd need maybe four seconds to get to the top. Pick up the gun, turn, aim, two more seconds.

Only six seconds. But if she saw him start to move too soon, he'd never make it.

"And Royce. Royce whom I loved with every young mother's simplicity. Royce whose fervid little brain was so very precocious, who blamed me for his father's leaving, for my keeping him here *because* I loved him, who could never forgive me for that. And who from a very early age was determined to kill his brother." The thought made her turn quickly toward Paul, eyes searching his face. "You know about that don't you? About Erik, Erik III?"

"I found some papers," he muttered.

"Royce hated him. Poor Erik was a sweet boy, my darling firstborn son." The tone in her voice told him: "You were lovers. You and your son."

"Does that offend you? But why not, Paulie? Erik was the only one who could do this dance with me. He was *real*. And who else would have had him, given what he was? He loved me in return."

"So you imprisoned him—"

"I *sheltered* him! I couldn't just farm him out to some anonymous *home* where they couldn't understand what was inside him, where they'd try to drug and shock it out of him. Even though he was a child, a slow child at that, we . . . understood each other!"

"Then why send him away? You had a perfect arrangement. His cell, right next to your bedroom."

"Oh, but there was Royce! And Royce was a jealous little boy, jealous of my . . . affection for his brother. And he'd figured out how his father's estate would work. I had to protect Erik. I had to send him away after all. It was a sacrifice I had to make if Erik were to live."

"How could Royce have hurt him?"

"I wasn't worried about hand-to-hand combat, Paulie," she said witheringly. "Royce liked things like razor-blade chips, remember? Once, Paulie, sweet innocent stupid Paulie, once I came home from a walk to find that Royce had run a garden hose from the car exhaust to the ventilator for Erik's room. If I'd been gone for five more minutes. . . . So then I sent Erik away, and then I moved him again and again—" Her voice rose in a grieving howl.

"So why didn't you turn Royce in? For killing him?"

Vivien swayed in the grip of an ecstatic grief. "If only it were that simple! *Because Royce didn't kill him.* You see, Erik did escape. With my help. And he did come here. And maybe he was still drugged, or they'd suppressed him so long he no longer had the reflex. But in my pleasure and excitement at having him again, I—he fell to pieces in my *hands*, Paulie, he came *apart* and there was nothing I could do." She held out her hands, left and right, a gesture of astonished helplessness. Then she looked at him, a gruesome coquettish glance. "Does that appall you? It appalls me too."

Paul felt sickened at the thought of it, the things she'd witnessed, the things she'd done. The things that welled up from inside her. "And your killing him gave Royce the opening he needed. Ownership of the trust went to him, the waiting period for Erik's death began. And five years later, you got a letter from the attorneys, this June twenty-first or twenty-second, that legal declaration of death was complete. And that's what triggered you—that's when it got too much for you. When you couldn't contain it anymore."

"You're very shrewd."

"Tell me how it worked. I mean the cycles. Every forty-four days."

"You are so perceptive! The longing, it *grows* on you, Paulie. You cannot know the need for release, or the pleasures of that release. At some point I recognized my own rhythm—yes, forty-four days, give or take a few days, I could hold it back for a time if necessary. It is easy enough to anticipate."

The true berserker, knowing her own patterns, her triggers. Becoming a connoisseur of her own catharsis. An artist of carnage. Conditioned to want the endorphin flood too, the opiate high. She knew she'd need it, and when. She knew the house was the best triggering environment, the place where all the grief and loss and hate awakened. She'd take a flight from San Francisco when she felt it coming near, wait like a spider in her darkened house for the sacrificial trespassers to come, to provide her that pleasure. Until even that became unreal. And when she began to realize that killing innocents was no longer sufficient, she knew that only doing the hyper-kinetic, hyperdynamic dance with another berserker would be real enough, deep enough. And then she telephoned Kay, succeeded in snaring Paul.

Vivien had begun to vibrate again, triggered by the memories.

"But what I don't understand," he said quickly, "is *why*. Why would you do this to yourself? Why would you wreck your own house?"

Vivien's face had taken on the look of a wrathful mask, a mix of rage and sorrow. "You really don't understand, do you? What a naive, fortunate little man you are! I had been happily married. I had two sons. I had a house, a *life*. And then it was all taken away! Everyone I loved. And here I lived, a prisoner in this house, unable to go away from it. *Solitary confinement*, Paulie. *Forty-five years of solitary confinement will do that to a person.* Don't you see? This is a prison!" She gestured in a circle at the ravaged house. "*This is a prison!* It's a cage of grief and loss and sorrow and betrayal! *This*"—she struck her temples with two hands, struck herself in the chest—"*this* is a prison!"

She had turned again, facing toward the far end of the room, beginning her acceleration to full-blown HHK/HHD. She didn't seem to notice the momentary change in the light of the room. Paul was puzzled by it briefly until he realized what the dull flash had been: A car had come into the circular driveway, passing the tall front windows and reflecting sunlight up into the raftered heights of the ceiling.

Lia and Mark had arrived.

68

He felt the panic start to shake him, took several steps toward the stairs. He was only a dozen feet away now. If he could make it to the bottom, if she would just turn away from him one more time, it was possible. It had all come together, the whole ghastly pattern clear at last. The only problem remaining now was how to survive.

From outside came the muffled chunk of a car door, then another. They had gotten out of the car. Paul saw the flick of Vivien's eyes as she noticed it, and he realized he was out of time.

He bounded for the stairs and made it to the landing when Vivien hit him from behind, buckling his legs and sending him smashing against the oak wainscoting of the wall. He spun and struck at her and was surprised to connect with her cheek, actually turning her head. In that instant he broke free of her and lunged up the second flight of stairs. He caught the gun in one hand before she grabbed him from behind and dragged him back down.

She swung him through the banister and out into the air of the room. Balustrades and lengths of banister flew like straw in a tornado, and then he was bouncing and rolling on the main floor. The gun was gone from his grip, lost. His conscious thoughts were minute, a tinny, small voice in the deep bass rumble of his own metabolism, of the chemical and neurological detonation in him.

Vivien began to descend the stairs, back straight, regal, chest pumping, on her face an expression of disappointment beyond words. She was coming to execute him.

And then Lia and Mark were coming in from the dining room doorway.

"Paul? Are you here?" Lia called, her voice a strange drawl. Her movements were eerily slow, graceful but ponderous. Paul realized that his metabolic rate was vastly greater than hers, everything but Vivien existed in a separate, much slower time scheme. In slow motion Lia turned and saw him across the room. A look of startled concern began to cross her face. She was wearing blue jeans and her rubber-bottomed L.L. Bean boots, and her hair was tied up and off to one side with a red scarf and she was very beautiful. And Mark was holding her hand, looking uncertain. A pale child, watchful, intelligent, an array of complex feelings in his eyes as he saw the ragged, dust-covered creature that was his father. A beautiful child. The whole scene was eerily gorgeous, somehow backlit, as perfect and luminous as a stained-glass window.

Above them, Vivien smiled. She had realized who Lia and Mark were. What potentials lay therein.

He realized it just as she did: *the ultimate trigger.*

And then thought vanished. The dam that had held every yearning and hunger and anger bulged and broke and the dark ecstasy came over him, the unmixed, uncompromised purity of being just one thing, one impulse and sensation and intention, unconflicted, unrestrained.

Vivien was coming down the stairs toward them. A noise like a waterfall filled Paul's head. He found himself in motion, Lia and Mark moving glacially, still staring at where he had been. He passed them and collided with Vivien just as she came off the stairs onto the floor.

They rebounded from each other, and then she was moving again, not toward Paul but toward Lia and Mark. Her flailing body would cut them to pieces like a wood chipper. They had only partially turned, faces beginning to take on expressions of alarm and confusion. Paul reached Vivien, hitting her with his whole body, knocking her against and through the great main door. He followed her through the ragged opening as splinters of oak and broken hinges and shards of glass flew slowly out and drifted toward the ground. When he burst into the sunlight, she was already upright again, charging back toward Mark and Lia. Her red eyes glowed, a smile gripped her face.

Paul's legs felt like coiled springs. He could feel the muscles in his chest and shoulders, a glorious strength, as if he were made of living steel. Euphoria spread through him, a glowing warmth that seemed to expand outward from his arteries into every muscle and even his bones. The endorphins, natural opiates, like an injection of morphine. Better, more ecstatic by far, a single white fire of purpose burned in him, obliterating everything else, burning him clean. Simplicity. Unity. *To be one thing, one urge.* A white electric fire burned in every nerve and brain cell.

As she'd wanted. The dance she'd wanted to share for so long.

Then he plowed into her again and they grappled on the terrace, turning as if in a frenzied tango. He felt her body hard against his, the only solid thing in a ghostly world, resisting him, her pelvis moving urgently against his. They spun into the marble balustrade, which gave way and toppled slowly into the driveway, and the unreality of it struck him with a killing fear: *The world is insubstantial as mist and you, my enemy, are the only real thing.* Then the neurochemical avalanche obliterated all feeling.

He pivoted her and flung her into the driveway. She landed on her feet on the gravel. As she charged him again, her eyes never left his, knowing him, seeing the state blossom fully in him, and he caught a glimpse of the pretty young woman in the photographs. A blood-red look of deep communion, the bride lifting her veil at the altar, lustrous with desire and gratitude. A state of cruel grace.

For a moment a shred of conscious thought kept him back from the forbidden thing that had to happen, that she so wanted, and then he was holding her again, caressing her and feeling her bones start to break, and he took her body apart as if it were a scarecrow, just wet straw and brittle twigs and rags. He opened her. Reverent, grateful, hating her, he reached into her and let her out of the prison that had contained her.

The world began to gain density. The driveway began to feel solid beneath him, the pull of gravity began to be perceptible again. He looked at his bare red arms, the steam rising from the spray of gore that had been Vivien.

The dead leaves in the oak trees began slowly to move, to accelerate their vibration in a slight breeze as his metabolism slowed toward normal. Momentarily dizzy, he closed his eyes, and despite the nauseating smell of blood felt the paradoxical joy still in him. The afterglow of the unity, the euphoria caused by the endorphins coursing in his veins.

When he opened his eyes again he caught a movement inside the gaping hole in the shingle wall.

"Lia?" he called. His voice came out a hoarse bark. He tried it again. "Lia? Please take Mark into the kitchen. Call the police from the kitchen phone."

There was no answer. He went up the terrace stairs and peered into the big room. Lia and Mark weren't in view. The house was a shambles once more, destroyed by his battle with Vivien, and the tension began to rise in him again. The last few minutes of the fight were hazy in his memory, incomplete. Maybe they'd been hurt, maybe he'd—

And then he found them in the kitchen.

Lia stood at the far end of the room, holding Mark's face to her chest with one hand, the .38 held levelly at Paul's face as he came through the door. The outside door batted open and shut in the wind. Mark's shoulders were shaking and his arms clung tightly to Lia's waist.

"We've got to call the police," he said. Relief poured over him at the sight of them.

"I already did," Lia said.

"You're both okay?" He started toward them, wanting to embrace them, comfort them, enfold them.

"Stop," Lia said. It came out quietly but with tremendous force. "Don't come any closer." She took a step backward. Her eyes were diamond bright, piercing, her alertness at laser intensity.

"Lia, it's me, Paul!"

"I don't know who it is. I don't think *you* know who you are. Stay back from us."

Paul wished that Mark would turn to face him, then realized that with Vivien's blood soaking him, his eyes no doubt still engorged with blood, his clothes just rags, he wasn't a sight Mark should see. He'd seen far too much already. The overwhelming desire to comfort Mark, to shelter and embrace him, had no possible outlet. Pain lanced through the euphoric haze, and Paul thought: *This is how it feels to become human again.*

"Okay." A weariness began to come over him. "She killed Mo. She tried to kill me. She would have killed you both, all of us. I entered a special kind of accelerated metabolic state. It's hereditary, Vivien had it too." He took a step toward her, entreating her understanding.

"Get back, Paul!" Lia barked.

He did as she ordered. "It comes on in response to anger or fear or protective concern. She tried to provoke it in me, but I couldn't get into it until I had to protect you two. You're right not to trust me after . . . that. But it was self-defense. And it's over now."

Lia's gun hand didn't waver.

Paul found a rag of curtain and began wiping his arms and hands, which were becoming sticky. Who would ever understand? How could he ever explain, even to Lia? No one would believe. The police would think he was insane. And the endorphins were starting to fade, slipping just a little. Behind the euphoria he glimpsed the abyss, the vast dark emptiness that Vivien had lived in: how nothing would seem real enough again. How no experience could match that clarity and power, how he'd hunger for it. How he'd long for another human to share the knowledge of it, the fusion.

Looking at Mark sobbing against Lia, he wondered if he'd ever regain the trust and closeness of his son. His breath caught in his throat as the abyss threatened to swallow him. The horror overtook him, images replaying in his mind's eye—Vivien's face crumpling as he reached into her skull. *How could you live, knowing that was inside you?*

Then he pulled away from the brink. Lia's fine jaw was set, but there was something in her face, vaguely familiar. It brought a rush of feeling to him, warmth, liquid softness.

"God, you're gorgeous," he told her. "I know it's an inappropriate moment for endearments, but I swear you're the most beautiful sight I've ever seen."

"Just stay back until the police come, Paul," she said. There was no give in her voice, but some nuance was slightly different.

Of course, Paul thought. *She thinks I'm dangerous.* Maybe it was just the residual opiates in his bloodstream, but the thought pleased him greatly. *I really* am *dangerous.* Any concern on that score could be safely discounted, the old nagging doubt banished. He almost laughed at the understatement of the thought. Very very definitely, no more wet-blanket, reliable, *safe* Paul.

He looked at her, feeling an enormous affection for her. *Lia is truly hopeless.* That's what was in her face, that indomitable curiosity of hers, that crazy attraction to danger and its attendant revelations. The moth to the flame. She'd come around. The more he thought about it, the more it seemed inevitable.

"You knew this was going to happen," she said. "You knew and didn't tell me."

"Not until this morning. Not for sure." Paul almost smiled. Already, the argument had become an intimate one, about his violation of their trust, their candor with each other. Not about his status as a monster.

He was the luckiest man alive. Provided the police would ever let him go. In the distance, as if in response to the thought, the first faint sirens came into hearing. The first of what would no doubt be many, many sirens today. They were coming to a slaughterhouse the likes of which nobody had ever seen.

Yes, Lia would eventually come around. But what about Mark? He'd be traumatized, in shock. How could he forget what he'd seen? How could he understand anything Paul told him about it? How could he ever again trust his father as a source of comfort, of protection, when he'd seen what Paul did to Vivien in the driveway, when he'd glimpsed the hidden thing that lived in Paul?

It might take a while—years, probably. But Mark would understand when he came of age, when he began to know the origin of his own neurological problems, the predilection he'd inherited. When he began to realize that the same thing lived in him too, and that Paul was the one person in the world who could ever really understand.

Even as the first cars braked hard and scattered gravel in the driveway, he still felt waves of irrational optimism. There'd be a lot of explaining to do for a long time, but eventually things would work out. And Lia was giving him a look, as if she were beginning to see it for what it was.

He was one lucky son of a bitch.

Her gun had lowered, barrel pointing obliquely away from him: They'd made progress already.

69

Paul sat in the chair next to his bed, impatient for the visitors to come. A tic came with the anticipation—his hands flicked up and touched his eyebrows and moustache—which he observed with a certain affection. Old Faithful. The windowless room was plain, tile-walled, without even the pretense of aesthetic concern that ordinary hospitals showed—not even the usual noncommital pastel prints on the wall, the plastic ferns hanging from the ceiling in macramé slings. Oh well, he thought. What could you expect from a state-run psychiatric detention facility? At least the handcuffs and leg irons were gone.

It was the third day after, or maybe the fourth. He couldn't be sure: For a long time he hadn't been able to think past the incredible pain that had racked his body, the combination of exhaustion and muscle strain and bruises and going cold-turkey off the best chemical fix the world had ever known. And all the time he'd had somebody in his face, questioning him, threatening, cajoling, bargaining, trying to snare him in his own contradictions, all the clumsy and transparent ploys of interrogation. He told them what he knew. Fortunately, there was nothing to hide, no contradictions for anyone to exploit. *Only ambiguities—and good luck with those, boys.*

His heart skipped as keys turned in the lock and a policeman swung open the door. Surprisingly, it wasn't Lia who entered.

"Royce," Paul croaked.

Royce took off his coat and tossed it on a chair. "I'm happy to see you too, Paulie." He was dressed perfectly, as always, but seemed different, a look of worry or weariness on his broad face. *Wounded,* Paul decided. "They said relatives only, and I told them I was your dear cousin, very close. Sorry to disappoint you."

"You've been to Highwood?"

"In a manner of speaking. The driveway's cordoned off. But I got the general drift, found out where you were." Royce's face twitched almost imperceptibly. "I know how Vivien died."

"Look, your mother was going to kill me. She was going to—"

Royce held up his hand. "You don't have to persuade me she had it coming, cousin. I know something of her . . . habits. At first, I'll admit, I was rather affronted that someone, that you, had the presumption to kill my mother. Rather surprised at the feelings that welled up, frankly. But they're offset somewhat when I consider the benefit to me of her . . . absence." Royce seemed freighted, Paul decided, as if his brisk persona were more difficult to maintain. "I also know that what you did was probably the best thing anyone could have done for her."

In his mind's eye Paul saw her striking herself, the wild fists on her own invulnerable chest: *This is a prison,* she'd screamed. He shivered involuntarily, recoiled from the horror and into anger.

"How's your prick friend, Rizal? He happy now?"

Royce made a calming gesture. "My mistake for talking to him about you. I should have known he'd try something heavy-handed. Trooper Rizal is cunning but is ultimately not up for anything too complicated. I'd figured that my mother would self-destruct eventually. So I asked Peter to keep an eye on the place, let me know if Vivien left, and so on—"

"And told him to rough me up and threaten me, to make sure the repairs never got completed."

"No, actually, that was his own overzealous idea. Give me some respect, cousin, at least for having more intelligence than to try anything so *obvious. I* simply tried to lure you away with a more lucrative offer. Perfectly aboveboard. For that matter, I tried to warn you about my mother."

"Good of you."

"But you were too high-minded to respond to either effort. Speaking of Trooper Rizal, you'll be amused by an ironic turn of events. Peter was apparently among the State Police called to the scene of the . . . drama . . . at Highwood. In his enthusiasm for getting there in a timely way, he managed to drive his cruiser into a telephone pole in Golden's Bridge. Broke his arm in three places, crushed a couple of ribs. Probably a needed dose of humility for Peter, hmm?"

"Is there anyone you *do* care about, Royce?"

Royce flashed a look of anger at him. But it subsided quickly, giving way to the worn look, the vulnerability, the resignation. He said nothing.

"It's okay to mourn her," Paul said quietly. "She was a remarkable woman. 'A singularity,' she called herself. I hate her. But I know it isn't easy to be a singularity."

Royce swept the hair back from his head, looked away for a moment, then came back with the reflexive counterattack: "It's okay for you to mourn Ben too, cousin. You've waited long enough."

It was Paul's turn to look away. Yes, there was that. Ben, blameless after all, a man who had done his best and not done so badly. Yes, Ben was definitely on the agenda. But not just yet, not with Royce here. Damn Royce and damn his mother. And damn the Skoglunds too, damn all family for being too dear and too difficult and too hard to be shut of, ever, no matter what they did or what they were, their unending claim upon you.

In silence, they looked at each other warily for a moment.

"Why'd you come here, Royce?"

"There's something you can do for me."

"What's that?"

As if against his will, Royce fell into a half whisper. "You can tell me what you finally found, cousin. When you went to the bottom, the starting place." He leaned closer to Paul. "What was it?" he whispered. "What was in there?" The single fold in his forehead deepened, and suddenly Paul knew the nature of Royce's solitary obsession. *Poor Royce: to be afflicted with the big questions. And to hope that anyone could offer a shortcut to the answers.*

For a moment Paul remembered the killing rage, the ecstatic explosion inside him. He felt again the sensation of her naked heart convulsing in his hand as he tore it from her chest. He shuddered, looked away, unable to meet Royce's eyes.

"I think," he managed at last, "that it's something you'll have to figure out for yourself."

Royce continued staring at him, unmoving, as if waiting for him to say more. When he didn't, Royce nodded, straightened up. "I'll do that, Paulie. Okay. Hardly worth my drive up here, but probably the best I'm going to get from you. So with that I'll take my leave—and get to work on all the messy details you left me with at Highwood." He gathered his coat from the chair.

"Wait, Royce," Paul said. "I've got a question for you too. It was you who told Aster, wasn't it? About your mother and Ben?"

When Royce turned, his thin, uneven smile had returned. "Considering your unwillingness to answer my question, Paulie, I think I will just leave you as you've left me. Wondering. Uncertain. A little tit for tat, cousin." He savored this little advantage for a moment, then gave a sour backward glance and rapped sharply on the door to be let out.

Lia stood against the wall near the door, beautiful, reserved, distant. "So they've been treating you all right?"

Paul sat on the edge of the bed, restraining his desire to go to her and fold her into his arms. Best to wait until she was ready, let her make the first gesture. "After the first day, everybody's been very courteous and respectful. Ever since the Army Intelligence and CIA people talked to me, the police have been treating me with kid gloves. These three intelligence-community types, dark suits and impassive faces, interrogated me all day yesterday. They're the ones who told the cops I should be allowed to have visitors. Also that the handcuffs and leg restraints were excessive and unnecessary."

"Did they also add 'useless'?"

Paul smiled. "They made it plain to the police it would be, uh, unwise to get me riled. That reasonable accommodations were in order."

Despite her caution, the sight of her was a balm that poured over him. The days of pain, after the initial euphoria had died, were over. With her here, with that mixture of tenderness and wariness and curiosity in her face, his optimism returned.

"They've been grilling me too," she said. "I told them what I saw. I think they believe me—that your killing Vivien was self-defense. That you weren't the one who killed the others. I doubt you'll get charged with anything."

"Probably not. Especially with my new friends pulling a few strings." Paul frowned. "But in exchange for all their solicitude, the Army Intelligence people would like me to take some tests. 'Voluntarily,' they said. I'm not sure I believe *that*. I haven't made up my mind. I don't know if I want them to know too much about it."

In a rush, he started to explain the whole thing to her, but she held up her hand, hushing him. "I got it, Paul. I put it together, okay? Anyway, I've been staying at the Corrigans'—I read the letter from Dr. Stropes." She stepped to the end of the bed but still didn't come to his arms as he needed her to.

"You know Mo's dead," Lia said. The corner of her mouth twitched, Paul noticed, a pang of sadness she governed quickly.

Paul nodded, feeling the sorrow too. There was a painful gap, the place where their friendship had just begun to grow. He thought of the wistful expression on Mo's face as he lay dead, and suddenly the whole scene came rushing back to him: Vivien in the big room, the horror of their fight, the strength rising in him. More than anything, the terror of the empty chasm he'd glimpsed. Without thinking he took Lia's hand, looked at it, held it tightly, desperately. He needed to gaze at her face but could hardly bring himself to, afraid to see a phantom there, one of the insubstantial people that with so few exceptions had been the only inhabitants of Vivien's lonely world. Afraid that maybe Vivien had destroyed him after all.

But when he did raise his eyes, her face was as always beautiful, alert, *present*. The strength of her hand, returning his grip, wasn't arguable. And there were her no-nonsense eyes. The relief was almost overwhelming. Whatever else he'd inherited, he hadn't gotten *that* through the blood. Gratitude filled him.

"What?" she asked.

"You're . . . real," he said.

"Of course I'm real!" A small, ironic smile: "As much as anyone in these existentially challenged times, anyhow—"

"Listen, Lia. Two things. I want to see Mark. Soon. I need him to see me, now that I'm, I've leveled out."

"He's out in the waiting room. I gave him the choice to come here or not, and he more than agreed, he insisted on coming. But then he got a little, well, nervous about coming in right away. He's letting me scout you out. I'll go get him."

"Yes, please." As always, knowing that Mark was near filled him with relief, gratitude, *gladness*. "But in a minute. Second thing: you and me. This is hard for me to say. I want you to know that I'm going to be better able to . . . better able to accept that you love *me*. I mean I won't fuck us up with my own insecurities. Ah, this sounds like—"

"Why is that?" She held his eyes with hers, somber now.

He rolled his shoulders, dropped his eyes, suddenly embarrassed.

She caught the expression on his face, deduced its origin. "You are so full of shit, Paul. Yes, you scare me, okay?"

"I can believe that, yeah."

"Goddamn it, I mean you've *always* scared me! Can't you see that? Can't you see that I could give away everything to you, that I *want* to, that everything's at risk here?" She was crying now. "The big jump, into another person. No parachute. Around you I'm always at the edge of that. Scared out of my mind." At last she came to him, into his arms. Holding her against him—that felt real too. *Yes,* Paul thought, *when you surrendered to love, when you let someone become as important to you as life itself, then you were really at risk. Oh yes.*

"I've got a favor to ask," she said after a time.

"Anything."

"You've always come with me to my . . . difficult places." She steeled herself, took a breath to rally. "I know it hasn't been easy for you, knowing there's a thing that . . . threatens to run away with me. That you've seen it and still loved me has . . . made all the difference."

Paul was stunned. This was the closest she'd ever come to admitting that she recognized its dark dimensions, that it wasn't entirely under her control. He stroked her hair, desperate for a way to assure her.

"So, the favor I'm asking you is to do the same with me. You held out on me, about the things you didn't trust in yourself, the scary things you weren't sure of. Never hold out on me again, Paul. Bring me there with you."

He was able to find his voice. "I promise," he said.

They gave it some time. Eventually she pulled back to look at him. "So we're going to be okay?" she asked.

He just looked at her.

She managed a quick smile. "Well," she said, wiping her eyes, "I'll get Mark."

Mark came into the room alone: Lia stood behind in the doorway, catching Paul's eye and shrugging as if to say, *I don't know how this is going to go.* Surprisingly, although Paul had expected him to be as wary and distant as Lia had been at first, the boy came right over and hugged him, small arms squeezing him so that he gasped. *Talk about paradoxes,* Paul thought: *Lia the danger lover being so wary, Mark the fragile eight-year-old facing straight and hard into it.*

They couldn't talk for a while.

Finally, Paul held him at arms' length. "I wanted to tell you two things," he said. "First, I'm sorry. Second, thank you."

"Sorry for what?"

"That's what I wondered too. When I thought about it, at first I thought it was about letting you come to that house, where something bad might have happened to you, where you had to see . . . all that. But then I realized it went much further. I'm sorry you always have to come so far, cross so much territory, to be with your father. You're doing it right now, and you've had to do it every damned time you come to the farm, going from one world to another. You know what I mean. And that's what I wanted to thank you for. For always doing it—crossing over to be with me. For being brave enough to do that. For loving me enough to do that. It means more to me than I could ever tell you."

Mark didn't say anything. He took an exploratory turn through the room, touching lightly the blood-pressure monitor, the lamp bolted to the wall, the bulletproof window in the door, and ended up as if by accident near the bed again.

"Did Lia explain all this to you?" Paul asked him.

"I've got it too, don't I?" Mark asked in a hoarse whisper. His eyes flicked up to Paul's face, then away.

Paul blew air out through pursed lips. "I guess so. It seems to run in our family. Your symptoms are the same ones I had when I was your age. But—"

"Does that mean I'll get Tourette's too? Say swear words and stuff?"

"What? God, no! At least, the odds against it are enormous. There's no connection at all between Tourette's and . . . this other thing. I somehow managed to inherit two rare, unrelated neurological conditions."

Mark looked relieved. "Lucky you, huh?"

"I got lucky in other ways, though," Paul said, touching Mark's arm.

"So does me having that other thing mean that I'm going to start flipping out and killing people?" He said it with a certain bravado, but the concern was real.

"Mark, it was only when someone tried to hurt you and Lia! That's the only thing that could have made me do something like that." *And that's not so bad,* Paul thought, momentarily stunned with the relief the insight brought. Here was the real answer to Royce's question. The HHK/HHD reflex was in there, yes—powerful, so powerful he could rip somebody apart. *But it's awakened, driven, only by something stronger and deeper, something all human beings have in them. It lives at the very bottom of every person, a force, yes, but not necessarily a monster. Love's shadow, neither good nor bad, just very, very strong. Ultimately, it is what you make of it.*

Mark tried a tentative smile. "So even if you get mad at me because I don't clean my room or something—"

They both laughed. Mark was doing it again: His troubled eyes told Paul that his mood was serious, that he hadn't recovered from what he'd seen, there was a lot of sorting out to do, and yet he was setting up their routine, the half-bogus banter that would make it all right, complete the bridge between them. *If only Ben could meet this kid!* Suddenly, the scope of Mark's strength took his breath away: his courage, the way he rallied from setbacks, the profound depth of his desire to care for those he loved. If it came to a contest between the kind of storm that had spun up out of Vivien's anguish and the very different sort of power that resided in this kid, he'd bet on Mark, no question.

The thought cheered him. True, there might be a problem resuming his life, his role as a father, given the interest of the CIA and Army Intelligence in his capacities: What they called "some voluntary tests" was almost certainly doublespeak for a permanent role as guinea pig, isolated in some top-secret laboratory, far from Lia and Mark—

But just the thought brought on a flicker deep inside him, as if some huge creature had shifted minutely in its sleep, and recognizing the sensation, Paul had to smile slightly.

About the Author

··

DANIEL HECHT spent twenty years as a guitarist in a musical career that included albums on Windham Hill Records, concerts at Carnegie Hall, and international performance tours. He received an M.F.A. in Writing from the Iowa Writers' Workshop, where he was awarded the prestigious Teaching/Writing Fellowship. He now writes from his home in Vermont. This is his first novel.

Author's Note

....

The association of Tourette's syndrome (TS) with other neurological conditions described in *Skull Session* is entirely fictional, and is not intended to imply an actual link between TS and violent behaviors, specific psychological conditions, or particular personality types.

While the number of people in the United States with TS is estimated at 250,000, most show only mild symptoms, such as simple motor tics; only 10 to 15 percent exhibit coprolalia, the involuntary outburst of obscene language. In general, people with TS lead productive lives as teachers and technicians, bus drivers and bankers, actors and athletes, surgeons and secretaries. TS is genetic in origin and is considered part of a spectrum of conditions that include attention-deficit disorder and obsessive-compulsive disorder. As a growing body of medical literature attests, TS research offers many fascinating insights into normal human cognition and behavior.

Once diagnosed properly, TS can be treated effectively with medication. For more information, get in touch with the Tourette Syndrome Association, Inc., 42–40 Bell Boulevard, Bayside, NY 11361; telephone (718) 224-2999, fax (718) 279-9596, or by e-mail: tourette@ix.netcom.com. Or visit the TSA Web site at <http://tsa.mgh.harvard.edu/>